THE KING OF CLAYFIELD

SHANE GREGORY

A PERMUTED PRESS book

Trade Paper ISBN: 978-1-61868-112-6
eBook ISBN: 978-1-61868-113-3

Cover art by Roy Migabon.

CHAPTER 1

I harvested sweet potatoes today. The first frost was this morning, and you're supposed to dig sweets on the morning of the first frost. I'm glad I know stuff like that. It's a bad time to have to learn about important things like when to dig your sweets. I got two wheelbarrows full—I've only got one wheelbarrow, but I filled it up twice. I don't know if it will be enough.

I took them to the little greenhouse, put them all out on the rack and covered them with wet towels to cure. They've got to stay warm and moist for a few days to cure properly. I'm glad I know that too.

Sometimes I get to thinking about the people out there who don't know this stuff and how they have to learn it the hard way and how they might die because of it, or how they might kill me for what I have because they didn't learn how to take care of themselves before everything happened.

It's been eight months since Canton B took people's minds away. It was quick too. In less than 24 hours, it had spread through my hometown of Clayfield, Kentucky, population twelve thousand and something. It didn't originate in Clayfield, but that doesn't matter.

I remember scanning over a story online a few days before everything happened. It was about an epidemic in Europe, something that affected the brain. I didn't pay much attention, because the media were always trying to scare us with some new thing that was going around. It wasn't until after everything happened that I learned about it ... not that there was much to learn.

Canton B was airborne, and the infected could be contagious as much as 36 hours before exhibiting symptoms. That was how it spread so fast. By the time they knew someone was infected, it was too late to quarantine him.

A couple of days after that news story, the headline on the front page of the Clayfield Chronicle said, "Canton B Suspected in U.S. Patients." There was a picture of a woman being held down by men wearing surgical masks. I still didn't think much of it.

Less than a week later, all hell broke loose in town

* * *

I am—well, I was—a museum director. It was the only museum in the whole county. In the permanent collection, we had artifacts from Clayfield's past, including Civil War cannon balls and a replica of a Prohibition-era moonshine still. There were some much older items too, like arrowheads and fossils of prehistoric sea creatures. Every three months, we hosted traveling exhibits in our gallery space.

The museum was a nonprofit, relying on donations; otherwise it would have never made it. Some days I was there by myself with nothing to do; other days, I'd have a house full of school kids on a field trip. It was a great job. Now, my only job is staying alive.

I remember exactly what I was doing when I became aware of Canton B's arrival in Clayfield. It was a Thursday around 11:00 a.m. I was supposed to have a group of senior citizens coming for a tour after lunch, and I was in the gallery, sweeping. The show in the gallery was about the history of tobacco in Kentucky. That exhibit is still up, and it will be until the building falls in or the artifacts turn to dust.

The local oldies radio station was tuned in, and they were playing Marty Robbins's classic, "El Paso." I used to love that song, but now I just associate it with that day. I suppose it doesn't matter, since I'll probably never hear it again.

* * *

Somebody crashed a car on North Eighth Street. I didn't know what it was at first, because there was no sound of screeching tires; it was just a loud *boom!* It kind of sounded like a garbage truck emptying a dumpster. The building shook a little. It startled me, and I ran to the door to see the source of the noise.

The Grace County Museum sits on the corner of North Eighth Street and North Street, with the front of the building and parking lot facing North Eighth. Directly across the street is an empty building with a "For Sale" sign in the window. Jay's Transmission Repair is across the street to the left, and across the street to the right are the offices of the Clayfield Chronicle.

I stepped out the front door, still holding my broom. It was a cloudy February day, and leftover dirty snow lined both sides of the street. The temperature was just below freezing, and I was uncomfortable in only my shirt sleeves.

Off to my left, in the corner of the lot, a red Chevy S-10 was ramped up onto the museum's sign. The sign was splintered in half horizontally. I feel bad saying this, but the first thing I thought about was how it was going to be a hassle to get it replaced. My second thought was to check on the driver of the vehicle.

I ran out to the truck. The driver must have had her foot on the accelerator, because the engine was roaring and starting to smoke, and white exhaust plumed out of the tailpipe. I guess it was in park or neutral, or the wreck had messed up the transmission, because the tires weren't spinning. A young woman sat behind the wheel, her head resting on the back of the seat. The deflated airbag lay across her lap.

Smoke from the engine poured into the cab through the vents. I tried to open her door, but it was locked. I ran around to the other side, but it was locked too. I could see her stirring, so I pounded on the passenger-side window.

"Wake up!" I shouted. "Get out of the truck!"

Another car pulled into the parking lot. An older man, I guessed in his late 60s, got out.

"Break the window!" he said, his breath fogging out of his mouth.

I drove the end of my broom handle into the window, but it wouldn't break. Then I turned the broom and swung it like a baseball bat. The other man opened his trunk, retrieved a tire iron and started working on the driver's-side window. After several swings, the broom handle broke in half. Then I saw the driver's-side window shatter. I ran around to the other side, where the man was already opening the door and trying to unbuckle the driver's seat belt.

"Call nine-one-one!" he yelled at me.

I dropped my broken broom, took my cell phone from pocket and dialed the number. It rang, but no one answered.

Another crash. Farther up North Eighth, a white delivery van had driven up onto the sidewalk and struck the front of the Chronicle building. Just as I looked, the van tipped over onto its side. The only thing I could think of was that there must have been ice on the road.

I had just started toward the van when I heard a scream to my left. The older man was on his back next to the wrecked truck, and the woman he had been trying to rescue was straddling him. It looked like she was kissing him. I stepped toward her, and she looked up at me.

Her mouth was bloody, her eyes wild. I looked down at the man and saw that blood was dribbling from his neck and pooling around his head and shoulders. The woman stood and stared at me. She had light brown hair pulled back in a ponytail. No coat, just jeans and a flannel shirt, which were soaking wet. I could see steam coming from her wet clothes. Panting like an animal, she took a wobbly step toward me and fell.

My brain wasn't making sense of any of it. It was surreal. I just stood there, watching her crawl toward me, the man's blood smeared on her chin. Then another crash snapped me out of my stupor. It was farther away, but it was definitely a car wreck. A siren sounded.

"What is happening?" I whispered to myself.

The young woman attempted to stand again. I picked up my broken broom handle and backed toward the front door of the museum, keeping my eyes on her. I detected movement across the street. A man was staggering around in front of the transmission shop in his boxers.

Something was very wrong.

I retreated into the museum and locked the door behind me. Through the glass, I watched the woman. She got to her feet and looked around with an expression of bewilderment, like she'd forgotten what she was doing, then turned and limped across the parking lot and into the street. Another crash, this time from the direction of North Street. Someone screaming outside. Three gunshots.

I ran into my office in the back of the building to see what I could see. The Everly Brothers were on the radio, singing "Cathy's Clown." I switched it off. My office window looks out onto the rear parking lot of Kentucky Regional Bank. I can see across that lot to North Seventh Street. Past that is another empty lot, then North Sixth, where City Hall and the fire station are. There was a lot of activity going on between the fire station and City Hall. I could see four police officers in their black uniforms shooting at something out of my field of vision. The gunfire sounded like little pops from this distance.

Closer, two nicely dressed women sprinted around the corner of the bank. The second one had on a dust mask. They were both wearing heels, but it didn't slow them down. Not far behind them was another well-dressed woman. The third woman was barefoot and moved like she was drunk. One of the first two skidded to a stop next to a black car that was parked near the drive-through ATM. She said something to the second woman and began digging in her purse. The second woman stopped beside the first woman's car. The third woman kept coming in a limping jog that reminded me of the movements of an ape. The first woman found her keys and unlocked the car. The woman in the mask took off a shoe and threw it at Woman Three. It was a move that cost her time, and Woman Three tackled her. The two of them fell out of view on the passenger side of the car. The first woman screamed, but didn't make a move to help. She got in the car, tore out of the lot and headed up North Street toward the fire station.

The two remaining women wrestled around on the asphalt for a few seconds. The masked woman finally broke free and stumbled over to another car, which I presumed to be her own vehicle. Leaning against it, she started crying. Unlike the other woman, she didn't have her purse or keys.

CHAPTER 2

The woman in the mask recovered quickly from her breakdown and moved around her car, feeling under the fender wells and behind the bumpers. The whole time, she kept an eye on Woman Three, who was now seated next to the ATM, watching her.

The masked woman finished her sweep for spare keys with no luck, then leaned on the car again in frustration. It was hard to tell with the mask, but she looked like she was in her late 40s to early 50s. She was wearing a knee-length brown coat, black dress slacks, a red hat and a matching red scarf.

A siren approached, and she turned to look in the direction of the bank. An ambulance sailed past on North Seventh. She waved both arms, trying to attract their attention, but they didn't slow down.

Woman Three jumped to her feet again, seemingly agitated either by the noise or by the masked woman's movements, and began to shuffle toward her.

This whole time, I had been watching through the window, as if the series of events were a television program. I was still trying to process whether or not what I'd been watching was even real. A blue pickup truck came down North Seventh, going the wrong way, and the masked woman waved to them too. Woman Three was getting closer. It finally struck me that I had to help her.

I ran out of the office, through the gallery and out the back door of the building. I wasn't really thinking at all, and I didn't even feel the cold. I know I was yelling, but I don't think I was saying any words. Both women looked in my direction. The masked woman screamed, realizing how close Woman Three was to her, and now seeing this newcomer charging at her with a broken broom handle. She ran around the car, putting it between herself and us.

I wasn't thinking. I don't know why I did what I did or how I even managed to make myself do it, but when Woman Three noticed me, she came at me, and I hit her in the face with the broom handle. I kept hitting her. It was fear that drove me, and I didn't stop hitting her until the handle broke again and she lay in a heap at my feet.

I stood staring down at her, overcome with guilt for what I had done. I dropped what was left of the broom next to her body. I caught movement out of the corner of my eye. The woman in the mask had discarded her other shoe and was running away, headed toward the fire station.

"No!" I shouted, "Stop! I was trying to help you!"

She kept going. I started to run after her, but I noticed a group of people coming across the empty lot between North Sixth and North Seventh from the direction of City Hall. There were about ten of them, and they were moving funny.

The woman in the mask noticed them too. She immediately turned and headed for the back of the bank. I stood by the ATM, wondering what I should do. The group noticed her, and four of them broke away, picked up their pace and moved in her direction.

"No!" I yelled at her, "You can hide over here! In the museum!"

That attracted their attention, and they came toward me. Two more of the original group perked up when they heard me, and they came as well.

There was no rear entrance to the bank. The woman stopped by the building and looked at me. I could tell she wasn't sure about me.

"I'm not one of them!" I said. "Please!"

The group had just crossed North Seventh Street. One of them tripped and fell over the curb, but the others didn't stop.

She made up her mind that she would rather deal with me than with them.

By the time we got inside the museum, the group was at the ATM. She ran in first, then I backed in, slammed the door shut and turned the deadbolt. The was no window in the back door, so I couldn't see if they were still coming or if, like the woman from the wreck, they had moved on once the door was shut.

When I turned toward the woman in the mask, she was already on the opposite side of the room. She had picked up a tobacco stake from one of the displays.

"Stay the hell away," she said.

"It's okay," I said, hands raised. "I won't hurt you."

"No," she said. "It ain't okay. You could have it."

Just then, there was a heavy thump against the door. The woman yelped a little, then backed farther away from me and the door.

At the time, I was still oblivious.

"Have what?" I asked. "What is going on?"

"You know. Canton B."

I thought for a moment, and remembered the news reports to which I'd only given cursory attention.

"That flu that's going around?" I asked.

"Ain't no flu," she said. "Haven't you been watching CNN at all?"

"No."

"It's bad," she said, maintaining her defensive posture with the tobacco stick. "I need to use your phone. Where's your phone?"

I pulled out my cell phone and offered it to her.

"You got some Lysol or something?" she said.
"Yeah, in the supply closet."
"Spray the phone first," she said.
"What?"
"Spray the damn phone! I need to use it."
Up to that point, I'd been addled, but now I was pissed.
I put the phone back in my pocket.
"Go bum a phone from one of your friends outside, lady."
I expected her to soften, but she didn't.
"I don't have time for this shit. In case you haven't noticed, it's the end of the world, asshole!"
There were scratching noises at the back door.
"Where's the damn supply closet?" she said.
I stared at her a moment, thinking how much she reminded me of my ex-wife. They didn't resemble each other, and this woman was older, but they had the same personality. I seem to bring out the best in women.
"In the other room," I said, "behind the agricultural display."
She eased into the room housing our permanent collection without turning her back to me. I continued to stand there pondering what she'd said.
The end of the world?

* * *

She came out of the supply closet with a can of generic disinfectant and a rag. She sprayed the rag and pitched it toward me. It made it half the distance between us.
"I'm not trying to be rude," she said. "Please just come get the rag, then put it over your nose and mouth."
She seemed to know more about what was happening than I, so I did it. The rag was damp with disinfectant, and the concentrated fragrance was sickening.
"Here," she said and tossed me the can. "Please spray your phone. I need to call for help."

"I already tried the police," I said, taking my phone from my pocket and spraying it.

"Not the cops," she said. "They're never any help. I'm calling my brother."

I stepped toward her with the phone, but she held up her stick.

"Just put it on the floor, if you don't mind. You and I need to keep our distance ... just in case."

I shrugged. "Fine. Make your call; I'll be in my office."

I walked around her, staying as far from her as possible, to make her feel at ease, and went into the office. I put the rag on my desk, picked up the office phone and dialed my mother's number, but there was no answer.

Through the window, I could see that the group that had chased us into the building was in the parking lot. Some were shuffling around, some were fighting. It reminded me of those animal programs on TV showing activity in a pack of wolves. All ten were there–seven men and three women. Of the men, one was a city police officer. Three of the men were dressed like me, in long-sleeved shirts and ties. The rest of the men were dressed casually. I recognized one of the casual fellows as Stuart Wall, one of the city-council members. I knew two of the women to be employees at the mayor's office. None of them was wearing a coat.

I could hear the woman in the gallery having a discussion on the phone, but I couldn't tell what she was saying. I sat down at the computer and typed in the address for CNN.

This event was the *only* news. Every article and every video was about Canton B. I clicked the play button on a video at random. Knoxville, Tennessee was burning. In another video from Little Rock, Arkansas, people tore at each other like wild animals. In another from a small town in South Carolina, the dead lay in the streets like a Matthew Brady battlefield photograph.

I pressed play on one more, and the masked woman stepped into the doorway of the office. She watched the monitor over my shoulder. In the clip, bridges were being blown up.

"They're trying to contain it," she said. "They're bombing every bridge and ferry on the Mississippi and Ohio Rivers. The South is screwed."

"What the hell?" I said to myself.

"My brother will be here in half an hour," she said. "Here's your phone."

She put it on a shelf just inside the door, then stepped out.

"What's your name?" I asked.

"I'd rather not say," she said. "Things being what they are."

"What are things that you can't give me your name?"

"Again, I'm not trying to be rude, but if I gave you my name, it might give you a way to find out where I live. It's the only safe place I know."

"How could this happen?" I said, turning back to the monitor.

"Have you been in a cave or something?"

I looked up at her and quickly reviewed the past few days in my head.

"Well," I said, "let's see …Today is Thursday. No visitors yesterday. We had snow and ice on Tuesday, and the museum is closed when the schools are closed. I'm also closed Sundays and Mondays. No one came in on Saturday. Other than me, you are the only person to set foot in here since last Friday."

"Hell," she said. "Working here's a friggin' cake walk."

I stared at her. She probably thought I was offended, but really, I was wondering how I could have been so unaware of what had been happening. I thought back. When I wasn't here, I was at home …

"When did this all start?"

"The craziness started in the U.S. on Monday down in Florida," she said. "They stopped all air traffic after that, except for military. But it's been spreading north anyway."

I looked down and noticed her bare feet. One of them was bleeding a little.

"You okay?" I asked.

"Not really," she said, looking at her feet. "I knew better than to come into town today dressed like this, but we didn't expect this shit to go down until Saturday at the earliest. It spread quicker than they said it would."

"You need the first-aid kit?"

"Yeah," she said. "And shoes if you got them."

"Can't help you there," I said, trying to muster a smile.

"Please use the rag," she said.

I put the rag over my face and went to the supply closet.

When I returned, she had removed her coat and hat and pulled my chair out of the office. She sat in the chair, examining her bleeding foot.

"It's not scraped much," she said. "It'll be fine, but it'll be sore for a couple of days."

I stood away from her and held out the kit and a wet towel. She took them.

"Thank you," she said. "I'm not as bitchy as I seem."

I didn't respond. I just stepped past her and leaned against my desk.

"That shit on CNN is all old news," she said. "What you need to be thinking about now is where to go from here."

"For me, this all just happened. I don't know ..."

She paused a moment from cleaning her foot with the towel.

"This is serious," she said. "Ain't nothing going to ever be the same. All those people out there killing each other ... they ain't getting better."

"There's no cure?"

She shook her head and resumed tending to her foot.

"That shit on the news ain't helping anybody now," she said. "You remember the ice storm, don't you?"

Around here, if anyone ever says "the ice storm," they're talking about the storm of 2009.

“Do you remember how everybody acted over that?” she said.

I nodded.

“That was nothing,” she said. “This right here, this that’s happening today … this could be the end of everything we know. It’s going to be like the Wild West out there pretty damn quick. Maybe worse. The Wild West wasn’t full of zombies.”

CHAPTER 3

"Zombies?" I laughed.

"What else would you call them? They ain't the undead, but they ain't right neither."

"How long do they have?" I asked. "How long before the disease kills them?"

"It doesn't kill them," she said. I noticed her looking into the other room. She stood and walked into our permanent collection. There was an old Red Cross nurse's uniform on display in the corner.

"There's some shoes," she said, "and about my size."

I followed her, and she raised her tobacco stake to make sure I didn't get too close.

"You can't wear those," I said. "They're part of the display."

She picked them up, stood on one leg, and compared them to her foot.

"They might be a little big," she said.

"They're part of the display!" I said.

"Who cares now?"

"I care."

"Don't you get it? This doesn't matter anymore. All of this ..." She waved her stick around. "All of this is junk.

Nobody wanted to see it before, and they sure don't give a shit now. I'm taking the shoes."

She sat on the floor and, after blowing the dust out of the decades-old relics, slipped the shoes on her feet.

If everything I'd seen and heard today was true, then she was right. I could still hear the muffled pops of gunfire and people yelling outside.

"So what happens to them?"

"What do you mean?" she said, tying the laces.

"The sick people. The crazy people."

"They stay that way."

She stood and walked around in her new shoes.

"From what they said on the news, the disease fries the brain," she continued. "Higher brain function is shot to hell. The neocortex, the limbic system, they get fried … not completely, but enough. They're like animals now, but not *scared* like animals. They're aggressive, dangerous."

"They're still people," I said.

"They're not in there anymore," she said, pointing to her head. "Their memories, reason, compassion … they're gone. All that's left is a human body inhabited by a rabid dog."

She noticed me wincing at that.

"I'm just saying what the doctor said on the news yesterday when he was warning people to stay away from them. Right now, they're contagious. If you get too close, if they bite you, whatever. I don't know how it is after the virus has messed them up. You could be contagious right now, even if you aren't acting like them."

"Maybe you're contagious," I said. "I'm divorced. I don't have kids. I haven't been close enough to catch anything from anyone for a week … except you. I haven't even been out to buy groceries."

"Jesus," she said. "Don't you have a social life? What are you, one of those porn addicts or something?"

"Listen," I said. "I know you keep saying that you don't mean to be rude, but you are. Of the two of us, you are more likely to be infected than I. You were out there rolling around on the ground with one of them."

She sighed and looked down at her new old white shoes.

"You're right," she said. "And you helped me. I am thankful. You have been very … kind."

That was better.

"When my brother gets here, you can't come with us, but …"

"Why would I want to come with you?"

"Good," she said, raising a hand to stop me from getting offended. "But I still want to help you with a little advice."

I shrugged. "Okay."

"Make a plan. All those people out there … they all have jobs. What happens when they don't show up to do their jobs? How long do you think we'll have electricity or food shipments or Internet access? It's a scary thought. It could turn into the Dark Ages again. Can you handle that?"

"I'm not a kid," I said. "I don't need the Internet. I like it, but I don't need it."

"The Internet is more than music videos and porn, hon. Go in your office right now and start printing off hard copies of everything important, and I'm not talking about financial statements.

"If you don't know how to purify water, find a website that will tell you how, and print out instructions. If you don't know how to store food, find out how. Print out manuals for shit—guns, generators, stuff like that. Print until the power goes out or you run out of paper. If you have an extra computer, get them both going."

"Are you serious? There's no way I can do all that."

"Do what you can. I'm helping you the best way I know how. I'm divorced too. I've had to move in with my younger brother. He's around your age." She moved over to one of the shorter display pedestals and sat on the edge of it. She wasn't supposed to sit on those, but I didn't say anything.

"My brother is one of those survivalist types," she continued. "He's got lots of guns and food and stuff like that stashed away for occasions like this. I always thought he was nuts, but when the ice storm happened, he was ready. While everyone else was without heat and electricity for nearly a month, we were warm and watching TV. He's ready for anything. He's ready for this, as crazy as that might sound.

"He has binders full of stuff at home. Most of it seems ridiculous. I mean, why would I need to know how to operate a forklift? Why would I want to make soap or butcher a pig? Since I've been watching this stuff play out on the news, I've been seeing how this information might come in handy very soon. Knowledge is power. How-to knowledge will be the most important. It might be a while before help comes. If this thing jumps the rivers, then help might never come.

"Start with the important stuff like water, food and shelter, then work your way out from there. Shelter shouldn't be as much of a problem. There will be thousands of empty houses, but definitely learn about water. Where will you get it? When the power goes out, the water will eventually stop coming out of the tap.

"Electricity would be a good one too. If nothing else, learn how to wire a generator into a well. Then you could pump water and store it as long as the generator is running. In fact, you should be filling every available container in this building with water right now."

I was kind of dazed. So much to do ...

"Do you know anything about any of this stuff?"

"I try to plant a little garden every year," I said, "and I have a subscription to Mother Earth News."

She rolled her eyes, but then composed herself.

"Okay," she said, "that's a start. Just go from there."

What she said made sense, but I didn't know where to begin. I started toward my office, and then turned back to her.

"I don't understand," I said. "If everyone was informed, then why are so many people in town today?"

"I can't speak for everyone else, but I was at the bank closing my accounts. We thought it might be a good idea to have a large amount of cash on hand in case we needed to leave. We might be able to bribe our way across the river. Now I see we *will* need to leave soon, but I never got my money."

"Your brother should be here by now."

"He was at Wal-Mart, trying to get some extra food before everything got bad," she said, "He told me it was crazy there. He'll be here."

* * *

I went into my office and tried my mom's number again. Still no answer. She lived near St. Louis, so I wasn't too worried about her yet. I did think about calling my ex to check on her, but decided not to.

The woman stepped into the doorway.

"Have you got a trash can in here?" she asked.

I pointed under the shelf by the door where she'd put my cell phone. She picked up the small plastic waste can and removed the bag.

"I'm going to fill this with water," she said. "Just in case."

I nodded and dialed another number. It was my friend Blaine.

Blaine, his wife and their two small children lived in a manufactured home out in the county near the little community of Gala. He had a few acres of land, grapevines, fruit trees, some chickens, a pond stocked with fish, and he always planted a big garden. I thought that if I needed to stay somewhere until this all blew over, Blaine's would be the place to do it.

I knew I couldn't realistically stay in my little house on 17th Street. I had electric heat, and if I had to stay there for very long, I would either freeze or starve. The woman was right; I needed a plan.

The call went straight to voicemail. I hung up and dialed his home landline. It rang a few times, then the answering machine picked up. This concerned me, but I decided to go out there anyway, and hope he wouldn't turn me away.

I left the office to have a look out the front of the building, and that was when the power went out.

"Shit!" the woman said from the back room. "Well, there it goes. Damn it!"

I looked out the window in the front door. That little red truck on the museum sign was still running. I could see faint exhaust fumes coming out of the tailpipe. The driver's door was still open, and the older man who had tried to help me was gone. Even his car was gone. Only a dark puddle of his blood and a shoe remained. There were several people out in the streets now. I looked south to Broadway, and I counted twelve standing in the intersection under the stoplight. Some were dressed for winter, with coats and hats, but one man was completely naked.

"I filled every container I could find," the woman said. She put the tobacco stick down and started putting on her coat. "I've plugged the sink, and I'm filling it now. Who knows how long you'll have water? Of course, if it gets cold enough, the pipes will freeze and burst, anyway."

She went into the office and looked out the window.

"He's here," she said, pulling her hat down on her head. "He's out back."

I went as close as the doorway to the office. I could see past her, through the window and into the parking lot. There was a white Dodge Ram 4×4 pickup idling outside. I could see a man in the vehicle looking at his phone. Then my cell phone rang on the shelf.

"It's for me," she said.

I stepped back so she could get the phone without getting too close to me.

She grabbed the phone and went back to the window.

"Yeah, it's me. I'm in the window."

She waved.

"I see you. The power is out here."

Pause.

"No, come around front. There's too many of them back there."

I could see some of the infected coming around the truck now.

"Watch them, hon. Lock your doors."

One of the infected women crawled into the back of the truck.

"No! Don't you dare get out. Just come around front. We'll deal with her later."

The truck began to back up, and then Stuart Wall ran at it and jumped onto the hood. The cop started pounding the driver's window with his fists.

"Just go!" she shouted into the phone.

The truck surged backward, and Stuart rolled off the hood. The cop grabbed the mirror and ran alongside the truck, continuing to beat the window. The woman in the back was joined by a second, and when the masked woman's brother stopped to shift into drive, the two women fell into the bed. For a brief moment, their feet sticking up in the air almost looked comical.

"Go, Danny! Damn it, just go!" The woman in the mask was crying now.

Danny went. The rear tires of his big truck smoked as he mashed the accelerator and peeled out onto North Street. The cop fell, taking the mirror with him.

She pushed past me and ran to the front door.

Before I could join her, she had already opened the door and run outside. I got outside just as Danny was pulling over the curb and into the museum's parking lot, just barely missing my car. He circled the truck around so the passenger door would be closest to us. The truck jerked to a stop, and the passenger door flew open. The masked woman jumped in and started to shut the door, but one of the women in the back stood, reached around and stuck her arm into the cab.

The masked woman slammed the door on her arm, and the infected woman howled in pain, but didn't pull it out.

By this time, the cop had recovered and was limping around the corner of the building.

"Go!" I shouted, "Just drive!"

The cop grabbed the truck door as Danny put it in drive again and pulled away. The woman who had reached in fell out of the truck as Danny turned onto North Eighth Street. She landed on her head and stayed there. The cop continued to run beside the truck, but he couldn't keep up. Danny cut through the corner lot at Jay's Transmission and headed west on Broadway.

The infected crowd from the intersection was agitated by the commotion and chased after the truck. I quietly backed into the museum and locked the door.

I was alone.

There was a splattering sound from the other room. My heart jumped as my imagination told me it was something horrible. I looked around in the small gift shop for something I could use as a weapon. I grabbed a short metal postcard rack from a display case. The postcards spilled to the floor. Then I peeked around the corner into the permanent collections. The sound was coming from the back room next to the supply closet.

She'd left the water running, and the sink was overflowing onto the floor.

I walked past the nurse's uniform on my way to turn off the water. She'd taken the shoes … and my phone.

CHAPTER 4

I turned the water off and went to the supply closet for a mop. I would have to leave the building soon. With the electricity off, the museum would get cold quickly. Plus, I didn't have enough food in there to wait until things died down outside. I kept a couple of cans of soup and a partial box of crackers in the bottom drawer in my desk in case I ever forgot my lunch. Then there was today's lunch, a salami sandwich, in the mini-fridge. I also had a couple of bags of microwave popcorn, not that they'd do me any good now. I could hide in the museum for a few days, ration my food and try to ignore the temperatures, but I didn't want to.

I mopped up as much of the water as I could. I didn't have a place to put the wet mop, because she'd filled my bucket. There were also three small plastic trash bins full of water, and of course, the sink. I propped the mop against the wall. I had to remind myself that it didn't matter if I made a mess, because life as I knew it was over. The weight of that thought made my knees weak. I suddenly felt so alone. I wished someone were with me, even if it was the rude woman with the dust mask.

I needed to sit, so I went back to my office, pulling my chair in with me. I sat at my desk and stared at the black, blank computer monitor. With the power off, it was amazingly quiet in the building. I could hear myself breathing. I tried to calm myself. I needed to think.

I had to get to Blaine's. First, I would go home and get a few things ...

Just then, I was startled out of my thoughts by a scream outside. I stood and looked out of the office window. Off to the left, on the other side of North Street, I could see a man and a woman on the sidewalk, clawing and slapping each other. I could tell by their movements that they were both infected. I pulled the blinds closed on the window. I didn't want to see any of it anymore.

It was after 1:00 p.m., and the sun would set in less than four hours. If I was going to go home and get to Blaine's before dark, I needed to go right then. Blaine's place was less than a ten-minute drive outside of town, but who knew what sort of problems I would face between here and there, or what problems I might encounter once I got there.

The more I thought about it, the clearer it became that I just needed to go straight to Blaine's house and see what kind of plan he had, then maybe he and I could venture back into town later for the things I might need.

I put my coat on, and then I went to the mini-fridge to get what was in there. I pulled out my salami sandwich and two small bottles of water. All that was left were three fast-food ketchup packets. I brought the stuff back to my office and put the sandwich and water along with the soup and crackers in a plastic garbage bag the woman had left on the floor. She'd left the first-aid kit sitting on the floor just outside the door. I grabbed it too. I tied the rag over my face, picked up the bag of supplies and her tobacco stick, and went to the front door.

To the south, I could see a man over at the transmission shop, but he was far enough away not to be a problem. To the north, I could see a group of people gathered around the overturned delivery van by the newspaper office. They, too, were far enough away, so long as I got to my car quickly and got out of the lot before they blocked my path.

It looked like a good time to go. As quietly as I could, I exited the building. Out of habit, I started to lock the door behind me, but stopped myself. I might need a place to which I could retreat.

I made it to my car without attracting any attention. I knew that once I started the vehicle, they would come. I unlocked the door, put my food on the floorboard behind my seat, the tobacco stake in the passenger seat, and climbed in. The seat was cold, and I could see my breath. I pulled the door shut gently. My hands shook as I slid the key into the ignition.

"God help me," I whispered.

I cranked the car, and immediately, the group at the newspaper office turned toward the noise. There must have been twenty of them. They came at me fast. I put the car in drive and jumped over the curb onto North Street. I turned right and headed east, toward the fire station. I could see them chasing me in my rearview mirror. Then the couple I'd seen fighting earlier jumped in front of my vehicle. I tried to swerve, but I hit the woman. She flipped up onto the hood, struck the windshield, and rolled out into the street. I didn't slow at all. The crowd shrank in my mirror as I sped down North Street.

I kept looking in my mirror at the woman's body in the road. I'd already hurt two people that day. The masked woman had said they weren't people anymore, but I still didn't believe that. The night before, when they went to bed, they'd been human beings with families. What if their families were looking for them or worried about them? What about their kids? The thought brought tears to my eyes.

* * *

When I got to North Fifth, I took a right so I could connect with Broadway. I immediately wished I hadn't.

The intersection of Broadway and North Fifth, by Clayfield Water and Electric, was blocked by a head-on collision. It was bad. The driver of the car on the right was halfway out the windshield. The front end of the other car was crumpled so that the hood was pushed into the interior of the car.

There was a crowd of infected around the wreck, some of whom were crawling on the vehicles. They were all in various states of dress. I couldn't understand how some of them could stand to be in the cold without their coats … or pants. They all turned toward me. I stopped the car. I knew I had to get out of there quickly. I put the car in reverse and threw my arm up on the back of the seat to head back the way I'd come, but there was a little boy behind the car.

He couldn't have been more than six years old. His vacant stare told me he was infected like the others. I faced front again and saw the crowd approaching. I turned back, and the little guy was still standing there.

"Move damn it!" I yelled. "Move!"

I lay on the horn. The boy jumped a little, but didn't move from his spot. Then the crowd started hitting and rocking my vehicle. They didn't like the horn. They gathered in a crescent around the front end of the car. Some of them were actually snarling. I looked in the mirror; the boy bared his teeth.

Rabid dog or no, I wasn't going to run over a kid. I put the car in drive and stomped the accelerator. I didn't punch through the crowd as I'd hoped. I wasn't going fast enough. An elderly man went down and under the car. I groaned inside, but I couldn't think about it right then. Suddenly, the car just wouldn't go. I kept the gas pedal on the floor. I could hear the rear tires squealing. The people crawled up onto the vehicle, fists and faces pressing against the glass.

I looked into the mirror again, and the little boy was on the trunk. I didn't hesitate. I took my foot off the gas and put the car in reverse, then stepped on the pedal. The vehicle jumped backward, but I was crazy with fear and lost control. The car hooked around to the left and T-boned another car parked on the street. The boy flew off the back and bounced off of the other car. The crowd was coming. I crawled across and out of the passenger side of the car, grabbing my stick on the way out.

I just ran. I had no plan at that point; I just needed to get away. They chased me, but the disease had affected their coordination enough that they weren't fast enough to catch me.

I ran two blocks north to Ann Street before I looked to see how close they were. I had outdistanced them by a full block. This made me feel better about my chances. My lungs burned from the cold air. There was no way I'd make it to Blaine's on foot by nightfall. I could either go home or head back to the museum. I allowed myself a slower pace and jogged west down Ann Street, trying to get a clear thought in my head.

My house was on 17th Street, and that was a long way on foot. I jogged two more blocks until I reached North Seventh. There was no traffic on the roads by that time, just wrecked or abandoned cars.

I stopped at the corner of Ann and North Seventh to catch my breath. My pursuers weren't even in view anymore. I wondered if they weren't smart enough to follow me that distance, or if once I was out of sight, they'd forgotten about me, or if they'd found other prey.

I'd left my keys in the car, along with my food and water. I went up to a couple of empty cars, hoping I could find one with keys, just to get me home, but no luck.

I looked south down North Seventh, and I could see the Old Hill Hotel in the distance, and next to it, Kentucky Regional Bank. That would put me next to the museum. The Old Hill had been a hotel in the early 20th century, but now it was used as office space.

I could see that the stoplights for the next two intersections were black, but I did see one working a block past the courthouse. The power wasn't out everywhere.

Looking toward Kentucky Regional Bank, I remembered what the woman said about closing her account and how she didn't get her money. I also remembered that she didn't have her purse with her. I presumed it must still be in the bank. I assumed that the car she was searching earlier belonged to her. I decided to venture into the bank and retrieve her purse and, hopefully, her keys.

I jogged south to North Street and stopped. I made sure I wasn't followed, and that there wasn't anything waiting for me ahead. The crowd that had chased me after I left the museum was gone, but the woman I'd hit with my car was still there. I felt sick about that. Part of me wanted to go check on her, but I knew I couldn't help her.

I proceeded to the bank. As I drew closer, I got a better view of Broadway. There was a small group on the courthouse lawn, but they didn't notice me. Once I got to the bank building, I hugged the wall until I got to the tinted glass door.

It was dark inside, darker than I expected it to be ... and quiet. I stood still for a moment, allowing my eyes to adjust. There were glass-walled offices to my left. To the right was the area for tellers. Papers littered the floor. The place appeared to be vacant. I looked in each teller stall for the purse, but it wasn't there. In one stall, I did find two stacks of twenties bound with paper wrappers. A little voice told me that I would need it and that no one would ever know, but I left it.

I was just about to leave, when I spied a purse in one of the offices, on the floor next to a chair. I stepped inside and picked it up, then came out next to the front door. I opened the purse to examine the contents in the dim light coming through the front of the bank.

There were keys, a wallet, two tampons, a partial pack of gum, an ink pen, and some loose cough drops. I opened the wallet and checked the driver's license. It wasn't the woman with the mask. It was the woman I'd beaten with the broom handle. I felt a twinge of guilt, then sadness as I looked at the face in the photo. She was smiling. Her name was Rhonda Leslie Stern. She lived out on Foster Road. She was five foot six and 135 pounds. She was two years younger than I. I didn't recognize her, but we might have gone to high school together. I might have seen her around town. She might have visited the museum. She was still alive, judging by the fact that she wasn't on the ground behind the museum anymore, but her life was over.

I took her keys and left everything else.

Once outside again, I had to figure out which car was hers. I could hit the unlock button on the key chain, but that might alert the small group of infected at the courthouse. The key was large, with a Chevrolet symbol on the back. I remembered a black Chevy Blazer parked around the rear lot. I crept around the corner of the building and bumped into a man.

I stepped back away from him. I knew he was infected. Even though it was ten degrees below freezing, he was in short sleeves. He growled and stepped toward me. I raised my stick.

When he attacked, it took me by surprise, even though it shouldn't have. He grabbed my stick, and we twirled around and slammed against the back wall of the bank. I stumbled and went down backwards. He fell with me, snarling in my face.

CHAPTER 5

His face was inches from mine. I'd managed to push the tobacco stick against his throat crosswise, and that was the only thing preventing him from biting me. Saliva hung from his bottom lip in a long syrupy strand. I couldn't allow it to get in my eyes. There was an unnatural heat coming from his body. I couldn't imagine a person surviving a fever that high.

I don't know how much he weighed, but my adrenaline was pumping, and I was able to shove him away from me long enough scoot backwards and get out from under him. By the time I got to my feet, he was in a crouch, ready to lunge at me again. I swung the stick like a bat and connected with his shoulder. He made a noise that was somewhere between a scream and a moan, and charged me. I was ready this time. I turned the stick again and leaned in.

The stick caught him across the chest. He grabbed it, but I was able to turn him and press him back against the wall. I got the stick against his throat again and put my weight against it. He didn't have the leverage to push me away. Slobbering and eyes bulging, he slapped me and tugged at my coat. I just kept leaning in. I didn't even feel like it was me doing it.

I noticed a couple of men approaching from the direction of the museum. They didn't seem interested in me just yet. I had to go, but this guy was still fighting me, and ... Where were the keys? I'd dropped them during the scuffle. Keeping my weight against the stick, I looked around. They were on the ground by the corner of the building.

I glanced toward the approaching newcomers again. They'd seen me. I pulled the man away from the wall a little, and then slammed him back until his head smacked the bricks. While he was dazed, I grabbed the keys. I hit the unlock button on the keychain. The lights flashed on the Blazer, and there was a little *toot* from the horn.

The newcomers were very interested by that time. The other man had slid down the wall. I could see blood at the corner of his mouth, and he was making a loud rasping sound. I got to the truck in plenty of time. The interior of the vehicle smelled like the coconut air freshener hanging from the mirror. I noticed a toddler's car seat in the back. I tried to ignore it. The truck started without a problem, and I pulled away, going west past the museum. The men didn't chase me. The last thing I saw in the mirror was them standing over the man by the bank. I didn't want to think about what they might be about to do.

* * *

I didn't see many people on my way home. I stuck with the side streets, which took a little longer. The only direct way for me to get over to 17th Street was to use Broadway, and I knew better than to do that. There was too much activity over there. I had to go north on Ninth, and then cut across Gardner to 12th, then 12th to Depot Street, and that would take me to 17th. Twice, I had to go around abandoned vehicles, but otherwise, the streets were empty.

As I crossed over 14th Street, I could see thick black smoke billowing from the northwest. There would be no one to put out the blaze. I prayed it wouldn't spread.

When I pulled into the driveway of my little house, the clock on the Blazer's radio said 3:09 p.m. I have a small one-car garage, but the automatic opener was still clipped to the visor of my car. Besides, the power was probably out anyway. I almost parked the truck in the driveway, but changed my mind. I would be leaving within the next couple of days, and I would need to load it with supplies. I looked around to make sure no one was close by, and then I jumped out and opened the door manually.

Once inside, with the door shut, I felt an incredible emotional release. I broke down. I just plopped down on the cold concrete floor by the closed door, next to oil stains and spider webs and cried like a baby. Once I was able to compose myself, I continued to sit there, listening to the Blazer's cooling engine pop, smelling the stale fumes of gasoline.

I hadn't noticed it right away, but the light on the motor for the garage-door opener was on. This side of town, or at least my house, still had power.

I walked between the car and a narrow metal shelving unit, to the interior door. It was locked, but I kept a spare key under the mat. The house was warm; it felt good.

The first thing I did was to try to call my mom again. There was still no answer. I told myself she was shopping.

Then, I stripped down and took a hot shower. It might have been frivolous, but I needed it. It comforted me. It was the last hot shower I would have for a long time.

I turned the water off when the ends of my fingers started to wrinkle. I stood there for a moment, watching the steam swirl and listening to the dripping water. There was a clean, clear drop hanging from the shower nozzle. It grew, then fell, and another replaced it.

I could hear the voice of the woman in the mask in my head. *Start with water ...*

I didn't know how to purify water. I knew I could add bleach to it, but I didn't know how much. I knew I could filter it, but I didn't know if that was enough.

I stepped out of the shower and dried myself off quickly. I had a lot of work to do, and I'd already wasted too much time. I grabbed a pair of pants from the pile of dirty clothes on my bedroom floor, put them on and went into the living room. It was dusk. I was afraid light would attract the infected, so I didn't turn any on. I shut all the blinds and curtains, and I made sure all of the doors were locked.

Okay. Think. What are my priorities?

Water, food and shelter. She'd said to fill every container with water. So I did. I plugged the tub and filled it. I filled every bucket and plastic trashcan, but I couldn't imagine drinking from any of those things. I also filled the empty juice and water bottles in my recycling bin.

With that done, I turned on the TV and put it on CNN. I just wanted to listen while I worked on other things. They were reporting that the disease had been contained, and that it hadn't spread any farther north than Pennsylvania in the east and Kentucky in the west, but I wasn't sure I believed that.

I turned on my laptop. The Internet was still working. The news stories on my Internet provider's home page were about Canton B. One headline said PROTECT YOURSELF WITH ALCOHOL. The blurb underneath said, "Doctor tells people to get drunk." I rolled my eyes. Even then, with the most sensational story of all time, they felt the need to get more sensational.

I moved on and checked my email for something from Blaine or my mom, but there was nothing there but advertisements. I logged into all the social networking sites. I hadn't been online since Wednesday, and only then to check my bank statement. I hadn't visited any of the social sites since Sunday. There was a lot of talk about Canton B, but none of my local friends had posted anything for a couple of days … except one. Jen Warren, a woman I knew from my high school days, had posted three hours before.

Things are really bad. People are killing each other outside. We're at home. 131 College St., Clayfield. Please send help.

Sixty-eight comments followed the post. Many of them said, "Praying" or "Sending positive thoughts your way" or some pointless variation thereof. A few people talked about themselves and how things were where they lived. A few said they were going to help, but I visited their profiles and saw that they lived north or west of the rivers or too far away for that promise to be realistic.

* * *

I typed, "Jen, I am at home now. It's getting dark, and I'm not going out. I will come by your place in the morning. I will be in a black SUV. Have some things ready to leave. Please respond to this message so I know you got it."

I hit "send." Then I checked Blaine's profile. There was nothing posted since the week before, and it was a link to a seed catalog with a comment about how it was time to start his tomato seeds indoors.

I visited the profile of his wife, Betsy, and the week before, she'd posted a link to a Stevie Wonder music video.

Failing to find any pertinent information, I got busy with the masked woman's advice.

I typed "how to purify water" into the search engine. Every result was a link to a site pertaining to disaster preparedness.

The first one was a government site. It had already been updated to deal with the current crisis. From what I could gather, it was posted for those outside of infected areas. There was no advice as to how to deal with the infected except to keep your distance and notify authorities. We were past that. I got the impression that they'd written off the infected areas as a loss. There was actually a sentence toward the end of their home page that said, *"Once the affected areas have been fully depopulated, testing should indicate whether these areas are habitable again."*

Depopulated? I stared at that sentence, trying to figure out what they meant. Did they plan to wait it out or depopulate it themselves? I didn't like either option. There wasn't going to be a rescue. At best, I could expect to stick it out here alone until the infected died off. At worst, the federal government was going to do something to eradicate us.

I couldn't think about that right then. I had a job to do. I dug around in my desk and came up with a partial package of paper–30 sheets at the most. It would have to do. I started printing out the information. I printed from the government site for a while, but then I found some sites that seemed better suited for my situation. These were sites that used acronyms like WTSHTF (When the Shit Hits the Fan) and TEOTWAWKI (The End of the World as We Know It). Those terms described my day exactly.

These sites were like a gold mine for me, but since it was all so new to me, I wasn't sure on which information I should focus. I kept it simple with food and water. I looked through their guns sections, but I thought some of it was ridiculous. I mean, where would I come across an automatic weapon? I already knew how to shoot; my dad took me hunting when I was a kid. It had been a while, but I could still do it. As far as using the guns for something other than hunting … I didn't even want to think about it.

I did remember the masked woman talking about hooking a generator up to a well pump. I knew Blaine had a well at his place. It was under one of those little white fiberglass well houses. I did some searching and found a relevant discussion in a forum. I'd have to hardwire the generator into the pump. I printed off some information on that too.

One site had a list of "necessities" that everyone should have in case of the end of the world. Another site told how much food was needed to supply a family of four for a year. I printed the front and back of every sheet, and it didn't take long.

I tried to call my mom and Blaine again. They didn't answer. Then I checked to see if Jen had responded to my message, but she had not.

I searched online a while longer and started writing information in the margins of my pages. I wrote until my hands hurt.

I thought about exploring more sites, but I was exhausted. I realized as I turned off the computer that I hadn't eaten anything since breakfast. It was now close to 11:00 p.m. Only twelve hours before, I'd been sweeping my museum.

CHAPTER 6

Before going to bed, I looked at the TV. There was a video of men in biohazard suits, lifting body bags onto a truck. Then the image switched to the news anchor standing at a large map. All of the Southern states east of the Mississippi River were shaded in red, and the red spread all the way up through D.C., Maryland and parts of Pennsylvania. Looking at the map, I really didn't see any way they could stop it from taking every state east of the Mississippi.

The anchor said, "An Ohio doctor claims inebriation could have an affect on Canton B.

"Dr. Sharron Harris of the University Hospital in Cincinnati has spent the past two days assisting medical personnel in Louisville, Kentucky. She is with us now, via satellite. Dr. Harris, this is has the potential to be something big. How did you come to this conclusion?"

The doctor looked tired and solemn. She said, "I examined a woman last night, a rape victim. Her assailant was later brought in by police, exhibiting symptoms of the virus. Tests concluded that he was infected, but his victim tested negative. She had been drinking.

"This morning, I treated a homeless man who had been attacked. He'd been beaten and bitten by two individuals in the advanced stages of the virus. The homeless man is an alcoholic and was intoxicated at the time. I ran tests on him, and they all came up negative for Canton B …"

The reporter interrupted her. "Yes, but doctor, does this really indicate that alcohol had anything to do with it? I'm sure there are people out there with a natural immunity."

The doctor shifted in her seat. "Right now, this is just a theory. I have contacted hospitals across the Southern states, but as you know, much of the South is without power, and communication is spotty. I did receive an email from a nurse in Atlanta who stated that she had treated an intoxicated woman following a car crash, and the woman had tested negative.

"I don't think it is a cure, but I think that perhaps alcohol's interaction with the brain might prevent the virus from initially taking hold. We don't know enough to say for sure, but I think it should be investigated further."

"Doctor, isn't there a danger in telling people to drink? I would think that now more than ever, especially in the infected zones, people wouldn't want their judgment impaired."

"I'm not telling anyone to drink; I'm trying to get information out there that has the possibility for saving lives."

"Doctor, how much should we drink to fight off the virus?"

"I'm not saying anyone should drink … I don't know …"

I turned the TV off. I had a bottle of bourbon in the pantry, but I didn't want to get plastered just on the hunch of a tired doctor. I had to keep my wits.

I started to try my mom again, but decided to wait. Part of me questioned why she hadn't called to check on me.

* * *

I slept hard. When I woke up, daylight was peeping through a gap in my bedroom curtains. There was a faint smell of smoke. The house was cold. It wasn't cold enough for me to see my breath, but it was uncomfortable. My alarm clock was dark. I'd set it to go off at 6:30 a.m., so I could go help Jen. I tried the lamp by my bed, and it wouldn't come on.

I peeked through the curtain, and there was about an inch of new snow on the ground. A body lay in the street in front of the house next door, also covered in snow. I'd hoped it had all been a dream.

I went to the kitchen, where I could check a battery-operated clock. It was a little after nine. I looked out a window in the back of the house. I could see a lot of smoke coming up over the trees to the west.

I wouldn't be able to stay. Maybe I could bundle up enough to sleep there, so long as that fire didn't spread, but eventually, the water would freeze. It might warm up this afternoon, or it might stay this cold for a week. I didn't know, and I doubted the local weatherman was still making forecasts.

I went to my closet and put on some warmer clothes–a blue-and-yellow Murray State University sweatshirt and some jeans. Then I took out five more changes of clothes to take with me to Blaine's. I piled them all on the bed, and then I went out to the spare room to get my suitcase. On my way through the living room, I stopped to try my mom again. The phone relied on electricity and was dead. I felt a little empty and worried. I wondered if I would ever know if she was okay. I was suddenly angry with the woman in the mask for taking my cell phone.

I was angry all around.

I went into the spare room. I never called it the guest room, because I never had any guests. I'd always thought about turning it into a little library or a study, but that was just another plan that never materialized. The room was stacked with boxes and junk. When I divorced two years prior, I'd bought this place. I unpacked the necessities when I first moved in, but this other stuff had never made it out of its boxes. Some of the boxes had been packed when I left home for college many years before. I was just too sentimental or too much of a pack rat to let any of it go.

One of the boxes contained my old comic books. Some were collector's items, but I never sold them, because I always thought I'd read them again. I tried once, but they just weren't the same. No, I wasn't the same. Another box had some of my back issues of Mother Earth News. I never threw them away either. I always had this little fantasy of living in the country and growing my own food. I could live that dream vicariously through Blaine and reading those magazine articles. I grabbed the box. I figured that I'd need them.

I packed my clothes in the suitcase. I emptied out one of the boxes of junk from the spare room and put the contents of my medicine cabinet in there. I took everything—even a bottle of expired vitamins. I had three rolls of toilet paper and a partial; I put them in the box. Toothpaste, mouthwash, disposable razors, nail clippers … it all went in.

I had some lace-up Wolverine work boots in the closet that I didn't wear much, but I kept them around in case I ever needed to do any work outside. I put them on and took the box of toiletries, the magazines and the suitcase out to the Blazer.

While I was out there, I removed the child's car seat. There was still a sippy cup in the little cup holder. It made me sad. Once it was out, I brushed out the stale Cheerios and raisins that were in the back seat. Then I went back in to pack my food.

I thought I had been running low on food and had been planning to go to the grocery since Tuesday. But when I got in the fridge and cupboard, I found a lot there. I always had food in there that I forgot about or ignored, like boxed rice mixes or cans of vegetables that I rarely ate. It had become a little like the clutter around my desk, and eventually I didn't see it in there anymore. Some of it was close to or a little past the "use by" date, but it was food. It all fit into three file boxes.

I opened a granola bar and ate it. I hadn't realized how hungry I was, and I wound up eating two more and finishing off a bottle of grape juice.

Once the food was in the back of the Blazer with the other supplies, I loaded all the water I had bottled up the night before, which took up half the floorboard in the back seat—two half-gallon juice bottles, and six smaller bottles. Then I went back in for another sweep of anything I might need.

I bagged up a couple of blankets and a pillow, and put them by the door. I put my laptop and the stack of papers I'd printed next to that. I put on my heavy coat, and tied a dishtowel around my nose and mouth. I couldn't think of anything else.

I loaded the last of the stuff. The back of the truck was crammed. Then I locked the house and opened the garage door.

It was so quiet. No car engines. No voices. No hum from the wires on the poles running down the street. Not even a dog barking. There was no one around, and the snow hadn't been disturbed, so no one had been around for a while. The smell of smoke was strong; it had settled low and close to the ground.

I backed the Blazer out, then got out and shut the garage door. The driveway was a little slippery. When I got back in, I put it in four-wheel drive.

I saw fourteen dead bodies as I headed south on my way to Jen's house on College Street. I didn't know if they'd been murdered by the infected or had succumbed to the cold. I saw only two people out walking around, but I didn't stop. I didn't want to risk it.

I did see an older tan Ford pickup truck driving one block over and headed north as I crossed over Walnut Street. The back of the truck was piled with supplies, and there was a tarp tied over it. I just caught a glimpse, and they didn't slow down. I turned at the next intersection and circled around to chase them down, but by then, they were gone.

When I got to College Street, it was after 10:30. Jen lived in a little white house, not that much different than mine. I pulled the truck up into the yard, with the passenger side close to the front porch steps.

The front door was standing wide open. I waited a moment to allow her and anyone else inside time to come out, but no one did.

"Shit," I said. My own voice sounded odd. Then I realized I hadn't said a word since the day before, when I'd screamed at the boy behind my car.

The tobacco stick was still in the front seat. I grabbed it and got out, leaving the engine running. I noticed footprints in the snow on the steps, coming out of the house and headed down the street.

Cautiously, I stopped in the doorway and looked inside. To the left, along the wall, there was a door, and next to that was a couch that had been folded out into a bed. The bed was unmade. On the other side of the room, a lamp lay on the floor. Pictures hung crooked on the wall. I could smell feces.

I wanted to leave right then, and I almost did, but I'd promised her I'd come. Just inside, there was an opening to the right, which led into a small dining room, and behind that, the kitchen. A laptop sat open on the dining-room table. Next to it was a coffee cup with the string of a tea bag hanging out of it. One of the chairs was overturned, and there was a pile of human excrement on the floor next to it.

I entered the living room, and tried the switch by the door. No power there either. I went around the foldout bed to the other doorway. There was a bathroom in front of me and a bedroom on either side. All of the doors were open, and there was no one inside.

Both bedrooms were a mess, but the one on the left was worse. The dresser was turned over and leaning against the bed. The floor was littered with clothes and cash. I stepped in and looked around. I saw a stain on the wall that I presumed to be blood. I hadn't gotten there in time.

I went over to the dresser and righted it against the wall. The top drawer hung open, and women's underwear spilled over the side. I'd just started pushing them back into the drawer when I heard movement in the closet.

I held up my stick.

"Hello?" I said.

No response.

I stepped closer.

"Jen?"

Silence.

Then the bottom of the closet door exploded outward, and the lamp on the nightstand by the bed shattered. I peed myself a little.

"Jesus!" I said, falling backward over the corner of the bed.

"Get back!" said a woman's voice from the closet.

"Jen?" I said. "I've come to get you."

The long barrel of a shotgun eased out of the bottom half of the splintered closet door, followed by Jen's face. Her eyes were red, her hair was tangled, and she was shivering.

I pulled down the dish towel from my face, so she could see who it was.

"You came," she whispered. Then she lifted her gun at me. "Are you sick?"

"No," I said.

She disappeared back inside, and then the door opened. She stepped out with a shotgun in one hand and a bottle of tequila in the other.

Her brow furrowed. "Whatcha doing with those?"

I looked down to see what she was talking about. I was holding a pair of her panties.

CHAPTER 7

I dropped the underwear and looked up at her. She was still staring at me like she was expecting an answer.

"We've got to go," I said, stepping past her to the bedroom window. "That gunshot will probably attract them."

She just stood there swaying; her gaze had drifted a million miles away.

"It's been hell," she said in a hoarse whisper.

I could see three men at the corner of the street, two houses away.

"They're coming," I said. I grabbed her arm to lead her out, but she wouldn't move.

"I'm so drunk," she said, continuing to stare.

"Have you been infected?" I said.

She shrugged.

I took her shotgun and the bottle. She didn't resist. I stepped back to the window. The trio was still at the corner, but they would notice the noise of the Blazer's engine.

When I turned back, she was sitting on the bed.

"I'm so damn drunk," she said again. This time, she put her head in her hands and started bawling.

"We can talk about that in the car," I said. "Let's get some clothes for you."

"Zach ... oh God ... He just lost it," she said through the sobs.

I propped the shotgun against the wall and set the tequila beside it. There was a duffel bag by the closet. I put it on the bed and started filling it with the clothes from the floor. There were three or four hundred dollars in tens and twenties scattered on the floor too. I collected as many as I could.

"I was trying to pack some stuff after I read your message," she said. "Zach got sick, that asshole. God, he was such an asshole."

I looked out the window again. They were headed in our direction.

"They're really coming now, Jen. We have to go."

She just kept sitting there.

"As soon as he said he had a headache, and I mean the very second he said he had one, I opened the bottle and started drinking, just like that doctor said. I knew he'd get sick. That was just like him."

"Tell me in the car, Jen," I said.

I put the tobacco stick in her hand. She took it. I pulled my towel up around my nose and mouth, hung the strap of the bag around my neck, and took her by the elbow. I stood her up and grabbed the shotgun.

We made it to the living room but had to stop. There was the silhouette of a man in the doorway. Out the front window, I could see the other two by the Blazer.

"There he is," she said. "What an asshole. You hear me, you son of a bitch?"

She broke away and vaulted over the foldout couch and at the man in the doorway. When he stepped inside, she nailed him in the crotch with the stick. He folded up into a neat ball at her feet. The other two men were on their way up the porch.

I got to her before she made it outside, and pulled her through the dining room. I could see the back door in the kitchen on the other side of the refrigerator.

"We'll circle around," I said, but I knew I was just talking to myself.

Out back, there were shallow footprints in the snow that had been filled in with newer snow. A snow-covered gas grill sat to the right of the steps, and a snow-covered garbage can to the left. The back yard was fenced, so we headed for the gate. I realized then that she wasn't dressed for the cold. She was wearing sweatpants, a lightweight sweater, and some house slippers.

I stopped her underneath the kitchen window, next to the garbage can, and leaned her against the house.

"I'm cold," she said.

"I know. I'm going back for your coat and shoes. Stay right here."

She looked like she was going to say something, but I left before she could.

Back in the kitchen, I peered into the dining room, shielding myself with the refrigerator. There was no one there. As quietly as I could, I made my way toward the living room. All three men were out on the front porch again. I was about to try sneaking past the open door to Jen's bedroom, when I noticed a row of coats hanging on pegs behind the front door. Beneath them was a row of shoes.

The men were heading down the steps toward the Blazer. Quickly and silently, I ran to the coats. I took a bulky brown one from its peg and draped it over my arm, then I picked up a pair of pink-and-white running shoes.

I would need to get the men away from the truck so Jen and I could leave.

I went to the doorway. "Hey! I'm up here!"

Their heads jerked up, and they came at me. I ran back through the house. When I got to the fridge, I stopped to see if they were still following. As soon as they entered the dining room, I ran out the back door.

Jen was bent at the waist, leaning on the stick. The snow at her feet was brown and melting.

"They're coming," I said as I ran past her.

"I puked," she said.

I got to the gate and nudged it open with my foot.

"Now, Jen!"

The back door flew open, and one of the men fell out into the snow. A second man stumbled out on top of him. Jen seemed to come to her senses, and bolted away from them. She was having trouble getting traction in the snow in her slippers, and her feet would run in place for a few steps, make progress, and then she'd fall to one knee. The third man leaped out of the house. When his feet hit the ground, they slipped in the snow, and he landed on his butt. The whole scene had a grotesque cartoonish aspect.

I backed against the gate to hold it open. Jen made it to me before the men could recover. I closed the gate and looked for something to hold it closed. I started to use the shotgun, but Jen stopped me.

"Are you outta your mind?" she said, looking at me like I was an idiot. She jammed the tobacco stick into the ground and leaned it over so that it was wedged under the gate's latch. Then she took the shotgun from me.

More people were coming down the street. They didn't seem to be a group, just nine loners, spaced out and staggering toward us, attracted by the noise.

We got in the Blazer and pulled away before they could reach us.

I drove around and past the people in the streets. Some stopped and, with slack jaws, watched us pass; others chased us. I couldn't get over how little some of them were wearing. How could they stand the cold? The thermometer on the dashboard was showing the outside temperature at 18 degrees Fahrenheit.

I headed east on College to Sixth Street, then took that to Bragusberg Road.

"Are we going to your house?" Jen asked softly. She'd put the shotgun in the back seat and was resting her head against the window. The big brown coat covered her like a blanket, pulled up to her chin.

"No," I said. "A friend owns a place out between Gala and Farmtown, I'm going out there."

Her distant stare was back.

"Are you okay?" I said.

"No."

I didn't know what to say. She and I were "friends" on Facebook, but that was the extent of our relationship. We had only been acquaintances in high school; we didn't run in the same circles. I might have seen her three times around town since graduation. I didn't know anything about her.

"You grabbed the wrong coat," she said. "This is Zach's coat ... my boyfriend."

"Sorry," I said. "It was the first one on the rack."

She was silent for a moment. She pushed her hands down in the pockets of the coat, and a slight grin crossed her lips.

"Score," she whispered and fished out a pack of cigarettes. She stuck one in her mouth.

"Do you mind?" she asked.

I did mind, but I said, "No, go ahead."

"Want one?"

"No," I said. "I quit years ago."

"Hell, good for you. But I think we've earned it."

"If I smoke one, I'll smoke the whole pack," I said. "The last thing I need to is get re-addicted to something they might not be making anymore."

She pulled out a lighter and flicked it a couple of times until the flame danced.

"Ain't nothing worse than a smoker that's quit," she said, lighting up.

"Why's that?"

"They bitch and moan about smoking more than people that's never done it."

She took a deep drag and exhaled, filling the cab with smoke.

I opened my window, and the cold wind bit at my face.

"I should know, because I quit too. I gave Zach hell about these things every damn day. I wouldn't let him smoke inside."

She rolled her window down and threw the cigarette and the rest of the pack out.

"Tastes like dirt," she said.

We put our windows up and were quiet for a while. I pulled off of Bragusberg Road onto Britton Lane. The road had been snowy the whole way. There were no tire tracks or footprints.

"Have you been exposed?" she asked.

"I don't know," I said. "I've been around people who had it, so probably. I've been wearing this mask."

"If I'm going to turn ..." She paused as if she didn't want to finish. "If I turn into one of them, it'll be sometime today. Zach and I were probably exposed to the disease within a few hours of each other. He probably caught it at work, and I probably caught it from him. We should know by this afternoon whether this alcohol thing works."

"Do you think there's something to it?" I asked, turning onto Gala Road. "It sounds crazy."

"Crazy is all we've got right now."

"There's no way to know how much to drink," I said.

"I got wasted," she said. "I made sure I got my brain good and soaked."

She looked out the window.

"I've got a headache," she said. "I don't know if it's from the virus or the liquor. I thought you ought to know."

"Is a headache the first symptom?"

"Yeah," she said. "Zach got a headache. His sister and her kids were staying with us, because their power went out yesterday, and their neighborhood was getting bad. They were all in bed with bad headaches before long. I was drinking, but I don't know if it helped."

"I'm sorry," I said.

"Me too," she said. "He was an asshole, but he didn't deserve that. His sister and ... and the kids ..." Jen sighed heavily and started crying.

I pulled into Blaine's driveway. His truck was gone, but Betsy's minivan was there. Their long, tan manufactured home was off to the right of the driveway. They had a workshop behind the house with an attached chicken coop. I could see four chickens in the pen. There were other, smaller outbuildings here and there. The snow in the yard was pristine, and I didn't take that to be a good sign. I started to get out, and Jen put her hand on my arm.

"Don't let me become one of them," she said.

"Jen, I ..."

"If I start acting funny, if I start getting violent, you kill me."

"I couldn't do that."

"Before this is over, you'll probably have to kill some of them," she said.

I stared at her. I was afraid I already had killed, but I didn't want to tell her that. Her eyes were red from the booze and the tears; they were desperate and pleading.

"I don't want to wind up like Zach," she said.

"Blaine didn't know I was coming," I said, changing the subject. "I'm going to see if it's okay if we stay here."

She pulled her hand away and ran her fingers through her hair.

"I'll wait," she said.

Family and friends used the back door at Blaine's. Strangers always came to the front. I knew I should go around back. Blaine had a shotgun too, and if I tried the front door, he might give me the same welcome that Jen had.

I went up the back porch and knocked.

"Blaine!" I called. "Betsy!"

I couldn't hear any movement inside. I cupped my eyes and looked through the narrow window on the back door. I could see their small laundry room. I knocked again, louder.

I left the porch and walked around the house, looking in windows. No one was in there.

For as far as I could see, the snow lay perfect and untouched. During the ice storm of 2009, the family had slept in the workshop, because Blaine had a small wood-burning stove in there. I walked over to the shop. I waved at Jen. The windows were starting to fog up on the Blazer, but she saw me and raised her hand in acknowledgement.

I knocked on the workshop door, and then tried the knob. It was unlocked. I stepped inside. It was as cold in there as it was outside. I touched the wood stove to be sure. It was cold, unused. I tried the light switch, but there was nothing.

I returned to the Blazer.

"They're gone," I said, climbing in.

"So what now?" she asked.

"I don't think Blaine would mind us staying here," I said. "The power is out, so we'll sleep over in the workshop. Maybe I can get a fire going."

"Do you think your friend has anything to drink?"

"I don't know," I said. "Haven't you had enough?"

"Not for me," she said. "If I don't get sick, then we know alcohol works. If it works, you need to get good and drunk."

CHAPTER 8

We unloaded the truck and took everything into the workshop. The building was a metal pole barn on a concrete slab, tan to match the house. Along the two shorter walls to the left and right of the door were counters lined with tools–grinder, miter saw, vise, drill, and such. The building had three windows—two on the south side facing the road, and one on the east side looking out into the chicken pen. High on the walls hung garden tools, some lawn chairs and a bicycle. On the wall opposite the front door was a little square door three or four feet off the ground.

"What's this for?" Jen asked. "Hobbits?"

The joke coming out of the blue on such a grim day made me smile.

"It's an egg door."

"Egg door?"

"Open it." I grinned.

She unlatched the door and opened it. She was wearing the coat now, and it swallowed her up, making her look like a little kid. She stood on her tiptoes to get a better view into the opening, which further accentuated her childlike appearance.

It took her a minute.

"It's dark ... oooh, an egg door. It's the chicken coop." She turned to me. "There's one in there."

She reached in and pulled out a brown chicken egg.

"I think it's frozen," she said.

"Chickens don't lay much in the winter," I said. "I'm surprised there was one there at all."

"They don't like the cold?"

"No, it's not that," I said. "They need a certain amount of daylight, and the days are shorter in the winter. Some people put lights in the coop to trick them into laying."

* * *

The building was insulated, so that would help once I got the fire started. Jen was still kind of spacey. She sat on an upside-down five-gallon bucket and stared down at the egg.

Blaine didn't have any dry firewood inside, which surprised me. I stepped outside. There was a small pile of wood to the right of the door, but it was covered in snow.

C'mon, Blaine. I thought you were Mr. Prepared. Where's all the dry wood, damn it?

I came back inside with four small wet logs.

Jen didn't look up.

"There's some food in those boxes if you're hungry."

"I can't eat right now," she said.

I put the logs on the floor and looked around the shop for something I could use as tinder and kindling. There was a two-by-four next to the miter saw, and I seized that. Then I ripped out some of the advertisement pages from my magazines. After digging around in one of the drawers under one of the counters, I found a box cutter, and I used it to shave off curly slivers of the two-by-four.

When I had a handful of shavings ready, I opened the door to the stove. We had a stove like this when I was a kid, but I'd never actually operated it. I'd watched my dad enough that I thought I could do it. If I was lucky, I wouldn't burn the building down, and Jen would think I knew what I was doing ... not that she cared.

The bottom of the stove had a lot of ash in it. I found Blaine's ash bucket and shovel, and cleaned out the stove. I put down some of my shredded magazine ads in first. There was a small hatchet next to the door. I turned the two-by-four on its end and used the hatchet to bust it up into smaller sticks for kindling.

Then I opened the damper on the stove, so it could draw air.

"Still got the lighter?" I said.

Jen looked up absently, then dug around in the coat pocket and tossed me the little green BIC. I got the paper started, and then I placed my pile of shavings loosely on top of the flame. It started to smoke, then ignited. I put the smaller kindling on first, and when it caught, I put on the bigger pieces. Then I put one of the wet logs next to, but not on, the fire. Smoke poured into the room. I'd forgotten to open the flue. I looked over my shoulder to see if Jen had noticed, but she wasn't paying attention. I opened the flue, and the smoke went out the chimney.

"I've got to find more dry wood," I said. "I'm going to see if there's any in one of the sheds."

She nodded but didn't look up.

I stepped out and shut the door behind me. In the field across the road were several cows. They all stared at me as though I were the only human they'd ever seen. There were cows like this on farms all over the countryside. There were all sorts of fenced livestock out there. I wondered what would happen to them. Would they eventually overpopulate their boundaries? Turn feral? Starve?

I walked over to the closest shed. Inside, I found stacks of plastic flowerpots, four bags of potting soil and a bucket of sand. I was about to leave and check another shed when I noticed the wooden pallet on which the bags of soil sat. I moved the dirt quickly and pulled out the pallet. The top boards were dry, and that would do for now.

On my way back, I looked out across the open fields behind the house. In the far distance, I could see a figure moving around, dark against the snow. It was far enough away, and my depth perception was confused enough, that I couldn't tell whether it was human or animal. My imagination told me it was human. I watched it, trying to figure it out, but the whiteness of the snow was playing tricks on my eyes. I couldn't watch long, because I had a fire to feed.

When I came back into the building with the pallet, Jen was removing the power tools from the counter.

"What are you doing?"

"I'm not sleeping on that concrete," she said. "It's cold and hard, and there might be stuff crawling around down there."

I didn't argue. It made sense to me.

"How many shells do you have for that shotgun?" I asked as casually as I could.

"Two."

"Just two?"

"It only holds three, and I used one."

I didn't want to shoot anyone, but the reality was that I might have to defend myself and Jen.

I grabbed a claw hammer and pried the pallet apart.

I could feel her staring at me.

"We should save them," she said. "You know, for us ... just in case."

I looked over at her; she looked so incredibly sad and scared.

"It'll be okay," I said. "The alcohol worked. I'm sure it did."

"But my head is splitting," she said.

"You're just hung over," I said. "Eat something."

She picked up the egg and sat down on the bucket again.

"Part of me hopes I do have it," she said softly. "Things won't get no better than this."

"No," I said. "The government has contained the virus. We just have to wait here."

"Be real. They ain't coming for us."

I knew this. Deep down, I knew it had spread everywhere by now. But I had to give her some hope.

"Then we'll go to them," I said. "We'll head west and cross the river. Besides, we're not the only people left in this town."

"Yeah," she snorted, "There are plenty of people—all drunks and monsters."

* * *

Using the hatchet, I split the slats from the pallet into narrow strips, and broke the strips across my knee.

The fire was dying, but I fed it some more paper, then the pallet wood. I got my head close and blew on the embers. Soon it was a respectable fire. I went outside and brought in the rest of the wet wood, then piled it near the stove to dry. I closed the damper a little.

"The fire is going," I said. "Let's have a hot meal, then we'll try to come up with a plan. I haven't really eaten much since yesterday morning, and I'm starting to get a headache too."

She looked up at me warily.

"I get headaches when I don't eat," I said.

I pulled one of the food boxes in front of her to unpack, and then I started on another.

“Who the hell buys canned beets?” she said, pulling food out of the box. “Or lentil soup?”

“I've had those a while,” I said.

"Did you buy them on purpose?"

“We can save them until last, or eat them first and get them out of the way.”

“Or we could forget about them altogether.”

I pulled out a cylindrical box of oatmeal, and just looking at it made my stomach growl.

"We'll need to get in the house," she said. “Where does your friend keep his key?”

"I don't feel right about going in there when they're not home," I said.

"Did you bring a can opener to open this lentil soup? Or a pan to cook it in? Or a spoon to eat it with?"

"No," I said. It made me wonder how many things I'd forgotten. "I'll take care of it. That way I won't have to explain about a stranger in their house."

"I don't think they'll be back for a while," she said.

"Still," I said, "I'd feel better if I did it."

"Suit yourself," she said. "Knock first when you come back. I want to change clothes."

I found the spare key underneath the fourth rock that lined the walkway to the back door, just where it always was. The rock was frozen to the ground, so I had to knock it loose with the heel of my boot.

After I picked up the key, I looked out across the fields again. The dark figure I'd seen earlier was gone now. It made me uneasy. I knew they were out there. I knew they were around, just like in town.

I went into the house.

"Hello? Blaine?"

Even though I knew no one was there, I still thought I should announce my presence. I went into the kitchen and started collecting the necessary utensils for our meal. I didn't want to nose around in my friends' house without them there, but I decided to see if they had anything decent to eat, so we wouldn't have to eat canned beets. I would try to replace anything I took later.

The pantry was empty. Completely empty. I opened the refrigerator. There was a stick of butter on the door and an open jar of pickles in the back, but otherwise, it was empty too.

I left the kitchen and went into the living room. The pictures of the kids that Betsy kept on the bookcase were gone. Some of the bookshelves were bare. I went to the kids' bedrooms. Their closets held very few clothes. I went to Blaine and Betsy's bedroom. The chest of drawers was open.

Blaine's gun rack was empty. I stepped over to the walk-in closet.

"They bugged out."

The voice startled me, and I jumped. Jen had come in and was standing behind me in the doorway. She'd already changed her clothes.

"What?" I said.

"Got the hell out of Dodge," she said.

"It looks like they moved."

"Well, it looks like they plan to be gone awhile," she said. "Did they have family somewhere else?"

"Betsy's family lives in Missouri ... I don't understand. Why didn't he tell me?"

She looked around the room.

"Do the kids have twin beds?" she asked.

"Huh? I don't know."

"If they do, we should move them out there to sleep on. It'll beat sleeping on those countertops."

She left me. I sat down on the bed.

He could have told me he was leaving. He could have at least warned me about the virus.

"There are twin beds in both rooms," she said when she returned. "After we eat, we should move the mattresses into the shop before it gets dark."

"How could he do this to me?" I said. "He just left."

"Don't be hard on him," she said, sitting next to me. "He had kids to worry about."

I still felt a little betrayed.

"Come on," she said. "Let's eat those lentils. Maybe this headache will go away."

* * *

We didn't eat the lentils. We ate oatmeal instead, and it was the best oatmeal I'd ever tasted. It felt good to have my belly full. Jen seemed to feel better too.

We moved the kids' mattresses out to the workshop with the intention of moving the beds out there the next day. I went out and checked the clock in the Blazer, and it was after 2:00 p.m.

"Our priority now is to get you drunk. I think the tequila killed it. I feel good ... well, as good as I can, considering."

"I didn't see anything to drink in there," I said.

"We'll have to get some somewhere. Maybe one of the neighbors."

"Break into somebody's house?" I said.

"I'll do it if you feel weird about it," she said. "But we need to do it now. It'll get dark soon. We might want to find some candles while we're at it."

We headed outside.

"Another thing," she said. "We need a toilet."

"We can just use the ones in the house."

"I did use one of the ones in the house, but we'll have to haul in water to flush it at some point."

CHAPTER 9

There were no liquor stores in Clayfield. In fact, the whole county had been dry since Prohibition. I figured Grace County probably had a higher rate of infected for that reason.

It wasn't that there was no alcohol here; it just wasn't sold legally. People drove over the county line and bought it or got it from bootleggers. It was likely that one of the neighbors would have something stashed away, but finding the right neighbor would be the key.

Blaine's nearest neighbors were close enough that we could see their houses, but not close enough to walk there quickly. I drove, and Jen rode shotgun. Literally.

I pulled into the driveway of the nearest house. The name on the big black mailbox was Kaler. It was a brick home with a large red barn off to the side. There were two cars by the house under a carport and a small blue tractor by the barn.

"Next house," Jen said.

"Huh? Why?"

"Look on the gray car. There's a Jesus bumper sticker."

"So?"

"Not likely to have booze, so it'll be a waste of time."

"Okay," I said, putting the Blazer in reverse.

"We'll come back, though," she said. "There's a four wheeler parked in the barn. It's painted camouflage. You know what that means?"

"What?"

"Somebody in that house hunts, so there'll be guns in there."

I laughed for the first time in days. "You're a regular Sherlock Holmes."

"Well, yeah," she said. "Elementary, my dear dumbass."

She smiled. It was a real smile, like in her profile pictures. I hadn't been thinking about it before, but she was pretty in a rough-around-the-edges kind of way.

We passed another field of cows and pulled into the driveway of a large white house with a wrap-around porch. The mailbox at the end of the driveway was painted to look like a large-mouth bass.

"Ahh," Jen said. "Another sportsman."

I stopped behind an older pickup truck.

"Well, Sherlock, what's the verdict?"

"Let's try it."

I turned off the Blazer, and we got out. We both stood still a while to listen and wait in case someone was inside. We didn't want to bust in on an occupied home and get shot.

"I think it's fine," I said. "But I'll go knock on the door. You okay with the gun?"

She nodded and brushed her hair away from her face with her forearm. Her long coat sleeves were bunched up, stopping at her knuckles. The only thing preventing her hands from disappearing inside was her grip on the shotgun.

I stepped up onto the long wooden porch, and walked down to the front door. The screen door was closed, but main door stood open. I felt a sinking in my stomach. There was no reason for that door to be open.

I looked down the porch to Jen, who was standing by the truck. She raised her eyebrows and started forward. I shook my head for her not to come. There was a noise from inside.

Heeeeeh. Heeeeh. Heeeeeh.

I stepped back from the door.

"What's the matter?" Jen whispered.

I motioned for her to stay back.

Heeeeeh. Heeeeeh.

There was movement in the darkened room. I could see through the house to a window on the other side that looked into the back yard. The silhouette of a head and shoulders were framed in that window. Fine wispy hair stood away from the head. I stepped back to the porch railing. I began to make out the rest of the person shuffling toward the screen door.

Heeeeeh. Heeeh. Heeeeeh.

It was an old woman. Her long gray hair had been pulled back in a bun, but was coming loose, part of it draped across her shoulder. She wore a nightgown that was ripped from her left shoulder and one bare, shriveled breast hung out. Her chin was black with dried blood.

Heeeh. Heeeeeh. Heeeeh. It was her breathing.

I couldn't move.

Jen stepped onto the porch.

"What is it?" she said.

The old woman stared at me. Her eyes looked like those of a hungry animal. She charged, slamming into the screen door.

I yelped, flipped over the railing and tumbled out into the yard.

I could hear Jen running back toward the Blazer.

The door didn't open. The woman rammed it again. It still wouldn't open. It must have been latched. She let out a noise that stood my hair on end. It sounded like a cat's growl.

Jen came around the porch and ran to me.

"Are you okay?"

"She can't get out," I said.

Jen looked up to the door and got her first view of the woman.

"Holy shit," she said.

"She can't figure out how to unhook it," I said, fascinated and terrified at the same time. "Let's go," I said. "We'll try another house."

"No," Jen said. "We need to get you something to drink, and we are liable to find something like her at every house we go to. She looks kind of frail; we can handle her. I'd rather face her now than have to deal with you later."

"But there's no guarantee there will be anything in there. She doesn't look like a drinker to me."

Jen nodded and made a face.

"Okay, but we've only got a couple of hours until dark."

We went back to the vehicle. Before Jen got in, she went over to the pickup truck, opened the passenger door and searched it. I had the Blazer cranked when she returned.

"I was hoping to find a flashlight," she said.

We drove another quarter-mile past woods and a sleeping cornfield. We passed a little Baptist church. I was still shaken from my encounter with the old woman, and I knew I'd have nightmares about her.

"Maybe we should just head back the other direction and check houses that way," Jen said. "I'm starting to worry. When were you exposed for the first time?"

"Around noon yesterday, I guess."

"It's getting close for you, then."

"I feel fine."

"Zach did too," she said. "It'll hit you fast."

The next house was a mobile home. There were two junked cars in the front yard, and one had a blue plastic tarp over it. To the side of the house was a huge oak tree with an engine block hanging from one of its limbs by a chain. The driveway wound through trees and circled around to the back, then continued a few hundred feet farther into a wooded area to a concrete block building with a garage door. I pulled around and parked by the back door of the home.

When I got out, I could hear a sound like an engine running. It was coming from the direction of the block building.

"What's that noise?" Jen asked. "It kind of sounds like a lawn mower."

"We should leave," I said.

"Someone is there," she insisted. "Maybe they can help us."

"They don't look like the sort ..."

"You haven't seen them to judge whether they're the 'sort,'" she said. "Let's at least go take a look."

Reluctantly, I agreed. We walked out toward the building. The snow was all trampled down and muddy. There had been a lot of activity there that day. I stepped over near one of the trees and picked up a stick. It wasn't long like the tobacco stake, but it would make a good club.

There weren't any windows in the front of the building, but I could see a couple in the left side. There was a gravel footpath that led around that side of the building to the rear. There was a lot of rusted metal and junk piled along the way.

Jen nodded toward some broken beer bottles and said, "Looks promising."

"I think the noise is coming from behind the building," I said. "Let's go around."

I tried to look in the windows on our way past, but they were too high.

"Oh God," Jen said, grabbing my arm.

She was staring into the trees to our left, at a doghouse that had been pieced together with scraps of siding and plywood. A food bowl sat beside a stake that had been driven into the ground. Attached to the stake was a chain, and the chain was attached to the mutilated remains of a mutt. It had been ripped apart. There was blood in the snow.

This wasn't good. Now I'd have to check on the noise to see if someone was in trouble.

I stepped away from her and eased toward the back of the building.

"No," she whispered. "Let's get out of here."

I ignored Jen. I didn't want to leave if there were people who needed our help. I crept to the corner of the building and peeked around.

There was a small gas-powered generator beside the back door. The door was cracked enough to allow an orange extension cord inside. Standing next to the generator with his back to me was a large man in dark blue coveralls. He was hunched over a little, and I couldn't see what he was doing. I scanned the rest of the area behind the building for others, but all I saw was more junk and trees.

I looked over my shoulder. Jen was still by the dog, motioning me back. I returned to her side, but I didn't plan on leaving just yet.

"There's a man back there," I whispered. "I can't tell whether he's infected. I'm going around to the other side to see if I can see his face."

"Is anyone inside?"

"I don't know," I said. "But there's a generator running back there, so probably."

She didn't offer to come with me. I went around the right side of the building. There were no windows on this side. I looked around the corner. The man wasn't there anymore. I presumed he had gone inside.

The noise of the generator would mask the sound of my movement, so I wasn't concerned about that. I went up to the back door, and put an eye up to the crack. It was a garage, judging by the tools and oil stains. There were five cots set up in the middle; one was occupied. The extension cord coming from the generator was connected to a television, a space heater, and a small lamp.

Then there was a shotgun blast.

I ran around the building. Jen was still where I'd left her. The man in blue coveralls lay on his back on the ground between us.

"Mother fucker!" Jen cried. She stepped closer to him, pumped the shotgun and fired again. The coveralls near his stomach blew out like confetti. The sound echoed through the woods behind me.

"Mother ..." She dropped to her knees, the shotgun rolling down her lap to the driveway.

"Jen! Are you okay? Did he hurt you?"

She grabbed a handful of gravel from the driveway and threw it at the body.

When I made it to the man, I paused to look at him. He was a bearded middle-aged fellow with a buzz haircut. Something that looked like an uncooked sausage link hung from the corner of his mouth. In his left hand was one of the bloody dog legs.

Jen was sobbing now. I ran over, lifted her to her feet and pulled her to my chest.

"He was eating it," she said. "He came at me ..."

I didn't want to be insensitive, but we didn't have time for this. The gunshots would attract more of the infected, and it was getting late. Here in this wooded area, the light was already fading. I had to get some alcohol, and we needed to get back to Blaine's very soon.

I led her back to the Blazer and put her inside. She wouldn't quit crying. I shut the door and went up to the back of the mobile home. The time for discretion was over. I didn't knock; I just went in.

The interior of the house smelled like a combination of ashtray and wet dog. It was hard to see anything in the low light, but I could tell that I was in the kitchen. There was a small table in there piled with mail and small parts from car engines. The white refrigerator had greasy black handprints on it. The sink was full of dirty dishes, the floor littered with trash.

How do people live like this?

I started on one side and went around opening all the cabinets. A quarter of the way around, I noticed the bottles on the shelf over the refrigerator.

"It's about damn time," I said out loud.

I pulled up a chair, stood on it and got them all down. Some were empty, but three had a little left in them, and one was completely full. I didn't take the time to read the labels. They were liquor bottles, and that was all that mattered. I hugged them to me and ran out of the house, the bottles clanking together the whole way.

As I came down the porch, I noticed an obese woman coming out of the woods near the block building. She was bundled up for the cold, but that didn't mean anything. I ran to the truck.

"Jen, open the door!"

She did, and I passed the bottles to her.

The big woman limped toward us. A girl in pink pajamas came into view, followed by a man in his underwear.

I ran around and jumped into the Blazer. Jen was staring out at the approaching figures.

"I'm sorry," she said.

I backed down the winding driveway toward the road.

"I let you down," she said. "Sometimes I'm such a girl."

I backed into the road and put the Blazer in drive.

"It's okay," I said. "I like girls."

"I dropped the gun, and I used up all the ammo."

"This is Kentucky," I said. "I think we'll find more."

CHAPTER 10

We were both in a daze as we drove back. The sun had all but set, and the snow was taking on a blue hue. Jen opened the full bottle and passed it to me.

"Get started," she said. "It's Southern Comfort."

I took a sip from the bottle, and the sweet liquid trickled down my throat, warming me all the way to my belly.

"You'll have to do better than that," she said. "Drink up."

"I'm driving, you know."

"It ain't far, and I don't see no sobriety checkpoints."

I put the bottle to my lips again and took a bigger swig. It burned. I almost didn't get it down.

I passed the bottle back to her.

"I'm not much of a drinker," I said. "And I never drink it straight like that."

* * *

When we got back to Blaine's, she handed me the bottle again.

"You go work on that," she said. "I have to use the restroom."

I waited until she went into the house, and I took a leak behind the truck. The air was bitter cold, and the sky was clearing. The sun was down below the tree line, and the first stars were starting to arrive. Off to the west, I could see a glow where Clayfield was. Either the power had been restored, or there was a big fire in the town. I zipped up and went into the workshop.

The shop was dark, but warmer than it had been. I couldn't see to get around in there, and I didn't want to trip and hurt myself. I went back out to the truck and turned on the headlights so they would shine through the front windows of the building, then I went back inside.

At least I could see enough to get the fire going. I blew on the embers again until the fire flared up, then I fed it some wood and air. The wood I'd brought in earlier was dry enough, and I put three logs on it. I left it open to get the fire hot, and then before bed, I would close it up and shut the damper down. Maybe we'd have heat all night.

I took another drink. This one went down more easily. I was already feeling the effects.

Jen returned.

She looked out at the truck. "What about the headlights?"

"We can turn them off now."

She handed me a glass dish that contained a used scented candle.

"I found it on their nightstand," she said.

We lit the candle and turned off the headlights. Then we made sure the building was locked up so we wouldn't have any surprises while we slept.

It was only around 6:30 in the evening, but we were both exhausted. Jen hadn't really slept at all the night before, so she was in worse shape than I. However, we couldn't sleep yet; I had to get drunk, and she had to make sure I got drunk.

"It shouldn't take long," I said. "I'm kind of a lightweight."

Jen sat cross-legged on her mattress on the floor. She'd removed her shoes, but she was still bundled up in the coat.

"I killed him," she said, staring at the lit candle on the upturned bucket between us.

I took another drink. I had a strong buzz going by that time.

"He was eating that dog," she said.

"You had to," I said.

She shrugged. "I could have run. I didn't have to shoot him twice."

"You said yourself that we were going to have to kill ..."

"That was before I had to do it!" she snapped.

I took another drink.

"Pass me that bottle," she said.

I did, and she took two swallows. In the candlelight, I could see a tear running down her cheek.

I stepped over to her. I intended to sit by her and put my arm around her to comfort her, but she gave me a look that warned me not to even think about it. Instead, I took the bottle.

I went over to my own mattress, sat and removed my boots. I took another drink.

It was getting warm in the room.

"Put a big log on the fire," I said, "then close down the damper. I don't think I can do it in my state."

She slipped her shoes on and took care of the stove.

"Do you think it's working? Are you drunk?"

"I'm getting close," I said. "I prolly had 'nuff, just need to wait for it to do its think ... I mean, thing."

Outside, there was a howl—hopefully a dog or a coyote.

"If you feel uneasy 'bout me," I said, "you could restrain me. That way, if I turn, I won't be able to hurt you."

"No," she said, returning to her bed.

Another howl outside.

"I'm going to bed now," she said. "Can I put the candle out?"

"Yeah," I said. I took another drink, and the room got dark.

I screwed the lid onto the bottle and fell back on the mattress. My head was swimming. Just before I passed out, I could hear Jen softly crying on the other side of the room.

* * *

When I woke up, the sun was glaring through the window in the east side of the building. I could see water dripping past the windows from the snow melting off the roof. The shop was cozy, and the faint smell of wood smoke was comforting, briefly bringing back memories of Christmas morning. Jen's bed was empty. I figured she was in the house.

I sat up slowly, expecting a hangover, but I was surprised at how good I felt. There was no headache, and I was rested. I hadn't had coffee in two days, and I really wanted some right then. I put on my boots and stepped outside to relieve myself.

The Blazer was gone. I panicked for a second, worried about Jen. Then it dawned on me that she'd left me. My worry turned to anger. I guess I should have expected it. I barely knew her. We'd only spent one day together, but I felt hurt that she wouldn't want to be with me. I could hear my ex-wife's mocking voice in my head,

What the hell did you think would happen?

CHAPTER 11

There was nothing I could do about it. She was gone. It was probably for the best. It would make it easier for me to travel if I traveled alone. She was a big girl; she didn't need my help.

I went back inside and dug around in the food for something to eat, but nothing looked good, and I didn't have much of an appetite. I decided to go in the house and conduct a thorough search for useful items. I needed to find the keys to Betsy's minivan anyway. I didn't feel so bad about pilfering now, since I'd realized they'd abandoned me.

I was in a really bad mood.

On my way up to the house, I looked out across the fields again. It was still cold, but the sun was out now, so the snow was melting, and the ground was showing in places. I heard a car alarm very faintly in the distance—a horn blaring over and over. One of the infected must have set it off during the night.

I went inside. I wasn't sure what I was looking for. It appeared that Blaine and Betsy had taken the important stuff. After fumbling around in the dark the night before, I decided to look for a flashlight or more candles. I opened drawers in the kitchen, just to see what was there, but I didn't find anything that struck me as immediately useful.

I went into Blaine and Betsy's bedroom. I found a little book light and another candle in one of the nightstands. I stepped into the walk-in closet. Most of the clothes were gone, but there were still some left—mostly impractical things like suits and some of Betsy's dresses. I noticed one of Betsy's coats that I thought might fit Jen, then had to remind myself that it didn't matter. I pushed the clothes across the closet rod one at a time.

I slid a black dress over, and next to it was a lacy red chemise. I paused. It had been ... too long. I wondered how Betsy might look in it, and then I felt disgusted with myself for thinking it, especially now that the world had gone to hell.

I'd been divorced for a while, but it was still difficult for me to get in the "single" mindset. I hadn't put much effort into dating again. Betsy had set me up with one of her friends, but that didn't work out.

My mom was always on me about going to church so I could meet a "good" woman. Now the selection of available women had shrunk dramatically. The selection of good women ... well ... Right now, the world being what it was, a good woman meant a woman who knew how to take care of herself and would care enough about me to put a bullet in my head if it ever came to that.

I slid another dress in front of the lingerie and turned my attention to the shelf above the clothes. There were some small boxes and photo albums. I pulled the boxes down. One was full of old Valentine's Day and Mother's Day cards. Two of them held loose photographs. I pulled a picture from one of the boxes. It was Betsy and the kids opening presents two Christmases before. Tears welled up in my eyes. Seeing their smiling faces took away the anger I'd felt toward them. They'd been good friends to me. I hoped they'd made it someplace safe.

A vehicle pulled up outside.

"Jen."

I put the box of photos on the bed and ran to the back porch. It wasn't the Blazer. It was an older red-and-white pickup. I stepped back inside the house and looked around for something to use as a weapon. I ended up retrieving an umbrella from the corner.

I went out onto the porch to ascertain the intentions of the driver.

It was Jen after all.

I ran out to her, resisting the urge to hug her.

"What the hell?" I said.

"I thought I'd be back before you woke up."

"What the hell?" I repeated.

"Come help me," she said, walking to the back of the truck. She let down the tailgate.

The bed of the truck was packed with supplies, including a gas-powered generator.

"Is this the same one?"

"Yep," she said, grinning.

"How?"

She climbed up into the bed. The generator had two small wheels on it. She pushed it toward me. It took both of us to lift it out.

"How did you get this in here by yourself?" I said.

"I backed the truck to a low spot so that the tailgate was close to the ground, then I just wheeled it in. My granddad used to load his riding mower that way."

"But what about the people?"

I parked the Blazer down at that church early this morning, then I set off the alarm and hid. They started showing up within a few minutes, and gathered around the noise. There were a lot of them—probably thirty. They were really pissed about the horn; you should have seen them."

"Are you crazy?" I said. "You could have been killed."

"While they were busy with the Blazer, I ran up the road to that old lady's house and took her truck. The keys were in it. Then I drove back to get the generator. I saw more of them headed toward the church. They're everywhere; we just haven't been seeing them."

"Why would you do something like that by yourself?"

She handed me the extension cord.

"I needed to make up for yesterday," she said. "I wanted you to know that I'm not a liability. I can help you. I can do stuff."

"Jen, I don't think you're a liability."

She hopped out of the bed.

"I know we don't know each other very well, but I think we should stick together for a while."

"Of course," I said.

She pulled out the shotgun we'd left the night before and handed it to me.

"He was gone," she said.

"Who?"

"The man I shot," she said. "I must not have killed him after all."

We stared at each other a moment, both of us pondering whether or not it was a good thing.

"I got some good stuff," she said.

I looked in the bed. There were two more guns in there—another shotgun and a rifle—and several boxes of ammunition. There were also several plastic bags. She started pulling them out.

"I got food," she said, smiling. "There's bacon in there ... and coffee."

"Where did you ...?"

"I'll tell you about it over breakfast," she said. "I'm starving."

* * *

I finished unloading the truck while Jen got breakfast going. A lot of the food she'd brought back would need refrigeration, but we could just store it outside for a while. We'd probably eat it all before the weather warmed. I put the food that I knew we wouldn't use right away into the cab of the truck to keep it from attracting animals and cracked the windows to keep the sun from building up too much heat.

When I went into the shop, I was met with the wonderful aroma of frying bacon.

"I checked for eggs, but there weren't any," she said. "Maybe you should see if the chickens are doing okay. They probably haven't been fed in a while."

I headed outside.

"Also," she said, "you might see if there's a campfire coffee pot in the house."

I walked around to the pen and looked inside. It was muddy in there. The snow was nearly gone. There were three chickens in there, scratching around. It looked like two Barred Rocks and a Rhode Island Red. They would need water too. Their automatic dispenser that kept the water from freezing was operated by a little solar panel, but it was almost empty. I opened the gate and went in with them, then walked over to the coop, which was really just a back room of the workshop. It had a larger door for people, with a smaller door set in the bottom for the chickens. There was a wooden bin just inside the door that had a partial bag of chicken feed in it. There was another Rhode Island Red in the coop, and she made a big fuss when I came in. I scooped out some feed and poured it in a pan that was on the floor, then threw another handful on the ground outside.

There was no campfire coffee percolator inside. There was an electric drip coffee maker, though. I took it back to the shop.

When I got back, the bacon was almost done, and Jen was starting on some oatmeal. I put a pan of water on the stove.

We were down to our last bottle of water, and I didn't want to give it to the chickens, so I went outside with the five-gallon bucket to get some snow. There was still some in the shaded areas under the trees and behind the house. I scooped it up and brought it inside to melt for the chickens.

I put in the filter and measured out the right amount of coffee. When the water on the stove was about to boil, I poured it into the filter cup of the coffee maker and let it drip down into the pot.

* * *

"I went back to that brick house with the red barn," Jen said, chewing her bacon. "You know, the one that had the four wheeler. There ain't nobody there. The door was unlocked. The table was set, and there was food on it. It had been there a while. It looked like they were in the middle of the meal and just got up and left. Nothing was disturbed. It was kind of strange.

"I just loaded up with the basics, but they have a lot of good stuff. We should go back and clean it out ... maybe even move over there. They have a wood stove in the house."

I knew things were different now, but it just didn't sound right.

"I don't know," I said. "It doesn't set well with me."

"What?"

"Looting."

"This ain't looting," she said. "Looting is when you take TVs and shit. Looting is when you take stuff that belongs to somebody. This is scavenging. Salvaging."

"Feels a lot like stealing," I said.

"Yeah, well how does that bacon taste, huh? And how about that damn SUV you've been driving? I looked in the glove box at the registration. It ain't yours."

"That was different," I said. "I was running for my life, and I knew the woman was infected."

"Nobody was there, damn it! You ain't going to make me feel guilty about this."

"I'm sorry, Jen," I said. "You're right, but think about this: We aren't the only healthy people. We can't be. What if we break into a house and take stuff that belongs to healthy people? What if someone came in here while we were gone and took our stuff?"

Jen laughed. "Our stuff? This is Blaine's place, remember? You're justifying stealing when it suits you."

I sipped my coffee to keep from having to reply.

"Okay," she said. "From now on, we'll only go into homes we know are abandoned. Would that ease your conscience?"

I nodded.

Everything was so wrong now. I hadn't even had time to really think or process exactly how different life would be.

"I'd hate to leave this area," I said. "I grew up here. It's home. But maybe we should try to get across the river soon. Try to get to a safer place."

"I don't think they stopped it," she said. "I think the whole world is screwed. I tried the radio in the truck this morning. Most of the stations aren't broadcasting anymore, and the ones that are keep airing a recorded message telling people to stay indoors.

"But we have the generator and your laptop," she continued, "so let's see if we can get online. If there is any safe place out there, they'll still be broadcasting."

"Do you really think the Internet will be working?" I asked.

"Should be," she said. "I'll bet those servers have backup power. I don't know how it all works exactly, but my cousin used to tell me about Internet backbones ... or something like that. He said it would be impossible to destroy the entire Internet all at once. It's only been a couple of days since the disease hit Clayfield. I don't see why there still wouldn't be cities with electricity. I would think those power plants would run for a little while without people around. We probably just lost a substation in Clayfield or something."

"No," I said. "On the news, they were saying that a lot of the Southern states were without power."

"How would they know?" she said. "Everybody down here is sick. Besides, I don't think that will affect the Internet."

I shrugged. I didn't know. I guess it wouldn't hurt to try. Except ...

"That generator makes a lot of noise. How do we run it without everybody in Grace County showing up on our doorstep?"

CHAPTER 12

The ideal solution would have been to put the generator underground to deaden the noise, but Blaine and Betsy didn't have a basement or root cellar. Even if they did, we would have to be in a different location because of the gas fumes and carbon monoxide.

We considered running it in the workshop while we were in the house, but even then, it might be heard and alert everyone to our location.

The generator's previous owners had left it outside like they were supposed to, but they wound up dead from something far worse than fumes.

"Why don't we forget the generator," Jen said. "If you have enough charge on your battery, we could drive around, maybe find a signal."

"Those modems and routers need electricity, though."

"I wonder how the cell towers are doing."

"Neither of us has a phone, so ..."

"There are lots of people out there not using their phones," she said. "We can just search houses until we find one."

"That might involve coming in contact with them, and I'd like to avoid that as much as we can."

"How about this," Jen said. "We put the generator in the back of the truck and run the cord into the house. One of us sits in the truck with it running while the other is inside logged on and getting news. If they show up, the one in the truck just drives away, but slow enough for the infected to follow. Once they've been led far enough away, just speed up, circle around and come back home."

"That's a bad idea."

"Kiss my ass. I'm the only one thinking here."

"No," I said, raising my hand. "No, it really is a bad idea, but I think you are on the right track with moving it. We should just take it somewhere else, away from here, where making noise wouldn't matter. All we want to do is get news. Eventually, we might need to use it to pump some fresh water, but if we can find bottled water ..."

"So we just need a place that has an Internet connection and a basement," she said.

"Yes, or an easy escape. I'm thinking the museum."

"Where you worked? But that's in town."

"We were going to have to go into Clayfield for water and other supplies eventually anyway," I said.

"Why? The whole countryside is full of unoccupied houses loaded with supplies. There must be houses out here with Internet connections and basements or easy escapes."

"But going to the museum would save us from running into situations like we did yesterday where we don't know if we'll find what we're looking for. There's no need to risk it for an uncertainty."

"It's all uncertain now," she said. "I thought you wanted to avoid the sick people."

"There shouldn't be anyone at all in the museum. If we pull right up to the door, we can run in and lock up. The place is solid. Plus, the building is large enough, and the doors are spaced far enough apart, that if we distract them on one side of the building, we can get out on the other side."

"This sounds like a pain in the ass," she said. "I went out by myself and got all this good stuff without getting too close to anyone. I say we stay in this area and try to find a charged phone and access the Internet that way."

"We're also out of drinking water," I said. "The city water system might still be working, or we might need to go into some of the stores and get bottled water. We'll have to go into town for that anyway, at least until I figure out how to get water from that well out there without so much noise."

"So we're breaking into stores now?" she said.

"I know," I said. "I sound like a hypocrite, but we need water."

"I'm just giving you a hard time. In fact, now that you mention it, we might need to go to the county line and stock up on booze."

We got to work on our plan.

First, we removed the back seats from Betsy's minivan. The generator would go in there. Our thinking was that if we ran the generator from the van, no one could get to it to tamper with it or damage it.

We filled the generator from Blaine's lawnmower gas can, then plugged in the long orange extension cord. Once the generator was inside the van, I cracked the back windows. Then I fed a little of the extension cord out of the one on the passenger side so we could access it quickly.

Next, we loaded the guns. The shotgun and shells Jen brought back from the Kaler house were 12-gauges. Her gun was a 20-gauge, so we were still out of ammunition for that weapon. The other one she brought back fired .22 long rifle rounds—not a powerful gun, but it was better than the sticks I had been using. I really didn't want to use the guns at all, but we needed to keep the infected at a distance.

I took the .22 and one of the partial bottles of alcohol—about three fingers' worth of Captain Morgan. Jen took my laptop, the shotgun, all of our empty water containers in a garbage bag, a box of ammunition for each of us, and the mostly full bottle of Southern Comfort.

I drove the minivan, and Jen followed in the pickup. I kept glancing back at her in the mirror. She had a red bandana tied around her nose and mouth, and she looked like a bandit from one of those old westerns. I could see the shotgun propped up in the seat beside her. I was so relieved to have her back, though I couldn’t say if it was because of her company or if I was just glad I wasn't alone.

I adjusted my own mask. I still didn't know if the masks worked, but we could find out about that when we got online at the museum. I hoped we’d also find out about the necessary amount of alcohol. Hopefully we wouldn't need to get drunk every time we had an interaction with the infected.

Even though it was a longer route to the museum, I took Bragusberg Road again. Gala Road would have been faster, but I worried about encountering wrecked or abandoned cars that would block our path. Our last drive down Bragusberg Road had been clear, and I didn't want to stop until we got to the museum.

I took it slow. I wanted to check out the houses on our way into town. The infected were out, and there were a lot of them. I made a mental note of every house where I saw them. It didn't mean those houses were abandoned, but it was a pretty good bet.

The disease seemed to affect them in different ways. Some of the people were quite spry, but others were almost catatonic. I noticed a few with bad injuries, but they didn't act bothered by them.

Some ran out to the road as we passed. At one point, we had a small crowd behind us, like we were the press vehicles in a televised marathon. Jen was getting nervous about it. A couple of times, it looked like one of our pursuers almost caught up to her, but I don't think there was any real danger of that. Our slow pace was still quick enough to stay ahead of them.

When we reached an open, straight stretch of road, she sped up and pulled alongside me on my left. She gave me a dirty look, flipped me the bird and motioned for me to get a move on. I grinned as she dropped back behind me. After that, we drove 60 miles an hour until we approached the city limits and left the crowd of infected in the road between two cornfields.

CHAPTER 13

There was a lot of smoke over Clayfield. It looked like fires were still burning on the west side of town. My house was out that way, and I wondered whether it was still standing. I would check on it later, but right then, we needed to get into the museum without attracting too much attention. It didn't look like that was going to be possible.

As Bragusberg Road enters the city limits, it is lined with large trees and restored Victorian and shingle-style houses. I could see people out on the front lawns of some of the homes. They were interested in us, but only a few followed. One blue house was surrounded by at least a hundred people. Most stood staring up at the second floor, but some tried, and failed, to climb up the side.

Bragusberg Road ended, and I took a right onto Sixth street, headed north. As I approached the court square, my stomach knotted up.

They were everywhere. The only other time I'd seen so many people in the streets was in October, during the town's Pumpkin Festival.

The south side of the square was so thick with people as to be impassable. I looked in the mirror at Jen to make sure she was doing okay. I didn't see anyone near us at the moment, so I slowed and stopped when I got within half a block of the intersection with Water Street. That put me a block and a half from the crowd. I wanted to watch them for a bit before we took a detour around them.

Just like at the blue house, there were some who just stood and stared. Their interest was directed to one of the buildings on the back side of the courthouse. Others were very active. They behaved much like wild animals—chasing, clawing and biting each other. A dark-haired woman ran out of the crowd, dressed only in a pink sweater and one gray sock. Her left knee was bloody. A man ran out after her, tackled her and pushed her face to the pavement. He forced her legs open.

I'd seen enough.

I pulled down Water Street and planned to circle around the defunct Barret Clothing Mill, up Fifth Street and away from the crowd.

When I looked in my mirror, the red-and-white pickup shot past me, continuing toward the court square.

"Damn it, Jen! What are you doing?"

I slammed on the brakes, put the minivan in reverse and backed out into the intersection. Everybody looked at us, even the slow ones. A few had already started toward us. Jen ran the pickup over the curb and skidded to a stop on the sidewalk opposite the crowd. I turned to follow her.

Her door opened.

"No, Jen," I whispered. "Oh, no no no ..."

She stepped out into the street and pulled the shotgun to her shoulder. The end of the weapon bounced up with the recoil, and the side of the rapist's head blew apart. There was a collective gasp, and the entire crowd jerked in unison at the sound of the gun and then charged her en masse. Their snarls and whines went up like a roar. She slipped back into the truck. The backup lights came on when she put the truck in reverse, and then the beasts engulfed her. There were so many that I couldn't even see the truck anymore.

I leaned on my horn. A few of them looked up, but they didn't leave the pickup. I didn't want her to panic and do something stupid like shoot at them through the glass.

"Son of a bitch!"

I pulled the minivan around so I was broadside to them, and grabbed the rifle. I let down the window and aimed at a head in the crowd near where the truck was buried. I couldn't pull the trigger. I took a deep breath and pointed at the knee of one on the perimeter. I squeezed.

The sound was nothing like the shotgun. It was more like a crack.

A man buckled and fell to the ground, but the crowd still didn't move toward me.

The rifle was a semiautomatic. I didn't have to do anything but pull the trigger. I squeezed it again. A woman arched over, grabbing her side near her kidney, and stumbled away from the crowd. I fired three times in a row, not aiming. I saw two people drop. It became easier when I didn't think about it.

I looked to my right. I had a new group headed my way from the south.

Two more shots, and the mob finally became interested in me. They cleared up for her in front first, and when I saw the truck lurch forward, then pull away across a corner lot and down South Street, I mashed the gas and headed down Water Street. We were running parallel to each other, and we each had a group chasing us. We crossed over Fifth simultaneously, a block apart, and sped down to the next cross street, which was Second. By then, the crowd was far enough behind us not to matter. She stopped at the intersection and waited for me to turn north and pull back in front of her. When I got to the intersection of South and Second, where she sat idling, I stopped in front of her, perpendicular to her vehicle.

I glared at her. Her eyes narrowed. This time, I flipped her the bird.

* * *

Our original route changed, but our plan did not. I was pissed that Jen had put us in unnecessary danger like that, but I hoped that some good would come of it and that the noise of the gunfire and horn would draw people away from the museum.

I took a left onto Broadway, then a right onto Fifth. I had to drive up on the sidewalk, because that was where the head-on collision had taken place. It was also where I'd wrecked my car.

The cars were all still there, but not the bodies. The old man I'd hit with my car might have lived, but there was no way the man in the other wreck had survived. They were both gone. There must have been other healthy people out disposing of bodies.

I escorted Jen to the front of the museum. She pulled in close, with the passenger side of the pickup near the front door. She got out, pulled out the garbage bag of supplies and the shotgun, and ran inside. I sat in the van and watched to make sure she made it, and then I pulled the van to the side of the building on North Street underneath a window. I got the passenger side as close to the building as I could; I even scraped off the side mirror in the process.

When I got out, I could see Jen inside at the window, breaking out a pane of glass. I fed her the extension cord, and then I ran around and climbed into the back of the van, where I started up the generator. Then I grabbed the rifle and the Captain Morgan, hopped out and locked the doors. The sound of the generator was noticeable inside the van, but not as loud as I thought it would be.

I was about to run to the front door, when I noticed that the corpse of the woman I'd hit with my car wasn't in the street anymore. Someone was definitely removing the bodies.

I didn't have time to wonder about it right then. I went around to the front of the building. Across and up the street, the delivery van lay on its side at the newspaper office. In the museum lot, the little red truck rested on the splintered sign. It was so quiet and still and unnerving. I went inside, relieved that we were able to get in so quickly and without any interference. I locked the front door and looked around.

The place was as I'd left it. No one had been in. I walked through the small gift shop and the permanent collection, toward my office. The extension cord hung down the side of the wall below the window in the gift shop.

"Jen?"

No answer.

She was in the office, sitting in my chair.

"C'mon, Jen, we need ..."

She held up a hand. She was on my office phone. Her red bandana was pulled down around her neck like a kerchief. I pulled my own mask down.

"We need to ..."

"Shhh," she hissed.

I left her to her call, took the end of the orange cord and tugged it through the broken window and into the office.

"It's just ringing," she said.

"Who are you ..."

"Shhh."

The office computer equipment and modem were plugged into a power strip. I unplugged them from the wall and plugged them into the orange cord. The light on the modem came on.

Jen hung up.

"I was checking on my brother," she said. "He lives near Kansas City. Nobody answered."

I went straight to the phone and dialed my mom. I listened to it ring and watched Jen turn on the computer.

"What the hell were you thinking back there?" I said.

"I won't put up with that shit," she said, not looking at me.

"You could have gotten both of us killed."

"You didn't have to stay."

"You know, if what they say is true, and they're just running on base instincts, then we're going to see a lot more of that," I said.

"Then you're going to see a lot more killing," she said.

The phone rang almost twenty times, so I hung up.

"It's working," she said. "I'm online."

I got out my laptop and plugged into the power strip and one of the other ports on the modem.

"I'm on CNN's website," she said. "No new stories there since yesterday. The last story was posted yesterday morning at ten. It is about a state of emergency in Minneapolis."

She looked at me. "Which side of the Mississippi River is Minneapolis?"

"The wrong side, I think. Any mention of St. Louis? My mom lives there."

She shook her head.

I checked my emails. There was nothing there from my mom.

Check all the social sites," Jen said. "That's where we'll find out what's happening."

There were no new posts on any of those sites. The only notification I had was Jen's reply to me two nights before. I checked Blaine and Betsy's profiles, but they were unchanged.

Frustrated, I got up and peered out the window. I could hear the generator, but it was muffled. Thus far, we'd not attracted any attention.

"What time is it?" I called out.

"Almost three," Jen said.

"I'd like to get the water bottles filled if we can. If not, we might need to leave early and check some stores. We need to head back to Blaine's before five. That should give us plenty of time to get in before dark."

"Uh-huh," was her reply.

"Any of your friends posting?" I asked on my way to the sink.

"Not for a while ... wait, yeah! He's your friend too, I think."

I turned on the faucet, and water came out.

"We got water," I said. "Who's my friend?"

"Brian Davies," she said. "He posted last night. It's a link to his blog."

"I don't know him," I said, coming back to get the empty water bottles so I could fill them.

"Sure you do," she said. "Brian Davies. You know."

"No."

"From high school?"

I shook my head and picked up the garbage bag of bottles. I removed the Southern Comfort, put it on the desk and headed back to the sink with the bag.

"He was a couple of years younger than us," she said. "He's a professional blogger now."

"They have those?"

"Yeah, and he does that Michael Jackson act sometimes. He was in the paper last fall. He did that concert to raise money for those kids."

I topped off one of the bottles and started on another.

Michael Jackson act?

"He's a Michael Jackson impersonator?" I asked.

"I think it's more of a tribute act, but yeah, close enough."

"They have those?"

"He's completely changed his blog," she said. "All he's talking about is what's happening. There's a lot of information here. Links to stuff, so we won't have to search. He says the virus jumped the river yesterday."

"How would he know?"

"He said that alcohol works, but only if you drink enough before the fever sets in."

"What's enough?"

"He says wearing a mask helps but isn't always effective."

She wasn't listening to me. I filled the last of the bottles, and then took one with me back to the office. I handed it to her, and she took a drink. I checked on the van. We were still okay.

"I'm going to share the link," she said. "Get on your laptop and check it out."

CHAPTER 14

Brian Davies's "professional" blog didn't look very professional to me. The top banner was a still image from Michael Jackson's Thriller video, and most of the page was loaded with links. I recognized a few of the sites as ones I had visited that first night.

I supposed I shouldn't be too critical; Jen did say he'd completely changed his site since the virus hit. Also, he'd taken the time to provide a little description with each link, so visitors could find things easily—not that there were many visitors.

When he did do any writing, he was describing what was going on around him, what he'd experienced, what he observed out his window, and what others were telling him from other parts of the world.

His site didn't look like much, but it was actually loaded with pertinent information. I read through several posts and followed the links when they looked relevant to our particular needs.

According to the links he'd provided, it wasn't necessary to get drunk, but only to begin to feel the effects of the alcohol. Also, masks worked, but the disease could still be spread through bites, scratches and sexual contact.

I read one of his journal entries:

There has been a group of them outside for more than 12 hours. I've been watching them through the window. I feel like Dian Fossey observing her gorillas. There are eight of them: three men (I hesitate to call them men) and five women. There is a clear alpha male in the group. He has been having sex with all the women. The other two males are submissive but do attempt to initiate sex with the women when the alpha isn't looking.

It is fascinating and grotesque. Four of them are mostly naked, yet they don't act like they are uncomfortable. I have noticed what looks like frostbite on some of their feet. Last night, I saw them all huddle together under my maple tree. I presume this was for warmth.

I have to keep reminding myself that these were the same people I saw in restaurants and theaters. These were all people once.

"Where does he live?" I said.

"He's still in Clayfield," Jen said. "I see him and his boyfriend out all the time."

"Do you think they need help? His journal says he has infected out on his lawn."

"I'll send him a message," she said.

"I'm going to take the water out to the truck."

On my way, I took a look out the window. The minivan had an audience now. There were six of them out there, walking around. They weren't trying to get into the vehicle yet, but they were curious.

"They've found the generator," I said.

Jen joined me at the window.

"We should go before many more show up," she said.

"I'll get the water loaded," I said. "You get a message to your friend. If he doesn't reply within fifteen minutes, we'll just have to try him again another time."

I went into the supply closet and emptied out a cardboard box I'd been using to store cleaning supplies. I was able to fit most of the water bottles in it. I carried it to the front door. No one was out front, so I took it out as quickly and as quietly as I could and put it in the back. I could hear them pounding on the minivan now. Their noises would probably bring more.

I went back inside and locked the door.

"Make that five minutes!" I said.

"Do you have a router?"

"A router? Why?"

"Yes or no?" she said.

"There's one under the desk, but I quit using it because ..."

"Does it work?" she said, impatient.

"Yes."

She disappeared behind the desk.

I went to get the rest of the water. When I got to the front door, I looked into the office. She was brushing the dust bunnies from the router and plugging it in.

I loaded the rest of the water in the truck. I saw a woman over at the Chronicle office, but I didn't think she saw me. When I got back inside, Jen was on my laptop.

"We've got a signal," she said. "We can head out now."

"The range on that thing is really short."

"We'll sit in the truck," she said. "We'll stay close to the building for a while."

I went into the office to get the rifle and the liquor, and I looked out the window to the big lot behind the building, then farther out to Sixth Street. More were coming.

I got in behind the wheel, and Jen sat in the passenger side with my computer in her lap. We pulled the doors shut gently, so the people around the other side of the building couldn't hear us.

A boy in his early teens crossed the street near the transmission shop and headed our way. We sat very still inside the pickup, and he walked right by. He was shirtless, and there was a terrible gash in his chest. It had bled a lot, but at that time, the blood was all dried down his body and right leg.

"I think there were people in that blue house," Jen said. "Those things were interested in something there. On the court square too."

I nodded, suspecting she was right.

"There ain't many of us left," she continued. "We need to help each other."

"It's getting too late to help all of them," I said. "First, let's focus on your friend. We'll see what's going on in the blue house tomorrow."

The crowd around the minivan had grown enough that it was beginning to extend around the edge of the building. We were no more than twenty feet away from them, and they didn't even know we were there.

"Someone is removing the dead," I said, feeling the need to whisper.

Jen looked at me, but she didn't say anything. I know she was thinking about the man she'd shot the day before.

"That first day, I hit people with my car," I said. "I didn't mean to, but I did. They're not there now. Their bodies are gone."

We couldn't actually see the minivan from where we sat around the corner, but the crowd around it was getting agitated.

"What if they get in or jerk the cord loose?" Jen said.

I shrugged. "I haven't seen them smash a car window yet, and I pulled the van up close enough to the building that I don't think they'll be able to get to the cord. They could turn the van over, I guess. That would do it."

Two men tumbled out of the crowd near the corner of the building, and rolled together within a few feet of our truck. I recognized one of them. It was Mr. Aslam, who owned the gas station I always used. The other man didn't look familiar. They were biting each other. Another man came out of the crowd and joined the fight. He dragged Mr. Aslam off of the other man and shoved him into the wall, then against our truck.

Mr. Aslam saw us. There was a moment when we made eye contact and I could have sworn he knew me, but it was only a moment. The fight didn't interest him anymore; we did. He leapt up onto the hood, sliding on his belly until his face hit the windshield.

I cranked the truck and put it in reverse. Immediately, the mob came around the corner of the building.

"Ho-lee frickin' shit," Jen said.

There were far more than we'd thought; they'd been hidden from view by the building. I backed out into the street, almost to the transmission shop.

"How about your friend?" I said.

"Nothing yet," she said, looking at the laptop. "Can we drive around the building for a little while? Stay close to the signal and give him some more time?"

They were running at us. Mr. Aslam was trying to chew through the glass. I put the truck in drive and gunned it around the south side of the museum. The crowd followed.

"You'll have to get closer," she said. "I've lost it."

I got to the back of the building and stopped. The mob rounded the corner after me. I waited until they were almost at my tailgate, and I started off again. I went around the next corner, onto North Street, where the minivan was parked. The van was covered in people. There were a few still in the street, but most of the crowd was chasing me around the building.

I kept it up for five laps.

"He responded!" she said. "He sent an address and a map to his place. Head west."

I came around the building for the sixth time, then got onto Eighth Street and turned west onto Broadway. Mr. Aslam stayed with us for a while, holding on to the windshield wiper.

I slowed so that Mr. Aslam could get off, but he didn't want to. Jen tried rolling down the window and poking him with the rifle, but he still wouldn't budge. I didn't want to hurt him—he'd been a nice man once—but he had to go.

I did the only safe thing for us. I sped up and then slammed on the brakes. Mr. Aslam flew off the hood, the right windshield wiper still in his grip. I pulled around him and proceeded down West Broadway.

The air was hazy with smoke. We passed 15th Street, and I could see that several houses had burned to the ground. Blackened chimneys and refrigerators stuck up from the rubble.

"I'd like to go to my house," I said.

"Do you have stuff to get?"

"I do, I suppose, but I just want to see if the house is still there. I can come back later for the stuff."

I took a right onto 17th Street. My house had been spared, but farther down the street, the library had not. The building was brick, but it had been gutted by the fire. The windows were broken, and the roof had been consumed. I felt gutted too, thinking about what a place like that could mean for us at a time like this. I also felt ashamed. It had been more than a year since I'd even been in there. Lately, the Internet had provided all of my reading material and information. Soon, it would be gone too.

CHAPTER 15

Brian Davies lived just outside of Clayfield, near the little community of Belfast. He had a huge front yard and a long, paved driveway that led to a new brick home. The drive was gated, but the gate was open.

We counted seventeen people on his lawn. They came at us when we pulled into the driveway. I started to back out, but then the front door opened, and Brian stepped out and waved at us with both arms. I stopped, and he pointed to the three-bay garage. The door on the left started going up.

"Hurry," Jen said. "Get in there."

I waited until the people were near us, then I sped toward the garage. They chased us, but we were inside and the door was down before they could catch up.

"Wow," I said. "Professional bloggers do pretty well."

To my right were two cars: a black Porsche 911 and a silver Mercedes AMG. There was also a blue Waverunner in there on a little trailer, which meant there was probably another vehicle somewhere to pull the trailer.

The interior door to the garage opened, and Brian came out to greet us. He was holding a drink in one hand. I wish I could say that seeing him jogged my memory, but it didn't. I still didn't recognize him. He was about Jen's height and thin. He was extremely well groomed and nicely dressed for a man more than two days into the apocalypse.

"Jen!" he said. "It's been too long!"

He hugged Jen and kissed her cheek, holding his drink off to the side.

"It's been awful," he said.

"It's been hell," Jen said.

He looked at me sideways.

"I sent you a friend request like two years ago, and you rejected me," he said. "I've never gotten over it."

I didn't know what to say.

"Sorry, I ..."

"Shut up," he laughed. "I'm joking."

He got between us, hooked both our arms with his, and escorted us to his door. He sloshed a little drink on me in the process, and I think it was intentional.

The house was beautiful, showcasing art and antiques, aquariums and terrariums, specimen bonsai trees ... It felt more like a museum than my museum did.

"So how's my favorite nerd from the history club?" he asked.

It took me a second to realize he was talking about me. I had been in the history club in high school, but I was surprised that he remembered.

"Fine," I said. "Considering."

"Everything is relevant." He grinned.

"Relative?" I said.

"That too."

Jen was looking at an enormous aquarium set in the wall. It was lit.

"So how is it that you still have electricity?" she asked.

"We have a windmill out back," he said. "One of the big ones. Didn't you see it?"

"I didn't notice."

"Well, it's huge," he said. "It makes a lot of noise. We're used to it, but I'm sure that's what's drawing them here."

I was blown away by all the lovely things. It was hard for me to imagine a house like this in a town like Clayfield.

"Your home is beautiful," I said. "I'm really impressed. You've done well for yourself."

"You have too," he said. "I see you in the paper all time with stories about the museum. You're really doing something important over there. Clayfield needs culture, you know."

"I appreciate that, but this ..."

"Stop right there," he said. "My sweetie knows how to make a buck. Don't make more of it than what it is. I don't. It's just money, and right now it doesn't matter, does it?"

"Where is he?" Jen asked.

"The last I heard, he was in Hong Kong. That was yesterday. I have to believe he'll be okay, but the virus has moved into Asia ..."

His voice was starting to break, so I changed the subject.

"So Jen tells me you're a Michael Jackson impersonator."

"Jen tells you? Jen tells you? Damn, boy, I've been doing that act for a while. Didn't you know? I was on the telethon; I was at the fair ... Anyway, it's really more of a tribute act, and it doesn't matter anymore either. Come on to the kitchen; I'm cooking us some dinner."

We followed him through the dining room, into the ultra-modern kitchen. It looked like something from one of those cooking shows on TV.

"I'm baking some tilapia," he said. "We'll have steamed asparagus and rice."

"Thank you, Brian," Jen said. "But we want to get back before dark. We came because we thought you needed help."

"Get back where?" he said.

"We're staying at a friend's place out on Gala Road," I said.

"Electricity?" he said.

"No."

"Fresh water?"

"No."

"Food?"

"Some."

"Then what the hell are you going back there for? It sounds to me like you're the ones who need my help. We have everything we need right here. You two stay with me for a few days, and we can plan how to take over the world."

* * *

We accepted Brian's invitation to stay, but only for the night. We told him about the blue house and the building south of the courthouse, and he agreed that we would need to help anyone who might be inside.

We discussed things over dinner.

"I've got a couple of friends in the blogosphere—survivors—who are saying this is an actual zombie apocalypse, like in the movies."

"Things are crazy." I chuckled. "But not that crazy."

"I have a friend in Greece," he continued, pouring us some more wine. "He said he saw someone walking around, despite the fact that he knew the guy was dead a few hours before."

Jen and I looked at each other. We were both thinking the same thing, but it was too frightening to admit.

"My friend in Miami claims the same thing."

"What do you think?" Jen asked.

Brian shrugged. "I don't know what to think. It's all too bizarre to be real, yet I look out my window, and there they are. You two have been out there. What have you seen?"

"Well, the ones I've been close to have been alive," I said. "They're just gone in the head."

"How close did you get?" he asked, a concerned expression on his face.

"Close enough to feel their warmth, to hear their breath."

Brian was quiet.

"Don't worry, hon," Jen said, patting his hand. "We took care of it with Southern Comfort."

"Bless your heart," he said, returning to his meal. "That's some bad medicine."

"There are bodies missing," Jen said with some hesitance, looking at me, as if for permission. "We just figured there were people out clearing them away."

"Could be," Brian said. "Or I suppose coyotes or dogs could have dragged them off."

Jen and I nodded.

"Another possibility," Brian continued, "and I'm sorry to bring something like this up at the dinner table, but another possibility is that they are eating each other. My friend in Greece suggested that."

We were quiet for a while.

"I hope everyone has room for dessert," Brian spoke up finally, in a cheery tone. "I have a Sara Lee cheesecake in the freezer."

He got up from the table, and Jen helped him clear the dishes. I stepped over to the large dining-room window that looked out onto his back yard. It was dusk, but I could see neat rows of small trees to the left. To the right was a grape trellis. There was a small fountain between them. Farther to the right, surrounded by a patio, was an in-ground swimming pool. I could see the base of his wind turbine about fifty yards out. We probably didn't notice it coming in, because it was so large, and the blades were not in our field of vision. We just thought it was another tower.

If seen from far enough away, that thing would be like a beacon to every survivor for miles around. I suspected that within the next few weeks, he'd have more than the infected gathering on his lawn; he'd have refugees, and not all of them would be as nice as we were. I mentioned it to him as I closed the shades.

"The more the merrier," he said.

"But what about those who would take this place for themselves?"

"I think you've watched too many Mad Max movies," he said. "I think a crisis like this will bring us all together."

I didn't want to argue with him, but I feared that this would soon be a dangerous place to live.

We had our cheesecake and wine in the living room by the glow of the fireplace. The curtains were closed, and we avoided the topic of current events. When we were done, feeling full and relaxed from the wine, Jen stood.

"Brian, I'm going to impose on you."

"Please do."

"I would love a hot shower. Would it be okay?"

"Of course! Both of you make yourselves at home. At the end of the hall and on the right. I'd be happy to wash your clothes too, if you didn't bring more."

"That would be great," she said. "I'll leave them outside the bathroom door."

She smiled and left us.

When she was gone, Brian poured the last of the bottle into my glass.

"How long have you two been together?"

"Since yesterday morning."

"Hmm. I took you to be a couple. No?"

"No."

"Hmm. You have no idea who I am, do you?"

"Sure I do," I said. "We went to the same high school. You were a couple of years behind me."

"That's what Jen tells you, right?"

"No," I said. "I mean, I didn't remember you right away, but now I do." I didn't.

"It's okay," he said. "I saw you on Facebook a couple of years ago, and I didn't remember you right away either."

"I guess I didn't make a big impression," I said.

He stared at his empty glass for a moment.

"I'm going to go get Jen some clean clothes to wear in the meantime."

He left for a moment and returned with two jogging suits.

"These should be comfortable enough to sleep in," he said. "Henry is about your size. His is the maroon. Take it, go change, then bring me your other clothes."

"I'd hate to …"

"Just do it," he said wearily.

I took a candle from the mantle and did as he told me. When I returned to the living room with my dirty clothes in my arms, Brian was gone. I sat down to wait for him and finish my wine. The only sounds were the gas hissing in the fireplace and the muffled patter of Jen's shower down the hall.

Then a door in the dining room flew open, and Brian stumbled out. The color was gone from his face.

"They're in the house!"

CHAPTER 16

I jumped up and ran to him, my dirty clothes and wine glass tumbling to the floor. He'd been coming up from the basement. He turned and tried to shut the door, but an arm reached in and prevented it.

I joined him, pushing on the door.

"I forgot to turn the light off when I was down there today. I've been distracted with making dinner. I guess when it got dark outside, they could see it. They've broken through the basement window."

"How many?"

"There were three down there by the washing machine. More coming in."

"But the light is still on down there," I said, shoving my weight against the door.

"Yes," he said. Then it dawned on him what that meant.

They would just keep coming.

The infected man who had chased Brian up the stairs was forcing his way in. His head and left shoulder pushed through the opening. Brian and I leaned against the door, but the man had help. We could hear and feel more of them on the other side against the door and walls.

"If we can get the door closed, I think we can block it," I said. "Maybe we should let him through and then shut it behind him."

Brian hit the man in the head with his fist, but the man was unfazed.

"Oh God, he's getting in!" he yelled.

The door bulged outward, and we pushed back. The man fell, and a second person reached through the opening. The first man grabbed Brian's ankle.

"No! He bit me!"

I kicked out at the man, but missed. I didn't want to let up on my pressure against the door. Then Jen was there, dripping wet and wrapped in a white towel. She had the .22, and she put it against the man's head. There was a pop, and he quit moving. Then she stepped around him and shoved the rifle barrel through the crack in the door.

Pop! Pop! Pop!

The other arm slipped back through the crack, and we could hear them falling down the stairs. She pulled the rifle out, and the door shut. There was an odd smell in the air that I realized was the mixture of gunpowder and Jen's shampoo. Brian put his weight against the door, gripping his ankle. He stared at the dead man on the floor.

"Oh my God, you shot him."

Jen and I dragged the body out of the way.

"It's best not to think of them as people," she said.

"But they …" Brian started.

"They're not people anymore!" Jen said.

"It's okay, sweetie," Brian said. "I'm not judging you, I'm just ... well ... you were so brave. Thank you."

Jen nodded and forced a smile.

We moved the dining room table to block the basement entrance.

They continued to pound against the door, and every time they did, the table jerked. Brian crawled into the living room next to the fire, and Jen went with him to check out his wound. I stayed in the dining room, piling up every heavy thing I could find on and around the basement door.

When I finally got into the living room, Jen stood.

"It broke the skin," she said. "Get him drunk. I don't care what that website says; get him plastered."

She noticed me looking at her. She adjusted her towel and handed me the rifle.

"Get your eyes back in your head," she said. "I'm going to get dried and dressed. I'll look for a first-aid kit for that ankle."

I watched her walk down the hall. When she got to the bathroom door, she turned and looked at me before going inside.

"I saw that," Brian said. "You two ..."

"Where do you keep your booze?" I interrupted. "You've got some drinking to do."

* * *

Brian was pouring his third shot of Maker's Mark when Jen returned from the bathroom. She was wearing Brian's gray jogging suit. I handed her the rifle.

"I'm going to change back into my regular clothes in case we have to leave soon," I said.

"Where are my clothes?" she asked.

"In the basement," Brian said. He downed the third shot. "You know, you two should be drinking too. I mean, he's right there, bleeding on the floor. Jesus, there's a dead man in my dining room."

Jen took a drink from the bottle and held it out to me.

"I'm still feeling the wine," I said. "I'll have something when I get back."

I hadn't realized how bad I smelled until I changed back into my dirty clothes. It wasn't only sweat; I reeked of smoke from our fire at Blaine's and from the fires in town. I wondered how Brian stood to be around us without insisting that we bathe and change. He was a good host. I was disappointed; I'd been looking forward to a shower. I didn't want to risk it now. We might need to make a quick getaway.

When I came back, Jen was putting a bandage around Brian's ankle. I went into the dining room and checked the basement door. It was holding, but I could hear them on the other side of the door on the stairs. I could hear movement below us too.

"Brian, where's the breaker box? Maybe we could kill the lights down there with that."

"Garage," Brian replied.

I started for the garage and, on my way, peeked through the curtain of the front window. The crowd on the lawn was gone. They were all likely in the basement by then. I changed my mind. I'd leave the light on down there. By morning, everyone who gathered outside would have gone into the basement. Maybe they wouldn't be able to find their way out.

Jen looked up at me when I returned.

"His ankle is starting to swell."

"Does it hurt?" I asked.

"I have enough whisky in me that you could pull my teeth," Brian replied.

Jen stood and moved close to me.

"I think we should watch him," she whispered. "I ain't dealt with bites."

"When he falls asleep, we can tie him to a heavy piece of furniture, just in case," I said.

"You two talking about me?" Brian said from the couch.

"Yep," Jen said.

"Do what you've got to do, Jen," he said. "You've always been nice to me. I trust you."

"We'll sleep in here tonight," I said. "The garage isn't far, if we need to go. We should take turns keeping watch."

"Okay," Jen said. "You sleep first, since you're feeling your wine."

I nodded. "Wake me around one."

I stretched out on the floor in front of the gas logs. I didn't think I'd be able to sleep, because of what had just happened and the noise downstairs, but much too soon, Jen was shaking me awake.

"Brian has a fever."

I sat up, trying to clear the sleep out of my head.

"What time is it?"

"After midnight."

I went over to the couch and put my hand on his forehead. He was hot, but not hot like the others.

"Maybe it's a fluke," I said. "Maybe he just came down with something."

Jen shook her head.

"Then let's strap him down," I said. "Find some rope or …"

She shook her head again.

"Why?" I said.

"And then what?" she said, on the verge of tears. "And then I just tie him down and shoot him? Is that it?"

"Jen, I …"

"No," she said.

"Jen, maybe he just has a bug. Maybe he has a fever from the bite, but not the virus."

"I don't want to see him turn," she said.

"Okay," I said. "I'll sit with him. You go sleep. You don't have to stay in here, but stay close."

She stood and stared at us both, then went down the hallway and into the bathroom. I saw the light come on under the door.

I felt his head again.

"Brian, does your head hurt?"

He didn't answer. I took a candle and opened doors until I found a bedroom. I checked the closet for a belt. I found a bathrobe, and I took the belt from it. I went back and tied one of his arms to the couch leg. Then I sat in the chair opposite the couch with the rifle across my lap and watched him. Eventually, I fell asleep.

I awoke gradually to a tapping sound. My sleeping mind tried partnering the noise with a dream, but it was just too loud and persistent for me to stay asleep. I opened my eyes, and I was looking down at my lap and the rifle in the orange glow of the gas logs. I had a crick in my neck, and I felt like an ass for falling asleep on watch. It was still dark outside. I looked around for the source of the noise.

One of our downstairs visitors had figured out how to operate the knob to the basement door. The door would open an inch, hit the dining table, and then shut. Open, shut, open, shut, tap tap tap tap.

I looked at Brian. He was still sleeping on the couch. I rubbed my neck and stood to push the door closed again. When I stepped into the dining room, I became aware of another sound. It was a rustling noise, very soft, in the darkness near the kitchen. I backed out of the room to get a candle from the mantel of the fireplace. They'd all burned down to stubs, and only two were still lit. I grabbed one in a wide glass dish and went back into the dining room, straining to see. The rustling increased, and then stopped.

"Please be a mouse," I whispered.

I decided right then that the first thing I would do when morning came would be to find a damn flashlight. For the moment, however, I would have to make do. The curtains and shades were closed, so I thought I could risk turning on the light for just a second. I felt on the wall for the switch. I flipped it on quickly, and then off again.

The man had moved. He was now a few feet from where we'd left him, and there was a smear of blood connecting the two spots.

"Okay," I whispered to myself. "Okay, okay, okay, okay."

My hands shook.

I turned the light on again, and then off again. He had definitely moved.

"Okay. Shit. Okay."

I put the candle on the floor, then grabbed one of the dining-room chairs from the pile of stuff in front of the basement door. I approached him like a lion tamer, using the chair as a shield, rifle aimed forward from my hip, and scooting the candle along with my foot as I went.

When I got close enough, I poked him with the end of the gun. He didn't move. I poked him again, but still nothing. Maybe the movement was my imagination. Maybe Jen moved him again while I was changing or sleeping. I left the candle and went to find her. There was still light coming out from under the bathroom door. I knocked.

"Jen?"

"What?" She sounded hoarse.

"The man in the dining room ... Did you move him?"

Silence.

Then, "No."

The light went out, and the door opened.

"Is he gone?"

"No," I said. "Just moved."

"Just?"

We both walked softly back to the dining room and looked around the corner. He was where I'd left him, the little candle flickering a yellow light over his body.

"Shit," she whispered. "He's still alive."

"I haven't actually seen him move," I said.

"But obviously he has."

"We need to get him out of here," I said. "Let's drag him outside."

She looked exhausted.

"I don't know how much of this I can take," she said.

"Let's drag him out, and then you go get in Brian's bed and sleep. We can wait for you to get rested before we leave here."

She turned and looked at Brian.

"How is he?"

I shrugged. "Sleeping. I was thinking that it might be kind of early for him to be showing symptoms anyway, right?"

"I don't know," she said. "Bites might be different."

The rustling started again. We turned toward the kitchen, where it looked as if the man on the floor were having a seizure. His body jerked and rolled around. I stared. Jen grabbed the rifle from me and started to shoot, but a spasm brought the man's arm up, and he knocked the candle over. Then it was dark. Jen fired anyway, and a flash erupted from the end of the gun. The rustling continued. There was a click.

"Shit," she said. "We never reloaded it. We're empty. Go get the shotgun; it's in the truck."

I left her, taking the other candle on my way. When I returned with the 12-gauge, I could see Jen's head poking up from behind the couch. She motioned for me to be quiet, then pointed to the dining room.

The man was standing there, staring at the basement door as it opened, then closed, then opened again. His mouth hung open, and bloody drool dripped from his bottom lip. His eyes seemed vacant.

Jen made a shooting motion with her hands.

I didn't do it. It wasn't like the group I fired into at the court square. This was a man only a few feet away. It felt different. I knew that if I shot him at this range with the 12-gauge, I would be taking his life, such as it was, and I couldn't bring myself to do it.

Brian shifted on the couch, and the man's head turned toward him. The man made a noise similar to the feline growling that the old woman we'd encountered had made.

He stepped into the living room, staring blankly at Brian. He growled again.

"Do it," Jen whispered.

The door continued to tap against the dining table.

He stepped farther into the room. The light from the fireplace illuminated the coagulating blood on the side of his face. How could he be walking?

He took another step.

I looked at Jen. There was something in her eyes that got to me more than my fear and more than my dread over killing someone. It was disappointment, or maybe even disgust. She looked at me the same way she'd looked at her boyfriend, Zach, when she saw him in the doorway of her house and attacked him with the stick. It made me ache inside for her to look at me like that.

I put the shotgun to my shoulder, aligned the end of the barrel with the man's chest and squeezed the trigger.

CHAPTER 17

The recoil from the shotgun hammered my shoulder.

It wasn't like in the movies; the man didn't fly across the room, and there wasn't a bucket of gore. It was as if someone had kicked him in the chest. The white stuffing from his coat puffed out, and he fell back against the dining table, then to the floor.

The tapping of the basement door against the table stopped for a moment. I could hear moaning in the stairwell, and there was still movement below us, but otherwise, it seemed so quiet. I felt sick. I looked over to Jen. She was on her feet. Brian was awake and trying to sit up, but the belt tied around his arm kept him in place.

"Let's get that thing out of here," Jen said.

That thing.

The tapping started again. Jen got to the door and pushed it closed, then pushed the table closer to stop the door from opening at all.

That thing.

In the past three days, I'd beaten people, choked people, shot people, hit people with my car, and I had probably accidentally taken lives—but this made me feel like a killer. The man was on his side next to the table. His eyes stared ahead at nothing. I looked at his clothes and his silly hat. I wondered what he'd been thinking about when he was getting dressed in those clothes, what his plans had been for the day. I wondered if he'd been married and if he'd told his wife he loved her that morning. I wondered if he ever suspected that he might be sick. I wondered what his last thought was before the disease took his mind.

Jen stepped in front of me and waved a hand in my face to snap me out of it.

"Don't do it," she whispered. "Don't think about it."

She took the shotgun from me and propped it against the chair.

"Let's get him out of here," she said.

Brian had untied his arm and was sitting up. He didn't look good.

"Brian," Jen said, "does your head hurt?"

"Ooooh God," he said. "I drank too much."

"Brian?" Jen said.

He jumped up and ran at us. Jen grabbed the shotgun, but he pushed past us, down the hall to the bathroom.

"Brian?"

We could hear him vomiting.

"We'll check on him when we get back," I said. "It's too soon for him to show symptoms anyway, I think."

The sun was coming up as we dragged the man out into the back yard. We left him by the grape trellis, and Jen started back inside.

"I'll catch up to you," I said. "I want to check something."

She hesitated, then nodded and went inside.

I walked past the swimming pool and went around the side of the house. I could see the broken basement window. There was no one around. I noticed that there was a fence across the front of the property, but the rest of the land was enclosed by a line of trees. There would be no way to keep them out, even if we shut the gate.

I stepped up to the basement window and squatted to look in. It was packed. There were people crawling over each other on the stairs. Everyone was focused on the basement door. In front of the door at the top of the stairs, the people had climbed up on each other all the way to the ceiling. They didn't notice me there.

I looked around for something I could use to seal the window to keep them from getting out, but I didn't see anything nearby. I decided to check the garage.

On my way back around the house, I was shocked to find the man I'd just shot standing beside the swimming pool. I ducked back around the corner before he could see me. It might have been possible for him to survive the .22 to the head, but that and a 12-gauge blast to the chest from only a few feet away? Maybe the shells had been reloads of rock salt.

I peeked at him again. He was just standing there with his back to me. I went back around the house, past the broken window, and knocked on the front door. Jen looked through the curtain and let me in. I didn't mention the man out back. I wanted her to rest.

Brian was back on the couch with his head in his hands.

"How is he?" I asked.

"He failed to mention that he gets hot like that when he has too much to drink."

"That can happen?" I asked.

"I don't know," she said. "My roommate in college had an allergy to red wine. She got hives."

"I'm not allergic," he said. "I just get flushed, that's all."

"You were hot, dear," she said.

"You're not too bad yourself. Now keep it down; my head is pounding."

She turned back to me. "The fever is gone, but that headache bothers me. Plus, his ankle is still swollen and red."

I nodded, distracted by thoughts of the man out back. I wasn't really concerned about Brian. The alcohol had worked for us; it would work for him.

"What were you doing?" she asked.

"I thought maybe we could close the gate and stay longer, but now I don't know. Why don't you go to bed, and I'll talk things over with Brian."

She looked at Brian, a worried expression on her face.

"Just go," I said. "He's fine."

After she closed the bedroom door, I went into the dining room and looked out the back window. The man had stepped out onto the pool cover, and the cover had collapsed. He was in up to his waist, surrounded by floating leaves and chunks of ice. He looked content to be there.

I returned to the living room and sat down.

"You had to kill him two times," Brian said.

I nodded. "Two times."

* * *

I cooked some sausage, eggs and toast for breakfast. As I prepared the meal, I periodically walked past the kitchen window, which gave me a view of the pool. The man hadn't moved. His skin and lips were turning blue. I didn't want to look at him, but I needed to know when and if he decided to end his soak.

I took a plate into the living room to Brian. He balked at eating.

"It'll make you feel better," I said. "You need protein and bread. It'll take care of that hangover."

I got myself a plate, and we both had coffee and orange juice. I got to thinking about how coffee beans and oranges didn't grow in Kentucky, and how one day, I wouldn't have them anymore unless I relocated.

"It's not safe here," I said.

"But I have electricity here," he said, "and I need to stay near a computer in case Henry tries to contact me."

"I understand," I said. "I haven't heard from my mom either."

"I'll stay indoors. When I've heard from Henry, I'll load up the car and leave. They got in this time because I wasn't careful. I'll be careful now."

"Why don't you come with us and bring your phone. He can contact you that way."

"And what happens when the battery dies? And what about my ankle?"

It sounded like he was making excuses.

"You can't stay here, man."

He didn't answer.

"Okay," I said. "How are you set on food? I noticed you might have about a week's worth in the kitchen. Is that all you have?"

"I can stretch it," he said. "We have a lot more food, but it's in the basement. I always thought that would be the best place to keep it, in case of a storm or something. Now I guess I should have spread it out some. Maybe I should have stored it all over the house."

"Well," I said, "you'll know to do that for the next time the world ends."

He grinned.

"I'd feel better if you came with us," I said.

"I'd feel better if you stayed."

I nodded. I knew that, so long as Henry hadn't checked in, he wouldn't be convinced.

"Do you own a gun?" I asked.

"No way; I hate guns."

"Do you want us to leave you one?"

"Absolutely. That big one there would be perfect."

"It only holds three shells at a time, but it's a man stopper, unlike the .22. Do you know how to shoot it?"

"I had a dad. I grew up in Clayfield. Of course I know how to shoot. I can also show you how to take the plug out of that thing so it'll hold five shells instead of three."

"Oh," I said.

"Yeah," he said, winking. "I'm a riddle wrapped in an enigma wrapped in a ..."

There was an incredible crash from the dining room. We both jumped up. I went in with Brian limping behind me, but we couldn't see anything. Then I remembered.

"The stairs."

We moved the stuff off of the table, then moved the table just enough to crack the door.

The stairs had caved under the weight of all the bodies. We pushed the table farther and opened the door. The well was just an empty space now. They were all piled on each other ten feet below us. Some of them had confused, almost comical expressions on their faces, while others had already recovered and were reaching for us.

It smelled like a sewer down there.

"Ugh," Brian said, looking at me. "The stench alone might ..."

His voice trailed off. He was looking past me, out the window.

"What the hell?" he said.

He moved over to the window. He'd seen the man in the pool.

"Oh my God," he said. "It's true."

"No," I said. "It doesn't mean anything."

"He's been dead twice, and now he's standing in my swimming pool—my icy swimming pool."

"Yeah," I admitted. "It looks bad. I didn't want to upset either of you."

"We're not children."

It was Jen, woken by the collapse of the stairs, and standing behind us. "You don't keep stuff like this from us."

She peered down into the hole where the stairs had been, made a face at the odor and shut the door.

"If there are dead people walking around, we all need to know," she said.

"We don't know if he's dead," I said. "I'm thinking that maybe I shot him with rock salt."

"Rock salt? I had that rifle to his head," she said. "That might not have done it—I've heard stories about that kind of thing—but you shot him again, and now he's just out there, standing in freezing water. Something isn't right."

"Nothing is right about any of this," I said. "I can accept that a disease made everybody crazy, but I'm not willing to believe that dead people are coming back to life. It's just too much."

She went over to the spot on the floor next to the basement door where she'd shot the man. She started to stick her finger in the thick, sticky blood.

"Jen, no," I said. "The virus. I don't want to have to get drunk again because of something careless."

"I don't have to touch it anyway," she said. "I can see the hole in the floor. The bullet went clean through."

"So?" Brian said.

"Well," she said, "I saw on TV once that a .22 bullet has the power to get into the head, but not enough to get out. It just bounces around in the skull and kills the person by destroying the brain. This bullet wasn't able to do the damage it could have done, because it went all the way through the head and into the floor. It doesn't mean it couldn't have killed him, but ... I don't know."

"There you go," Brian said. "Take off your sunglasses, aaaand ... CSI: Grace County."

"Asshole," Jen said. "I'm this close to shooting you anyway, just to be on the safe side."

"Come on to the couch, sweetie," Brian said, limping and leading her by the elbow. "This good man made us some breakfast. He tells me you two will be leaving soon."

"Does he?"

"He does."

Jen looked at me, but I couldn't read her.

"Maybe the two of you could run by Wal-Mart for me while you're out," Brian said. "I'm getting low on milk ... and ammunition for my new big gun."

CHAPTER 18

Brian gave us three bottles of wine and a case of bottled water. His well was still working, and he felt confident that he would not need to go to bottled water for a while. We left him the 12-gauge and the box of shells we'd brought. Jen was quiet as we prepared to go. She had tried to talk him into coming with us while she picked at her breakfast, but he refused.

None of us discussed the man in the swimming pool.

After we'd loaded the truck, Jen made one more push to convince him to come along, while I went outside to take care of the window to the basement. I took the rifle with me.

I found a piece of plywood in the garage that would fit over the opening, but I didn't have any tools to affix it to the block foundation wall. Ideally, I would have put a screen over the window, so it could get air—not for their sake, but for Brian's. I figured that within a couple of days, the smell would be unbearable. I didn't know how many people were down there, but there wasn't even room for them to move unless they crawled on top of each other.

Maybe the smell would force Brian to leave before something happened to keep him from ever leaving.

First, I got down on my belly. The people tried to get at me, but the window was too high for them. If I'd stayed there long enough, they would have crawled on top of each other and grabbed me, but I wasn't going to be long. I shot out the two light fixtures in the ceiling. Then I propped the plywood against the wall over the window and wedged it a little in the ground. It wouldn't hold forever, but maybe they wouldn't figure out how to move it.

As I came around the front of the house, I could see a group of four coming down the road. They were the faster ones. They'd probably heard the rifle. They were far away, and I had plenty of time, so I went around back to check on our pool guy.

He was trying to get out. He would never make it. He was splashing along the side of the pool as if trying to find an opening. It reminded me of a zoo animal pacing in its cage. He'd walk the pool cover down, and then it would float up again behind him. He tripped and went under. After a lot of splashing and slapping the water, he was able to get up again. His hat had fallen off.

He'd been standing still in that frigid water for almost two hours by that time, yet he was able to move around. Perhaps it was true; perhaps he wasn't human anymore. I doubted any human could do that.

I went in through the back door and made sure it was locked.

"We've got some on their way," I said.

Brian hugged Jen.

"If Henry hasn't called in a week, I'll just leave," he said. "I have directions to your new place."

"I'm going to worry about you out here by yourself," Jen said.

"I'll be fine," he said. "Your new beau schooled me on the ins and outs of firearms. I'm a regular commando now."

She looked over her shoulder at me, as if to see if I had been listening. I pretended that I hadn't been.

"A week is a long time," she said. "We'll come check on you before then."

"I'm fine," he said. "Go check on that blue house first."

* * *

We got into the truck, and Brian stood in the doorway with his finger on the automatic door opener. Jen rolled down the window.

"When you come, drive the Porsche," she said. "I've always wanted to ride in one of those."

Brian smiled and pushed the button. The door went up, and as soon as we had enough clearance, I drove out. He waved to us as the door went down again.

The four new visitors chased us, and I drove slowly enough to give them hope of catching us so I could lead them away from his house.

Jen was quiet. She didn't even acknowledge that, for a short time, there was a woman running right outside her window.

"We should have made him come," she said. "We should have just taken him."

"Are you okay with leaving?" I asked.

"Yeah," she said. "We couldn't stay there. I had hoped we could, but after they got in, and then there was the smell ... And I got to thinking about what you said about people taking the place. I've been so focused on the infected that I never thought about how dangerous the uninfected might be."

"I wouldn't be too worried about that, but it is something to keep in mind," I said. "I hope Brian is right, and this brings us all together. Who knows, maybe when it all settles down, we'll have Utopia."

She looked in mirror at a woman jogging just behind the truck.

"Poor thing," she said. "She has no control over herself. All she wants to do is get us. I wonder why? Do you think she wants to eat us? Do you think the virus has a mind and sends her after us so it can spread?"

"I don't know," I said.

"I wonder why they don't try to kill each other," she said.

"I've seen them fight," I said.

"Yeah, but they ain't fixated on each other the way they are on us. With each other, it's almost like they're establishing a pecking order."

She rolled down the window and turned around in her seat. Then she grabbed the rifle and picked them off one by one. She was shooting left-handed, so it took her several tries. Every time she fired, the rifle ejected the spent casing into the cab of the truck. One of the hot shells hit me on the cheek.

She left the woman for last.

"She just keeps on coming," she said. "All of her group has been shot, but she doesn't stop to check on them."

She fired, and the woman fell in the ditch by the road. Jen rolled up her window and faced front.

"It gets easier," she said. "They ain't people anymore; they're monsters. Anyway, it can't be murder when they don't stay dead."

CHAPTER 19

There was still smoke in town, but not as much as there had been. It was a cloudy morning, but it felt a little warmer outside. We pulled into town on Broadway. As we crossed the railroad tracks and neared the post office, we could see a large group off to our right.

"Looks like they're going to church," Jen said. "This is Sunday, ain't it?"

The group milled around the Community Christian Church. I took a left at the post office, heading away from them.

"We're going to need more guns," Jen said. "I don't want to go check on that house and that building with just this twenty-two."

I took a right on North Street, headed back toward the museum.

"We could go back out and search some houses," I said. "But we're getting low on gas. We've got less than a quarter of a tank."

"There are vehicles everywhere," she said. "Take your pick."

The minivan was still parked by the museum. The mob had dispersed. The generator would have burned through its gas quite some time ago.

"Want to stop and get it?" she asked.

"Let's leave it," I said. "We can always bring more gas up here and use the computer another time."

She nodded, and we proceeded to North Seventh Street.

"The police station," she said. "I'll bet there'll be guns in there."

"I've never been in there," I said. "Where do you think they keep them?"

"Beats me," she said. "But it's not like there's anyone around to stop us from looking."

* * *

I went up two blocks and accessed the parking lot for City Hall and the police station from the Fifth Street entrance so the crowd at the court square wouldn't notice us. My wrecked car was right there too.

"That's me," I said. "That blue car."

"Were you in that wreck?" she asked, nodding toward the head-on collision.

"No," I said. "I came upon it right after."

I parked behind the building, and we got out. There were two police cars parked there, along with three other cars and a pickup.

"Check it out," Jen said, bending over and retrieving something off the asphalt. She grinned and held up a pistol.

"Look," she said. "There's another one over there by the grass."

I went over and picked it up. It was scratched up and had some water in it from the melted snow.

"I wonder if this is a nine millimeter," Jen said. "Cops use nine millimeters, don't they?"

"I don't know."

"I don't know either," she said. "This one looks like Zach's gun, and his was a nine millimeter. They all kind of look alike to me."

"They were doing a lot of shooting here when it all started," I said. "I guess they were overpowered."

"Or they turned into them," she said, sliding the clip out. "It's empty."

"Do you know how to shoot one of those?" I asked.

"Yep."

"I've never used a semiautomatic handgun," I said. "I could figure it out; I've seen it enough on TV."

"I guess I'll have to school ya," she said. "I gotta make sure the new beau knows the ins and outs of firearms. Ain't that right?"

"That was all Brian," I said.

"I know," she said, "I'm just joking ... Hey, there's another one."

This one was under a shrub next to the building. It was a snub-nose revolver. I knew how to use a revolver. I picked it up and opened the cylinder, but there were no live rounds, just used casings. I pulled one out and read the rim. It was a .38. I put it in the pocket of my coat and stuck the other one in the waistband of my pants.

The doors were unlocked, and we went inside. There was a round desk in the middle of the room that acted as an information center. There were some potted plants here and there, and big, poster-sized photographs of how Clayfield looked in the 1890s, 1920s and 1950s. I had similar, smaller prints at the museum. The police-station section of the building was to the left, and the city offices were to the right. I saw a closed door with a placard that said OFFICE OF THE MAYOR.

The office was in the front of the building, with a view of the court square. There was a window that looked into the interior of the building too, but the blinds were closed.

"First, let's go in here so we can look out the window and see how big the crowd is over there," I said.

I tried to open the door, but it was locked. I was about to forget it and go to the police station, when I heard movement in the office.

"Someone is in there," I said.

I knocked. The blinds moved.

"Are you okay in there?" I said.

"The mayor is probably infected," Jen said. "Let's just go. It'll never figure out how to unlock it."

Then I heard the lock clicking. The door stayed shut. I looked at Jen. She shrugged and held up the rifle. I tried the knob again, and the door swung open. I stepped inside, and the last thing I saw was a black blur coming at my face.

The next thing of which I was aware was Jen looking down at me. I had a horrible pain across my right eyebrow.

"Are you okay?" she asked.

"What happened?"

"This jerk hit you in the head with the butt of his shotgun."

Another face came into view. The man had a white-and-gray beard, neatly trimmed. He grinned down at me.

"Mr. Somerville?" I said.

"You know him?" Jen said.

He held out his hand to her.

"Hi, I'm Nicholas Somerville."

She just stared at him.

"He's on the city council," I said, sitting up.

There was a dawning on her face.

"Oh yeah," she said. "Saint Nick. You dressed up like Santa for that thing."

"Every year for ten years," he said.

Somerville wasn't dressed like Santa this time. He was in full camouflage. He had a rifle with a scope slung over his right shoulder and a shotgun in his left hand. A pair of binoculars hung around his neck.

"How's the noggin?" Somerville asked.

"It hurts," I said. "You could have said something before you clubbed me."

"You're lucky I didn't shoot you," he said. "What are you two doing in here?"

"Looking for guns," Jen said bluntly.

"Won't get any here," he said. "They're still locked up. I tried getting to them myself."

"What are you doing here?" I said, rubbing my head.

"Well, right now, I'm the acting mayor," he said.

"Says who?"

"Says me," he laughed, "but I'm not sure having a mayor matters anymore."

He turned toward the window and put the binoculars to his eyes.

"There's someone in that building over there," he said. "They're on the second floor. I just get glimpses of them every now and then. I don't know what they're up to in there, but they sure do have a fan club."

"We were coming to get guns to help them," I said.

"I've been thinking about helping them too," he said, "but I couldn't do it by myself. You know, if we get enough of us together, we might have a chance of putting Clayfield back together again. The three of us could start up city government and get things organized."

"The hell we could," Jen said. "I was just starting to get comfortable with anarchy."

CHAPTER 20

Somerville noticed the pistol in my waistband.

"How many rounds do you have for that?"

"None," I said. "I found it in the parking lot."

"All we have is a twenty-two," Jen said, "with a little over fifty bullets."

"Oh," Somerville said, frowning.

"It's not like we're going in there shooting everybody," I said. "We just need to lure them away like you did with the car alarm."

"Did that work?" Somerville asked.

"Oh yeah," Jen said, "but it also attracted a bunch more."

He put his binoculars to his eyes again and looked out.

"There are probably three or four hundred of them over there."

Jen was looking around the office.

"Have you been in here all this time?" she asked.

"No," he said, sounding distracted. "I got here early this morning. I shot one of them in the street in front of my house the night before last. I noticed it was gone yesterday afternoon, so I thought the mayor had a crew working. I thought I'd come up here and help out any way I could."

"No cleanup crews," Jen said. "They're just walking away."

Somerville laughed. "Not this one. I shot him with my thirty-aught-six. He was stone cold dead."

"I'm telling you, he walked away."

"She's right," I said. "Either they're not dying, or they're coming back to life."

"Nah," he chuckled. "There's a cleanup crew. They're probably just operating from another location. I'm thinking the fairgrounds or one of the high schools."

"Whatever," Jen said. "If we're going to help the people over there, then let's do it. There's a house out on Bragusberg Road that has someone in it too."

"There are two police cars outside," I said. "Why don't we just turn on a siren?"

"Or better yet," Somerville said, "let's turn on the emergency siren—the one the city uses to warn people about tornados."

"That one is really loud, though," I said. "I've been out at Blaine's house and heard it way out there."

"Who's Blaine?" Somerville asked.

"That'll be too loud," Jen said. "We don't want to draw them in from everywhere, do we? Besides, wouldn't it run on electricity?"

"I don't know," Somerville said, "but I've always wanted to be the one to turn it on."

"Feel free," Jen said. "Just wait until we're out of town, okay? Right now, I think the siren on the police car will do."

"Okay," Somerville said, turning toward a map of the city that was hanging on the wall in the office. "Where do we want to sound the alarm? Which way do we want them to go?"

"There are three groups that we know about," I said. "The best thing would be to put the siren where they would all come together without coming into contact with us."

I marked the house on Bragusberg, the building behind the courthouse, and the Community Christian Church.

"It looks like Walnut Street might be a good spot," Somerville said. "It's a couple of blocks from all three groups, and away from each other. Too bad we couldn't contain them there."

"They should stay for a while," Jen said. "We'll have plenty of time to get into the buildings and get out."

Somerville retrieved the keys for the police cars from the other side of the building. Then he put his .30-06 into the cab of a black pickup in the parking lot.

"I'll drive one of the cruisers," he said, still holding his shotgun. "One of you follows me in the other one. One of you stays here with my truck. We'll set a siren off at the corner of Walnut and Ninth, and then we'll pull down the block and see if it works."

"It'll work," Jen said.

"If it doesn't, we'll have a second cruiser as a backup. If we need the truck to come pick us up, we'll honk our horn three times."

"Then what?" Jen said. "If it doesn't work, what good will a second cruiser do? And how is honking three times going to let anyone but the monsters know where you are?"

"We'll stay on Walnut. How about that? If you hear honking, drive down Walnut Street until you find us."

"Fine by me," I said. "Give me the keys."

"To the truck," Jen said. "I want to drive one of those cop cars."

"No," I said. "You're not going out there. It's too ..."

"Don't you dare say it's too dangerous," she said. "I'm going."

Somerville tossed each of us a set of keys. I got the truck.

"I'll leave you the binoculars," he said, "so you can watch them and see when they've all gone. If you can get in there and get them out, then do. That rifle is loaded. It's bolt action."

I watched them pull away. They went back the way we'd come in. When they turned left onto North Street, I took the opportunity to run over to my wrecked car. I thought I might be able to drive it out of there, but I'd left it on, and not only was it out of gas, but the battery was dead. I grabbed the bag of supplies I'd packed a few days before and ran back over to Somerville's truck.

I could not see the building from where he was parked, so I had to start the truck and pull it around to Sixth Street. When I got to the intersection with Broadway, I killed the engine and waited with the window down. A few of them noticed me and started toward me, but halfway there, they seemed to lose their way, and they eventually returned to the mob.

I was intrigued by what could be in that building that had them so interested. The movement in the window was rare and brief. I couldn't hear any loud noises coming from it, but I was a block away, and there might have been sounds I couldn't hear at this range.

I wondered if, at one point, a few of the infected stopped there because of the movement in the window, then others stopped because of them, then others until they reached a sort of critical mass and were there because of each other more than anything else.

I opened up my salami sandwich—my lunch from Thursday. It was a little stale, but good.

Then I heard the siren.

The crowd began to move toward Seventh Street. First it was just the ones on the western side. Some of them seemed torn between staying and going. I looked through the binoculars.

There were a few who were jogging away toward the siren, but others were only shuffling along. I hadn't given it much thought, but I'd been avoiding paying attention to their faces as much as possible. Like Jen, I was trying not to think of them as people anymore, and looking at their faces didn't help with that. Also, on some level, I was afraid of seeing people I knew. I wondered how it would affect me when I had to point a gun at one of them.

There was a difference between the slow ones and the ones who moved faster. Something in the eyes was different.

I noticed that they could all move fairly quickly when they wanted to, but for some, it took a little more encouragement.

A couple was having sex in the street near the corner of the county jail. It didn't look consensual. Is it ever consensual with animals? It was probably best that Jen wasn't there so she wouldn't feel the need to do something about it and screw up our plans. The man, naked from the waist down, stood up and walked over to the others. The woman lay there for a few seconds, then followed.

I saw old Mrs. Gordon in the crowd. She'd donated items to the museum, and was a big part in our last fundraiser. Toward the end of the group, I saw three men in ripped and burned military fatigues. One of them was wearing a helmet like the ones pilots wear.

Then I saw two people who almost made me reconsider the whole undead hypothesis. On the ground, dragging himself along, was a man with only one leg. All that was left of his right leg was a bloody stump that left a trail behind him. He didn't act like he was in pain; he was just trying to keep up with the others. The second man was the rapist. Jen's shotgun blast had claimed the right side of his face. He was up and walking, but he was having trouble and kept veering away from the others and bumping into things.

I felt a chill that wasn't from the air. A wave of nausea hit me, and I opened my door and puked up my sandwich.

When most of them had disappeared from my line of sight, I cranked the truck and crept forward to get a better view. I watched all but the one-legged man go around the corner at Seventh Street. The rapist Jen had shot was the last of those still on two legs to go, as his meandering causing him to fall behind.

I pulled the truck up in front. It was a three-story building that was one of the old downtown businesses. It was even in one of those photographs from the 1920s that were hanging in City Hall. It might have been older than that. It had been difficult to keep businesses downtown, since all the big chains constructed their super stores on the south side of town. Everybody wanted to be part of the little strip malls that sprang up around the giants.

The right side of the old building was home to an antique store, but the left side of the building had been vacant for several months. We'd seen the movement on the second floor of the vacant side. The building itself was situated between two others similar to it in age and architecture. One side was occupied by a photography studio and the other by a pawnshop.

The one-legged man was past the pawnshop when he heard and saw me. He looked back at me, then to the corner where he'd last seen the others. He decided I was more attainable, and turned around, dragging himself with his hands.

It would be a while before the mob got to their destination, so I didn't expect Jen and Mr. Somerville back for several minutes. Rather than wait for them, I decided to go on inside and see who was in there. I pulled up my mask and got out of the truck.

CHAPTER 21

This could never have happened in real life—me going into an old building off the court square wearing a mask and carrying a .30-06 while a one-legged monster crawled after me. Never in a million years. If I'd been told the week before that this was what I'd be doing …

Then I remembered what I'd been doing the Sunday before and laughed a little to myself. Exactly one week before, about the same time, I'd been sitting on my couch in my sweatpants with a game controller in my hand, playing a first-person shooter. The game was set in France during World War II, in a town about the size of Clayfield. My weapon had been a 7.62 mm Mosin-Nagant, and my targets were Nazis, but still, the similarities were striking.

The one-legged man had made it to the front of the antique store just a few feet away. I didn't want to attract more of them by firing the gun, so I just let him be.

Unlike in my video game, I didn't get extra lives. If they got me, I'd just start fighting for the other side.

The man hissed at me.

I stepped up onto the sidewalk in front of the building and tried the door. It was locked. I stepped back a little and looked up.

"Hello, up there!" I said.

The man hissed again.

"Come down! We're here to help!"

The man tried pulling himself up on the sidewalk, but he slipped and hit his chin. He growled.

I stepped back to the door and knocked. Nothing. I went to the truck and got out my bottle of water. It still had a little in it. I threw it at the window on the second floor. It hit, then bounced down to the street. I heard a noise from inside. It sounded like a bell or a gong.

"Hello?" I said.

The curtains moved, and then the bell sounded again.

I was going to try again, but the one-legged man was already chewing on the bottle.

Then I decided to walk around the photography studio on the corner and go to the rear of the buildings to see if there was a back door.

The back door was locked, but there was a fire escape. I couldn't reach it from the ground, so I ran back to get the truck.

On my way back, I met the one-legged man coming around the corner—the little engine that could. When I ran past him, he changed direction again to follow. I pulled the truck around underneath the back windows.

I slung the rifle over my shoulder and the binoculars around my neck, climbed on top of the cab of the truck, then pulled myself up onto the rusted fire-escape stairs. The metal was so cold. When I climbed up on the fire escape, I could see a mass of people south of my location coming from the direction of Bragusberg Road, headed toward the siren. Good.

I was right there—the second floor. I got down on one knee. The window was curtained, so I tapped on it.

"Hey!" I said. "I'm here to help you!"

The gong sounded inside. I knocked on the window again. I heard what sounded like a strangled scream. I knocked louder.

"Are you okay?"

Nothing.

I tried to open the window, but it wouldn't budge.

"I'm going to break the window! Step back!"

I stood and hit the window with the butt of the rifle. It shattered the first time. I cleaned away the remaining shards with the gun, and then I pushed the curtains aside. I squatted down and looked inside.

The room was filled with old furniture. There was a door to my left that was open to a staircase, and another door beyond that that accessed the other side of the building. It looked like the antique store was using the second floor of this side of the building for storage. There were a lot of old bed frames stacked up in the middle of the room and leaning against a couple of wardrobes that stood back to back. The stack of furniture cut the room in half crosswise. To the far left was an old claw-foot bathtub set at an angle. It was dirty and missing all of its hardware. A couple of chests of drawers stood between me and the bed frames. The furniture created a little maze in the room with a narrow walkway that wound through to the window on the other side.

There was a sick woman near the far window. I could tell that she had been beautiful once, but now, she was a mess. She stank. Her clothes were torn and dirty. She paced, looking for a way to get to me. When she would get near the bathtub, the gong would sound. I looked down to see a pile of loose bed slats on the floor. She had stepped on the end of one of them, causing it to pop up and hit the tub.

I eased through the window onto the broken glass and old hardwood floors. I had no intention of getting any closer to her. I just wanted to leave the building via the front door.

Then, three honks in a row. Jen and Mr. Somerville were in trouble.

"Shit."

I stepped back out the window to the fire escape and looked through my binoculars to the southwest. Trees and buildings obscured my view. I was tempted to go up to the third floor, or even up on the roof to get a better view, but I didn't. If they were honking, then they needed me to come get them.

The gong sounded inside again, louder. I parted the curtains with the barrel of the gun, and there she was. She came out of the building fast. The end of my rifle caught her in the chest and snagged on her blouse, and as she came forward against the tip of the gun, she pushed me backwards. I got as far as the railing, then went down in a crouch to keep from being pushed over the side. She kept on coming, and the muzzle slid right up her chest and under her chin. Her fingers were inches from my face when I pulled the trigger.

The rifle jumped out of my hands, and the top of her head came off.

One one thousand, two one thousand ... Then bits of her rained back down.

The horn honked again just as the woman's body slumped down. I pushed her, and she fell backwards through the window and landed hard. Her feet and legs, in black shoes and gray tights, still hung over the windowsill from her knees. One of her shoes had fallen off, and the tip of her big toe poked out of a hole in her tights. The red polish on the nail was chipped. Something about that made me feel an overwhelming compassion for her. It was those little things—those human things—that got to me.

I couldn't keep doing this to myself.

The curtains sucked out of the window and fluttered in the breeze, and the horn honked again. I picked up my rifle.

There were little bloody pieces of the woman's head all around me and on me. I would need a bath, and I'd probably have to drink again, just in case. Much more of this and I might become an alcoholic ... for more reasons than one.

Climbing down was going to be harder than climbing up. It seemed like no matter how I situated myself, I couldn't get in a good position to drop down to the top of the truck.

The horn honked again, followed by two gunshots.

I'd have to go through the window after all. I tried to step over the woman, but I wound up stepping on her. The way her body felt under my feet was sickening—firm, yet soft at the same time. Once inside, I ran down the stairs and out the front door.

When I got to the truck, I found the one-legged man underneath the fire escape and right next to the door of the truck.

"Figures," I said.

I went around the passenger side, but it was locked. The keys were in the ignition.

Four more gunshots. They were a mixture of the .22 and the shotgun, clustered together and overlapping one another. I could still hear the police siren too.

"Son of a ..."

I went to the end of the truck and got the man's attention so he would drag himself away from that spot and I could get in. He took his sweet time.

"Come on!" I yelled.

He hissed at me.

Then I heard the roar of an engine. I turned and looked south. A block away, on Water Street, a white car shot by. I couldn't see who was driving.

Impatiently, I waved my arms at the one-legged man to pick up the pace.

Then, two blocks away, one of the police cruisers came down Walnut with its blue lights flashing. When it got to Sixth Street, the driver slammed on the brakes. The tires screeched as the tail of the car fished around, then squealed again as the driver stomped the accelerator and headed up Sixth. When the car got to me, the driver hit the brakes again.

It was Jen. I went over to the car.

"I heard gunshots. What's going on?" I said.

"We had a little trouble, but it's okay now," she said. "Are you okay?"

"Yeah," I said. "Where is Mr. Somerville?"

"He's with that girl," she said. "What is that on you? Is that blood? Are you hurt?"

"No, I ..."

"Oh shit!" she yelled, and brought the rifle up and fired.

I turned to see the one-legged man on his face at the rear of the truck. He twitched a little, and Jen shot him again.

"Are you okay?" she asked again.

"Yeah, I'm ..."

"Did you get them out? Were they up there?"

I shook my head. "There's no one up there."

"But we saw someone."

"No," I said. "She was sick. I shot her."

"Oh," she said. She looked sad for a moment, and I knew it was sympathy for me and not for the person I'd shot.

"Are you okay?" she asked.

"You keep asking that," I said.

The white car pulled up, coming from the north. They had circled around.

Somerville got out. There was blood splattered on his right pant leg, but it wasn't his.

Then the driver got out. She looked like she was in her late teens or early twenties. She was plump, but in all the right places. Her reddish blond hair was cut short. She was wearing a red-and-black Clayfield High School letter jacket. There was a smudge on her cheek and a two-foot length of rebar in her hand. Unlike the rest of us, she wasn't wearing a mask. She was very cute.

"Everything all right?" Mr. Somerville asked.

I nodded, still staring at the newcomer.

"This is Sara," Somerville said.

"Hey," I said.

She raised her hand timidly.

"Nice to meet you, Sara," Jen said politely.

"Hey," I said again.

Jen turned to me and said under her breath, "Don't get all googly-eyed; she's just a baby."

I ignored that.

"Have you been up there yet?" Somerville asked, looking up to the second floor of the building.

"Yeah," I said. "They were infected."

"Oh," he said. "That's too bad. I had hoped there were more of us."

"Looks like there are," I said, nodding to Sara.

"Yeah," he said. "Sara told me she's been hiding over at the Community Christian Church. She really saved my butt back there."

"Are there more over at the church?" Jen asked.

"No," Sara said. "Just me."

"How long have you been there?" Jen asked. "Have you been eating?"

"Since Friday morning," she said. "They had food in the fellowship hall—mostly crackers and ketchup."

"What happened?" I asked. "Why were you honking and shooting?"

"I set off the siren," Somerville said. "Then we pulled down the street in the other car to watch. For some reason, the ones from the church came in from behind us instead of in front of us. Before we knew it, they were all over the car ..."

"I honked so you could get them off of us," Jen interrupted. "Then she came. They left us for her really fast. It didn't take long for her to be covered too. Mr. Somerville got out to help her, and he got cornered ... Anyway, it didn't go exactly as planned, but it went."

Somerville nodded. "It went. Well, that's two buildings down and one to go. Let's check on that other house while they're distracted with the siren. The more of us there are, the better chance we have."

CHAPTER 22

Mr. Somerville drove his truck, I rode with Jen in the police car, and Sara followed behind us in her vehicle. It wasn't that far to the blue house, and other than a couple of stragglers, we had clear streets.

I got to thinking that it might be possible to get something to make a loud enough sound to attract a whole town's worth of infected people to one spot. I thought it might be a good idea to experiment over the coming days, to see how long they fixated on the sounds and how long they would stay. Maybe it would take more than just sound to keep them there.

"When we're done at the blue house, maybe we should go back to the court square and check that building again," I said to Jen.

"Why?"

"I didn't really search it. I saw the woman on the second floor, but I didn't have time to search the whole building."

"You think someone else is in there?" she asked.

"I don't know. From what we've seen, it doesn't make sense that the crowd would be hanging out down there because one of their own was making a little noise."

She took a left onto Bragusberg Road.

"Did you leave the car with the siren cranked?" I asked.

"I don't know," she said. "Mr. Somerville did it. Why?"

"I was thinking that when the battery died, so would the siren. Leaving it running would extend it some."

She looked over at me.

"You've got that stuff all over you," she said.

"I know. I need a shower."

"Amen to that," she said. "So, what are we going to do about the others?"

"What do you mean?"

"Are we all going to camp out at Blaine's? Do you think we should all go back to Brian's house?"

"Oh," I said. "Well, I haven't had time to think about it. Mr. Somerville obviously hasn't been out of his house much, if at all, since this all started, and Sara doesn't seem to have a home. I guess we should at least offer."

"I don't know," Jen said, parking in front of the blue house. "Councilman Somerville seems to have good intentions, but maybe it would be nice to just be free to live for a while without having to mess with government. I mean, there are only five of us that we know of. If government does come, I don't want to be in charge of anything. I just want to be left alone."

Mr. Somerville knocked on my window. I opened my door.

"You two coming?" he asked.

I nodded, and we got out.

I looked behind us, and Sara was standing in front of her car, holding the rebar.

"I told her to wait out here," Somerville said.

I nodded again and smiled at Sara. She smiled back, but it looked forced.

Before we even got to the porch, we could hear the generator running. It was up on a second-floor balcony on the side of the house.

Somerville knocked.

"Hello! This is Nicholas Somerville."

Nothing.

He knocked again.

"Go away! I'm armed!" said a woman's voice.

"We don't want any trouble," Somerville said. "We're just checking on you. We've lured the sick people down the road. Now would be a good time to come out."

"Go away! I can see your guns!

"They're just for personal protection, ma'am," Somerville said. "We don't want to hurt you; we're here to help. I represent the mayor's office."

"Don't need help. Go away!"

"Ma'am, they could be back any minute. It's best if you …"

She fired through the front window. Somerville flattened himself against the wall beside the door. I dropped down in front of the porch, and Jen took cover behind a tree in the yard. I looked to the street, and Sara was crouched behind the car.

"There's no need for this, ma'am!" Somerville said. "We're just …"

She fired again.

"Okay!" he said. "Stop shooting! We'll leave."

Silence from inside.

Somerville put his hands over his head, but he didn't drop his shotgun.

"We're going, ma'am," he said. "We won't bother you anymore. If you ever do need help …"

"I don't need your help!"

Somerville motioned us back to the cars.

As we walked back, Somerville said in a low voice, "We'll pull down the block and come back on foot—go in through the back of the house."

"What for?" Jen asked.

"She can't stay," he said. "They'll be back."

"That's her decision," Jen said.

"There are not enough healthy people around for us to allow idiots to make their own decisions," he said. "It's for her own good."

Jen stopped at the car and faced Somerville.

"I left a friend this morning because he made the same decision," she said. "His damn basement was full of them things. If I left him, then I'm leaving her. If she wants to stay, let her. We can come back and check on her in a few days. Maybe she'll change her mind."

"It's a bad decision," Somerville said.

"Yeah," she said.

"Let's head back to the court square," I said. "I want to check out that building again."

Somerville looked back at the blue house, then got into his truck.

Jen and I led the way back to the square.

I was relieved to see the one-legged man in the same spot and position in which we'd left him. We pulled around the building and went in through the now-unlocked front door.

It was a large room with a black-and-white tile floor. There was a counter at the back of the room and a couple of display cases against one wall, but otherwise, the place was empty. The entrance to the stairs was in the back.

"Let's split into two groups," Somerville said. "Sara and I will go look in the antique store, and you two search this side. The building has three floors that we know of, but we'll check for basement and roof access. If there are survivors in here, we need to find them."

As we approached the stairs, I noticed a yellow business card on the counter. The name on the card was Frankie Jakes—a real-estate leasing agent. Then I saw a purse on the floor behind the counter, and an overturned McDonald's coffee cup next to it. The coffee had spilled out, forming a dark little puddle that had dried around its mouth. I opened the purse and looked in the wallet for the driver's license. It was the woman upstairs. The name on the license was Frances Ann Jakes.

"Maybe the person she was showing the place to is still inside," I said, handing the card to Somerville.

"Let's hope so," he said.

We separated into two groups at the second-floor landing.

Jen stepped into the room full of furniture and stopped at Ms. Jakes's body.

Jen didn't mention the corpse.

"Did you search this room?"

"No. Actually, I didn't make it in any farther than this window."

We stepped around the body and wound our way through the furniture to the window on the courthouse side of the building.

Frankie hadn't been sick the whole time. It looked like she'd been hiding here for a little while. On the floor beneath the window, there was a pallet that she'd made for herself out of a couple of antique quilts. She'd slept there at least one night. In the corner near the old bathtub was a drawer from a piece of furniture. She'd used that as a toilet. The only sign that she'd had anything to eat was a Snickers wrapper.

I felt even sadder for her than I had before. Jen stepped on the quilts and looked out the window.

"It must have been horrible to look out there and see all those things waiting in the street," she said. "No way out. Nobody to help."

"Let's look on the third floor," I said, eager to get out of the room.

We took the stairs to the third floor. There was an access door on the landing, but it was locked. Jen knocked.

"Anyone in there?"

She knocked again.

"I'll go up the fire escape and see what I can see," I said.

I went back down to the second floor, did my best not to step on Ms. Jakes, then climbed out the window and back up to three.

There were no curtains on the third-floor windows. I cupped my eyes and pressed my face to the glass. The room was completely empty except for a small table lamp sitting on the floor next to the door. I broke the window with the rifle and climbed inside. I opened the door for Jen, but she wasn't there.

"Jen?"

I found her down on the second-floor landing, talking with Somerville. She looked up at me as I came down the stairs.

"They found another woman," Jen said. "But we'll have to carry her."

"Let's carry her out, then," I said.

"She's really heavy," Somerville said. "I don't know if we can carry her down the stairs."

"What happened to her?"

"I don't know. Sara found her in a back room. She's unconscious, and her ankle is bruised and swollen."

"I don't mean to sound callous," I said, "but can we take care of her even if we get her out?"

"We can't just leave her," Somerville said.

Sara cleared her throat.

"Maybe a sled? We could get her down the stairs like that."

Somerville and Jen looked at her with confused expressions, but I knew what she was getting at.

"Okay," I said. "There are some old beds in here. If we can get her on one of the headboards, we can slide her down the stairs on it. We could tie something to it to lower her down slowly. But once she's down there, we'll need a way to get her in the car. Then after that ... I don't know."

She was a big woman, but not that big. Once we managed the stairs, I didn't see any reason why the four of us couldn't carry her to the car.

Jen and Sara retrieved the old quilts from the other room.

Tugging on her clothes on one side, Somerville and I were able to lift her up enough for Jen and Sara put the quilts under her.

We dragged her to the landing on the quilts.

Somerville and I went into the other room for a headboard.

"These are all too wide to go down those stairs," he said.

He looked around the room. Then he went over and picked up a couple of bed slats.

"We might just have to make a stretcher and try carrying her."

Then he parted the curtain on the window.

"Damn it all to hell," he said. "There are two of them out by the vehicles, and I see two more coming down the street."

"Are they headed toward the siren?"

"Nope."

CHAPTER 23

"Everybody grab a corner!" Somerville ordered as he pushed past me onto the landing. "We have to go right now!"

He grabbed the corner of the quilt by the woman's right foot and looked back at us until we'd all grabbed our own. It was a bumpy ride for the woman. It was a good thing she was unconscious.

Once we had her on the first floor, Somerville reached inside his jacket, pulled out three 12-gauge shells and started loading his gun.

"Are you two loaded?"

We nodded.

"Are you ready? Here we go."

We dragged her from the stairs to the front door. Somerville pulled the door open.

"Sara, darlin', hold this door for us."

Then he stepped outside and pumped off two rounds, dropping both of the close ones. The other two, who were up the street, came toward us in a trot. He fired again and caught one of them in the face.

Jen and I got the woman onto the front sidewalk while Somerville reloaded. There was a drop from the sidewalk to the pavement.

"We'll never be able to lift her into the car," I said. "We'll have to put her in the back of the truck."

I ran to Somerville's pickup and backed it up to the sidewalk. Somerville shot the fourth of the infected. Jen let down the tailgate. It was above the sidewalk about a foot, but that was manageable. The shotgun fired again. I looked up and there were three more coming down South Street.

Jen, Sara and I pulled the woman into the back of the truck.

"Sara, hop in and drive," Jen said. "Pull us up behind City Hall, next to the red-and-white pickup."

Somerville fired again, and I got out of the truck to help him.

As the truck pulled away, Jen was wrapping a quilt around the woman to keep her warm.

I put the rifle to my shoulder. I didn't like the scope; it was awkward trying to aim. I did my best to get one of the approaching figures in the crosshairs, and I squeezed the trigger. It wouldn't fire. I tried again.

"It won't shoot!" I said.

"Get in the car," Somerville said. "We'll just leave."

He took the rifle.

"You never ejected the last shell," he said.

We got into the police car and drove to City Hall.

"What now?" Jen said.

"We need to get this woman some medical treatment," Somerville said. "I'm guessing since there are cleanup crews clearing bodies, there must be medical help too."

"There ain't no crews!" Jen said. "This is it, damn it! We're it! The people are getting up and walking away."

"I know what you say," Somerville said. "But we should at least take a look over at the hospital."

"No," Jen said. "There won't be anyone at that hospital. We might want to go out there for medicine, but there ain't no help. Ain't nobody going to save us."

Somerville stared at her.

"Okay," he said. "Cover her up good, and I'll take her to the doctor by myself."

"Jen's right," I said. "It'll be a wasted trip, probably a dangerous one too."

"I said okay," Somerville said, angry. "I'll take her by myself."

"Why don't you come with us? We're staying at a friend's place out in the county. We've got a wood stove and ..."

"No," Somerville said. "I'm going home this evening. Judy is expecting me back before dark."

"What?" Jen said. "Your wife? Is she safe there?"

"She'll be fine," he said. "She's got a three-fifty-seven and a taser."

"Do you have booze? You've been exposed, you know."

"We can't stand around here shooting the shit all day," Somerville said. "They're coming down the street. Sara, are you coming with me?"

Sara was over at the police car, digging through the trunk.

"Look what I found," she said, holding up a large first-aid kit. She bent over the trunk again and pulled out a black 12-gauge with a pistol grip.

"Better let me have that, darlin'," Somerville said.

Sara slid the fore stock back slowly. A shell poked out of the ejection port, and she pushed it back in. Then she clicked it back into place.

"Nah," she said. "I think I'll keep it."

Somerville grinned. "Okay, then. You coming with me?"

Sara nodded and climbed into the passenger side of his truck.

He looked at us one more time.

"We'll follow you out to the hospital," I said, "but we're not staying in town tonight."

He grinned again and winked at us.

I looked over to Jen. She rolled her eyes.

* * *

Jen and I followed behind him in the old pickup. We had our water and wine from Brian's house in there, and we didn't want to leave them behind.

"Maybe we'll get out there and find some more survivors," I said.

"Whatever," she said, looking out her window.

"We need to stick together," I said. "There aren't many of us."

"Sounds like he has a convert," she said.

"What's the problem?"

"The problem," she said, "is that you keep letting him call all the shots. And he's going to do it, too, because he's used to doing it."

"What do you have against him?"

"It's nothing personal," she said. "I just don't like getting bossed around."

She looked over at me. From the look in her eyes, I thought she was about to apologize for being so grumpy. Instead ...

"Damn, you need a bath."

We took a left onto the bypass, and the woman in the back of Somerville's truck sat up.

"Whoa!" Jen said. "She's awake."

"Did you give her enough quilts?" I asked. "She's probably cold."

She didn't look around. She just sat there staring at us, the wind blowing her shoulder-length hair in her face.

"I'm thinking that she ain't cold," Jen said.

I flashed my lights at Somerville. The woman stood.

"Oh shit," Jen said.

I stepped on the gas and moved into the passing lane.

The truck swerved a little; Somerville had noticed her.

The woman turned and faced forward, with her hands on top of the cab, then hit the rear window with her fist. The truck swerved. She lost her balance a little, but recovered. She hit the window again, and her fist punched through.

The truck cut hard to the left, dropped off into the median and flipped onto the passenger side, then over again, slinging mud and grass into the air. It came to rest on the driver's side.

I drove past the wreck and stopped. I could hear Sara screaming and crying. I started toward it. Then, around the back end of Somerville's truck, the woman appeared. She was muddy and bloody. A bone stuck out of her left arm. She crouched a little, which sort of spread her out. She snarled, howled and charged at me like a linebacker.

CHAPTER 24

I wasn't armed at all. All I could do was run, and I did. I ran to my left, out into the road.

Jen fired the .22. If it hit the woman, she didn't act like it. Jen fired again, and the woman changed direction and came at her instead. The .22 wasn't stopping her, and all of the big guns were in Somerville's truck. Jen shot one more time, and the woman bulldozed over her.

"Jen!"

The woman was on top of her. Jen had her hand around the woman's throat, but that was the best she was able to do. The woman was too heavy for Jen to hold off.

Jen screamed just before I got to them. I kicked the woman in the head. She rolled off, but came back. I kicked her in the face. Her head whipped back, and she fell over, stunned. I grabbed the .22, and with no thought at all, put it to her head and pulled the trigger twice.

Jen got to her feet, holding the side of her neck, stumbled sideways and fell. She started to get up again, and I held her by the elbow so she could get her balance.

"Let me see," I said.

She pulled her hand away. Her palm was bloody, and there was a little chunk of flesh gone from her neck. She pulled off her bandana and pushed it against the wound.

"I think she might have cracked one of my ribs," she said.

I put my hand on her side, and she brushed it away.

"I'm fine," she said.

Sara was still crying from inside the truck. I ran around to the back window.

"Are you hurt?"

"Help me!" Sara yelled.

"Mr. Somerville? Are you hurt?"

I got my face near the hole in the window through which the woman had put her fist. Somerville was against the driver's door. I didn't see any blood, but all of the guns, the first-aid kit and other smaller items had fallen on top of him. Sara was hanging from her seatbelt.

I still had that pistol in my jeans, so I pulled it out and used it like a hammer to break the glass.

When I had beaten out a big enough hole, I moved the debris off of Somerville. Then I took the .30-06 and used the stock to beat out the rest of the glass.

I grabbed one of the old quilts out of the mud and put it over the opening to guard against any shards sticking up. Then I crawled halfway into the cab.

Mr. Somerville had no obvious injuries, but he was unconscious. He wasn't wearing his seatbelt, so I started trying to pull him out. I couldn't get him to budge.

"Let's try turning the truck over," Jen said. She was standing behind me, a little wobbly.

"Push it with the other truck," she instructed.

I didn't want to do it, but I didn't see how else I would get them out.

"Sara, you hang on," I said. "I'm going to try to turn the truck over on its wheels."

I pulled our truck around so that the front of it was perpendicular to the top of Somerville's truck. I eased in slowly, and bumped the truck. Sara screamed. Slowly, I applied more gas. I could hear my tires spinning. Then Somerville's truck tilted. The passenger-side tires landed, and the vehicle bounced. It was righted.

Somerville's door was crushed and wouldn't open. Sara's door didn't look any better than the driver's door, but I managed to pull it open halfway. Other than a big knot on her forehead and the beginnings of a black eye, she seemed okay.

When I got in to pull Somerville out, I still couldn't move him. Then I saw that his left forearm and hand were pinned between the door and the seat.

"I can't get him out," I said, crawling out of the truck. "I can't even get to his arm to pry it loose. We'll have to force the door open from the outside."

"With what?"

"Jen?" Sara said.

Jen and I looked at her. She was staring far down the road, toward the hospital.

It was the biggest group I'd seen so far. There were several hundred at least, spread out across the two right lanes of highway and over the median. The sound of so many arms and legs and bodies moving was like a thousand whispers. Their occasional howls reminded me of the lowing of cattle.

I ran back to Mr. Somerville, grabbed his sleeve and pulled, but his arm wouldn’t come free. Jen and Sara were on the other side, trying to open his door.

Somerville stirred.

"Mr. Somerville!"

He opened his eyes, but his head was lolling.

"You've got to pull your arm out!" I said.

He looked over at me, then past me. His eyes widened. He tried to pull his arm out, wincing in pain. He looked past me again.

"You've got to go," he said, shaking his head. "I can't get it loose."

I looked back over my shoulder. They were too close.

"You've got to go," he said again.

I climbed out and shut the passenger door as well as I could.

"Come on!" I said. "We're leaving. Grab these guns and stuff and get them into the truck."

"Work on it some more, damn it!" Jen said. She picked up the .30-06, braced herself on the side of the truck and fired into the crowd.

She'd never do any good; we all knew it.

I picked up the shotgun Sara had found in the police car and fed it through the back window to Somerville. He continued to stare out at the approaching horde, but he took the weapon.

"I appreciate it," he said.

I grabbed Jen by the arm. She jerked away. I grabbed her again and yanked her back. She looked over at Somerville, pulled away from me again, and got into the truck. Sara seemed unsure what to do.

"Get in the truck, Sara. We're leaving."

She stared out at the mob for a moment longer, then joined us in the truck.

I put the vehicle in reverse and backed away a good distance, then put it in drive and headed in the opposite direction. Sara turned in her seat.

"Don't look," Jen said.

Sara faced front, but I looked back in the mirror.

The black truck was swallowed up in the throng.

CHAPTER 25

I headed back toward Blaine's place. I'd had more than I could take for one day. Jen and Sara both had the thousand-mile stare. Jen still held the bandana to her neck, and Sara's eye was swollen and bruised. My eye had swollen a little too, where Somerville had hit me earlier in the day. There'd been so much excitement that I hadn't even noticed the pain. I probably would later, but that would be deadened by the alcohol.

I was actually looking forward to a drink.

I barely knew Mr. Somerville. Before that day, I'd met him only once, at a museum fundraiser. It was campaign time, and he was there schmoozing. I was okay with it, because when government officials showed up to those things, it lent credibility and helped people feel better about making donations. I'm not sure that he even remembered me when he saw me that morning in the mayor's office.

It didn't matter. Almost nothing that was before seemed to matter anymore.

I kept thinking about Mrs. Somerville. She'd be waiting for him to come home, and he wouldn't. After a day or so, she'd probably go out looking for him and wind up dead or sick too. I couldn't allow that.

I was about three miles from Blaine's, and I pulled into the driveway of the first house I saw.

"What are you doing?" Jen said.

"Sorry," I said. "I've got to tell Mrs. Somerville. It wouldn't be right not to. I'm going in here to find a phone book. Maybe it'll have his address. If you want, I can drive you and Sara out to Blaine's, and I can go ..."

"No," she said.

I got out, grabbed Somerville's shotgun and went up to the porch of the little yellow brick house. Jen and Sara stayed in the truck.

I knocked on the metal storm door. I didn't get an answer, but I didn't expect to. There was a little open shed off to the side of the house. There was a riding mower parked in there and some firewood stacked along the wall. The yard was small for that of a country house—not more than a quarter-acre—and ended abruptly, with woods on every side but the street side.

I looked around for a spare key in all of the obvious places a person might keep one—under the mat, on the fixture of the porch light, under flowerpots. I finally found it beneath one of the planters that flanked the entrance to the porch.

I went in. I was standing in the living room; the dining room and kitchen were off to my left. I didn't take a lot of time to investigate right then. I made a quick sweep of the house to make sure there were no surprises waiting for me. It was empty.

I went back to the porch and waved at Jen to get out.

"What?" she said.

"You and Sara come in and check the place for food and water while I find Somerville's address," I said. I didn't see any reason why we should pass up an opportunity to get supplies. I was getting over my aversion to scavenging, as Jen called it.

Jen seemed reluctant, and even a little angry, when she came in the door. Sara was quiet.

"Can't we just do this food and water thing later?" Jen said. "I'd like to take care of my neck, and my side really hurts."

I looked up from the phone book. I felt like an ass for being so insensitive.

"Yeah," I said. "Sorry. We can do it later. Why don't I drive you two out to ..."

"I've already said no to that," she said. "Let's just find his address and take care of this."

Then I heard something so familiar that it didn't register at first: water running in the sink.

When what we were hearing sank in, Jen and I made for the kitchen in surprise. Sara was standing at the sink with a glass of water. When we came in, she turned around.

"What?" she said.

"The water is working?" Jen asked. "How?"

Sara turned it on again.

I tried the light switch, but nothing happened.

Jen went to the sink and looked out the window.

"There's a big tank out back," she said. "Maybe it's a cistern."

"That's good to know," I said. "We'll come back."

Sara opened the cabinets and pulled down a box of Pop Tarts. I went back into the living room to search the phone book.

I found Somerville's name and address.

"His house is on Depot Street," I said. "He and I are practically neighbors."

Jen came in and sat on the couch, but she didn't say anything. I picked up the telephone to see if it worked. There was a dial tone, but I got a busy signal when I dialed Somerville's number.

"Phone works," I said. "Do you want to try your brother?"

Jen shook her head.

"Sara? Do you want to try to call your family?"

Sara stepped into the living room.

"I tried at the church. No one ever answers."

I stared at the two of them for a moment. They looked so battered and defeated.

"Why don't the two of you stay here until I get back?"

Jen shook her head again, but I continued.

"Yes," I said. "There's running water. You can get cleaned up and have something to eat. I'll go talk with Mrs. Somerville, and I'll be right back. I'll see if she wants to come back here too."

"No," Jen said. "What happens if you don't come back? What are we going to do then?"

"I'll be right back," I said. "Sara can bandage up your neck. I'll leave the wine."

"I kind of want to stay," Sara said. "I don't want to be around them anymore."

"Don't want to be around them?" Jen said. "They're everywhere. We can't get a frickin' break."

"I'd still rather stay," Sara said. "I haven't eaten real food in a couple of days. There's a gas range in there. If you have a match or a lighter, I could fix us a hot meal."

"Shouldn't we at least break the news to poor Judy Somerville before we have a damn banquet?" Jen said.

"Jesus, Jen, go easy on her," I said.

"Just leave," Jen said.

I looked up at Sara. She was staring at the floor.

"Sara, a hot meal sounds nice," I said. "I look forward to it. Heat some water on the stove for me too, and I'll get a bath when I get back."

* * *

All manner of thoughts ran through my head as I drove to Depot Street. Mrs. Somerville was armed, so approaching her would be tricky. Then I'd have to deliver the bad news. Then I'd have to convince her to come with me. On top of that, I had to contend with these monsters showing up unexpectedly. Then there was Jen ...

I didn't have a clock, but I guessed it was around 4:00 p.m. when I pulled up in front of the house. I left the shotgun in the truck and started to the front door. I heard voices coming from the garage.

"Hello? Mrs. Somerville?"

There was silence for a moment, then, "Yes?"

"Mrs. Somerville, I'm a friend. I was hoping I could talk with you."

I heard muffled voices inside.

"Mrs. Somerville?"

She lifted the door. She was standing there in a housecoat and slippers, the .357 Magnum in her right hand. She pointed it at me.

Behind her, parked in the garage, was Nicholas Somerville's muddy, dented, black pickup. He was in the driver's seat.

"Mr. Somerville?"

I couldn't believe what I was seeing.

"In or out," Judy Somerville said. "I need to shut the door."

She kept her gun trained on me as I got inside. She closed the door, and I came to Mr. Somerville's window. Blood had been splattered all over the inside of the cab. There was a man in there with him, upside down, with his head on the floorboard. Another dead man lay in the bed of the truck.

Somerville looked over at me. He looked like he was in pain, but he still managed to grin.

"What the hell? I said.

"There'll be no language like that," Mrs. Somerville said. "Not in my house."

"I'm a tough son of a bitch, that's what," he said.

"Nick! Watch your mouth."

"Oh, Judy, judging by how things turned out, I don't think Jesus is listening anymore."

"Don't talk like that!"

Mr. Somerville rolled his eyes.

"There's a pry bar out there," he said. "Start working on this door for me. She hasn't been able to get it open."

"How did you get away?" I asked, working on the door.

"Well, I was all ready to go. They were all over me, coming in the window. They must have bitten me a dozen times. I was trying to decide whether I should use the last shell on them or myself. Then I did the obvious thing and tried to start the truck. It cranked right up, so I got the hell out of there. I brought home a couple of souvenirs."

"Can't get the door from here," I said. "I'll have to get in."

I went around and pulled the body out of the truck, then scooted through the gore so I could get the pry bar between the seat and the door.

"It means a lot that you came here," he said. "You're a good man to check on Judy like that."

"Well, I figured she'd worry," I said.

"Yeah, she's a worrier," he said. "Where are the girls?"

"I left them in a house outside of town. They're pretty banged up."

"Are they all right?"

"They will be once I tell them you're still here." I grinned.

I pulled against the bar.

"Try it," I said.

He groaned in pain and pulled his arm free. His arm and hand were massively swollen. We'd have to cut his sleeve to get his coat off. Judy helped him inside while I dragged the two bodies outside.

When I came inside, I found him sitting on the couch in a wife-beater undershirt. He had bite marks on his neck and arm, but it looked like his coat had kept them from breaking the skin. His wife brought in a plastic baggie full of ice.

"I think his arm is broken," she said.

"Nah," he said. "It's just swollen from having the circulation cut off, that's all."

"You need a doctor," she said.

He looked up at me.

"I don't know where the doctors are, hon."

"What if the bone needs to be set?"

"You'll have to do it," he told her.

"I don't know anything about that, Nick."

"Don't worry about it."

He looked up at the window.

"It'll be getting dark soon," he said. "You're welcome to stay, but I guess you'll want to get back."

"Why don't you two come with me? It'll be safer."

"Write your address down, and maybe we'll see you in a few days," he said. "As soon as I'm up to it, I'm going to check around town for more survivors."

Judy got up and left the room.

"She'll be fine," Somerville said. "You should probably get going."

I nodded and handed him the address.

"You should probably get a bath too," he said. "You're rank."

"Could I get a towel or something to put in my seat? I don't want to get this mess all over the truck."

"Sure," he said. "Judy! Bring a big towel!"

"Do you have any alcohol in the house?" I asked.

"Yeah," he said. "I've got a bottle hidden in the garage. I saw that on the news. I don't know if it works."

"It works," I said.

"Well, it ought to be fun either way. I've never seen Judy drunk before."

"And you never will," Judy said, coming in with a towel.

"You'll get drunk tonight, darlin'," he said. "And if you don't watch out, I might just take advantage of you."

"Nick! Don't talk like that in front of company," she said.

I took the towel and said goodbye.

CHAPTER 26

When I pulled into the driveway of the yellow brick house, it was getting dark. I'd driven the whole way with my headlights off so I wouldn't attract any of the infected to our location. The shades were closed. I knocked on the door and announced my presence. Sara opened the door. She was wearing different clothes, and I got a faint sweet scent from her. The room behind her was lit with the flickering of three candles. I could smell kerosene too, and I saw a lit kerosene heater in the middle of the living room. It hadn't gotten very warm in there yet, but it would. She looked past me to see if Mrs. Somerville was with me.

"How did it go?" she asked, holding the door open for me.

"Better than I expected," I said. "He's alive. He's home."

Jen emerged from the kitchen. Her hair was up in a towel, and she had changed out of Brian's jogging suit into some jeans and a sweatshirt. They looked a little big on her. There was a bandage around her throat.

"How can he be alive?" she asked.

I came inside and told them the story.

"We should have just tried the key to begin with," Jen said.

"Are you hungry?" Sara asked. "I cooked some beef stew. It's the canned stuff, but it smells pretty good. We've been waiting on you before we eat."

"First, how about that bath?"

"Definitely," Jen said. "And let's burn those clothes."

They had two big pots of water boiling on the stove. I ran a little water in the tub, and then poured in the water from the stove. Then I added some more cold water until it was bearable. The water felt good, but I knew the warmth wouldn't last long, as cold as it was in the bathroom. I washed quickly, then got out, shivering.

We scrounged some changes of clothing from the closets in the house. The clothes didn't fit very well, but our own clothes were just a few miles down the road, and we'd be able to get something for Sara somewhere else.

They'd found other useful things in the house too. We now had two flashlights, a .22 revolver with another hundred or so rounds of ammunition, blankets and the kerosene heater. Plus, there was several days' worth of food.

We sat down for a candlelit dinner of canned beef stew, corn on the cob and Saltines. The mood was much lighter than it had been; the gloom that had been hanging over Jen was gone. Even with all that we'd been through that day, the news of Mr. Somerville's escape had perked everyone up a bit.

Jen opened a bottle of Merlot and poured me a tumbler. She started to pour some for Sara, but she put her hand over her glass.

"No," Sara said. "I don't drink.'

"You've been exposed. Don't think of it as drinking," Jen said. "Think of it as medicine."

"No," Sara said. "It's wrong to drink."

"No," Jen insisted. "It's wrong to turn into a mindless monster when you don't have to."

"I'm only nineteen," she said.

Jen laughed. "Is this a religious thing? Because Jesus made wine, you know."

"My pastor says that what Jesus made wasn't really wine. It was just grape juice."

"Yeah, well your pastor is a friggin' zombie now."

Sara looked like she was going to cry. I knew I had to step in. The three of us might be together for a while, and we all needed to get along.

"Jen," I said. "Don't."

Jen gave me an angry look, then poured herself a glass. She put the cork in the bottle and went back to the counter.

"Sara," I said. "Jen is right. We've all been exposed to the virus today. You don't have to get drunk. I think the Bible says not to get drunk, doesn't it?"

"But it's wrong," she repeated, shaking her head.

Jen returned to the table with a glass in her hand.

"Here," she said. "Apple juice."

Sara took the glass warily.

"But let me tell you something," Jen said. "If you get sick, it's your own fault."

Sara sniffed the glass, then took a drink.

"Thank you," she said.

"We're just trying to help you," I said.

"How about we change the subject," Jen said. "Sara, what's up with the letter jacket? Are you on the basketball team or something?"

She smiled. "It was my boyfriend's jacket. He let me wear it. He's in college now at U of L."

"What about you?" Jen asked. "Are you in school?"

"I go to the community college part time, and I work at the church part time."

With all of the questions, I realized that I really didn't know much more about Jen than I did about Sara. We'd been together since Friday, but we hadn't really talked. We'd never gotten to know one another.

We continued to eat and converse. Jen waited on us, refilling our bowls and glasses. After a half-hour, I noticed that Sara was really coming out of her shell. She was more talkative and smiled more. I was glad to see that she was warming up to us. Then she got an odd look on her face.

"I feel ... strange. My bottom lip is kind of numb. Is that a part of the virus?"

"I don't remember that being a symptom," I said.

I looked over at Jen, and she winked at me.

"Sara, hon, you really should drink a little something before you start getting the fever."

"I can't," Sara said.

"If you turn, then I'm going to have to shoot you, and I like you too much. Please don't do that to me. You don't have to drink much—just a little wine."

They stared at each other, then Sara nodded.

"Okay," she said. "Just a little wine."

Jen returned with the Merlot.

"This is a dry wine," she said. "That means it isn't very sweet. We do have some sweet wine, if you would rather have that."

"No," Sara said. "This will be fine."

Jen poured her half a glass. She sipped it and made a face.

* * *

We all moved into the living room. The kerosene heater was doing a good job of warming the room, but not the whole house.

"Why don't we stay here?" Jen said.

"Well, yeah," I said. "I don't want to go out in the dark."

"No," she said, "not just for the night, but for a while. It's a nice little house. There's a wood stove in the basement. I didn't start a fire, because the kerosene was quicker, but it looks like the vents in the floor open to the basement, so it ought to heat the whole house."

"I like it here too," Sara said.

"I don't like how it's enclosed by woods," I said. "We need to be able to see something coming from far away."

"True," Jen said. "But I don't think Blaine's is ideal for a long stay. It just isn't comfortable; we'll be crammed in that little shop. If this is going to be a while, then we should try to make ourselves as comfortable as we can."

I nodded.

Sara got up and went down the hall to the bathroom. When she'd shut the door, Jen grinned.

"I mixed some of that sweet white wine with her apple juice. She never knew."

If Jen had done that to Sara the week before, it would have been appalling, but a lot had changed in the last week.

I shrugged. "Whatever works."

When Sara returned, we both smiled innocently. She smiled back, sat down, and continued to nurse her Merlot.

"I don't want to go into town any more than we have to," Jen said. "I need time to rest and process this shit. It's just too much to have to deal with every day. They're out here too, but there aren't as many of them. I think we should make a list of things we might need, then go in and collect them in a single day if we can."

"Are we going to look for other survivors? Are we going to meet up with Mr. Somerville again?" Sara asked.

"I don't know if I have it in me to search the town for survivors every day," Jen said. "Somerville will probably need some help, though. I'm sure he'd take you in if you want to stay with him."

"I kind of like being with you two," she said. "You're closer to my age."

"I appreciate that, hon, but I don't feel that young."

"We could live almost anywhere," I said. "There will be more free houses than occupied houses. If it weren't for all the infected people walking around, it would be an exciting prospect—living however we want to. But the truth is, we have to live carefully, even more carefully than we did before."

"We can still have a comfortable and relatively safe place to come home to, can't we? We could store up some stuff so we don't have to get out there any more than necessary, right?"

"Sure," I said. "But there are more like us out there, and I think it's important to connect with them if we can. We don't all have to live together, but we're going to need each other eventually."

* * *

The three of us slept in the living room of that little house, around the kerosene heater. It ran out of fuel in the middle of the night, and we woke up the next morning cold and headachy. We were all concerned about the headaches at first, but we quickly realized that the smoking of the wick after the burner had run out of fuel had probably irritated our sinuses. Our chests felt congested as well.

It had started raining during the night. We didn't want to go out collecting supplies in the cold rain, so we decided to have some breakfast and wait it out. It was still raining after lunch, so we loaded up some of the stuff from the house and drove over to Blaine and Betsy's place.

I got a fire started in the shop while Jen went into the house to change into her own clothes. She and Sara planned to go through the clothes Betsy had left to see if something would fit Sara.

I checked on the food Jen had brought back when she went out by herself. The stuff that had been frozen was now thawed, but it was still cold enough that I didn't think it would be bad. I would need to find a thermometer somewhere so we could keep track of temperatures. We were in the latter end of February, and in this part of Kentucky, it could get down into the teens or up into the fifties. We would definitely need to save our canned and dry goods and start eating all this perishable stuff.

The chickens needed water again, and they were hungry. I considered letting them out of the pen so they could fend for themselves whenever we were away, but I didn't want to lose them to predators. We were going to need their eggs soon. In fact, I thought we should probably add more chickens to our supplies list, and a rooster too. A milk goat or cow would be good, but that could wait.

Jen and Sara returned. Jen had changed, but Sara was wearing the same clothes. They each carried an armload of novels. Jen also had a notebook.

"If it rains for a while, we're going to need something to distract us," Jen said. "I don't know what you like to read, but I got a little of everything."

I nodded. I wasn't really interested in fiction right then. I thought it would be more important to read some of the information I'd printed off at my house that first night. I could see the need for escape, though, so I didn't insist that they read what I thought we should all be reading. I grabbed my bag and went into the house to change into my own clothes.

It was too bad that Blaine's home wasn't equipped with a wood stove or some form of alternative energy. The house wasn't anything special—just a manufactured home—but the location was perfect. It was on a small hill, and there was nothing but open field to the front and back of the house, so we would be able to see anyone approaching. There was a large pond nearby that was home to bass, bluegill and catfish. There were mature fruit trees, pecan trees, blackberries and a small vineyard. It would be a good location to settle down. I was sure there were other places like this too, but how would I find them in February? I could probably identify certain trees and plants, but not in winter when there were no leaves.

On my way back out to the shop, I looked across the road to the cow field. In the distance was a dead cow. A pack of ten dogs was feasting on it. They weren't coyotes or coydogs. These were family pets. They were mostly mutts of different sizes, shapes and colors, but I saw a couple of purebreds in there too. Some were lying down or playing with each other, wagging their tails. They didn't look mean or vicious. I wondered if they'd brought the cow down or if they'd found it like that. If we were going to have livestock, then we would need to collect them soon. Animals like that would be easy prey with no one to protect them.

Jen and Sarah were sitting on the mattresses and talking when I got back. They'd made coffee.

"We're making our shopping list," Jen said, holding up the notebook.

I took one of the old lawn chairs down and sat.

"What do you have so far?" I said.

"Other than food and clothes, we're having a little trouble figuring out what we'll need."

I went over to the stack of papers I'd printed off.

"I have a list in here somewhere. It might not fit us exactly, but it should give us an idea. Actually, there are several lists in here."

I separated the stack into three smaller piles, one for each of us.

"Look through what I have, and we can make our own list from these."

I poured myself some coffee and took my papers back to my chair.

"But you're right about the house," I said. "We should be as comfortable as possible. Put a house at the top of your list."

CHAPTER 27

It rained steadily for the next four days. We ran out of firewood on the morning of the third day. It was a big relief, because we were all pretty bored by that time. We'd been doing nothing but sitting around reading and talking. We were all starting to get edgy, and we were ready for a diversion.

I had a real hankering for some TV or Internet surfing. I wondered how people managed to stay sane before the age of electronics.

There was plenty of firewood in the shed at the little yellow brick house, so the three of us loaded up in the pickup to drive over there and get it. The weather was miserable—soggy, cold and gray.

On the way, I looked at the houses on the road in a new light; I was shopping. I didn't see anything I liked, but there were thousands more from which to choose.

"You know what?" I said, "Let's go ahead and look for a new place now. It doesn't look like the rain is going to stop; we could spend the time driving around instead of sitting in that little building, staring at each other."

"I thought you said we were getting low on gas," Jen said.

"I thought you said we could steal whatever car we wanted," I shot back.

"It ain't stealing," she said.

"I know," I said. "I'm just joking with you."

"Okay. Let's find a roomy vehicle, and then we'll park the truck and use it to get the firewood later."

We drove a couple of miles, checking out houses and vehicles as we passed. We only saw one person, out in a field.

"Oooh," Sara said. "I like that car."

The red car, which appeared to be from the late '60s or early '70s, was parked under the carport of a big white farmhouse. There were newer vehicles parked up there too, but ... sure, why not?

We pulled up in the driveway, and we all got out. Sara ran up under the carport and looked in the car's passenger-side window.

"Isn't it beautiful?" she said. "My dad used to take me to car shows. This is a 1967 Cutlass Supreme. It's in perfect condition too."

"Yeah," I said as we joined her. "It's really nice."

"It'll drink the gas, won't it?" Jen said.

Sara shrugged. "Gas is free now, so who cares? Anyway, I imagine that truck you've been driving drinks it too."

"Gas is free, hon, but getting at it is the problem, and they ain't making it anymore."

"Come on," Sara said. "Just for today."

"Sure," I said. "Let's go back to the truck and get the shotgun; then we'll go inside and find the keys."

Jen stepped around the driver's side of the car to go into the house.

"Wow, look at this," she said.

I went around the car. Lined up between the car and the house were three five-gallon gasoline cans and four five-gallon kerosene cans. I went down the line, lifting them. All of the gas cans, and all but one of the kerosene cans, were completely full.

Next to them was something covered with a tarp. I pulled the tarp away and found a wooden pallet stacked with bottled water and toilet paper.

Jen and I looked at each other, trying to make sense of it, and then we both came to the same conclusion.

Sara was opening the storm door to the house.

"Sara," Jen whispered. "Get back to the truck."

"What? Why?"

Before Sara could move, the door to the house opened, and a gun barrel emerged, directed at her face.

"Get off my property," a man said.

Jen and I backed away to the side, out of the man's field of vision. Jen reached into her coat and pulled out the .22 revolver.

"We're sorry," Sara said. "We didn't know anybody lived here."

The man stepped out of the house, backing Sara up to the classic car.

"Well, somebody does."

He looked like he was in his mid to late 30s. He had dark hair, a new beard and a little paunch. He'd clearly gotten dressed quickly. His jeans were fastened under his belly but not zipped, his blue flannel shirt was open, his hat was on crooked, and he was wearing green rubber boots. He looked at Jen and me, noticed Jen's weapon and aimed his gun at us. We backed up even farther, until we were standing in the rain.

"No," I said. "It's okay. We don't want to bother anybody. We thought the place was abandoned. We're almost out of gas, so …"

"So you thought you'd steal mine."

"No," I said. "We didn't know you were here."

"It's a good thing I was, or you would have robbed me blind."

"We're going to leave now," I said. "We didn't mean any harm."

Sara sidestepped along the car until she joined us, and we all backed away toward the pickup. He kept his gun on us and walked up to the edge of the carport.

"Are there more of you?"

I stopped, "There are more survivors, if that's what you mean."

"How many?"

"Four more that we know of, but they're not with us."

He lowered his gun. "Is that all?"

I nodded.

"Do you have any news? Has the government stopped the outbreak? Are they coming to help us?"

"No," I said. "Nobody's coming. The virus is probably worldwide by now."

"Probably?"

"It crossed the Mississippi River a few days ago," I said. "It moved into Asia too."

His brow furrowed as he thought about what I'd just told him.

The three of us had stopped moving toward the truck; we just stood there in the rain.

"Aw, hell," he said.

"We really ain't here to hurt nobody," Jen said.

He didn't answer; he just looked up at us, distracted and sad.

"We're going now," I said.

We all climbed into the truck. The cold rain had soaked in, and we were shivering. I started the truck and turned on the heat and windshield wipers. I'd just started backing down the driveway, when the man ran out after us and slapped the hood.

"Wait!" he said.

I stopped, and he came around to Jen's window.

"I ain't got nobody left," he said. He looked so pitiful with rain dripping from his crooked hat.

"We don't either," Jen said.

He nodded.

"Y'all can have some gas," he said. "Why don't you come in for a while? I ain't seen nobody in almost a week."

CHAPTER 28

His name was Charlie, and he was a manager at the chicken-processing plant. There were stacks of canned goods and another kerosene jug sitting in his dining room. There was a kerosene heater in the middle of the living room. He'd been sleeping in there too. He had hung blankets over the doorways to help keep the heat in that room. There were blankets on the couch, and the ashtray on the coffee table was overflowing with ash and butts.

We all took off our wet coats, and he brought in a pot of coffee for us. Then he sat in one of the chairs and started talking.

"I work the night shift," he said, removing his hat. He was starting to go bald on top. "I woke up last Thursday, around four in the afternoon, and Wendy wasn't here. We knew things were supposed to get bad, so I figured she'd gone into town to get more food and water.

"I couldn't get her on her cell. Then it started getting late. I turned on the news, and I knew it had already begun. I tried to call in to work, but nobody answered the phones.

"My daughter, Katie, is a freshman at Purdue, and we'd told her to stay put, because we thought she'd be safer there than here. I tried to call her, but nothing. I saw what they were doing to the bridges and the ferries, and I knew there would be no way I could get to her.

"Around eight that night, I went out looking for Wendy. I found her car parked at Wal-Mart, but I didn't find her right away. God, it was crazy. There were people running around the parking lot. They were fighting and shooting each other. I went in the store, and it was even worse. I tried looking for her in there, but I couldn't find her. While I was in there, I decided to get a few things. We'd already collected a lot of food, but I figured we'd need kerosene. The power would go out eventually, and I remembered how we ran out of fuel during the ice storm.

"I got a cart and went back to automotive and piled it full of gas jugs. Then I got kerosene jugs. I tried to keep my head down so no one would notice me. I went around to sporting goods. All of the guns were gone. The case was smashed. There were loose bullets and shotgun shells all over the floor.

"There was nobody at the registers, so I just left. I still can't believe I got in and out like that without getting hurt."

He stopped and lit a cigarette.

"That's when I saw her. I knew it was her, because she had this ugly pink coat that she liked to wear. This guy was ... um ... he was on top of her, and he was assaulting her right there on the ground. I knocked him off of her ... then I ... I just beat him and kicked him. I think he might have died.

"When I went to check on her, she scratched me and tried to bite me. I tried talking to her, but it wasn't her anymore. All she could do was grunt and growl. I couldn't help her, so I left her there."

He put the heels of his hands against his eyes as if he were trying to mash away the memory.

"Um ... there's a gas station over by the county high school that sells kerosene, so I drove out there. There were lots of cars lined up to the station, but they were all abandoned. I found a gas pump that was on, and I filled up my cans with gas and kerosene, and then I loaded up some others that were sitting next to the other cars in line.

"I went in the little convenience store there to at least make an effort to pay, but nobody was in there. I went in the stock room and got all the canned goods, water, cigarettes and toilet paper I could fit in my vehicle. I left a note on the counter with my name and address so I could settle up with them later. Then I went home.

"I must have cried for two days straight."

"Sorry," Jen said.

"Thanks," he said. "But it ain't your fault. It ain't nobody's fault, I don't guess. Me and Wendy, we been together since high school. We had to get married—you know how that is. My folks were so embarrassed, but I really couldn't have had a better wife ... a better friend. I miss her, but I don't got no regrets when it comes to her."

He wiped away tears, put out his cigarette and lit another.

"If what y'all say is true about the virus, then I guess Katie has it too, or is like us and hiding somewhere. Either way, I'll probably never see her again either. I've already cried for her too."

"Have you been out since then?" I asked.

"I went over to check on some of the neighbors, but nobody answered the door. I thought about driving north—trying to find Katie—but I wanted to wait until things died down some. But now ..."

"Things aren't dying down," Jen said. "It's as bad out there now as it was on Thursday."

"What have y'all seen?"

"It hasn't changed from last week," I said. "Except maybe there are more infected people now."

He stared at the smoke coming off the end of his cigarette.

"I'm a mess," he said. "This whole thing with Wendy and Katie—I'm messed up over it."

"We can understand that," Jen said.

"But I'll help y'all any way I can. I don't know if I'll be any good to you."

"We all lost somebody," I said. "We're all messed up."

* * *

Charlie offered to help us collect supplies, and we accepted. We told him we'd be back when the rain stopped, thanked him for his hospitality and left. The five gallons of gas he'd given us brought us to just under half of a tank.

"What do you think?" I said as we pulled away from Charlie's house. "Should we invite him to come in with us?"

"He seems to be okay there," Jen said. "We know where he is if we need him."

"Don't you like him?"

"Honestly," Jen said, "it's the cigarettes. He just chained smoked the whole time. It would be okay if he'd go outside, but I don't want to make him do something like that. We can live however we want now, and I don't want to live with a smoker."

"I thought he was nice," said Sara. "Maybe he would smoke outside if we asked him to."

"He would be helpful," I said.

"I don't doubt that," Jen said. "He seemed like a really sweet guy, but I just can't do it. The smoke from the stove has me stuffed up enough. I'm not going to live with it if I don't have to. Besides, I'm liable to have a weak moment and start up again. That's the last thing I need."

"What if he asks to join us? We can't just turn him away."

"Then we need to lay down some rules," Jen said.

* * *

We found the perfect house on Ester Lane. It was a huge two-story brick house with a three-bay garage set well off the road with a long, paved driveway that circled up to the house, giving it access to the road in two places. It had two chimneys—one on the end and one in the middle of the house—which was something you didn't often see on newer houses. The property was open. There was a small lake with a dock behind the house, and there was a little building out back as well. There were also rows of trees to the side of the house. I wouldn't know until they leafed out, but it was likely that it was a little orchard. Plus, there was a new black Cadillac Escalade parked out front.

I didn't think the house or the property was especially pretty, but who cared about aesthetics when the place was built like a fortress?

"Now that's what I'm talking about!" Jen said. "Pull in, and let's check it out."

I felt kind of bad hoping the house would be unoccupied, because that would mean the owners were likely sick or dead.

We pulled up close to the front door. We all pulled our masks up. I retrieved the shotgun and knocked on the door while Jen and Sara went around looking in windows. When no one answered the door, I walked around the other side of the house and tried to lift the garage doors, but they wouldn't come up. I continued around and met Jen and Sara on the back patio. There was an in-ground pool. The building in the back turned out to be a guesthouse.

I tried the patio door on the main house, and it slid open. Jen grinned at me and went inside. It was a nice house like Brian's home, but much less tastefully decorated. We didn't care. Jen wanted comfort, and this place promised that, so long as those chimneys were functional.

We were standing in the kitchen. From there, we could see the great room and dining room. A suitcase and a garment bag sat next to the dining table. On the table was a small lockbox and car keys.

"What's that smell?" Sara asked.

"Yeah," I said. "I smell it too. We need to stay close to each other. Jen, give Sara that revolver."

Jen pulled the weapon from her waistband and handed it to Sara, and we began our sweep of the house.

On the ground floor, in addition to the rooms we'd already seen, we found two bedroom suites, a laundry room, a living room and a half bath. I opened the door to the garage. There was a tan Honda Civic in one of the bays, but that was the only vehicle.

Upstairs, we found two more bedrooms and a full bath. The last door was another bedroom. The smell hit us hard, and I thought Sara was going to puke. There was a fireplace on the far wall, and the bed was to our left. On the bed was an infected man. His hands were tied together and tied again to the headboard, and his wrists were raw. He lay there in his own excrement. His left ankle was opened up and scabbed over; it looked like it had been eaten. There was a dead cat in there too.

The man hissed at us.

"My God, what is this?" Jen said.

"They must have restrained him the way I did with Brian," I said. "Then I guess they left him after he turned. Maybe they were infected too."

Jen grabbed the knob and shut the door. We all stood in the hallway. We could hear the man making noises inside.

"Looks like we have a room to clear out," Jen said.

"This place is nice," I said. "But we can keep looking."

"It's just the one room," Jen said.

"Yeah," I said, "but we'll have to get him out, then carry out that filthy mattress."

"We'll just shoot him, then dump the body out the window," Jen said.

"That mattress isn't going to fit out the window."

It briefly hit me what an odd conversation that was. A week before, I would have never dreamed I'd end up discussing such matters.

"What do you think, Sara?" I said.

"It's really gross."

Jen rolled her eyes. "Well, there you go. It's not just gross; it's really gross. Thank you so much for your input, dear."

"Why do you have to be so mean?" Sara asked as she walked down the hall to the stairs.

We both watched her leave.

"Yeah," I said. "Why do you?"

"It was just a joke."

"It was uncalled for," I said. "And it's not the first time you've done it to her."

Jen walked down the hall and went into one of the other bedrooms. I followed her. She was standing at a dresser, looking through drawers.

"What are you doing?" I said.

She slammed a drawer shut and sat on the bed.

"Well, it turns out that we're not the last man and woman on Earth," she said.

"No, but that's good, isn't it?" I said, not really sure what she meant.

"Yeah, it's good," she said.

"You don't sound like you mean it."

I heard the front door, so I went over to the window. Sara was outside.

"We've been spending day and night together for ... what? Five or six days? You haven't tried anything."

"Tried anything?" I said, turning around.

"I've never been with a man this long without him trying to get in my pants. Do you not think of me like that?"

"What? Jen, look what we've been through. I mean, there's a damn monster tied to the bed in the next room, sitting in his own shit."

"I need to know where we stand," she said. "I think we need to be on the same page. I want to stay here, and you and Sara want to do something else. You and she have been agreeing a lot lately."

"What are you talking about?"

"Listen, I don't like what life has handed us here. This is some messed-up shit, but we can still try to be happy, can't we?"

"Sure."

She stood and went over to the window.

"I thought we were getting along. I thought that maybe I had a decent shot at a life, such as it is, with a decent man. Finally, after all the deadbeats and jerks, I found somebody who treated me like a person. Then along comes the young chick with the hot ass, and suddenly I don't exist anymore."

"Jen, I haven't ..."

"No, but you want to. Look at her out there. She's so damned adorable that I might just make a pass at her myself."

I didn't know what to say.

She turned to face me.

"As bad as things are now," she continued, tears coming to her eyes, "they were worse for me before. Zach was dealing meth on the side. His friends scared me. The cops scared me. Hell, Zach scared me. The sad thing is he was the best boyfriend I'd had in years. At least he had a job and a little money, you know? What an asshole.

"Then everything happened, and there you were. You even went back inside my house just to get me some shoes. Zach would have never done that for me.

"I hated my job. I had debt that I'd never have been able to pay off. Then all that went away, and it was just me and you. I felt like somebody really cared about me for once."

"I do care about you," I said, "but we've been kind of busy trying to stay alive. Anyway, I know we've been together for the past few days, but we barely know each other."

She stood up, grabbed my hand and shook it.

"Hi. My name is Jen. Pleased to meet you. Have you met Sara? She's the one outside with the boobs that you keep staring at. Or maybe you'd like to meet my friend Brian; maybe he's what you're looking for?"

"Why are you pressuring me like this?" I said.

"Jeez," she said, pushing past me to the hallway. "Grow a pair, would ya?"

I propped my shotgun against the wall and stepped out after her. I grabbed her arm and spun her around.

"Let me go," she said.

I pulled her in, pulled our masks down and kissed her.

Wow.

It was short-lived. She shoved me away.

"I don't want your damn charity," she said and started toward the stairs.

I grabbed her again and pushed her against the wall. She struggled a little, but I wouldn't let her get away.

I kissed her again, and she melted against me.

CHAPTER 29

We heard the front door open again. Jen pushed me away a little. She pulled her mask back up over her nose and mouth. She tenderly touched my cheek, then pulled my mask up too.

"Don't forget your gun," she whispered. Then she went to the stairs, leaving me staring after her. She looked back at me, her eyes smiling.

I went back for my shotgun.

When I got downstairs, Sara and Jen were standing in the kitchen.

"What's up?" I asked.

"I was apologizing. Sara was right—it is really gross. We can find a different house. It's not like we'd ever be able to clean that room enough."

"Okay," I said. "But we can come back. We know this is a house we can take stuff from."

"Like that Escalade out there," Jen said, picking up the keys from the table. "Let's leave the truck here, and we'll go house-hunting in style."

Jen wanted to drive. She didn't care where we looked for a new house. Initially, I'd wanted to stay near Blaine's, because of the familiarity, but if we found a perfect place, it didn't really matter where it was. We drove around for another hour, staying away from the city limits and exploring back roads.

We saw a few people stumbling around outside, but they never threatened us. We passed an open tobacco barn and saw a whole group of them crowded together inside for shelter. They weren't completely mindless. They did, as the saying goes, have enough sense to get in out of the rain.

"We ought to torch that barn," Jen said, driving by slowly. "That would be one group we wouldn't have to worry about."

"So we're going to be exterminators?" I said.

"I'm not talking about hunting them," she said. "But why pass up an opportunity?"

"It's too wet," Sara said. "But I agree; they all need to go."

That was surprising. Sara didn't talk much anyway, and we'd never had any indication that she was in a hurry to hurt anyone.

"See?" Jen said. "Sara's on my side."

"From what we've seen, there's no guarantee that anything will kill them forever," I said. "You might just piss them off."

"One thing I've been thinking about," Jen said. "We should all probably try to find some handguns. We're going to keep scaring survivors when we come to their doors with weapons. We need to be armed, but we need a way to hide it so they aren't afraid of us. I know I wouldn't answer the door if there was someone outside with a shotgun. If I did, I'd probably answer with a shotgun myself."

"We have the twenty-two. We also have that thirty-eight and the nine millimeters that we found at City Hall," I said. "But we need ammo."

"Just something to think about," she said.

* * *

We had traveled in a big circle, and we were headed back toward Blaine's place from the opposite direction when we came across something promising. There was a sign by the road that said LASSITER STABLES: HORSE BOARDING, FARRIERING, and RIDING LESSONS.

The entire property—probably thirty or forty acres—was enclosed in a white board fence, and then subdivided by more fences to form smaller pastures. The long driveway cut right up the middle and was fenced on either side. Horses grazed in a couple of the fields.

"This looks pretty good," I said as Jen pulled in the driveway. "We could put a gate up there at the entrance, and I think that fence should discourage the infected."

The driveway led to an old two-story house. The house reminded me of watching reruns of The Waltons with my mom when I was a kid. There were two barns and a little greenhouse. The property was immaculate. The owners had kept the place maintained and tidy.

There were five pickup trucks parked around the barns, including one with a horse trailer attached. There were also a couple of tractors, a four-wheeler and a golf cart.

"Sara," I said. "Hand me that revolver."

She passed it over the seat to me.

"I'm going to go up to the house and check it out," I said. "You two stay here."

"Since when did we become the frail little women?" Jen said.

"Since your conversation about handguns," I said. "We only have one, so only one of us will go knock on the door."

She just stared at me without expression.

"But please do cover me with the rifle from here," I said. "And stop looking at me like that. This was your idea, wasn't it?"

"Whatever," she said.

I got out, put the weapon in my pants and then covered it with my shirt.

I went up to the porch, opened the screen door and knocked. After waiting a few seconds and knocking again, I tried the door. It was open.

"Hello? Anyone home?"

No one answered, so I motioned for Jen and Sara to join me.

The interior of the house was just as clean and neat as the property outside. The decor in the living room was a Western motif. In the dining room, I found places set for four people. There were days-old biscuits, sausage and gravy on the plates. Next to one plate sat a copy of the Clayfield Chronicle. It was dated last Thursday. The only thing out of place was one dining-room chair that was overturned and a spilled cup of orange juice.

"No one has been in here in a long time," I said. "We can check upstairs, but I think we're good here."

"There's a fireplace in the living room," Jen said. "I like this place."

"What about all the horses?" Sara said.

"I love horses," Jen said.

"I do too, but how are we going to take care of them?" Sara said.

This was not something I had considered. Did we, by taking a property, become responsible for all of the pets and livestock on that property? And what about all of the other pets and livestock all over the countryside?

"We can't take care of them," I said. "So what do we do with them?"

Jen walked over to the window and looked out into the pasture.

"We'll need horses eventually, won't we?"

"I don't know," I said. "Maybe in a year or more. We have plenty of vehicles and gasoline around for a while—until the gas goes bad, I guess. I can't see the need right now."

"How many do you think there are?" Sara asked. "I saw five on that one side. I wonder if there are any in the barns."

"There are seven over here," Jen said. "Can't they just eat grass?"

"That's the thing," I said. "I don't know. I don't know anything about horses. I see big troughs out there. So someone has to give them water."

"Could we just let them go?" Sara asked. "Would they go?"

"Let's search the rest of the house. Then we'll go out to the barns and see what we're dealing with," I said.

* * *

The house had two bedrooms and a bathroom upstairs and another bedroom downstairs. The fireplace was clean and didn't look like it had been used in a while. There was a big propane tank out back, so we'd be able to use the stovetop in the kitchen. The gas line was likely hooked into the water heater and central heat as well, but the furnace had a blower, and they both had thermostats that required electricity, so they'd be useless to us.

There was more pasture behind the house, and there were more horses too. One of the pastures had a small pond. It had been raining enough that the horses were getting some water in their troughs, but when the rain stopped, they would probably go through that quickly. We'd have to let them out so they could find food and water on their own.

"There's going to be a problem with all these animals," I said. "I've been thinking about this off and on since this started. Domesticated animals have relied on people for a long time. Now the people aren't there for them anymore."

Jen nodded.

"I got to thinking about that when we found that dead cat today," she said. "My aunt has a house full of cats."

"Think about all the indoor pets—cats, dogs, hamsters, goldfish," I said. "They'll all eventually die of thirst or starvation trapped in their owners' houses. Then there are farm animals. They'll have a better shot, but not much better. Eventually, they'll start dying. I would think that, with all of the death, we'll have more disease to worry about. Canton B won't be our only problem."

"Let's check the barns," Jen said. "If there are more in there, then they've been in there for almost a week. Let's hope they've had enough food and water."

The three of us went out. On the way, Sara looked in the horse trailer.

"Aww," she said. "There's one in here. I think it's dead."

We joined her and looked inside. A gray horse lay on the floor of the trailer. Its head was stretched up, still secured to the front of the trailer by a halter and lead rope. Its eyes were open, and its tongue hung out of the side of its mouth. It broke my heart to see it.

Jen started crying.

"I'll check the barns," I said, taking the shotgun from Sara. "There's no need for you two to have to see anything like this."

"I've told you before," Jen said. "I'm not a child, and I don't need you to coddle me."

I nodded and started toward the nearest barn. She grabbed my arm, and I looked back at her.

"But thank you for offering," she said.

I nodded again and proceeded to the barn.

The building was cleaner than my house. There was a corridor down the middle with five stalls on the left side and four stalls on the right. On the right side, where the fifth stall would have been, there was an office. The barn also had a big loft stacked with hay that ran half the length of the building.

We were glad to find all of the stalls empty. Jen went into the office.

"Old Mr. Lassiter really cracked the whip, didn't he?"

"What do you mean?" I said.

"Look how clean it is in here," she said. "Textbook Virgo. Can you imagine working for this guy?"

"You believe all that zodiac stuff?" I said.

"It doesn't matter if I believe it," she said. "It's truth, and truth is truth whether you believe it or not."

"My pastor says that astrology is evil," Sara said.

Jen started to speak, then looked at me and held her tongue. I smiled at her.

"Could be that Mr. Lassiter's employees were all Virgos," I said. "Maybe Mr. Lassiter was a messy Pisces like me."

"See? Pisces are supposed to be messy, so it is true."

"I think it's just a coincidence," I said.

"There's no such thing," Jen smiled. "So a Pisces, huh? No wonder I like you so much."

The second barn was just like the first, except instead of an office, it had a tack room full of saddles, bridles and farriering tools. There was a pleasant smell of hay, leather, and ... well, I guess the other smell was horse. One of the stalls was occupied by a goat. There was still a little water in his trough. I climbed up into the loft and threw down some hay for him.

After I climbed down, the three of us stood in the entrance of the barn and looked out, listening to the rain tap on the metal roof.

"What's our horse count?" I asked.

"Sixteen," Sara said. "Not counting the one in the trailer."

"A whole damn herd," Jen said. "Now what?"

"There's a pond in the field behind the house," I said. "We can either put them all together in that pasture, or we can let them out. If we keep them, I guess we'll have to throw hay out for them every day until springtime, when grass starts growing again, but there will be no way to water them except with the pond."

"There must be a reason why they were all separated," Jen said.

"Yeah, I know."

"We should keep some and let the rest go," Jen said.

"How do we decide?" Sara asked. "And what happens to the ones we let go?"

"I don't give them very good odds," I said.

Sara took on a pained expression.

"I know," Jen said, "but it's better to keep a few, and have plenty of food and water for them, than to keep all of them and let them starve."

"Personally, I'd prefer to get rid of all of them," I said. "We have enough to worry about without have to take care of a bunch of horses. If we're going to have animals at all, we should have animals that will provide us with food."

They didn't seem too happy with my input.

"It's not something we have to worry about today," I said. "I wouldn't mind staying here for a while. If you two want to stay here, let's go back to Blaine's and get our stuff, then we'll get that firewood and come back. By the time we do that, it'll be about time to call it a day anyway."

CHAPTER 30

It was late afternoon by the time we returned to the Lassiter house with our supplies and firewood. We didn't have anything to put the chickens into, so we fed them and left them where they were, with the intention of coming back for them later.

As I pulled into the driveway, I realized it was the only entrance and exit for the property. We'd have to fix that. I wouldn't want to get cornered.

Sara volunteered to start on dinner while Jen and I unloaded the vehicles.

"When we've unloaded, I want to get rid of that horse trailer," I said.

"Do you think we'll need it?" Jen said. "We could always drag the horse out of here."

"No," I said. "There are horse trailers around at other houses if we ever really need one. I'd rather not mess with removing the horse."

Once we got everything into the house, I stepped into the kitchen.

"Jen and I are going to take care of that horse trailer," I said. "Will you be okay here by yourself until we get back?"

"I'll lock the doors," she said. "And I have a gun. I'm not too sure about the temperature outside. I don't know if this food is still good."

She held out a package of hamburger meat. It was cool, but not cold.

"Let's not risk it," I said. "Is there anything else?"

"We have plenty of canned goods," she said.

"How much of the cold stuff will we lose?"

"We ate most of it," she said. "There's this meat, and there's a bag of stir-fry vegetables. They're kind of mushy. We have some cheese and mayonnaise left."

"I'll feed the vegetables to the goat," I said. "Let's pitch the rest."

* * *

I drove the truck and trailer, which was a new experience for me. Jen followed me in the Escalade. It was already dark by that time, and it was much too dark to drive without the headlights. I just hoped we could do what we needed to do without being noticed.

I wanted to get the trailer far enough away from us that when the horse decomposed, we wouldn't smell it. I drove two miles away. I didn't know if it was far enough, but there was a church there with a wide lot, and I didn't think I'd find an easier place to park.

I didn't want to leave the truck, because it was practically new and had a full tank of gas, but I also didn't want to be out there in the dark trying to figure out how to unhitch a trailer.

I parked and got into the Escalade with Jen.

"You know," she said as we headed back to the house, "this might be the first time in a while that I will actually be able to relax a little. It's going to be nice to finally feel safe and be in a comfortable house."

"Yeah," I said. "I think this new place will be secure."

In the distance, I saw light. I couldn't tell what it was exactly. It was far away, and it just looked like a glow moving over the trees.

"What is that?" I asked. "Is that another car?"

"I don't know," Jen said.

"Quick, turn your lights off and pull off the road."

"But there isn't a place to pull off," she said.

"It doesn't matter," I said. "Just pull over on the shoulder."

"There is no shoulder!"

"Just stop the car and turn off the engine!"

She stopped and turned everything off. The light grew and moved. Then bright headlights came over the hill.

"Get down," I said.

We both hunkered down below the dashboard. The lights got brighter as they got nearer.

"I left a note for Brian back at Blaine's house," she whispered. "I didn't want him to look for us and not find us. Maybe it's him."

"We don't know who it is," I said. "And we don't know if they're friendly."

The light filled the interior of the Escalade. The vehicle slowed to a crawl as it came by, but it didn't stop. There were abandoned vehicles on the roads everywhere, and ours looked like just one more.

I sat up and looked out the back window once they had moved on. I watched the taillights disappear around a curve, then continued to watch the reflection of the headlights on the trees until they were gone.

"I don't like feeling scared," Jen said, sitting up. "I should be used to it by now, but I'm not."

"No," I said. "You shouldn't be used to it. No one should."

* * *

Dinner was Vienna sausages and canned tomato soup. I was hungry enough that I didn't mind it, but eating like this every day would get old quickly.

"I don't know why anyone would be out at night unless it was Brian or the Somervilles looking for us," Jen said.

"We were out after dark," I said, "but I see what you mean."

"Maybe you should have stopped them," Sara said. "They were probably okay."

"Probably," I said. "But I was being careful. Stopping cars on a dark country road just isn't something you do. I didn't want to lead them back to us here either. Like Jen said in the car, I feel safe here."

After dinner, I tried to start a fire in the fireplace. The smoke came back into the living room. I adjusted the flue, but the smoke continued to fill the room. We were all coughing and had to open the windows.

"I don't understand what I'm doing wrong," I said.

"My grandpa had a fireplace," Sara said. "He never used it, so he sealed the chimney to keep the birds and squirrels out of it."

"Sealed it permanently?"

"I don't know," she said.

"We're going to need a fire," Jen said. "We don't have any kerosene for the heater."

"What am I supposed to do about it?" I said.

"Someone needs to check the chimney," Jen said.

They stared at me expectantly.

"Oh," I said. "So you don't want to be coddled unless it's cold, dark and raining and you need someone to crawl up on the roof."

"You are the man," Jen said. "It's kind of your job, I think."

"Funny how these gender roles conveniently pop up," I said. "Okay. Let's find a ladder."

There was an aluminum extension ladder hanging on hooks on the side of one of the barns. I carried it back to the house while Jen walked with me under an umbrella, showing the way with a flashlight. I propped the ladder on the side of the house, took Jen's flashlight and climbed up while she held the ladder for me.

There was a piece of plywood over the opening of the chimney with a concrete block on top of it to keep it from blowing off. I pulled it off, and the smoke hit me in the face. My eyes burned, and I coughed a little. I left the plywood and block on the roof and climbed back down.

"Problem solved," I said.

"My hero," Jen said.

"Whatever."

* * *

The rain continued through the next day.

Over breakfast, we discussed what to do with the horses. Jen and Sara decided to keep six—one for each of us, and three backups. We had no knowledge about horses, so we didn't know which six would be best. Sara thought we should keep the most docile. She had an idea of calling them and keeping the first six that came to us, which made sense in a childlike way. Jen thought we should keep the healthiest. Once again, I made my point that we should rid ourselves of all of them, but I was outnumbered.

We spent our time that day doing much the same things that we'd done at Blaine's, but we did it in a real house, which made a huge difference in our moods. Plus, we had plenty of room to get away from each other when we wanted.

We also went through the house trying on clothes, looking through closets and drawers, and being generally nosy.

I found a single-shot .410 shotgun and a box of shells in a bedroom closet. In the drawer of one of the nightstands in the master bedroom, I found a loaded .22 revolver and some racy photographs of Mrs. Lassiter holding the same gun and wearing only a cowboy hat.

The Lassiters' reading selection was limited to the Bible, Zane Grey, Louis L'Amour, and Good Housekeeping magazines, but we'd brought Blaine and Betsy's book leavings with us, so we had some variety.

Around four that afternoon, the rain finally stopped.

"The sun is coming out. It looks like we can do our supply run tomorrow," I said, standing at the front window and looking out.

"Good," Jen said, coming up next to me.

"Are you sure you want to stock up and hole up?" I asked. "Haven't you been bored at all?"

"A little," she said, "but I'm a homebody. I've never liked going out much."

"I don't know if I'll be able to just hang out here all the time," I said.

"I won't make you do anything you don't want to do," she said. "But if we could ever get any real time alone, I think I could help alleviate your boredom."

* * *

We drove the pickup because we didn't want to alarm Charlie by arriving in a different vehicle. We pulled up in his driveway a little after 9:00 a.m. The old Cutlass was gone. The gas cans were gone too. I knocked on the storm door, but he didn't answer.

I opened the door, and a piece of paper that had been wedged between the door and the frame fell to the carport. It was a note from Charlie.

I have to know if Katie is okay. My brother has a little boat. I'm going to get it and cross the river. I probably won't be back. Take what you need from the house. Be careful. Charlie

When I got back to the truck, I handed the note to Jen. She read it and passed it over to Sara.

"We'll come back and get whatever is left of his kerosene and food," I said.

"He'll never make it," Jen said. "She's probably gone now anyway."

"I know," I said, "but I can't blame him. He's just been sitting in that house all this time. He had to be losing it in there."

"At least he was alive," Jen said, sounding kind of defensive.

"That's no life."

"What do you want to do, then?"

We weren't talking about Charlie anymore.

"I don't know," I said. "Right now, I want to go collect supplies."

"Only because I want to do that," she said. "What do you want?"

"Why doesn't anyone ever ask what I want?" Sara said. "Why do you treat me like I'm not here?"

It was shaping up to be an awesome day.

"Well?" Jen said. "Tell us."

"I think Charlie was right to find his daughter. I think we should find more survivors too."

"You could go live with Mr. Somerville," Jen said. "That's what he wants to do."

"You keep saying that," Sara said. "You don't like having me around. You think I'm a naive kid because I don't talk much, but I know why you want me to leave."

"I don't see any reason why you shouldn't be happy," Jen said. "If you want to look for others, then you should."

"You want me to leave because you feel threatened by me," Sara said. "I know what's going on."

"Bullshit! I ..."

"Stop!" I said. "We have a lot of stuff to do today, and it's going to be dangerous, and we have one less person helping us. Let's focus, okay?"

"No," Jen said. "If the two of you don't want to do this, then go do what you like. I can do this by myself."

"Jen, you can't do this by yourself," I said. "That's the point. None of us can do this alone."

They were both quiet.

"Jen," I said, "I agree that it is wise to go out and collect supplies. There's no need for us to have to go out every day, looking for food or fuel. It's too dangerous.

"But I also agree with Sara. We should be trying to find others. If you don't want to go out, then you don't have to. I won't go every day, but I will be going. I need more of a purpose than just existing."

"It wouldn't be just existing," Jen replied softly. "I plan on having a real life for once."

"I plan on that too," I said, taking her hand and giving it a gentle squeeze. "Now let's focus on what we have to do today."

CHAPTER 31

We approached Clayfield from the south. Our destination was the big chain stores and strip malls. The closer we got to the south side of town, the more obstructed our path became. There was a long line of abandoned vehicles in both directions leading to the front entrance of Wal-Mart. Across the street from Wal-Mart was a Lowe's and a little rental place. Both of their entrances were blocked.

We turned around and entered the Lowe's parking lot through the back and accessed the rental store that way. Our first goal was to get a moving truck.

There were infected everywhere. Some were still in their cars, unable to figure out how to open their doors. They'd been trapped in there for more than a week without food and water, yet they were still alive.

I parked in front of the rental store. There were two big box trucks parked out front. All of the infected in the street and in the Lowe's parking lot started making their way toward us. They were slow but deliberate.

I got out.

"Honk if they get close," I said. "Be sure to give me enough time to get back."

Jen scooted over to the driver's seat.

"Be careful," she said.

I ran inside the store. I had no idea where they kept the keys, but I figured they would be behind the counter or in the office. I didn't see them out in the open, and I was opening drawers in the office desk when the horn honked. I ran back outside, and got in next to Sara.

"I didn't find them," I said. "Let's draw them away from the building, and we'll come back and try again."

Jen pulled away slowly, and the people followed.

"The keys might be in the register," she said.

"If they are, then we won't be able to get them without electricity," I said.

She pulled around the other side of the building, back toward Lowe's. She neared the corner of the store, through a cluster of cars, and stopped.

On the outside edge of the group of cars was a black Porsche 911.

"As far as I know, there's only one person in Clayfield who has one of those," she said.

There were too many infected around for us to get out of the truck, so Jen drove slowly around to the rear of Lowe's. The crowd followed us. When she got near the loading bays, she sped up, leaving them behind.

"I don't know why he would be here," she said. "He should have gone to Blaine's house like he said he would."

"Maybe he's looking for supplies, like we are," I said.

"In a Porsche?"

"You told him to drive it," I said.

When we came back around the building, we saw three men hurrying away from the entrance farthest from us. One of them was almost to the Porsche. The other two were headed to a blue pickup truck. We presumed they were infected like the rest, but then they all turned to look at us, and they were wearing masks. One of them pulled a pistol from a holster at his side. Another waved at us with both arms as if to attract our attention.

Jen crept forward.

"What do you think?" she said. "That one looked like he was going to get into Brian's car."

"They're armed," I said.

"So are we."

"They could be nice," Sara said. "We should at least go talk to them."

"Stop the truck," I said. "I'll walk up there and say hello. If there's any trouble, I'll pull my mask down to signal you. Don't question, just do your best with the rifle, then get the hell away from here. Don't lead them back to the stables."

"Why don't I just pull up there and ..."

"No," I said. "Stop the truck. If something happens, in a couple of days, try to find Mr. Somerville. Okay?"

Jen nodded.

I stuffed one of the revolvers down the front of my pants and got out. I was more scared right then than I had been since it all started. At least I knew the intentions of the infected. These were healthy men, and I had no idea what sort of men they were.

My legs felt wobbly as I approached them. The one who'd waved came out to meet me. He was a big guy in new clothes. There was even a tag still on the sleeve of his brown Carhartt coat. He was wearing a black cowboy hat, and he had a machete hanging from his belt. I didn't see a gun, but I figured he had one stashed away somewhere.

"G'mornin'," he said.

"Good morning," I said.

"It's good to see there's more people out and about." He looked past me to the truck. "How many of you?"

"Three here," I said. "More around."

"More around," he repeated, staring at the truck.

"How about you?" I asked. "How many?"

"Oh, just the three of us," he said.

Another man came out of the store, pushing a cart full of stuff. He stopped when he saw me.

The man in the Carhartt coat turned to see him, then laughed.

"Looks like you caught me," he said. "Sorry. I didn't think it would be smart to tell you about everything."

"Yeah," I said. "I understand that."

I noticed that the man by the Porsche began to slowly move off to my left.

"You lucked out," Carhartt man said, laughter in his voice. "You got you a truckload of pretty girls."

"What's your name?" I asked, feeling uncomfortable and trying to change the subject.

"You can call me Hank."

The other man continued to move around to my left in a wide circle.

"Where's he going, Hank?"

Hank looked over his shoulder.

"Oh, he's just walkin' around," he said casually.

"He's making me nervous," I said.

Hank turned and motioned for the man to stop. He obeyed.

"We probably shouldn't stand around here very long," Hank said, pointing toward the road. Infected people were approaching.

"Where are y'all stayin'?" Hank asked.

"I don't want to tell you that right now," I said. "You understand."

"Yeah," he said. "Y'all have plenty of guns? It's real dangerous out."

My gut was churning. My bad feeling was getting worse.

"That's a nice car you got there," I said, nodding at the Porsche. "Where'd you find that?"

"Around," he said. "If you like it, I'd be willin' to trade it."

"I don't have anything for trade," I said.

"Oh, I think you do," he said. "You got all kinds of good stuff over there."

"No," I said, backing up. "Not interested."

"You don't need two of them," he said. "Tell you what, let's go ask them what they'd like to do."

"No," I said. "We're leaving now."

He opened his coat. I didn't know if he was going for his gun, and I didn't want to wait and see. I turned and ran back toward the truck, pulling my mask down.

Jen was on the ball. My mask hadn't even cleared my chin when I heard the gunshot. I looked up, and she was hanging out of the driver's-side window, shooting Mr. Somerville's shotgun left-handed. I didn't expect her to hit anything, but when I looked over my shoulder, I saw Hank stumbling around, clutching his face with both hands, his cowboy hat at his feet. The other men were pulling weapons and running for cover.

Sara opened the passenger door, stepped out with the .22 rifle and fired. I tried to pull the revolver, but it got hung up on my pants. I got around the door of the truck, and a bullet came through the windshield just above the wiper on the passenger side, spider-webbing the glass. I climbed in anyway and grabbed Sara, pulling her back into the truck.

"Drive, Jen!"

The truck lurched backward, the passenger door still open. The men advanced, shooting. I could hear the bullets hitting the truck, but I didn't know what kind of damage they were doing. Hank was still holding his bleeding face with one hand and firing a pistol with his other.

The infected came around both sides of the building and from the road. Some of them dragged their feet, but others surged forward in a limping jog, and others came at a full sprint. They were in different states of dress and undress. I saw five wearing red Lowe’s vests.

I leaned over Sara and pulled the door closed. A few were interested in us, pounding on our windows, but most of them were headed toward the four men in the open.

The men’s fear was evident, even from a distance. They turned their guns on the infected and backed toward their vehicles. Soon, their weapons were empty. They tried to run and reload, but there was no time.

Hank pulled out his machete. He hacked and chopped, but there were too many of them, and he was dragged down.

The man with the shopping cart tried to make it back inside the store, but they caught him and went to work on him like piranha.

"Dear God," Jen said. "What are they?"

"Please go," Sara pleaded as sneering, slobbering faces pressed against her window. "Please."

Jen looked over her shoulder and gunned it in reverse. Before we got around the corner, I watched one of the men break free and make it to the Porsche.

Jen continued backing up until she was well clear of the fray. Then she turned, put the car in drive, and pulled out onto the road behind Lowe's. I was shaking, and I couldn't make myself stop. Sara was crying.

"What happened?" Jen said.

"I asked him about Brian's car, and ..."

"Is Brian okay? Where is he?"

"I don't know. He told me he found the car. He offered to trade it for one of you."

"For one of us?" Sara said.

"That's why you pulled down your mask?" Jen said. "Hell, that ain't no reason to shoot somebody."

"No," I said. "I pulled down my mask because I thought he was going for a gun."

"He was," she said. "I saw that. I was going to shoot him whether you signaled me or not. I was just wondering what you did to make him go for his gun."

"Damn it, I can't quit shaking," I said.

"This is going to happen again," she said, pulling out onto the bypass that circled around the town. "This ain't a civilized world no more. People are realizing that they can do whatever they want and get away with it. There ain't no law or prisons to scare them into being good. For the rest, there ain't God no more neither. When there ain't no law and there ain't no God, then ... well, it's going to be like caveman days."

"You say that like you're okay with it," I said.

"I'm just facing reality—taking the bad with the good. We ain't got no government breathing down our necks; that's a good thing. Sara and me were lucky to come across you and Mr. Somerville like we did. There's more good folks out there like Brian and Charlie. There are also assholes out there with no moral compass. I ain't saying that I can't take care of myself. I can, and I have. But if I was to get backed into a corner ... surrounded ... outnumbered ... there'd be nothing I could do about it."

"I still believe in God," Sara said softly.

"Sara, hon, maybe you could talk to him about a few things. I think he dropped the ball on this one."

"Don't be so condescending," Sara said. "It'll all work out for the good. I believe that."

Jen laughed a little.

"Yeah," she said. "I can see that. It's worked out for my good so far."

Jen headed north on the bypass, the wind whistling through the bullet hole in the windshield. She knew of another place that rented moving vans on the other side of town. We crossed the railroad tracks, and I noticed smoke coming from under the hood.

"We're overheating," Jen said, looking down at the gauges. "They must've hit our radiator. I ain't stopping. We'll just run her until we crack the engine block."

It didn't take long. The engine started making a horrible sound and stalled. We coasted to a stop in front of Grub, one of Clayfield's better restaurants.

"That's that," Jen said. "Let's find another car before the zombies find us."

We all checked our guns and made sure they were fully loaded. Then we grabbed our small bag of supplies—extra ammo, a little food and water, and the bottle of Southern Comfort.

There were plenty of cars around; it was just a matter of finding one with keys that would start. Most of the vehicles that were abandoned with the keys inside were left running, so their batteries were dead, and they were out of gas. I went into the little restaurant to see if I could find a purse with car keys.

Both the dining area and the kitchen were trashed. The air inside stank. Old food and broken dishes littered the floor. I saw a couple of piles of human excrement and a raw, meaty bone with a partial human hand attached. Something really bad had happened here, just like everywhere else, but thankfully, it was gone now. I found Grub unoccupied.

There was a purse at one of the tables, and I found two more in the back. I took them outside so I could look through them in the fresh air. When I came out, Jen was standing sentry with the shotgun while Sara looked in the windows of cars and tried to start the ones with keys.

I turned the purses up and emptied their contents on the hood of the nearest car. Sara came up, and I handed her a set of keys.

"Try to find the car these go to," I said. "It'll be parked here in the lot."

She picked up one of the wallets and started to open it.

"Don't," I said.

"I'm not going to steal her money," she said. "I just thought I'd see who she was."

"I know," I said. "Don't. It's easier if you don't know them."

She did it anyway, then proceeded to open the other wallets too.

"Take them with you," I said. "We don't have time for this."

"Sorry," she said. She put them into a single purse and walked away.

"We need to move!" Jen said. "I see some coming down the road!"

I took the other two sets of keys and started trying them on cars.

"Got it!" Sara said, standing next to a green two-door Dodge Neon.

She slid in and shut the door.

I got to the car next and climbed into the back seat, leaving the door open for Jen. Jen ran over and got in the passenger side. Sara started the car, and the stereo started up too, with Flo Rida's Right Round. Sara ejected the CD, but Jen pushed it back in.

"I haven't heard any music in more than a week," Jen said. "I don't care what it is; we're listening to it. Hell, I'd listen to John Tesh right now."

"I like John Tesh," Sara said.

"Of course you do," Jen said. "Now drive."

She cranked up the volume, and I must admit that it brought a smile to my face and helped me forget for a little while. I still had the shakes, but they were subsiding. It was nice to see Jen enjoying herself. I was amazed at her resilience and detachment. I'd been trying to separate myself from all the excitement too, but I still felt shell-shocked. I feared it would eventually catch up to all of us. I just hoped it wouldn't break us.

Sara seemed to be having a good time too. It brought back memories of cruising with my friends in high school.

Then I heard something else. I thought it was part of the music at first.

"Turn it off for a second," I said.

Jen did.

"What?"

"Do you hear that?"

Jen rolled down her window and listened.

"It's the tornado siren," she said, laughing. "I guess old Saint Nick finally turned it on."

* * *

When we got close enough to see the rental store, Jen turned the stereo off.

"Pull in close," she said. "I'll run in and get the keys. I'll bet since the siren is on, we won't have any trouble now. I didn't think it was a good idea before—I still don't—but right now, I don't think we could have had better luck."

"I wonder what Mr. Somerville is doing," I said.

"He's probably giving himself some space so he can go door to door, checking for survivors."

"He'll need our help," Sara said.

"He's not getting my help today," Jen said. "I'm sticking to the plan. We can check on him when we're done. He knew where we were, and he could have run his plan by us before he did something foolish by himself."

CHAPTER 32

Sara pulled up to the front door. There were four trucks and a trailer parked off to the side of the building. They all had the words MOVING? RENT ME! emblazoned on their sides and backs. Two of the trucks were smaller, one was very large, and one was somewhere in between. I didn't really want to drive the big one. It was hard enough to maneuver around some of the cars on the roads as it was. Jen ran inside, and I got out too.

I stood by the car for a while, and then I decided to go in.

"Jen, you okay?"

"I'm in the office!" she called.

I walked around the showroom, looking at other goods. There were big-screen TVs, furniture and appliances. In another section of the store were tools like log-splitters, welders and augers.

I didn't see anything we could use.

I stepped behind the counter. Under the register was a row of hooks. The keys were there.

"Found them!" I said.

Jen came out of the back.

The hooks were labeled: 24', 17' and 10'.

The 10' hook had two sets of keys on it.

"These are the truck sizes," I said. "I think we should use one of the ten-footers."

"We can't get much stuff in there," Jen said.

"We're not hauling furniture," I said. "We're talking about food and clothes. I think it will be plenty big for that but small enough to get through tight places."

"I really wanted to get as much as we could," she said, hesitant. "What about the seventeen-footer?"

"How about both of the ten-footers?" I offered.

"I like that better," she said. "I like having a backup."

"I don't see a need to keep the car," I said. "Is Sara with you or me?"

I knew she wouldn't like either option.

"Sara can ride with me," she said. "It'll give us time to talk."

"I'm not sure if that's a good thing or a bad thing," I said.

"I'll be nice," Jen said. "I promise."

"Good," I said.

Jen rolled her eyes. "You heard what she said to me at Charlie's. I'm not threatened by her."

"There's no need for you to be, but ..."

"So you're going to take her side again?"

"No, Jen, there are no sides here. We're all in this together, remember? Why are we having this conversation again? Sara has done nothing to you. She's a good kid who has the terrible misfortune of being physically attractive. That's not something she can help, so why don't you give her a break?"

"Why don't you give me a break?" Jen scoffed.

"Would you be putting her through the same kind of hell if she weren't so good looking?"

"Would you be defending her if she weren't?"

"I have been avoiding talking to her and looking at her just so you wouldn't feel uncomfortable. Can you imagine how she must feel to be ignored like that? She's alone, just like we are. She's got nobody. She doesn't even have us, really. I feel bad about that."

"So it's my fault that she's not fitting in?"

"Jen," I said, frustrated, "I ... I don't know what to do here. I suppose I should feel flattered that you'd be so jealous, but ..."

"Oh yeah," she said sarcastically, "it's all about you."

I don't know why, but the conversation suddenly hit me as incredibly humorous. It was like I'd traveled back in time and I was arguing with my ex-wife again ... and every other woman with whom I'd ever had a relationship. Even during the apocalypse, I was attracting the same kind of woman. So far as I knew, all women were the same kind. There was absolutely no way I could win in these arguments.

I laughed.

I would never have done that in the past. In the past, I would have acquiesced and apologized just so I wouldn't have to talk anymore.

But I was a different man since the world had ended.

"Don't laugh at me!" Jen said. "What's so funny?"

"I should have traded you for that Porsche."

She stared at me over her mask.

I'd thrown her for a loop, and I was pleased.

"So this is a big joke? Why didn't you? Huh? Why didn't you trade me?"

I shrugged and said the first thing that popped into my head.

"I don't know how to drive a stick." I said it as dryly as I could, but I couldn't hold back the grin.

I could see her eyes soften a little. I started laughing again.

She stepped up to me and cupped my crotch. I gasped and froze. I expected her to squeeze and hurt me, but she didn't. Something like a jolt of electricity shot up my spine. She came in close, her eyes narrowing.

"I can drive a stick, funny man," she whispered. "I can drive it real good."

I couldn't breathe. I couldn't move. Every muscle in my body was tense.

She removed her hand.

"Sara is riding with me," she said, grabbing a set of keys and acting as if nothing had happened. "We'll work things out. It's none of your business."

She went to the door.

"You coming or what?" she said and walked out into the sunlight. She looked around, then headed toward the trucks.

I was still standing in the same spot, watching her through the large windows in the front of the store. I realized I'd been holding my breath. I exhaled.

Holy moly.

The trucks had CB radios, so we were able to communicate with each other. None of us had used one before, and it took a few minutes to get all of the particulars worked out, like setting the channels and not holding down the mike button when we were trying to listen. After playing with them for a couple of minutes, we realized why people in the movies said, "over" when they were done talking on them.

Once we figured out the radios, we hit the road. We knew that since the siren was going off, there would be no way to get through town, so we got back on the bypass.

"Where to first?" I asked.

I waited but Jen didn't reply. I realized I was still holding the button.

I said, "Over," then released the button.

The radio hissed static, and then Jen came on.

"That was quite a broadcast you made there, Bandit," she said. "Let's go to Wal-Mart. If we can't get everything there, then we'll go other places."

Static as she released her mike button. Then, "Over."

I led the way, backtracking past Grub to the bypass. I looked in the side mirror. The women had their masks down, and they were talking.

I was uneasy with this jealous side of Jen. Part of me was saying I should get out of this while it was still early. If I waited until after this thing was consummated, it would be a lot more difficult for both of us.

And she was more than just jealous; she was also a tad unstable and unpredictable. All three traits could be dangerous.

The other part of me—the part that usually did my thinking for me when it came to women—kind of liked that about her. Besides, did I really have the luxury of being picky? There wasn't exactly an abundance of fish in the sea these days.

I got to thinking about how things would be if Sara were replaced by a good-looking young man. Would Jen be acting the same way over me? Would I feel threatened in that situation? We were together out of necessity. But were we staying together for the same reason, or for something more? Had Sara's presence caused Jen to accelerate our relationship out of fear, and was I accepting that because I feared she'd leave and I'd be alone?

My ex-wife always accused me of overthinking things. Of all the times to be overthinking a thing like this.

It occurred to me that maybe I should accept Jen's assessment of the world and just be a damn caveman.

* * *

We had to access the Wal-Mart parking lot the same way we had to access Lowe's lot: through the back. We pulled past the entrance to the automotive section, around the front of the building, by the garden center. The main parking lot was crazy. Cars were everywhere. It looked kind of like it did the day after Thanksgiving, except there was no order to the parking. I was beginning to doubt we'd find anything left in there. Then again, all those people never made it outside with their purchases.

I couldn't get the van to the front door.

"Jen, we'll go in through the garden center here. The gate is shut, but maybe I can push it open with the van ... Over."

The garden center was enclosed in a tall chain-link fence. I pulled around and backed into it. Rather than the gate opening, the fence began to buckle.

"Stop," Jen said. "You're making it worse. Let's just go in through automotive. Surely we can open one of those garage doors."

Static.

"Over."

They waited in their truck while I tried the doors on the garage. The siren was still howling to the north, and there were infected headed toward it. I could see them here and there, weaving their way among the cars in the streets.

I got both doors up. In one of the bays, a car was up on the lift.

I directed Jen as she backed the truck up to the opening. Then she directed me while I backed up my truck to the second opening.

When I came around, the two of them were smiling.

"What?" I asked.

"Sara was just saying that it feels kind of like Christmas, and the store is like one big present."

The power was out in the store, but it was illuminated by the skylights. Sporting goods were to our right; automotive products were to our left.

"Should we stick to the list, or can we get extra stuff?" Sara asked.

"I think we should try to stick to the list," I said. "I want to be sure we get the necessities first."

"What if we see a necessity that isn't on the list?" Sara said.

"I don't know," I said. "Those lists I printed were pretty exhaustive."

"It doesn't matter," Jen said. "We're not separating anyway. We can discuss it if it comes up. Now let's get some carts and start shopping."

"Where do you want to start?"

"Food first," Jen said. "Then we'll work our way back."

Charlie had been right; the store was a mess. There were no guns left in the case in sporting goods, and the ammunition was nearly cleaned out. I looked down at the list to make sure I'd put .38-caliber bullets on there. I had—toward the bottom.

We made our way to the front of the store to get carts just like we would have on a normal shopping day, only this wasn't a normal shopping day, and there were no carts up front. The carts were scattered throughout the store and in the parking lot full of stuff. We couldn't find an empty cart anywhere.

We were between the checkouts and the greeting-card section when I stopped to look at one of the carts. I was curious to see what people were buying just before the end of the world.

That particular cart had five cases of Diet Coke, several cans of condensed soup, a new computer and a large bag of rice. The next cart held bottled water, three bags of cat food and lots of Spam and powdered donuts.

"We can probably find everything we need by picking through other people's carts," I said.

"We'll probably have to," Jen said. "Look at the grocery section."

The shelves were almost bare. We emptied those two carts of everything except for the water, donuts, rice and soup, then proceeded to the bakery. The front doors on the food side of the store were obliterated. Someone had rammed a truck through them, and it was still there, halfway in, the tires flat.

I found a bag of rolls on the floor. They'd been stepped on. I put the bag in the cart. Jen raised her eyebrows.

"For the chickens," I said.

Other than that, there was no bread. There was still the actual bread aisle to check, but I didn't expect much.

The produce section had been cleaned out too. There was a lonely bunch of beets and some black bananas left. I was going to miss bananas ... and oranges ... and avocados. There was so much produce that I loved to eat that didn't grow here.

"Look," Jen said, putting the beets in the cart, "your favorite."

I remembered the canned beets from our first day together and smiled. I spied a couple of small sweet potatoes on the floor next to one of the center produce displays. I picked them up and brought them to the cart.

"These aren't for eating," I said. "I'll use them to start plants for the garden."

"We have a garden?" Sara said.

"We will," I said. "We'll have to. I should have put seeds on our list."

"Won't we be able to collect enough food to live on for a while?" Sara asked.

"Maybe, but when that runs out, then what? Even if we don't need it right away, we should at least plant a garden so we can have seed for when we do."

"We'll check back in the garden center," Jen said.

"It's too early in the year," I said. "I doubt they'll have seeds out. We'll probably have to find them in houses. We can go back to my house. I have a few partial packets left from last year, but not enough to feed all of us."

We opened the freezer cases. They weren't full, but there was considerably more in them than on the other shelves. Nothing was frozen anymore, but it was still cold.

"We can get some of this stuff," I said, "so long as we eat it today or tomorrow."

"If we get another cold snap, it might last us longer," Jen said, pulling out a pizza. "I've been jonesing for pizza."

We got a pizza for each of us, a dessert for each of us, and tub of whipped topping for each of us. We knew this would be the last time we'd have anything like that for a while. I collected a few bags of vegetables for the goat. I noticed Jen standing in front of the juice concentrate.

"Have you ever made wine?" she asked.

"No."

"I had an ex who used to make it out of this juice," she said. "It tasted awful, but it did the job. We're going to need to have alcohol on hand at all times, and there are a few left in here."

"Do you remember how to do it?"

"I think so," she said. "It was just juice, sugar and yeast ... I think. One of those containers can make a whole gallon of wine."

"Get the supplies, and we can give it a try."

Next was the aisle with bread, coffee, tea and peanut butter. There was nothing left except some trampled coffee beans on the floor.

The canned-goods aisles were empty too. We went to every aisle and found nothing except broken bottles and spills.

"We'll have to do our grocery shopping out of the other carts or empty houses," I said. "Let's get the other stuff we need. I'm starting to get nervous about how long we've been in here."

"We're just getting started, hon," Jen said. "No need to be nervous. Mr. Somerville is throwing a party downtown, and we have the place to ourselves."

We spent the next half-hour or so collecting things from the store. Jen seemed comfortable and wanted to take her time, but I felt rushed. We got some batteries of different sizes, including two car batteries. We all got some clothes and boots in our sizes, but we didn't try them on or worry about fashion.

The pharmacy had been raided, but there were still some things left. We found a couple of bottles of amoxicillin, but that was all that remained in the way of antibiotics. I picked up a few bottles of pills at random, but I didn't know what the medications were, and I didn't have time to go through them all. I considered taking all of it anyway, but without proper identification, it would be useless to us.

We took what was left of the vitamins, protein bars, over-the-counter medications, and first-aid supplies—which wasn't much. Then there were things like eye drops, feminine-hygiene products, toothpaste, toothbrushes—things we took for granted that just wouldn't be made anymore.

Jen started tossing boxes of condoms into the cart. I could tell by the look on Sara's face that she was uncomfortable.

"Sara," I said, "would you mind looking on the next aisle to see if there is any soap left?"

She nodded and walked around to the other side.

Jen continued to pull condom boxes off the racks.

"Jen, don't you think that's enough?"

"I'm getting them all," she said. "I know they aren't on the list, but this is one of those unlisted necessities, don't you think?"

"You could be a little more discreet about it," I said.

"Does this offend you or something?"

"No, but Sara looked kind of embarrassed."

"She'll be okay."

I pushed the cart around and found Sara smelling a bottle of shower gel. She wouldn't look at me. She put some soap and shampoo into the cart and moved to the next aisle.

We filled three carts and parked them in automotive. We found four more carts that contained supplies we were looking for anyway, and we just pushed them back without going through them.

There were no seeds. We found two bodies in the garden center, but we didn't know if they were dead or if they'd be getting up at some point. We pushed some smaller display shelves on top of them in case they woke up while we were there. We thought it might slow them down.

The boxes of ammunition that were left were .223 and .30-30. I collected the loose bullets and shells from the floor too. I found three loose .38 rounds on the floor, and I loaded them into the little revolver I'd found in the parking lot at City Hall. They'd have a lot more stopping power than the .22.

The camping and fishing supplies were all gone. We didn't do nearly as well as Jen had hoped. We didn't even get enough supplies to fill one truck.

I didn't like how long it was taking us.

"Let's load this stuff," I said. "Then we'll go over to Tractor Supply. They'll have food for the chickens and horses. Maybe they'll have seed there."

As we started loading the supplies into the truck, I noticed the sound of distant gunfire. I went outside. It was coming from the north, just like the siren. There was also smoke from that direction.

"Jen! Sara!"

They came outside. We heard the sounds of multiple guns firing.

"Do you think he's in trouble?" I asked.

"Sounds like he has help," Jen said.

"We should check on him," I said. "That smoke concerns me."

"Shit," Jen said. "We have a plan, remember? Let's at least load this stuff first."

"He needs us," Sara said.

"We're going, Jen," I said. "We'll come back."

CHAPTER 33

We drove one of the moving vans and circled around, coming in on East Broadway. The siren originated at the fire station next to City Hall. It was loud enough to be disorienting. The smoke rose in great black billows. The gunfire was steady, and it sounded like there might even be an automatic weapon going off. We couldn't actually make it close to City Hall or the court square, because the mass of infected people pressing toward the noise extended for more than two blocks in every direction.

We stopped on East Broadway, between Second Street and Fifth Street. People were coming in from every direction to join the others. They'd been making their way here for at least an hour by this time, so some of these creatures had probably walked in from outside of town. They stumbled past us, more interested in the siren and guns.

"Can you tell what's going on?" Sara asked.

"I'm going up to take a look through the scope," I said.

I took the .30-06 and got out of the truck. A man nearby saw me and came at me. I was able to get around the front of the truck and climb up on the hood before he could get to me. I then crawled onto the top of the cab, then onto the top of the box. The man stared up at me for a few seconds.

"You want me to shoot him?" Jen called out from below.

"No," I said. "He can't get me."

I got down on my belly and looked through the scope.

The smoke was coming from the street, from the infected. The ones in the middle were on fire. They were walking around, bumping into each other as they burned. In the crowd were two fire trucks. People stood on top of them with hoses, pumping arcs of water against the buildings. Two people—merely silhouettes in the smoke from this distance—were on the roof of the C&S Drugstore. One was lobbing Molotov cocktails down to the street while the other fired into the crowd. Others on the fire trucks were armed and picking off people in the crowd as well. Bodies lay in the street, and the others simply walked on them.

"What the hell?" I said.

The smell of burning flesh and hair and clothes was sickening. Behind me, a vehicle approached.

"Jen, you two get down!" I said.

Not knowing who they were, I didn't want them to see me, and I didn't think they would notice me where I was. I lay still and watched them.

It was a Ford F-350 towing a flatbed trailer. It pulled up next to an infected woman who was staggering down the road. The driver let down his window and shot her in the head with a pistol. She dropped to her knees, then to her face. The truck's doors opened, and a man and woman, both wearing masks and rubber gloves, got out. The man shot the dead woman again in the head. Then the masked couple picked the woman up by her wrists and ankles and threw her on the trailer. The trailer already had several bodies on it.

The man who had been interested in me came out at them before they made it to the truck, and they dispatched him the same way. When they got close to the moving van, they stopped. The driver looked up at me. He'd noticed me after all.

"I just got word that the batteries are getting low!" he said, holding up a cell phone. "You might want to take up a new position!"

He'd mistaken me for someone else.

I nodded to them. He waved, then backed the trailer around and headed back, taking a right onto Second Street.

I wasn't sure what he meant, but I climbed down, thinking it prudent to obey.

"What are they doing?" Jen asked as I climbed in.

"It looks like they're trying to lure them all to one place so they can kill them. They're shooting and burning them. There are a few survivors out there. Somerville must have gotten some help."

"How many survivors did you see?" Sara asked.

"Nine, counting the couple in the truck."

"This is some major dumbassery," Jen said. "This is what happens when rednecks sit around and brainstorm."

"Did you see the Somervilles?" Sara asked

"I couldn't tell," I said. "Everyone was too far away, and they were all wearing masks."

"What do you want to do?" Jen asked. "Do you want to stay and help these morons?"

"I don't really want any part of this," I said. "I suppose killing the infected is necessary, but I don't know if I can stomach it like this. I don't even know if they're doing any good."

Then the siren stopped. My ears were ringing a little in the new silence.

"What are they doing?" Sara wondered.

"That must be what he meant about the batteries," I said. "The batteries running the siren have died."

The infected looked like they'd been awakened from a trance. I could hear the ones on fire screaming. The movement in the crowd reminded me of movement in water. The fire and smoke began to drift south. The men on the fire trucks turned their hoses on the burning people now, trying to put them out before they got away from them. The ones with guns focused their attention on the burning ones too.

Flames started licking out of the windows of the drugstore. The two people on top of the building ran around on the roof, looking for a means of escape.

"They're going to burn the whole town down," Jen said. "What were they thinking?"

"They were thinking they could contain it," I said.

Arms reached up to one of the fire trucks. The men on top tried to hold them off with the force of the water, but they couldn't push them all away. The infected started climbing up.

"This is about to get bad," Jen said, "and there ain't a damn thing we can do about it. Get the hell away from here."

I couldn't leave.

"We're going to try to help those people on the roof."

I could feel Jen looking at me, but she didn't say anything.

I put the van into drive and pulled up close to the back of the building. Sara wouldn't be able to open her door, but the infected couldn't get at her either.

"Jen, I'm going to get them on the roof of the truck. When I tell you, pull us out of here."

I jumped out of the truck again. The creatures were moving around more now, and I had three come at me all at once. I pulled the .38 from my pocket and aimed at the first one. The gun clicked. I pulled the trigger again, and it clicked again. It only had three rounds, and evidently they hadn't moved into place as the cylinder rotated. I could have tried one or two more times, and it would have fired, but they were too close. I stopped trying to shoot and just climbed up on the hood, then the cab roof, then the top of the box. Below, I heard a gunshot and knew that Jen was taking care of business.

The roof of the drugstore was still a few feet higher than the top of the moving van, but I could see. The two figures were moving around in the smoke. It hadn't gotten too thick on the far side yet, so that was where they were. They were looking over the edge with their backs to me. I could tell they were trying to discuss whether they should jump and face the monsters. There was really no choice; they'd eventually have to jump.

"Over here!"

They turned in the smoke. Only my head and shoulders stuck up over the roof, but they saw me. They thought I was one of the infected at first, and the one with the rifle pointed it at me. Then they noticed my mask, lowered the gun and ran to me. When they reached the edge, they sat on the roof ledge and dropped to the top of the truck.

"Go, Jen!"

Jen backed the van into the crowd, turned, then pulled away, heading east. The three of us on the roof held on as well as we could, trying to keep our backs to the cold wind. A large group of the creatures chased us, but were soon left behind.

When she got to the intersection of East Broadway and the bypass, she stopped the truck. This was the outer edge of the east side of Clayfield, where the town abruptly turned into farmland. There was no one around except an infected old man shuffling in.

"You two okay?" I asked.

One of them nodded.

"What about the others?" said the one with the gun. "We have to go back!"

"We can't help them," I said.

Jen got out, shot the old man and stood in front of the truck, facing us with the shotgun in a defensive posture.

"Come on down," she said.

We climbed down the front of the truck.

The two pulled down their masks. They were a boy no older than 15 and a woman in her 50s.

"We have to go back," the woman said again.

"We were barely able to help you," Jen said.

"Who are you?" the woman asked. "You're not with our group."

"What the hell were y'all thinking?" Jen demanded.

"Excuse me? We were thinking we'd take our town back."

The boy stepped up.

"We were doing something about it," he said.

"Hunter, no," the woman said, grabbing the boy's arm.

"We ain't going back," Jen said. "Y'all have them all stirred up. We'll never get in there. We even have a bunch coming this way."

We all looked down East Broadway. They were coming, but they were still far enough away not to present an immediate problem.

"Then let me take the truck, and I'll go in and get them," the boy said.

"It's too dangerous," I said. "You're safer with us."

"If we go back, then we'll all get caught," Jen said.

"If you don't want to go, then don't!" Hunter yelled.

He ran around to the driver's side of the moving van and started to get in. Jen ran to catch him. She got to him and tried to pull him out. He punched her in the face. I ran to help her.

"You little shit!" Jen said, holding her jaw.

She came back at him. A gun went off, but I didn't see it happen, because my view was blocked by the door. Jen stumbled backward and landed hard on her back. The door shut, and the van shifted into drive and started to roll.

"Hunter! No!" the woman yelled.

Sara opened her door and jumped out. Hunter wheeled around us as we encircled Jen. Then he sped off down East Broadway toward the mass of infected.

"The turd shot me," Jen shouted.

There was a bullet wound in the top of her right thigh. A spot of blood spread out around it, soaking her jeans. I took off my bandana and held it on the wound.

We were in the middle of the intersection, beneath the stoplight. We were completely exposed.

The moving van plowed into the approaching crowd, then stopped when too many bodies became wedged beneath the undercarriage. They started climbing up the sides.

"Hunter!" the woman screamed.

I grabbed the woman's mouth and squeezed it.

"Shut up," I said. "We're out in the open, and Jen is wounded. If you want to make noise, do it somewhere else. Do you underfuckingstand?"

She nodded, fear in her eyes. I let her go. Blood from Jen's leg was smeared around her mouth, where my hand had been.

I felt sick—sick over Jen, sick over how vulnerable we were, and sick over how I had just acted.

"I'm sorry," I said. "Please ... I'm sorry."

The woman was crying.

"We have to find a car," the woman said. "We have a doctor in our group and medicine. Maybe he can help her."

"Good," I said. "What's your name?"

"Brenda."

"Brenda, this is Sara. You two carry Jen off the road and hide in that ditch over there. Keep pressure on her leg. I'm going to find us a vehicle."

CHAPTER 34

I didn't know where to go. The only vehicles close were on the west side of the bypass, but the crowd of infected was there, trying to get at Hunter. There would be no way I could get in there, take a car and get out again. Even if I could get in, I had no guarantee that the car would even start.

We'd driven the bypass a few times that day. There were vehicles on it, but I feared they would be dead just like most of the other abandoned cars on the road. Still, I had to try.

I headed south down the bypass, running as fast as I could. There was a white car on the shoulder, about a quarter of a mile away. All I could hear were the sounds of my boots clomping on the asphalt and my own raspy breathing.

My lungs burned, and my throat was raw from running in the cold air. My heart kept punching me in the chest. I wasn't into fitness before the virus hit. I wasn't really overweight, but I wasn't in very good shape either. Taking the stairs usually winded me, and I liked my donuts. In this new world, everyone would have to get in shape, or they would die. It would be the new fitness craze: run for your life.

All I had was the .38 in my coat pocket and one of the .22 revolvers in the front of my pants. Hopefully I wouldn't meet a crowd of them.

I started doing math in my head. I didn't know how long it should take to run a quarter of a mile, but I seemed to remember people always talking about a ten-minute mile. It would take more than two minutes for me to reach the white car at that rate. That was like an eternity when there were zombies close to the people you cared about.

I looked over my shoulder. I didn't see the women anymore. They were hiding. Good. The white car was close. Gunshots and screaming. The creatures had gotten to Hunter. Poor kid. Poor stupid, reckless kid.

I got to thinking about one of the conversations Jen, Sara and I had had during the rainy evenings around the fire, back at Blaine's. Jen had been saying how there were two kinds of people who had survived the initial outbreak—the lucky and the smart. She said that the lucky wouldn't be lucky forever. They would have to get smart, or Darwin would eventually have his way. Stupid people might have survived and procreated in the soft and civilized world before Canton B, but in this world, nature wasn't going to allow it.

I had been one of the lucky ones. I hadn't prepared. In fact, I had been oblivious to all of it. I was lucky to have met the woman in the mask. Even she had been lucky. Her brother had been the smart one. I liked to think that, since that first day, I'd been smart. Maybe I wouldn't get culled out of the gene pool.

Sara had argued that God chose who lived and died, but she had no explanation for God's particular decisions. I could tell that she had been wrestling with her faith throughout the outbreak, and Jen wasn't helping with that.

I still couldn't get over the absurdity and randomness of all of it. I'd always believed in God, but none of this fit with my beliefs. Maybe all those fire-and-brimstone preachers were right, and God was punishing us all by letting Hell loose on Earth. Most of the world got off easy; with their minds gone, they didn't even know what was happening anymore. It was the survivors who received the harshest punishment.

Or maybe it was a mixture of the two. Maybe God was purging the world of the weak, and those of us who were left were being tried to see if we were worthy.

If this was God's doing, he sure picked a fine time to do it. We didn't know how to take care of ourselves anymore. Our parents hadn't seen the need to teach us how to do something as basic as feed ourselves. I wondered how many survivors would be able to start a fire when the world ran out of lighters and matches. I wondered how many would make it through next winter or the winter after that, when canned goods would be harder to find.

I wondered if I would be tried and deemed worthy.

* * *

When I got to the car, I found the doors locked. I took that to be a good sign. If the driver had succumbed to the disease and left the vehicle, he or she wouldn't have had the presence of mind to lock it. So there was a good chance that it would have some fuel and a good battery.

I hit the window with the .22, but it didn't break. I didn't have time to beat on it, so I stepped back and shot it twice. It was weak enough after that. I hit it with the gun, and it shattered.

I brushed some of the glass out of the seat and climbed inside. No keys, so I would have to hotwire it.

I had no idea how to do that outside of what I'd seen in movies. I opened the glove compartment, hoping to find something to use to pry the casing away from the steering column. There was nothing in there but papers. I pushed the button to pop the trunk, and got out to look. It was empty but for a spare tire.

"Shit."

This was taking too long. Jen was bleeding. I didn't know what I was doing, and our luck was running out.

I took off down the road again. The intersection with Bragusberg Road was just a little farther. There were houses and vehicles on that road.

My vision was blurring.

Stop crying, damn it!

I cut across the corner, onto Bragusberg Road. A little boy came out of nowhere and chased me. He was probably around nine years old. He was muddy and only wore one shoe. He couldn't catch me, but it was still unnerving knowing he was back there. I also realized that once I stopped, I would have to deal with him. I didn't want to have to do that.

I could still hear gunshots coming from around City Hall and the court square. The siren on one of the fire engines came on too.

I had to run past three houses before I found a vehicle in the driveway—a Dodge Caravan. The doors were locked, and there were no keys, so I went straight to the house.

I didn't bother knocking. I tried the knob, but it was locked. I ran around back. It was locked too, but it was a glass door. I shot it, then kicked it in. I found myself in a dining room. I could see through to the living room, where keys hung on hooks by the door. I went straight for them.

The house was occupied by a whole family of infected. A man, a woman and three kids came screaming down the hallway from the bedrooms and scared the shit out of me. I emptied the .22 on the woman, but she kept coming. I pulled the .38. It fired this time, and I hit her in the chest. She fell back into the hall, slowing the progress of the others, giving me time to get to the keys.

I turned the lock on the deadbolt as the man entered the living room, walking over his wife. I fired, but I just winged him. I fired again and hit him in the face.

I was empty. All I could do now was run.

I burst through the front door, onto the porch and over the railing to the front lawn. The little boy was waiting for me, and the three kids from inside were on their way out.

The kid came at me. I was still holding the .38. When he got close enough, I grabbed him around the throat, careful to avoid his teeth, and hammered the weapon against his forehead as hard as I could. He went limp. The other kids came down the steps, snarling.

I pushed the button on the keypad to unlock the door, and the side door of the van slid open. It wasn't what I was after, but it would do. I dove into the van and slid the door shut before they could reach me.

My hands were shaking again, but I knew I needed to reload before I encountered any more infected. I pulled the box of .22 rounds from my pocket, but I realized I had dropped the revolver, probably inside.

"Screw it," I said, and climbed into the captain's chair. Ignoring the little monsters outside, I cranked the van and sped away to help Jen.

I pulled up next to the spot where I'd told Sara and Brenda to go hide Jen. Some of the crowd on East Broadway was heading back into town to investigate the fire-truck siren. We got Jen into the van. She was being stubborn at first, trying to walk on her own, but she quickly swallowed her pride and let us carry her.

"Where?" I asked.

"What about the others? What about Hunter?" Brenda said.

"Hunter is gone," I said. "I'm sorry. I have to get Jen to your doctor. I'll let you out if you want, but I have to go."

"No," she said softly. "Let's go."

"Where?"

"Behind Grace County High School," Brenda said. "There's a maintenance building back there with a fence around it."

I looked at her in the mirror. She reminded me of my mom. She was younger than my mother, but there was something about her ...

"How many are in your group?" I asked.

"Sixteen."

"Wow. Really?"

"There were four of us from the high school. I worked in the cafeteria there. Hunter and Jamal were students. Wanda Green taught drama. Then there was a group of six that came over from the hospital. Doctor Barr was in that group, and so was Nathan Camp. Then there's ..."

"What about Nicholas Somerville?" Jen asked.

"The name sounds familiar, but he's not with us," Brenda replied.

"If Mr. Somerville didn't set off the tornado siren, then who did?" Sara wondered.

"That was Nathan's doing," Brenda said. "He's a firefighter. We noticed a few days ago that someone had set off a police siren, and we saw how the sick came in and stayed with it."

"That was us," Jen said. "We did that. Whose brilliant idea was it to set them on fire?"

"I know it didn't seem like a smart thing to do," she said, "but we know fire keeps them from coming back, and we thought we had it under control. Nathan assured us that the batteries on the siren would last. We really didn't expect to be out there that long, but they just kept coming in."

"Fire keeps them from coming back?" I said.

"Well," she said, "burning them up ... you know. You can kill them if you shoot them in the head, but they'd have to be disposed of anyway, and burning is the best way to make sure. We've shot them in the head and they came back, and we've shot them in the head and they didn't. I guess you've got to do it just right."

I drove past the spot where Mr. Somerville had wrecked his truck. We were coming up on the hospital.

"What about Hank?" I asked. "Do you know anyone named Hank?"

"No."

"Does anyone in your group drive a Porsche?" Jen asked.

"No," she said. "We know there are others around, but we don't know who they are."

We passed the entrance to the hospital, then crossed over the four-lane highway. The next road took us to the high school.

"You'll need to go around the school," she said. "It isn't with the main building."

I drove past the football stadium, then the high school. I could see the building she was talking about. There was a small parking area in the front with enough spaces for three cars.

There was already an ambulance parked in the spot nearest the front door. On the right side of the building was a big garage door, which accessed a bay for school buses. There were five buses off to the right, a short distance away from the building. Between the buses and the building was a diesel pump like you would see at a gas station. The building, the front lot, and the pump were all surrounded by a tall chain-link fence.

There was an elderly man armed with a shotgun on the other side of the gate.

"That's Ed," Brenda said. "Let me get out so he can see me. Otherwise, he might shoot."

I stopped the van well away from Ed and his shotgun, and opened the side door. Brenda got out and went up to the gate. She said something to him. He looked at us, nodded and opened the gate. Brenda went into the building while I parked the van.

When I ran around the van to get Jen out, Ed had already closed the gate and was approaching. Another man came out of the front door. He wasn't wearing a coat.

"Let me help you," the man said. "I'm Travis Barr."

He looked like he was a little older than I, but not much. His dark hair was gray at the temples. He was clean shaven, which was something we hadn't seen much of lately. He was slim and muscular. His physique wasn't like that derived from hard physical labor, but more refined and sculpted, as though he spent a lot of time in a gym.

He helped me lift Jen out of the van.

Jen yelped in pain.

"Sorry," he said. "We'll get you fixed up. I'm a doctor."

"What kind?" Jen asked.

"The real kind." He smiled.

"Do you know how to remove bullets?" Jen said.

"I've never done it before, but I've seen it done on TV many times."

Jen's brow furrowed.

"It'll be okay," he said, still grinning. "If I can't figure it out, I'll get Ed in to take a look."

He looked over at me.

"We're going to put her on the desk in the office," he said. "Brenda and Connie are getting it ready for us."

Sara held the door for us as we went inside.

It was warm in the building, and there was electricity. We carried Jen into the office. A sheet and a pillow lay on the long desk. The computer and papers from the desk were stacked on the floor in one corner. A pudgy young Asian woman left the room as we came in. I presumed that was Connie. She soon returned with a cardboard box full of medical supplies.

"Let's get these jeans cut off her," Dr. Barr said.

Connie removed Jen's boots and got to work with a pair of scissors, cutting up the leg of her pants.

He turned to me.

"Do you know what caliber weapon it was?"

"No," I said.

"It was Hunter who did it," Brenda said. "He had that twenty-two pistol he found."

"Okay," he said. "Maybe it won't be too bad."

Connie peeled away Jen's jeans and started cleaning her skin with a damp towel. Dr. Barr removed Jen's mask and unzipped her coat. When he pulled her scarf away, I could see the wound where the woman had bitten her a few days before. It didn't look very good.

"Jen," I said, "why didn't you tell me that wasn't healing?"

"What could you do about it?"

"Is this a bite?" Dr. Barr asked.

"Yeah," Jen said. "A woman tackled me and bit me. It'll get better."

"It looks infected," he said. "Do you have any other injuries?"

"What about your ribs?" I asked.

"No big deal," Jen said. "They're just a little sore."

"Travis, she has two bullet wounds," Connie said.

CHAPTER 35

I could see it too. There were two small holes in Jen's leg—one at the top of the thigh and another in the side. Both oozed blood.

"Were you shot twice?" Dr. Barr asked.

"I don't think so," Jen said, wincing when he touched the wound with his latex-gloved hand.

"I only heard one shot," I said.

"I need everyone except Connie to get out. I need room to work in here."

Brenda, Sara and I left the office, and Dr. Barr shut the door behind us.

Immediately to our right was the entrance to the bus garage. I glanced inside. There were rows of cots in there.

The room we were in was a sort of break room. There were two round tables with chairs, a countertop holding a microwave and coffee pot, and a small refrigerator in the corner. On the wall was a large map of Grace County with bus routes marked off in different colors. There was also a bulletin board with announcements for events and training that weren't ever going to happen.

"May we have some coffee?" I asked Brenda.

"Of course," she said.

Sara and I poured some coffee and sat at one of the tables.

"How do you have electricity?" I asked.

"We have generators in a little building out back. We don't run them all the time."

"They sure are quiet," Sara said.

"I'm really worried about the others," Brenda said. "Would you go back out with me?"

I didn't want to, but I nodded anyway.

"Yeah," I said. "But we're not doing anything too risky, and I'm doing the driving."

Brenda went to the office door to tell them our plans. I looked at Sara.

"Will you be okay here?"

"Yeah," she said. "The guns are in the van."

Brenda and I returned to the van, and Ed opened the gate. As soon as I put it in reverse, I could see the big Ford F-350 coming up the drive. The trailer full of bodies wasn't attached anymore.

"Some of yours?" I said.

Brenda looked in her mirror, then got out.

"It's Jack and Wanda," she said. "They were doing disposal."

She shut the door on the van and went out to meet them. I turned the van off and got out too.

Jack parked the truck, and the two emerged. They both had their masks down. Wanda was crying. She ran up to Brenda and hugged her.

"Oh God, I thought you were dead," she said.

Jack looked at me and nodded a greeting. He looked like he'd been crying too.

"Where's Hunter?" Wanda asked. "Is he okay? I saw the two of you on the roof and …"

"Hunter went back in," Brenda said. "I told him not to, but Jamal was on that fire truck ..."

The women hugged each other again.

"Are they coming?" Ed asked.

"Some are," Jack said. "But we lost ... we lost ... um ... some didn't make it."

Ed shook his head.

"I told him it was too dangerous," he said. "That cocky sumbitch."

"Well, we agreed to do it," Jack said. "So I guess it's on all of us."

"It ain't on me," Ed said. "Don't you put it on me neither. I had my say on it."

Jack looked up at the sky, then down at his boots. I felt like I was intruding, so I went back inside.

* * *

A few minutes later, I was sitting at the table with Sara when I heard a vehicle pull up outside. Loud voices drew close to the front door, which presently opened. Wanda and Brenda came in first. Wanda was still crying.

"If y'all did what y'all was supposed to do, it wouldn't have happened!" said a new voice.

"What are you talking about?" Jack exclaimed. "We did everything right."

"That engine siren should have started up the very second they got word about the batteries, and you and Wanda should have been drawing them away with your horn. We talked about that."

Jack and the new guy walked in.

The new guy looked at us.

"Who are they, and why are they drinking our coffee?"

"Don't be like that, Nathan," Brenda said. "They saved my life and Hunter's life."

Nathan stared at us a little longer, then nodded.

"Sorry," he said. "It's been a bad day, but I guess you know that."

"Yeah," I said.

He stepped up to us, extending his hand.

"Nathan Camp," he said. "I appreciate your help out there."

"Sure," I said, shaking his hand.

He was loud when he talked, loud when he walked, loud when he moved, and his handshake was entirely too hard. I didn't like him.

"Thanks for the coffee," I said.

He stared at Sara a little longer than necessary, then went to the office.

"Don't go in there," Brenda said, "Dr. Barr is helping one of their friends …"

Nathan opened the door anyway. I could see Jen on the desk in just her underwear. Dr. Barr was checking her ribs while Connie bandaged her leg.

"Hey!" Dr. Barr said. "I have a patient!"

Nathan didn't apologize or make an effort to leave.

"I need to talk to you, Travis," he said.

"I'm naked here! Shut the door, asshole!" Jen yelled.

He closed the door and, without another word, went into the garage.

He came back with a shotgun.

"I'm going back for them," he said. "Jack, Ed and the new guy are with me."

Jack went outside.

I didn't move.

Ed looked at the floor.

"Come on, boys," Nathan said. "You earn your keep."

"I've earned my keep plenty today," I said. "I'm not going with you. I need to be with Jen."

"The hell you're not."

"I am not," I insisted. "Anyway, we're not staying. We just came to drop off Brenda and see the doctor."

He glared at me.

"There are real people out there," he said. "You understand? Real people that ain't sick. They need help."

"I do understand," I said. "I'm sorry."

He pushed Ed aside and walked out without another word.

Brenda, Wanda and Ed were quiet after Nathan left. No one would look at me.

* * *

After a few minutes, Dr. Barr came out of the office, poured himself some coffee and sat at the table with us.

"Connie is helping Jen get dressed," he said. "She said I could talk to you. My guess is that the bullet went into her leg, struck the femur and then changed direction, exiting out the side of the leg. She was lucky, because if it had gone the other way, it could have hit the femoral artery, and there would have been nothing I could do about that; she would have bled to death. Also, it is fortunate that she didn't go into shock. She's a tough girl."

I nodded.

"Obviously, I don't have x-ray equipment here. I'm going to guess that her femur is fractured. She needs to stay off that leg for a while. I'm going to put it in a splint to immobilize it. I'm not going to stitch the bullet wounds; they need to drain. I gave her a tetanus shot too. Connie and I went into the hospital and pharmacy and took a lot of meds a couple of days after everything happened, so even though it's not ideal, she got the best treatment I was able to provide here."

"What about her neck?" I asked.

"I was coming to that. It looks kind of nasty. We have someone in our group—a boy named Jamal—who had a bite like that on his arm. The human mouth is full of bacteria anyway, and I guess for these ... things ... it's ten times worse. It just didn't want to heal. I'm going to give her a course of antibiotics to take over the next few days. Nathan and Jack probably wouldn't like me doing that, so we aren't going to tell them."

He gave me a look to make sure I understood. I nodded.

"Okay," he said. "Also, her ribs might be cracked or bruised. They were very tender. I wrapped them, but that's the best I can do."

"So we can go now? I get the impression Nathan doesn't like me much."

"Nathan comes on kind of strong," Dr. Barr said. "No, I would prefer it if she stayed here for a day or so, so I can keep an eye on those holes in her leg and see how the antibiotics are working."

"Okay," I said.

I looked at Sara, and she nodded.

"On the upside," Dr. Barr said, "at least I didn't have to dig around in her leg, looking for that bullet."

* * *

Connie came out of the office and told us it was okay to see Jen.

Jen was sitting up on the desk, her injured leg stretched out in front of her on a splint and her other leg hanging off the side.

She was wearing a blue-and-white long-sleeved dress. It was a little big on her, but she looked nice in it.

"You doing okay?" I asked Jen.

She shrugged.

"The doctor said we should stay," I said.

"Yeah," she said. "I'm sorry."

"I'm just glad there was a doctor and medicine. I was really worried about you."

"Shut the door, okay?" she said.

Sara went over and closed it.

"When Connie was in here without Travis, she was asking me if she could come with us," Jen whispered. "She doesn't like it here."

"What did you tell her?" Sara said.

"I told her it wasn't up to me. I really don't want her to, but she's a registered nurse, and it might be good to have her around."

"Why hasn't she left?"

"By herself? She can't get anyone to leave with her. She said a couple of others aren't happy either, but they like the electricity, and they're afraid to go out on their own."

"They do have a nice setup here," I said.

"She told me she overheard some of the men talking one night after everyone had gone to bed. They were talking about trying to find young women in their childbearing years. You know, to continue the human race and all that."

"Oh," I said, puzzled.

It seemed kind of early to be talking like that. This was a bad time to be having children. Frankly, if the talk did indeed happen, their motives were probably baser. They were probably all thinking about the sex they weren't having and were using the perpetuation of the species to justify something less than consensual. Jen was right; they were turning into cavemen.

"She's the only woman in her group who falls into that category," Jen continued. "All the other women here are either close to or past menopause."

I didn't think that mattered.

"Oh," I said again. "Have they tried to pressure her?"

"I don't know," Jen said. "She didn't really have time to tell me more. I don't want a bunch of extra people living with us, but I don't want a woman to be forced into being a baby machine either."

"She should come with us," Sara said.

"Sometimes men sit around and bullshit," I said. "They were probably drinking and shooting off their mouths. There may not be anything to it."

Sara and Jen rolled their eyes at the same time.

"Still," I continued, "I don't like that Nathan guy at all, and the sooner we can get away from him, the better."

"Nathan," Jen said. "That's his name. Connie doesn't like him either."

"Whatever you two do, don't mention where we are living now, and ..."

"I lied to Connie and Travis," Jen said. "I told them we were living north of town, near the chicken plant."

"Good," I said. "We don't know if we can trust them."

"I'm sorry we can't go ahead and leave," Jen said. "I suppose we could ..."

"No," I said. "I don't want to risk you getting worse. Then we'd have to come back out here. It's best if we stay cordial; we never know if we'll need Dr. Barr's help again."

"I think he'd help us again," Sara said. "He's really nice."

"He's a sweetie pie," Jen said.

A look passed between Jen and Sara that was easy to interpret.

I didn't say anything.

"Travis asked if we'd be joining them," Jen said.

"You mean staying here with them permanently?"

"Yeah."

"No," I said. "I'm not interested in that."

"Good," Jen said with a smile.

"I really think Connie should come with us if she wants to," Sara said.

There was a knock on the door. Sara opened it. It was Brenda.

"I'm sorry to intrude," she said. "Would y'all like something to eat?"

"I don't want to eat your food," I said. "I know you all will need it."

"It's all right," she said. "You're guests. I don't think three extra burgers are going to break us."

"Burgers?" Jen echoed.

"Yes," Brenda said. "We brought in two chest freezers about three days ago. We have lots of meat and ice cream and …"

"Ice cream?" Jen said.

"You'll eat with us," Brenda said. "It'll be a very late lunch or early supper. I really don't have much of an appetite after today, so if Nathan says something, we'll just tell him that y'all are eating my, Hunter's and Jamal's rations."

She started crying.

"I'm sorry, Brenda," I said.

Sara went up to her and hugged her.

"We're okay, Ms. Brenda," Sara said. "We ain't hungry."

Sara and I left the office so Jen could rest. We sat in the break room and looked at magazines. I was hungry, and I could hear Sara's stomach growling too. We could smell the burgers being cooked in the garage, and I wished we had accepted Brenda's offer.

Connie came in, carrying a tray. She opened the office door and presented Jen with a plain hamburger and some beans. Jen looked out at us.

"Eat as much as you can," Connie said. "You need the protein to help you heal."

She left the office and looked at us.

"I'll bring yours right out," she said.

I was relieved.

The front door opened, and three new men walked in. Two were just a little older than I, and one was sixty or more. They looked haggard and sad.

When they saw us, they stopped and said hello. Connie came in with our food. When she saw the newcomers, she called out into the garage that the men were back.

"We've been so worried," she said to the men. "We didn't know who made it and who didn't."

"It was bad," one of them said. "We tried to lead them away, but it took a while. We never did find Brenda or Hunter."

"Brenda is here," Connie said. "Hunter didn't make it."

"Jamal, Anne and Willy didn't either," one of them said.

"Nathan and Jack went out to look for you and the others," Connie said, setting our food in front of us.

The three men stared at us. I didn't know what they were thinking, but I doubted they liked that we were eating their food after a day like today. They were probably angry and looking for someone to take it out on.

"We drove out to the church like we were supposed to, but nobody ever showed," one said. "Mr. Peterson, Linda and Pat were supposed to be waiting there for us."

"We haven't seen them," Connie said. "Maybe Nathan will find them."

Nathan and Jack returned an hour later, alone. They'd had no luck locating the other people missing from their group. I suspected the others had decided to live somewhere else and had slipped away.

Everyone was upset over the losses. Seven people from their group had failed to come back, and even though they'd only been together for a little more than a week, it was easy for me to imagine how difficult it must be for them.

Sara and I tried to stay out of their way by hiding out in the office with Jen. We could hear some loud discussions going on in the garage. I couldn't hear all of what was being said, but some of it addressed the failed plan to eradicate the infected, and some of it was about us. Nathan played a big part in both.

After a few minutes, Nathan stepped into the doorway. Jack and one of the other men were behind him. Nathan was at least a head taller than the other men, and half as broad. His wavy reddish-brown hair was singed on the left side of this head, and his left ear was bandaged.

"What are you still doing here?" he asked.

"The doctor said Jen needed to stay."

"What are you still doing here?"

"We're with her," I said.

"If you don't pull your weight around here, you have to go," he said. "All you've done is mooch our food and take a coffee break when people needed your help."

"I don't …"

"You ain't welcome here," he said. "It's been decided that you should go."

"Decided by whom?"

"There is a chain of command around here. We have to keep things orderly to keep people fed and safe. I'm not going to have anyone here who doesn't do his share. Like the Bible says, if you don't work, then you don't eat."

"I'd be happy to go, just as soon as the doctor says Jen is able."

"No," Nathan said. "She's hurt, and she's hurt because Hunter shot her. I figure we owe her a little something for that. I'll let her stay until she's well enough, but you have to go now."

"I'm not leaving her."

"Then take her with you. Either way, I want you gone."

"Stop," Jen said. "They'll go."

"What?" I said.

"It's okay," she said. "Come back in a couple of days and get me."

Then she looked at Nathan and the other two.

"Would you three excuse us?"

"You've got five minutes," Nathan said.

"Make it four," Jen said.

They stepped away from the door, and Sara closed it.

"Assholes," Jen said.

"Jen, are you crazy?" I said. "I'm not leaving you."

"Please shut up for a second," she said. "I want you and Sara to go back to Wal-Mart before it gets too dark and get the stuff we collected. I'm not going to be getting around much for a while, and we need those supplies more now than before."

"But we can get that later. I'm still going to have to find food."

"I'll be fine," she said. "That stuff might be gone later. I'll ask Connie to sit with me. It'll give me time to talk to her."

I pulled the .38 out of my coat pocket.

"Here," I said. "Take it. It's empty, but they don't know that."

She took the weapon and hid it under her sheet.

"I'll be okay," she said. "Come back in a couple of days. I'll leave then, whether Travis says I should or not."

"We'll be back tomorrow to check on you," I said.

"Before you leave, ask him if there's any medicine you should find for me."

"Jen, this is a bad idea."

"Well, it's screwed up, that's for sure, but I'd rather hang out here with these jerks and keep my leg or my life than leave and lose one or both to infection. Travis said that could happen."

CHAPTER 36

Nathan and two of the other men stood out front to see us off. Ed held the gate for us as we pulled out.

"I really don't like leaving Jen here," I said.

"She can take care of herself," Sara said.

"I know," I said, "but I feel like I'm abandoning her."

"It's only for a couple of days," Sara said. "Connie and Brenda both said they would sit with her."

"It doesn't bother you?" I asked.

"If it was someone else, I might be worried, but not Jen. Anyway, you know she and I aren't exactly best friends."

I nodded. I felt the urge to apologize for Jen, but I didn't.

We had not gotten very far from the high school when the big pickup showed up in my mirror. They were clearly following us. Oddly enough, I don't think they knew they were being obvious. These were the ones Darwin would get.

"Why would they follow us?" Sara said.

"Maybe they want to know where you and Jen live."

"We were already with them," Sara said.

"Yeah."

It seemed to me that they would have been better off feeding us, being nice to us and making our stay in the maintenance building as comfortable as possible. It would have made their group very appealing, considering they had electricity and a doctor. Jen and Sara might have wanted to stay with them. They had a couple—or more—bad apples that were making a miserable life even more miserable. It crossed my mind that the rest of the group should lock the gate while they were gone and let the infected have them.

I didn't want to lead them back to the stables or Wal-Mart, so I stuck with Jen's story and headed north. I didn't want to go too far, because it was already late afternoon, and it would be dark soon.

I pulled off on a side road, and then entered the driveway of the first house I saw. The pickup didn't follow us down the side road. They were satisfied with knowing where we "lived" and headed back. What a bunch of knuckleheads.

We waited a few minutes, then drove south, toward Wal-Mart. We circled around downtown again. It was still smoky over there, but it didn't look like any other buildings were burning.

* * *

The full shopping carts were still waiting where we'd left them. We didn't bother unloading them; we just pulled out the dolly ramp on the truck and pushed the carts inside. They only took up the front portion of the box. We used the straps in the truck to keep them from rolling around. It took us about half an hour, and we were starting to lose daylight.

"Are we doing Tractor Supply today?" Sara asked.

"No," I said. "Let's take this stuff back to the stables, and we'll come back tomorrow."

I pulled down the rear door on the truck and latched it.

"We can leave the minivan here," I said.

It occurred to me that it might be a good idea at some point to park cars at strategic places around town. Then if we were ever in a bind and without a vehicle, we'd know where to find one. I made a mental note to put that on our list of things to do. We could take a map of the city—maybe even the whole county—and spend a day or two parking cars. It might just save our lives one day.

We moved all the guns we had with us—Somerville's .30-06 and 12-gauge, and the .22 rifle Jen had found at the Kaler house on our second day together.

We didn't talk much on the way back to the Lassiter house. This was the first time Sara and I had been alone together, and it felt kind of awkward, especially since Jen had been acting the way she had.

"Do you still want to go out with Mr. Somerville and look for survivors?" I said.

"You mean after what we've seen today?" she said. "It makes me think twice about it."

"I've been wondering if he's okay," I said. "Jen's bite wasn't healing, and he had several bites on him. We should check on him tomorrow. We might want to get him to the doctor."

* * *

It was getting dark when we pulled into the driveway. I was in no rush to unload the truck, so we left it for another time.

Sara got a pot of water warming on the stove for us to use for bathing while I worked on the fire. There were still some glowing embers left from the morning. I got the flames going again, and put in some split wood.

Jen's absence felt strange. I'd grown accustomed to having her around, and I was already missing her. We'd all planned to have pizza, and I didn't want to do that without her.

I went into the kitchen.

"The bath water is hot. You can take it," Sara said. "I'll start another one."

"No," I said. "You go first."

She smiled. "Really. I'll make something to eat while you get cleaned up, and I'll wash up after dinner."

"We'll wait on the pizzas until Jen is back, okay?" I said.

I took the pot of water into the cold bathroom. I stood in the tub and gave myself a sort of sponge bath. I'd bathed like this several times over the past few days. It wasn't comfortable at all, but it got me clean. I was thinking about all of the water I had used in the past to shower or bathe, and here I was getting clean with not much more than a half-gallon. I could probably have used less. Still, I would have loved a long hot shower right then.

When I came back to the kitchen, Sara had vegetable soup on the table. There was another pot of water on the stove, already steaming.

"Thanks for the food," I said.

"I just warmed up some canned stuff," she said. "I'm not a real cook."

"Thanks for doing it, though."

She smiled.

"Jen's going to be okay," she said. "Don't worry about her. She's tough."

I wanted to talk to her about Jen, but I didn't know how.

"I'm sorry for the way Jen has been acting," I said.

She shrugged and frowned.

"She can be kind of ... um ..." I couldn't find the right word.

"Crass?" Sara said.

"Well …"

"How about rude? How about bitchy?"

"Yeah." I laughed. "She can be all of those things."

She smiled again.

"Do you two have a history or something?"

"No," I said. "No history. We went to high school together. We actually only started getting to know one another since the virus."

"She doesn't like me," Sara said.

"I think she's just ... I think maybe she's ... I don't know."

"She's afraid you're going to like me more than her," Sara said bluntly.

She went back to eating her soup.

"Tomorrow, we can let the extra horses go," I said, changing the subject. "Do you have any ideas on that?"

"No," she said. "I don't know a lot about farm stuff."

"That's okay," I said. "We're all learning."

"Thank you for being so nice to me," she said. "I know you've been taking up for me with Jen."

"Sure," I said.

"I think my water is ready," she said. "You can have the rest of my soup."

She left the room with the pot of water.

When I finished eating, I poured myself some Southern Comfort and went into the living room to sit by the fire. I was just about over my TV withdrawal, and staring at the fire had become a nice way to wind down in the evening.

The room was warm, and I was relaxed. I listened to the fire pop and hiss. I heard Sara moving around in the other room.

She came to the living room wrapped in a blanket.

"It's so cold in that bathroom," she said. "I'll be glad when it's summer."

"Yeah, but then we won't have air conditioning," I said. "We could start using that kerosene heater in there when we're bathing."

She sat on the end of the couch nearest the fire.

"That kerosene stinks," she said. "I like the fireplace better."

"How did you stay warm at the church?"

"They had a gas range in the fellowship hall. I stayed close to it."

She looked at my glass.

"Do we need to drink something tonight?"

"I do," I said. "I came in contact with some infected when I was looking for the minivan. Besides, I'm a little shook up from today, and this helps."

She stood and stepped closer to the fireplace.

"It's so different now," she said, staring into the fire. "It makes me wonder about everything I've ever been taught. All the people I ever knew are gone … or changed. It's not fair that my family should get sick while those men at Lowe's this morning didn't."

"They didn't make it either," I said.

"I know," she said. "Maybe they got it worse than the rest, but ... I don't know. Why would my pastor get sick? He was a good man. He'd never hurt anybody before, but I saw him hurt people after. I had to lock him out of the church so he wouldn't hurt me."

She turned toward me.

"Does that seem right to you?"

"No," I said.

"I'm glad I met you," she said. "I feel safe with you."

"I'm glad I met you too," I said.

She took a step closer to me and let the blanket fall to the floor.

"Whoa" was all I could say.

She had a body like one of those pin-up models from the 1950s—soft, curvy. I'd never seen a more perfect example of the female form in real life, and I'd never been this close to an unclothed one. Flawless fair skin, full lips, soft down of pubic hair, every part of her perfectly shaped and proportioned. Standing in the firelight, she looked like a goddess. My mouth went dry, and my heart raced.

Her reddish-blond hair was short, but her bangs curled down over one eye. She brushed them away, and they bounced back.

I put my glass on the floor, stood up and stumbled a little.

"Whoa, Sara ... What are you doing?"

She came in close to me. I could smell the warmth of her body.

She didn't speak; she just took my hands and put them on her waist, resting them on the swell of her hips.

She felt like heaven. I pulled my hands away and stepped back.

"I want you to touch me."

"Sara ... I ... What about Jen?"

"Jen is a bully. She's not your type."

I chuckled a little. "Actually, she is my type. I always go for women like her."

"Well, maybe you should try something different," she said, stepping close to me again. "What about it? You want to try me out?"

"But you ... um ... you're ... What about your church? What about your boyfriend?"

"That's all gone now. I'm not a virgin, if that's what you think. I haven't been the slut that Jen has probably been, but I know what I'm doing. I'm very much a woman."

"Oh ... I can ... I can see you're a woman."

"I've noticed how you look at me," she said. "I know you want this."

I stepped away from her again.

"Wanting it and doing it are two different things."

My body was screaming at me: Are you crazy? Do it! Be a caveman like the rest!

"You want it, and I'm offering it, so what's the problem?"

She moved in again and put my hands back on her hips. I swallowed hard. I tried to step back again, but I was against the wall. She pressed herself against me. I felt lightheaded.

"You have no idea how bad I want it," I said. "But …"

"Oh, I can feel how bad you want it," she whispered back.

"But I can't," I said. "I ... I'd be betraying Jen."

"So you two are really together? She told me you were, but I just figured it was her being pushy again."

"Well, we never did anything official. I mean, we just kind of ..."

She smiled and put her hand on my face.

"It's okay," she said, smiling. "You're being loyal. At least there's still a little right left in the world."

My hands were still on her hips, and she was still pressed against me. I didn't want it to end, but if it didn't ...

She stood on tiptoes and kissed my cheek.

"You're a decent man. Maybe one day, you'll want a decent woman."

She stepped back and picked up her blanket. I was weak in the knees.

"I'll leave in the morning," she said. "I'll move in with the Somervilles like Jen wants."

"Sara, don't do that," I said. "What about the horses? What about ... what about everything? How can I do all of this by myself?"

"I can't stay here," she said, wrapping the blanket around herself. "It'll be too weird."

"I'm sorry," I said.

"I know I'm a little younger than you, but I think I could make you happy."

I suspected that she could.

"After seeing what's left out there ... never mind. I'm going to bed now," she said.

"Okay," I said, continuing to stare.

"Are we still sleeping in here by the fire?"

"Oh," I said. "I'm sorry, of course."

I went into the kitchen and poured myself another drink. I had the shakes again. It was going to be a long night.

CHAPTER 37

I woke up later than usual the next day. To say I'd had trouble sleeping would have been an understatement. The fire was blazing, and Sara's blankets were folded on the couch.

I couldn't find her in the house, and I feared that she was already gone. I didn't like the idea of her being out there on her own, trying to find Mr. Somerville's house.

I looked out the window. The rear door on the moving van was up, and the ramp was down. She had already pushed two of the carts outside and was coming out with a third.

I put on my boots and coat and went out to help her.

"Good morning," she said. "I thought you were going to sleep all day."

"It's only eight," I said.

"I know." She smiled.

She had traded in her letter jacket for one of Mrs. Lassiter's coats. She had a green homemade crocheted hat pulled down over her ears. Her nose was red from the frosty air.

"We could have done this after breakfast," I said.

"It is after breakfast," she said, still smiling. "Breakfast was served at six-thirty. Didn't you get your wake-up call?"

She was acting as if nothing had happened the night before. Maybe nothing did. Maybe it was a dream. Maybe it was all the alcohol.

I just came out with it.

"Please stay, Sara."

She was headed back up the ramp. She stopped, stood there a second and then resumed walking without saying anything.

"The whole reason we chose a big place like this was so we could all be comfortable and make a nice life for ourselves. You were part of that."

"This was all Jen's idea," she said from inside the truck. "This was what Jen wanted."

"What do you want?"

"I can't have what I want."

"I'm sorry about last night. I just ..."

She stepped forward out of the shadows.

"No," she said. "I didn't mean that. I want my parents back. I want to go back trying to decide what my major should be when I transfer to the university. I want to see my boyfriend on the weekends and eat at McDonald's and all that."

"I'm sorry."

"You don't have to keep saying that."

She went back into the shadow of the box and tugged on another cart.

"I had planned to ask the Somervilles again to live with us," I said. "I think we would all be safer if we stuck together like that."

"You might want to clear that with your girlfriend," Sara said, on her way out with another cart.

"I know Jen is being antisocial, but ..."

"Please don't make excuses for her," Sara said. "Anyway, that bunch at the high school isn't too happy. Jen might be right with keeping it small. The more people you have together, the more conflict there will be."

"They just have a couple of people who are making it bad for everybody."

"So if we had a larger group, do you think we wouldn't have people like that?" she said.

"No," I said. "We could be selective about who we ..."

"We already have someone like that," she said. "Jen is our Nathan."

"Oh," I said. "I don't think she's that bad."

"She's bossy and rude, and it's her way or nothing."

"I'll talk to her about that."

Sara shook her head and laughed.

"I'll help you today with the horses, and I'll help you get some more supplies, but then I'd like you to drive me out to the Somervilles' house. Okay?"

"And if the Somervilles decide to come out here?"

"I don't know," she said. "I hear there's a group in town looking for a baby machine."

"Don't even joke about that."

* * *

Sara and I leaned on the fence and looked out on one of the pastures.

"I don't know which ones to keep and which ones to let go," I said.

"I think the girls and boys are separated," Sara said. "I think these are all boys. Do you want a mixture, or all one sex?"

"What do you think?" I said.

She turned and leaned her back against the fence, elbows up on the rails.

"I told you; I don't know about farm stuff."

"Well," I said, "I suppose if we get to the place where we need horses, then we're going to want males and females."

"Do horses go into heat like dogs?"

"I don't know," I said.

"If they do, you should just keep some of the girls. They'll attract the boys at the right time."

"If any boys are still alive."

"Yeah," she said. "Also, how can we tell if they haven't been neutered? Do they do that to horses?"

"I don't know that either," I said. "I suppose they do."

"Sounds like you don't know much. Sounds to me like you don't need to own horses."

"I concur."

"So whatcha gonna do?" she said, turning to face me.

"Okay, the ones in that field over there are females, you say?"

"Yep."

"There are six of them, and they have access to that pond. I say we keep those and let the rest go."

"That sounds easy enough," she said. "How do we let them go?"

"We'll just knock out a section of fence. There should be hammers in the barn."

The easy thing to do would have been to open the gates. However, the gates opened to the interior of the property, where the house and barns were. I didn't want a herd of horses standing around in the yard and driveway; I wanted them gone. They might find their way around and back up the driveway, but at least I wasn't making it easy on them.

We each got a hammer, and I found a pry bar. We entered the pasture on the east side of the driveway. It was muddy. The horses looked up from their grazing but didn't find us very interesting.

"Let's pop off the boards over there," I said, pointing to the corner away from the driveway but near the house. "I don't think we need to herd them out. They'll probably find their own way out."

"What if they don't?"

"Then they don't." I shrugged.

They would find their way. The fence separated this land from a neighboring farm, and there was another large pond over there. They were smart animals, and if they got thirsty, they'd leave.

We beat and pried at the boards until there was an opening between two of the posts. We walked down toward the road where the pasture had been subdivided and opened a place there for the horses on the other side.

Then we crossed over to the west side of the driveway and did the same on that side. This would also provide us with another escape route. It would be a muddy one, so we probably wouldn't be able to drive out. I'd have to make another exit on the back side of the property eventually.

We were picking up the boards from the last opening and propping them against the fence when we noticed a man on the road. He was wearing ragged clothes, and judging from his movements, he was infected. He stopped at the end of the driveway and stared at us for a few minutes, and we stared back.

"We shouldn't shoot him," Sara said. "The sound of the gun might bring more in."

"No. You're right. Let's just see what he does."

He kept looking at us, then down at the ground, then back at us. He just stood there.

"We have other things to do," I sighed. "I'll go take care of him."

I pulled up my mask and grabbed the pry bar, then started toward him. He didn't move except to look around. One of the horses nickered, and he looked toward the sound.

"Be careful," Sara said from behind me.

When I'd covered half the distance, he became fixated on me. His mouth hung open, and he kept pushing his tongue in and out. He took one step toward me, but that was all.

"So you're going to make me do all the walking," I said.

He moaned when he heard my voice.

I was going to have to hit him in the head. Brenda said shooting them in the head killed them sometimes. I needed to make sure he wasn't coming back. I wasn't looking forward to it.

He hissed at me.

"I'm sorry," I said. "I have to do it."

He took another step. He was standing next to the big white mailbox that said LASSITER on the side. I was close. He hissed again.

Just do it.

I closed the remaining space in a jog. He started to reach for me, and I slammed the claw of the pry bar into his skull. He smelled like roadkill.

He kept reaching for me, but I held him away from me with the pry bar.

"Come on, man," I said. "Die."

I couldn't get the claw out. I worked it, but I couldn't pull it loose. His brains had to have been scrambled to mush as much as I moved that bar, yet he kept on reaching.

The claw had gone in just above the forehead. Maybe it was the lizard brain that needed to be destroyed. It had been a long time since I'd taken biology, but I thought I remembered that being near where the brain attached to the spinal cord. Was it the basal ganglia or the cerebellum or something else?

"I don't suppose you would know, would you?" I said.

He made a sound in his throat that I can't quite describe.

"I'm sorry," I said.

I pushed the pry bar away. He stumbled backward and fell on his butt. The bar hung down in front of his face. He grabbed for it, but couldn't grasp it. I could hear Sara walking up behind me.

"I haven't been able to kill him," I said.

She came up beside me. We both stood there, staring down at the poor man.

"Here," she said, offering her hammer. "I have the twenty-two on me too."

"Shit," I said. "Give me the gun."

I took the revolver from her, then walked behind the man. He just sat there on the road. I kicked him in the back of the head, and he fell over. Then I rolled him onto his face with my boot. He didn't move much. I put the gun against the base of his skull.

"I'm sorry," I said again.

Then I put two bullets in his head. The gun didn't sound as loud as I thought it would.

"I'll stay with him," I said. "Go back to the barn and get one of those trucks. We'll leave him at the church with the dead horse."

CHAPTER 38

We loaded the corpse into the back of one of the trucks and drove down to the church. My plan was to unload the body into the horse trailer and lock it in there. That way, if it did come back to life, it would be trapped in the trailer.

But the truck and horse trailer were gone.

"Are you sure it was this church?" Sara asked. "It was dark, and there are so many churches in Grace County."

"Yes," I said. "This was the one. Too bad. I was going to try to unhitch the trailer. That was a nice truck, and it had a full tank of gas."

"There are lots of trucks," she said. "What you ought to be thinking about is where it went and who took it."

"Let's get him out of the back," I said. "We have more things to do before you go."

* * *

By 1:00 p.m., I was watching Sara pack a bag of things she wanted to take with her.

"Stay," I said again. "It won't be weird. It never happened."

"I know it never happened," she said. "That's part of the problem."

"We've spent all morning together, and aside from the man at the end of the road, it wasn't bad at all. I really need you here. Jen and I both need you. I think you need us too."

"I tried to be friends with Jen," she said, looking through some of the new clothes we'd picked up at Wal-Mart. "I know we can live under the same roof—we've been doing that—but I don't want to make a home somewhere and feel unwelcome in it. There are so many other places I could live. One of the few good things now is that we can all live however and wherever we want."

"Why don't we convert one of the barns? Maybe the one with the office—turn it into a house? We have free building materials."

"Seems like a lot of trouble when there are already so many houses out there."

"But ..."

"No. Okay? I have everything packed. Let's go out to Tractor Supply and get the chicken food. Then we can go check on Jen. Then you can drive me to the Somervilles'."

* * *

Tractor Supply didn't have skylights like Wal-Mart. We had to use flashlights. It hadn't been hit as hard by looters as Wal-Mart had, but they had been there. I was happy to find a lot of the animal food left, including three 40-pound bags of whole-kernel feed corn. I could feed that to the chickens, but in a pinch, we might be able to eat it too.

We took that and the rest of the feed—some for horses, some for poultry and some for goats and sheep. We even got all the birdseed. We wound up with twelve 40-pound bags and ten 20-pound bags.

We also collected rope, chain, work gloves, boots, different hand tools and some books on livestock. I grabbed some of the large dog carriers to put the chickens in so we could move them to the new place. We'd need chicken wire too, so I got that.

On our last sweep of the store, my flashlight shone on a little wood-burning stove. There were several stoves of different sizes, but this one attracted me because it was small enough that I thought Sara and I might be able to lift it into the truck.

"Do you think we can manage it?" I asked.

"What for? Winter is almost over."

"I don't know," I said. "Maybe I'll go ahead and convert one of those barns in case you change your mind."

"That's very sweet of you, but …"

"Besides, in the summer, we're going to need a place to cook our food without heating up the whole house."

"You could use a grill, but sure, let's try it," she said.

It was heavy, but we got it on the truck. I went back in and got stove pipe too. I saw some other supplies related to woodstoves. I didn't know what I should get, so I just took it all.

It was almost three by the time we finished up there, and I was very happy with our haul.

"It's getting late," Sara said. "Let's go check on Jen."

* * *

When we got to the maintenance building, we could see a man on the roof. He looked like he was holding a military rifle. He made a call on his cell phone when he saw us coming up the drive, and four men came outside into the little courtyard between the building and the chain-link fence. I stopped the truck. I was starting to wish we had parked our truck somewhere else and driven a different vehicle. I'd hate to lose what we'd collected.

"I'm going to talk with them," I said. "Same rules as Lowe's. If something happens, get the hell away from here. Find the Somervilles later, okay?"

I started to get out, and she grabbed my hand. When I looked over at her, she kissed me. It was just a peck, but it was on the lips, and it addled me for a second.

"Um ... I'm ... I'm going to leave the engine running. When I get out, slide into the driver's seat."

I had the Lassiters' .22 revolver in my coat. I got out and walked to the fence.

Nathan, Jack and two of the other men were standing at the gate.

"I've come to visit Jen," I said.

"She's sleeping," Nathan said.

"Wake her up," I said.

"Nah, the doctor says she needs her rest."

"Let me talk to the doctor, then."

"He's busy."

"Come on, man," I said. "There is no need for this. We're all that's left. We need to help each other."

He just stared at me.

"Doctor Barr!" I yelled. "Doctor Barr! Come out here!"

"I told you," Nathan said. "He's busy."

The front door opened, and Brenda came outside.

"Nathan, you open that gate!"

"Get back inside like I told you!" he shouted over his shoulder.

"Oh," I said. "I see how it is. You're a little Hitler."

"Shut up, ass wipe," he said. "I talked to Jen last night, and she wants to stay here with us. She likes what we have to offer here."

"Okay," I said. "Let me hear it from her."

"Nathan! Open that gate, or so help me ..."

"Brenda, get your ass back in that building! Now!"

"Brenda," I said. "Is Doctor Barr in there? Send him out. Is Jen okay?"

"Brenda! Inside, now!"

Nathan stepped up to the gate.

"Leave," he said. "Jen is with us now."

My fear made me lightheaded, but my anger gave me courage. I stepped up too, so that we were nose to nose.

"Are you sure you want to fuck with me like this?"

Did I actually say that?

He laughed.

"I know who you are. Some of the others told me. You're that pansy-ass museum guy. You ain't going to do jack shit. I suggest you get in your truck and leave before that little blonde you came with decides she wants to stay with us too."

I kept standing there, unsure what to do. I felt like I did when I was a kid getting harassed by bullies. I was helpless back then, and I felt helpless now. They had me outnumbered and outgunned.

I hated feeling helpless. It made me angry and ashamed.

"Don't make me shoot you," he said. "That wouldn't help any of us. You'd be dead, and we'd have those things breathing down our necks. Now go."

Then it became perfectly clear what I had to do. I turned and walked away, back to the truck.

"Don't come back," he called out to me. "She'll get everything she needs right here."

I kept walking. When I got to the truck, I opened the door.

"Scoot over," I said to Sara.

"What's going on?"

"They won't let me see her."

"What?"

I climbed in and put the truck in reverse.

"Are you coming back later?" she asked.

I backed down the winding drive past the school. There were still people in the school—mostly teenagers—pressing themselves against the windows, trying to get to us. It must have been a real horrorfest in there. When I got to the football stadium, I stopped the truck.

"Hop out," I said. "Take the shotgun, and hide in there until I get back. If I don't come back, you have the Somervilles' address."

"What are you doing?"

"Get out."

"But ..."

"Get out!"

She looked afraid, but she obeyed. I opened the glove compartment and pulled out a box of 12-gauge shells.

"Here," I said. "Go hide."

She took the box.

"Don't do something stupid," Sara said. "There are innocent people in there."

"They've had plenty of time to do the right thing. There's only one person in that building I care about. Shut the door."

I put the truck in drive and put the gas on the floor. The big truck was a little slow getting started, but I had enough space to build up some speed. The men at the gate saw me coming and turned their guns on me. I leaned over behind the dashboard and put my hand on the horn.

I hit the fence, hard. It had some give to it, but the impact still threw me into the dashboard and down to the floor. The man on the roof opened up with his weapon. It was firing in bursts and chewing up the windshield.

Where did they get a gun like that?

I sank down onto the floorboard, shielding my head with my hands as the stuffing from the truck seat filled the air around me like snow. There was screaming outside. The gunfire ceased.

I groped above myself and found the steering wheel, then the gear shift. I shifted it, then pushed the gas pedal with my hand before they could open the door and get me. It didn't move. I shifted it again. The truck creaked back over the fence posts and chain link, tires squealing. It rocked and then finally rolled.

I was moving backwards. I let my hand off the gas and took a peek over the dash. The fence was pushed in. There was no hole, but it was down like a ramp and could be walked over. It had collapsed over the front entrance of the building, and two of the men were trapped beneath it.

I stopped the truck and grabbed the .30-06. I stuck it through the open space where the windshield had been. I put it to my shoulder and put the crosshairs of the scope on the man on the roof. I didn't even think; I just squeezed it off and dropped him.

I lay on the horn again and put the truck in drive.

The infected would be on their way.

CHAPTER 39

I didn't hit the fence again. Instead, I hung a right and headed toward the school buses. I wouldn't be able to go in the front after all. Nathan was corralled in the far side of the courtyard, with no exit. With the entrance to the building blocked, and the fence leaning, he was caged in. He took a shot at me with his pistol, but he missed. As I circled around the back of the buses, I saw him leap on the fence, trying to climb, but because of the angle, he couldn't hang on.

The springs from the seat were sticking out, and I had windshield glass down my collar. That gun had to have been illegal. I wondered where they had gotten it.

I parked the truck behind the buses, so I could have some shielding. I left it running.

The rear of the building had an exit too. It let out into the fenced-in area near the door to the generator building. I knew there were a couple of windows back there through which I could climb if the door was locked, and it probably was. There was a large gate on this side for the buses to access the garage and the diesel pump.

I didn't think anyone would come out. For one thing, people were shooting outside. Plus, they knew as well as I did that the creatures would be coming, drawn to the noise.

They were safe so long as they didn't open the doors to the building.

Now that Nathan and at least three of the other men were either fully or partially out of commission, I wasn't as willing to put the rest in jeopardy as I was before. That was the first moment since getting in Nathan's face at the gate that I'd had a rational thought. Up to that point, it was like I was outside of myself. My fear and rage had me all muddled.

What the hell was I doing? Had I really just put all those people in danger because one man humiliated me?

I was too far into it by this time to be having second thoughts. I slung the rifle over my shoulder and ran to the fence. I tried the bus gate. As expected, it was locked with a padlock. I ejected the spent casing from the .30-06, put the muzzle up to the lock and fired. The lock, now a jagged wad of metal, spun around on the latch. I pulled it loose and opened the gate.

As I ran around the back of the building, I could hear people yelling inside. They had to know why I was there, but they probably didn't know what to expect from me. I anticipated some fear-fueled resistance. I slung the rifle back on my shoulder, pulled the revolver from my coat and tried the door. It was locked.

"If you can hear me in there, let me in!"

No answer.

"I am going to shut off your generators! I'm going to break your windows! I'm going to drive my truck through your door! I'm going to get Jen, and I'm going to leave you all to die!"

I was bluffing. I was already starting to feel guilty about shooting the guy on the roof.

No answer.

"You made your choice!"

I could hear the lock. I stepped back and pointed my weapon. The door opened. It was Brenda. She was weeping.

"Please stop," she said.

"Where's Jen?"

Connie stepped past Brenda and came outside. She looked at me but didn't say anything. I pushed past Brenda into the garage. Dr. Barr was wheeling Jen toward me in an office chair. She was still wearing that dress.

"Jesus," Jen said. "What the hell were you doing out there?"

"They wouldn't let me in to see you," I said. I felt embarrassed.

"Take her," the doctor said. "I have to go out and check on the others."

I pushed Jen to the door.

"Help me over the threshold," I said to Brenda.

Jen stood on her good leg.

"I can hop," she said.

I looked at Connie.

"Coming or staying?"

She looked at Brenda, then at Jen.

"She's coming," Jen said. "We've already discussed it. Connie, go get your stuff."

Connie shook her head.

"I've changed my mind," she said.

"We don't have a lot of time," I said.

"I have to go help Travis," Connie said, running back into the garage.

"Brenda," I said, feeling the need to explain myself. "I would have never hurt anyone in here, but Nathan wouldn't let me in, and ..."

"Take her and go," Brenda said, looking at the ground.

That pissed me off too, but for different reasons. I wanted her to absolve me, or at least validate my actions. I needed to hear her agree with me about Nathan. On some level, I even wanted her to thank me for freeing her from tyranny. I'd just done her a huge favor.

Maybe if I explained it a little more.

"Brenda, I ..."

"Just go."

She stepped back into the building, and the door shut behind her.

I put the revolver in my coat pocket and picked up Jen.

"I told you, I can hop."

"Shut up," I said.

Jen was lean and fit. I had noticed that about her at Brian's house, when she was only wearing the towel. She looked good in a pair of jeans too, but that was really all I had seen of her, because she was usually hidden under a lot of bulky winter clothes. We had not talked about it, but I had pegged her to be a runner or gym member. Bodies like hers did not just happen. She wasn't that heavy at first. But I wasn't carrying her over the threshold, if you know what I mean. I had to lug her from the back door of the building all the way out to behind the buses, where our ride waited.

She could tell I was struggling. When we passed the diesel pump, she said, "I know you're trying to rescue me and all, but I can make it on my own."

"I'm good," I said.

"You're proud," she said. "Just don't drop me."

Somehow, I got her to the moving van and let her down next to the passenger door. My arms were numb.

"Came in guns blazing, didn't you?" she said, looking at the truck.

"Can you climb in by yourself?"

"How are we going to drive in the cold without a windshield?" she asked.

"All of our stuff is in here," I said. "We have to drive it."

"There ain't nothing left of the seats neither."

"Jen ..."

"What if the zombies come?" she asked. "They'll climb right in, won't they?"

"What the hell do you want from me?" I said. "They told me they weren't going to let me see you."

"Where is Sara?" Jen asked.

"Waiting for me at the stadium," I said. "She's pissed at me too, so you two might actually agree on something."

"You left her by herself?"

"We need to go," I said.

"What's going to happen to Travis and the others? How will they ever be able to get out now that you've got the attention of all the local monsters? They'll surround this place and starve them out."

I looked around to see if there was any way the people in the building could escape.

"Get in the damn truck, and I'll take care of them."

I ran over to the buses, looking for one with keys. I found one and started it up. The big diesel engine rattled to life. I shifted into gear, then made a very wide turn in the parking lot to get the rear of the vehicle pointed at the building. Then I backed it through the gate and past the diesel pump. I got the side door of the bus as close as I could to the back door of the garage.

Unfortunately, the bus blocked the entrance to their generator building, but it was the best I could do, given the time constraints. I got out of the bus and squeezed myself through the narrow space between it and the building, then ran back out to the moving van.

Jen was still standing on her good leg, leaning against the van.

"Is that okay?" I said.

"Why didn't you pull it into the garage?" she said. "Wouldn't that have been better?"

"Sure," I said. "Maybe they'll be smart enough to do that for themselves."

"We should take one of the buses."

"No," I said. "All the stuff Sara and I collected today is in here."

"What kind of stuff is it?"

"Tractor Supply," I said. "Animal feed, tools, boots—stuff like that."

"Can we find it somewhere else?"

"There are other farm supply stores, but we already have this stuff."

"Let's take that short bus."

"Son of a bitch!" I yelled.

I opened the door and killed the engine, then went over to the short bus, climbed in and cranked it. She hobbled over, and I let her. She hopped up the steps into the bus rather pathetically, but I pretended not to notice. As soon as she was seated, I pulled away toward the stadium.

It was getting late. I really hated the short winter days. It wasn't that the infected were more active during the night; I didn't know if they were or not. I just preferred to see them from a distance. I didn't want to only be the space of a flashlight beam or headlight beam away from them before I knew they were there. Since the power had gone out, it got dark at night—really dark. This was a dark to which we were unaccustomed. There were no longer streetlights or security lights. The glow over nearby towns was gone. If it was cloudy or moonless, it was downright scary.

We encountered our first arrivals on our way to the stadium. They stopped and followed us instead of continuing to the maintenance building. I passed the school and the teenagers. When I got to the stadium, Sara came out. I kept the bus moving until she was close enough to get in. She didn't speak to me when she climbed in; she just went back and found a seat.

"How are you feeling, Jen?"

"I've been better," she said.

"We'll go to the Somervilles' tomorrow, Sara," I said, looking in the big rearview mirror at the two of them. "It's getting too dark now."

Sara nodded.

The closer we got to the road, the more of them we saw. Once I pulled out on the highway, I started honking the horn to get them to follow me, and they did. When I thought they were far enough from the school grounds, I sped away.

CHAPTER 40

When we pulled into the drive of the Lassiter Stables, the headlights shone on three horses standing near the house. They had found their way out and around the perimeter fence, then back up the driveway. I didn't know if they would do any damage, except to my own conscience as I watched them wither away from neglect.

I carried Jen into the house and put her on the couch. I moved Sara's blankets and thought about the night before. That was going to be a topic to avoid.

"Can I get you anything?" I asked.

"No," she replied.

"Let me get the fire going, and I'll work on dinner."

"Do we still have those pizzas?" she asked.

"Yes," Sara said. "We saved them for when you came back. Do you think we can cook them in the fireplace or what?"

I hadn't thought of that. We didn't really have an oven, only a gas stovetop.

"I don't know how to cook them," I said. "It's going to take a while for the fire to burn down enough to cook on it."

"I'll figure it out," Sara said. "You take care of her."

She took the flashlight and went outside to get the food.

I started poking in the embers and ash.

"I know you don't want to hear this," Jen said, "but I think you shouldn't have done what you did today. It was really stupid."

"Yeah, I don't want to hear it."

"You could have gotten yourself killed, or me or Sara killed, or even one of the others killed."

"I did," I said.

"I don't understand."

"I shot the man on the roof," I said. "The one with the automatic weapon."

"I was in the office the whole time, so I ..."

"I shot him," I said. "He's probably dead. So I guess if I wasn't a murderer before, then I am now."

"It was self-defense," she said.

"No," I said. "Him shooting at me was self-defense. What I did ... I don't know; maybe it was."

"Are you okay?"

"Yeah," I said. "But I'm not okay with being okay with it."

"What about the other men? When Travis wheeled me out, they were all gone."

"I don't know," I said. "I tried to kill them too. I think I ran them over with the truck when I crashed into the fence."

She stared at me, and it made me uncomfortable. I turned back to the fireplace.

"You did all that just to see me?" she said.

"I guess so."

Sara came back into the house, carrying the pizzas and desserts, and she took them to the kitchen.

"So how did it go last night?" Jen whispered.

"What do you mean?"

"Well, you and Sara ... alone ... you know."

"It went fine," I said, putting kindling on the glowing embers.

"I'm sure it did."

I looked over my shoulder at her.

"How did things go with you and the handsome doctor?"

Jen laughed. "He is that and then some, but he ain't what I'm looking for. Maybe before, but not now."

I blew on the embers until they ignited.

"And what are you looking for? I thought handsome doctors were the ultimate prize."

"Well, yeah, but that's so last week." She laughed at her own joke.

"So what's trendy in men now?" I asked, adding wood to the fire.

"You gotta know how to build a fire, for one thing. All I ever saw Travis do was adjust the damn thermostat. Another fashionable thing in men this week is the willingness and ability to dispatch zombies."

"Dispatch?"

"And it would be good if he knew how to drive a stick shift too, but I'll let that one slide. The most important thing, though, is that he'll stand up to assholes and run them over with his truck. Travis never stood up to Nathan. Not once. I appreciate that he was there to fix me up, but he ain't earned my respect yet."

I sat in the chair across from the couch.

"So tell me," Jen said. "Did you and Sara cuddle? Share body heat to keep warm?"

"You'd think a bullet in your leg would have slowed you down some."

She pulled a small plastic bag from the pocket of her coat and held it up to show me. It contained pill bottles.

"Travis gave me some drugs before he brought me out. I've got some pain meds and antibiotics. I don't feel anything. I think you're avoiding my question."

"Yes," I said. "There was lots of nudity. Lots of naked nudity and body heat."

She smiled and threw a pillow at me, not knowing I'd just told her the truth—not that it mattered.

"I'm going to see how she's doing with the pizzas. Are you sure I can't get you anything?"

"Any wine left?"

"Yes, but not for you. You're on pain meds."

I went into the kitchen. Sara was using a serrated steak knife to saw the thawed pizzas into small sections so she could fit them in a pan to cook them on the stovetop.

"I wonder if there is a store around that has wood ovens," Sara said. "I'm really going to miss bread. Eventually, all the bread in Clayfield is going to get stale or moldy. We'll have to bake our own."

"I think one of those magazines I brought has plans for building a wood oven. Listen, I'm sorry for earlier, back at the school. I kind of lost my head for a second."

"Don't worry about it. I hope it doesn't keep us from seeing the doctor, though."

I got a bottle of water for Jen and took it back to her.

"Sara is leaving tomorrow," I said softly. "She's going to live with the Somervilles."

"Why?" Jen asked. "What changed her mind?"

"We talked last night, and she doesn't feel comfortable here."

"Well, if that's what she wants."

"I know this is what you want, but there will be a lot to do around here, and I don't know if I can do it all by myself."

"What am I?"

"Injured," I said. "Did the doctor tell you how long it would take the leg to heal?"

"He said the fracture might take as long as six weeks."

"That's a long time, Jen."

"I'll be getting around before then, but ... I know. I'm sorry to be a burden."

"Don't start that," I said. "It's probably too late, but maybe you could go easy on her, okay?"

* * *

We didn't stay up very late that night. We ate our pizza and tried not to discuss heavy topics. Mostly, we talked about movies we had wanted to see but never got to. Jen's pain medication was hitting her hard. She kept nodding during the meal, and she fell asleep with her plate in her lap.

Sara wanted to turn in early too. There's not a whole lot to do after dark when there is no one to talk to. My usual routine of staying up until midnight and watching TV or working on my computer was over. I tried to read by the firelight, but that was a strain on my eyes.

The next morning, we were all up before sunrise. Jen needed help getting to the bathroom. I helped her to the door and went into the kitchen to start some hot water for coffee. Jen called from the bathroom a couple of minutes later. When I knocked, she asked me to get Sara.

I went back to the kitchen, and I could hear them talking, but I couldn't make out what they were saying. Sara went upstairs, where we'd taken all of the non-food Wal-Mart supplies. She returned with a bag and headed for the bathroom.

"Is she okay?" I said.

"Yeah. Just woman stuff, and she needs to change the dressing on her leg. Would it be okay if she used that water you're heating?"

I gave it to her and started another pot. We were down to our last gallon of water. I would need to go fill bottles again. The yellow brick house was nearby and still had water in the cistern, and we'd still had luck getting water from the Clayfield city water supply. Eventually, that would all quit, and I'd have to find another source. We were getting low on alcohol too. We had just a little of the Southern Comfort and one bottle of wine left.

I could collect these things on my own, but it would be better if I had help. I was debating whether I should ask Sara to assist me. I knew she would, but I also knew she was ready to go, and I didn't want to impose.

I would need to go check on the chickens too. It had been a couple of days. They would need to come back with me soon. I didn't want to have to go back and forth. They were only a couple of miles away, but they would be neglected if they weren't there with me.

When the water was hot, I poured it through the filter pod of the automatic coffee maker, watched it slowly trickle through the grounds, and then poured some more until the carafe was full. I fixed myself a cup and went into the living room to make out my to-do list by the light of the fire. I'm a big believer in lists, and there's something sort of therapeutic about it now. It makes me feel "normal."

It would take me a while, and it might be a little more dangerous, but I could do everything on my list by myself. I wouldn't ask Sara to help. As soon as it was light enough, I would drive her to the Somervilles'.

I heard some noise in the kitchen, then Sara came in with her own cup of coffee.

"She'll holler when she's ready to come out," she said.

"I thought we could leave as soon as the sun is up," I said. "That'll give me time to get some things done today. I don't want to leave Jen alone any more than I have to."

"I can help."

"No," I said. "I've kept you long enough. You're still welcome to stay, but if you do want to leave, then let's go ahead and do it."

We got Jen comfortable on the couch. All around her, within arm's reach, were a loaded 20-gauge shotgun, a loaded .22 rifle, an additional box of ammo for each, the rest of the water, some snacks, and a stack of magazines and books. I found a set of golf clubs in one of the closets and gave her one to use as a cane.

I added crutches to my list of things to get.

Sara and I took one of the other pickup trucks that had been parked near the barn. The three horses were still there in the yard, but they were the only ones to find their way back. I hoped they would be smart enough to leave on their own; otherwise I'd have to lead them away and block the drive to prevent them from coming back.

We didn't have much to say on the way to the Somervilles'. I took a chance and headed into town, near the court square. It was the shortest route, and I was curious about how things looked there since the fire.

There were still clusters of people in town, though most had dispersed. The corner near the drug store and City Hall was clogged with burned bodies—some of them still walking around. The drug store was just a blackened brick shell, but no other buildings had burned.

* * *

On the street before we got to Depot Street, we noticed that the houses were marked. A big white or orange "X" had been spray painted on the front of every house, most on the front door. I'd seen something similar before on the news after hurricanes and earthquakes. Rescue personnel did that so they'd know which houses had been searched for survivors. The houses on Depot Street were marked the same way.

"What does it mean?" Sara said.

"I'm not sure," I said. "Maybe the group out at the high school did it."

"Do you think maybe there is still a government, and they're in town?"

"I don't know."

I doubted it.

It bothered me. It could just be a mark used by another group of looters so they wouldn't have to raid a house twice. It could be a tag that claimed a house to be looted later. Maybe it was Mr. Somerville, and he'd been going door to door like he'd talked about doing.

I pulled up in front of the Somervilles' home. A big white "X" was painted on the garage door.

"This is it," I said. "This is Mr. Somerville's house."

"Does this mean he and his wife are gone?" Sara asked.

"Let's go see, but we need to be careful. They're both armed."

We climbed out of the truck and walked into the small front yard.

"Hello!" I said as loud as I dared. "Somervilles!"

We waited to give them time.

"I'm going to the door. Keep watch here and make sure no one is coming."

I went to the door and knocked. I waited. I knocked again. I tried the knob, and the door opened.

Something violent had happened in the house. Some of the furniture was turned over. There were holes in the walls, some of which might have been caused by a shotgun. Others looked like something had rammed through the drywall. I didn't see any blood.

"Nicholas? Judy?"

I went into every room. The living room was the worst, but the rest of the house had damage too. The kitchen cabinets were all open and empty of food.

I went back outside.

"The house is trashed," I said. "Looks like looters. The food is all gone."

"Were they hurt?"

"I don't know," I said. "Let's drive around and see how many houses are marked. If we find an end to the spray paint, we might find the looters."

"Do we want to find them?" Sara said.

"No," I said, "but they should know about the Somervilles."

* * *

Every house on Depot Street was marked, as were all of the houses on West Ridgeway and North 16th Street. We found two houses marked on North 15th, where it connected to West Ridgeway. We didn't see anyone out, but it was still early. My own house was just two blocks away, so I headed over there to clear out anything I might want. They would hit my street eventually too.

Sara opened the garage door to my house, and I backed the truck in. We'd be able to load it without being bothered.

It felt like I hadn't been there in years; it was like I was in a stranger's home. I went to the sink and turned on the faucet. There was still water.

"We can fill the jugs here," I said. "There's a bottle of bourbon in the pantry too. Don't let me forget that."

"I see you got that new game system," she said, standing in front of my entertainment center.

"Yeah," I said. "I guess I should have spent that money on canned goods and a Swiss army knife."

"It doesn't look like a woman has lived here in a while," Sara said.

"A woman has never lived here," I said. "At least not with me. Hence the game system. I could never have had one before; my wife would have nagged the hell out of me."

"I would never have done that to you."

"Yeah, well ..."

"So you've been living alone. Were you taking advantage of being divorced and playing the field?"

I laughed, "If I were a player, you ... well, never mind."

She smiled and started filling water jugs.

I went into my bedroom. There were still clothes in my closet. I grabbed a few more things and put them on the bed. I heard a low noise from outside.

"Look out the window!" Sara said from the kitchen.

I peeked through the curtains. A UPS truck drove by very slowly. The back door was open, and there were two armed men standing in the opening. I thought I could make out more inside.

I turned, and Sara was standing in the doorway.

"No," she said. "Please let them go."

"What?"

"I know you want to talk to them about the Somervilles, but let them go. They don't know we're here. Let's just go back to the stables. I'll stay with you and Jen. I won't be any trouble."

"You're not any trouble, Sara."

"Those people out there could be like those men at Lowe's. They could be bad people, and I don't want them to know we're here."

"Okay," I said. "It's okay. But what about the Somervilles?"

"Maybe they got away and went to Blaine's house."

"All right," I said. "We'll sneak away."

She came into the room and hugged me.

"Thank you," she said. "They scare me more than the sick people."

"Sure," I said.

She looked up at me. I thought she was going to kiss me again.

"I'll finish the water," she said. "See if you can find more containers."

She left me and went back into the kitchen. She'd never been any trouble, yet she was a world of trouble.

* * *

When we were sure the men were gone, we left and headed south to Broadway. We'd already accomplished two things on the list—water and alcohol—and it was only 8:00 a.m.

"I want to drive out toward Belfast," I said. "Jen's friend Brian—the one with the Porsche—lives out there."

* * *

We could see Brian's wind turbine from a few miles away. It was turning slowly. When we got close enough to see the house, I stopped the truck. The house had been burned. It wasn't smoking, so it must have burned days before—probably before or during all the rain. There were three trucks, a four-wheeler and a motorcycle out front. A van was parked crosswise so as to block the entrance to the driveway.

I put the truck in reverse and got away from there.

If the house was burned and the men at Lowe's had Brian's Porsche, there would be no good up there. They were probably still going to try to use the wind turbine somehow. I knew I would have if I could.

"Are we going back to the stables now?" Sara asked.

"No," I said. "We'll go ahead and collect the food and other supplies we didn't get the other day. We'll just do our shopping out away from town so we won't run into these people."

"So we're going to go looting too?"

"You have a lot to learn, my dear," I said. "When we do it, it's called scavenging."

CHAPTER 41

So long as we needed our water jugs filled every few days, we would need to leave the house, and if we left the house, we increased our chances of getting into some sort of trouble. I think we were coming around to Jen's line of thinking; we needed to hunker down for a while. I was going to have to find us another source of water.

Before heading completely away from town, I decided to go to Founder's Farm and Hardware. They would have chicken feed and tools, just like Tractor Supply. I knew they catered to the local Amish community too, so they might have a wood cook stove. Then it hit me.

"Why didn't we think of that before?" I said aloud.

"What?" Sara asked.

"We should relocate to one of the Amish farms. They're already set up to function without electricity. They'll have wood cook stoves and heaters. They'll have hand-pumped wells. It would be perfect."

"But they're out past Belfast," she said. "And I would think other people would have the same idea."

"We didn't," I said.

"You just did," she replied. "If they haven't thought of it yet, they will as soon as their generators and windmills quit working."

"You're probably right," I said. "But if we can't find a wood cook stove at Founder's, then we should drive out there and take a stove from the Amish."

"We should take an Amish," Sara said.

I laughed, but it wasn't a bad idea. If we found an Amish survivor, he or she could be helpful by teaching us about living without modern conveniences.

"Yes," I said. "Let's put an Amish on that supply list."

Founder's Farm and Hardware had been in Clayfield for decades. It was off on a side road, away from the big chains. It didn't get as much traffic as the other stores, and it had been overlooked by looters. We were able to get the same supplies we'd gotten at Tractor Supply, just more of them. They also had three 40-pound bags of oats. We took it for the horses, but I figured that, as with the corn, we could eat it if we had to.

We were going to need a truck to haul it all in. We set everything we wanted near the door, and then we went out to the pickup so we could drive around and find a bigger truck.

To the side of the building, where they kept fence posts, landscaping timbers, concrete blocks and other things that didn't need to be indoors, were several large plastic tanks. I didn't know what their purpose was—maybe to hold large quantities of herbicides or pesticides for farmers to spray on their fields. Regardless of their intended purpose, they would make great cisterns. They were new, so they hadn't been tainted with toxins. They even had attachments at the bottoms for hoses or spigots.

I was never good at those math problems where we had to find volume, but these tanks were a little over four feet tall, and their diameter was around ten feet. They would probably hold several hundred gallons.

"We're getting one of those too," I said. "We'll need a flatbed truck or a trailer."

"How are we going to lift it?" Sara asked.

"We'll worry about that after we find the truck."

* * *

I'd seen a flatbed delivery truck parked behind Lowe's, but I didn't want to go back over there if I didn't have to. It would probably have a little forklift with it so the delivery driver could unload building materials. That would be helpful too. It would have really been helpful if I'd followed the masked woman's advice and read up on how to drive a forklift.

Instead, I drove away from town on Havana Road. We traveled five or six miles before we found what we were looking for. It was an old hay truck parked between a barn and a silo. It was painted powder blue, and it was eaten up with rust.

"It probably won't even run," I said. "It must be fifty years old."

"It'll run," Sara said. "They knew how to make them fifty years ago."

There was a ranch-style house on the same property.

"While we're here, let's see what they have inside," I said.

The doors were locked. We searched for a spare key, but never found one. We wound up breaking a dining-room window. I lifted Sara in, and then she opened the door for me.

It was a good score. The family must have just gone to the grocery before the outbreak, because they had enough food to last us for at least two weeks. There was a gun case too. We found two .22 rifles, a 12-gauge shotgun, a .30-30 and—my favorite—an AR-15.

"Cool," I said, taking it out of the gun cabinet.

"Badass," Sara said. "Let me hold it."

I handed it to her.

"How do I look?" she asked, posing with the weapon.

"Like you're holding my gun," I said.

"I don't know," she said. "I seem to remember something about possession being nine-tenths of the law."

"What law?" I said.

"Well," she said, "I guess as long as I hold this, I am the law."

I grinned. "Yes, ma'am."

I knelt in front of the cabinet and opened the drawer at the bottom. Half of it was full of ammunition, and the other half held two handguns—a Glock 9 mm and a .45 revolver, both with holsters.

"Thank God for gun owners," I said, strapping the .45 to my hip.

There were two gun-cleaning kits and a very large, very sharp fixed-blade knife in the cabinet too. We took it all.

I still hadn't had a real lesson in the use of semiautomatic weapons, but I'd done some reading during our down time when it was raining. Jen would be able to show me how to use the Glock and the AR-15.

"Let's check the garage for gas and kerosene, and then let's go get the stuff at Founder's."

* * *

We loaded everything in the pickup truck. I had to drive it while Sara drove the hay truck. The hay truck had a manual transmission. That was another thing I needed to learn how to do. Sara kept telling me how easy it was, so I hopped in. I drove for about a quarter of a mile, grinding the gears. Then the engine stalled. Red-faced, I got out and told Sara to take over.

She didn't say anything right then, but I could tell she was getting a big kick out of it. I led the way to Founder's, then got out so I could direct her as she backed in. She brought the truck up close to a tank and climbed out.

"How do we get it in the truck?" she said.

"We can lift up one side, then back the truck under it and then slide it the rest of the way."

"How do we lift the side?"

"We'll use those fence posts as levers."

"Okay," she said, but she didn't sound convinced.

"Archimedes said he could move the whole world with a lever," I said.

"Awesome. You should go on Jeopardy."

"Just get a damn post."

* * *

We wedged some of the smaller metal posts under the tank. We each lifted one and put a block under it so the tank was angled up off the ground. Then we got some of the longer, thicker posts and put them under the tank, raising them high enough to prop them on the back of the truck, forming a ramp.

Next I went back in the store and got a big spool of rope. I tied one end to the tank, and then I ran the rope over the truck, around a light pole, then back to the truck. Finally, I tied it to the front bumper.

"Okay," I said. "Now all you've got to do is back up. The truck should pull it up."

"You're way smarter than Archimedes," she said. "And he probably couldn't drive a stick either."

I grinned. "Shut up."

She backed the truck slowly, and the big tank slid right up onto the bed. We used the rope to secure it. Then we got the rest of the stuff loaded onto both trucks, including some attachments for the tank, some hose and a couple of plastic barrels to use to catch rain.

It was around one in the afternoon by this time.

"I think we can head back to the stables now," I said. "We're going to have a lot of work to do over the next few days getting set up, but it'll be worth it."

"How will we fill the tank?" she said.

"We have access to a generator," I said. "It should still be over by the museum. I have instructions on how to hardwire it into a well. We can pump out enough water to fill it, and then shut it down."

"We'll have to come back for the generator, then."

"Yeah," I said. "One more trip, but we can wait a few days. We should stop by Charlie's on the way back and get his kerosene. We also need to get the chickens from Blaine's house. You go ahead and go out to the stables, and I'll go to Charlie's and Blaine's."

"You sure? I don't like the idea of being alone."

"You'll be okay. Just don't stop for anybody, and don't lead anybody back to us."

CHAPTER 42

I followed Sara as far as Charlie's house, and then she proceeded to the stables. Charlie had not returned, and I suspected that he never would. I took the fuel, food and toilet paper he'd left behind, then headed over to Blaine's place.

I noticed the smoke before I got there, but what I was seeing didn't sink in right away. There was smoke coming out of the chimney of the workshop behind the house. There was a beat-up little hatchback parked in the driveway.

I would rather have seen ten infected people standing in the yard. At least with them, I'd know what I was up against.

I parked the pickup and got out, my hand on the butt of the .45. I expected someone to come out to greet me—or shoot at me—but no one did.

I knocked, but no one answered, so I went in.

Brian Davies was lying on one of the mattresses on the floor. When I opened the door, he lifted the shotgun Jen and I had left with him. He looked like hell—a far cry from the well-groomed, nicely dressed man I'd seen several days before.

Next to the wood stove was a pile of sticks and broken pieces of Blaine's dining room furniture.

"Brian?" I said.

"Thank God it's you."

"Are you okay? We saw your car and ..."

"No, I'm not okay," he said. "Where the hell have you been? I've been here since yesterday. I thought you two were dead. Where's Jen?"

"Jen is ... Jen is fine. She's at the other place."

"You didn't tell me there was another place."

"Jen said she left you a note," I said.

"I didn't see a note."

"What happened?"

"I never did hear from Henry," he said.

"I'm sorry," I said, "but what happened to you?"

"A couple of days after you left, these two men came to my house. They seemed friendly at first, and asked if I could spare some drinking water. I gave them some. They asked me about the turbine, and we talked about that for a while.

"The next day, they came back. They brought others. There were nine of them in all. There were six men, two women, and a little boy. They said they were moving in, since I had electricity. They said they were doing it whether I liked it or not. I didn't like how they were acting about it, but like I told you and Jen, I was glad to see others, and I welcomed them.

"They weren't too happy about the basement, and they started talking about what they were going to do about it and the changes they were going to make. I didn't like that either. It was my house, after all, and I should be the king of that castle. We were butting heads by the end of the day."

"We went to check on you this morning," I said. "There were a lot of vehicles there."

"Really? How did it look?"

"The house had been burned," I said.

He shook his head.

"I knew they would do that. They kept saying they needed to do that. God ... my library, my bonsai trees, the paintings ... I hope they at least saved some things. Some of those trees were several decades old. It would be a shame for them to have been destroyed like that."

"Where did they plan to live?"

"They were talking about building a tall fence and several new houses—like a compound. Sounded like a lot of trouble to me just to have electricity. But they were morons, so whatcha gonna do?

"One of the women had a big problem with me personally. She told me the whole reason the plague came was to purge away people like me.

"They put me out of my own house. They gave me a plastic Wal-Mart sack with a bottle of water, a peanut-butter sandwich, a few matches and a single shotgun shell. They let me take my shotgun, but wouldn't let me load it until I was away from the house. They gave me a piece-of-shit car to drive. I couldn't keep it running; it kept sputtering.

"I wound up spending the night in the car and using my only shotgun shell to keep from being zombie food. Anyway, I'm here now."

"I'm sorry," I said.

"I'm hungry. All I've had to eat since I got here were two eggs I found in the chicken coop. I didn't have anything to cook them in, so I just cooked them directly on the stove, and then scraped them off. It smelled really bad in here for a while. I would have had a chicken, but I couldn't bring myself to kill one."

"I have food in the truck. Do you want to eat now or go over to the other place?"

"Eat."

I went out to look for some things that didn't require cooking. I brought him back some Vienna sausages, a sleeve of Saltines and a juice box. He didn't complain.

While he was eating, I took the large plastic dog carrier Sara and I had gotten from Founder's Farm and Hardware and went out to catch the chickens. It wasn't that easy. I finally got them herded into the coop. Then I got in with them and shut the door. It was easier to corner them that way, but also more difficult to dodge them when they decided to escape by "flying." They made a big fuss over it, but I finally got all of them in the carrier.

When I came back into the shop, Brian was finished with his meal.

"Did you kill a chicken or something?"

"No," I said. "I'm moving them to the other place."

"I take it the other place is better than this?"

"Much better," I said. "But not as nice as your place."

"Does the offer still stand for me to live with you and Jen?"

"Yeah," I said. "Jen will be thrilled. We have a young woman named Sara living with us too. She was supposed to move out today, but that didn't work out."

"I had decided to leave today," he said. "The only reason I stayed was because I hoped you would be back. I figured since the chickens were still alive, someone must have been feeding them, but when you didn't come ..."

"We've been busy," I said. "Jen was shot in the leg."

"What?"

"Yeah," I said. "She can tell you all about it later. But I'm curious about that bite you got on your ankle. How is it healing up?"

"It's not," he said. "I'm having a hard time getting around."

His leg looked bad. It was swollen and red, and where the teeth had gotten through, it was oozing pus.

"I know where there's a doctor," I said, "but they probably won't let me in to see him; you'd have to go there alone."

"I think it'll get better. I just have to get some rest."

"Jen got bitten too, and the doctor had to put her on antibiotics."

"Where is this doctor?"

"He's out at Grace County High School with some others."

"Are there a lot of others?" he asked.

"Some," I said, "but they tried to kidnap Jen, so I ..."

"Well forget that shit," he said. "You'll just have to go out and find me some antibiotics."

"I have some amoxicillin, but I don't know if that's the right kind, and I don't know the dosage."

"What kind is Jen using?"

"I don't know," I said.

"Help me up," he said. "I can't walk very well."

The infected were very active that day. I attributed it to the weather. It had warmed up some outside that day, and the sun was shining. It was breezy, but it must have been in the upper 50s or low 60s—one of those late February heat waves.

We passed several individuals on our way out to the Lassiter house. Some were in the road, but most were in the fields. They were all headed in the same direction that we were, and I presumed there must have been a noise drawing them.

When I came in with Brian, Sara was sitting in the living room, but Jen wasn't there.

"She's in the bathroom," she said.

She looked at Brian.

"This is Brian Davies," I said. "We drove out to his house this morning. You know—the Porsche."

"I know you," she said. "You're that Michael Jackson guy."

"See?" Brian said to me. "I'm famous."

"My church helped with that benefit you did last year. My name is Sara."

"Very nice to meet you again," Brian said. "If you will excuse me, I need to sit. My ankle is in bad shape."

"They keep talking about you, but I never realized you were the same person," Sara said.

Jen hobbled in, and her face lit up.

"Holy shit!" she said. "We thought something bad happened to you!"

Brian smiled.

"I happened to something bad."

"Okay," I said. "You two cripples catch up. Sara and I are going to unload the truck. Jen, show Brian your antibiotics. His ankle isn't healing, and I might need to get some more."

"Let me see it," Jen said.

He pulled up his pant leg and peeled away the bandage.

"Ewww. You need to see Travis."

"The doctor? But I thought he tried to kidnap you."

"No," she said, "not Travis. He could have kidnapped me, and I wouldn't have minded, if you know what I mean."

Brian looked up at me and grinned.

"What about it?" he said. "Do you know what she means?"

"I haven't a clue," I said.

"Don't you think he needs a doctor?" Jen said.

"Sure, but he'll have to drive himself. They'd never let me get close to that place again. What kind of medicine did he give you?"

Jen read the bottle.

"Amoxicillin," she said. "That's what you got from Wal-Mart wasn't it?"

"Then it's settled," Brian said. "I'll take the stuff from Wal-Mart. If Dr. Travis is going to kidnap me, I want to be in the best of health."

* * *

Sara and I unloaded the trucks while Jen and Brian told each other about their week. We put the chickens in the stall next to the goat. I threw some food out for them while Sara got them water.

"I still don't know if I'm going to like this farm living," she said.

"Eventually everyone will have to live like this," I said. "It's good that we're able to get a head start. Some of the people are going to realize next winter, or maybe the winter after that, that the food supply is dwindling. We're fortunate to be where we are and have these resources."

"When do we need to plant the garden?" she said.

"Now, actually," I said. "Really, you want to wait until after the last frost, but we can go ahead and start things indoors right now. I picked up my seeds that were left over from last year when we were at my house. We'll need to find more, but they'll get us started. Blaine has some potting soil in one of his sheds. We can go get that too."

"I feel kind of useless," she said. "I don't know anything about any of this. I was just a student who worked in a church. I don't have any skills."

"I'm just a museum curator," I said. "Brian was just a blogger. Jen was ... hmmm ... I don't know what Jen was. Did she ever mention it?"

"Wow," Sara said. "You don't know what she did for a living?"

"No," I said. "Do you?"

"No, but I'm not the one in love with her."

"Well, I don't know if I'd go that far. I like her, but …"

"What are you? In the ninth grade?"

"My point is," I said, "that none of us were really ready for this. We're all learning, and we'll all find our place."

"Do you just keep me around so you'll have someone to help you unload trucks? Is that my place?"

"No," I said.

"It's okay," she said. "I know what my place would be if I were somewhere else. I like you …"

"We don't have to talk about this."

"But I don't want that to be my place. If I'm going to stay here, I need to be more than a third wheel. I need to learn a skill."

"We all need to learn some skills."

We walked out of the barn. Behind the house, on the other side of the fence, were three women. Their clothes were torn and muddy, and they were looking for a way to cross over to us. A man came stumbling up behind them. It was the first man Jen had shot—the one in the blue coveralls, who had been eating the dog. He snarled at us and rushed toward the fence.

CHAPTER 43

The man hit the fence and fell backward. Some of them could be fast when they wanted to be, but they weren't that bright. The wind shifted, and I got a whiff of the group or of someone in the group. It was the smell of decay, of a dead body.

Could it be possible that some of these people were more than just people with brain damage who were able to survive things that would kill a healthy person? Could it be that they were the actual undead as depicted in movies? Jen and the others had accepted that as a given, but I hadn't been willing to believe in animated corpses.

Sara backed up against me.

"Have we been making too much noise?" she said.

"No more than before," I said.

"What do we do?" she said.

"We might not need to do anything," I said. "They might not be able to get to this side of the fence."

"Do you think they'll hurt the horses?"

"I don't know. Let's get the food into the house. We'll keep an eye on them."

We pulled the pickup away from the barn and parked it next to the front porch. When we got out, we saw two more figures walking down the road.

"We've never seen this many out here before," she said. "What is attracting them?"

"I think it might be the warmer weather," I said.

"Look," Sara said, pointing to the road on the other side of the driveway. "There's another one."

"We need to block the driveway," I said. "We should have picked up a gate while we were at Founder's. I'm going to pull the school bus down there, but I don't think it will be long enough to completely block the entrance. You'll need to follow me down in the hay truck."

By the time I got down there with the little school bus, the three from the road had made it into the driveway, but they weren't very far in. I hit one of them as I cut the vehicle around. Sara was right behind and parked the hay truck on the other side. We faced each other at an angle like the head of an arrow.

Sara climbed out with a rifle in her hand. I got out too, and we met in the middle.

"This isn't going to keep them out," I said. "We'll need to do something else."

"Too bad we got rid of the horse trailer," she said. "That would have made a great gate."

I looked down the road in both directions. More were coming. They were in the field across the road too.

"What the hell is going on?"

"Should we start shooting them?"

"No," I said. "That'll just make it worse. Let's get back to the house. Pack some things to go. We might have to leave soon."

We both ran back up the driveway. Jen and Brian were on the front porch.

"Get inside, and get your things!" I yelled. "We need to be ready to go!"

They both limped into the house.

It didn't make any sense. We'd been careful not to make any loud noises. I didn't understand what was drawing them to us. All this time, it had seemed to be sound, but now it was evident that sound wasn't the only thing that got their attention. There had been a steady breeze all day; maybe it was the smoke from the fireplace.

The bus would be our best option at escape. The pickup would need to come too; it was already loaded from today's scavenging. We could all fit in the pickup. It wouldn't be comfortable, but we could fit.

Sara ran up on the porch, and I ran to the barns. I wanted to shut the doors, both to keep them from using the barns as an avenue through the barrier and to protect the goat and chickens.

There was a larger group at the fence by that time, and they were pressing against the railing. There were eight, but I could see three more coming in from the back field. They managed to cross the fence back there, and they would be able to cross here, too, when they got enough weight on the rails.

I shut the barn doors and headed back to the house just as the mob crushed through the fence. The first few fell into the yard, and the ones behind them crawled over them to get to me. I was afraid some of the faster ones would intercept me before I could get to the house.

I pulled the .45 from its holster, but before I could shoot it, I heard a shot from ahead of me. Brian was standing in the back door with a shotgun. When I got into the doorway with him, I turned to look behind me. Only two of them even stood a chance at catching me, and even they weren't fast enough. We could always outrun them. The rest of the creatures were just walking or stumbling or dragging their feet.

"Why are they here?" he asked. "Why so many?"

"I don't know," I said. "Maybe it's the smoke. We need to leave."

I holstered my handgun and went to find Jen. Sara was in the kitchen, putting food and water into cardboard boxes. Jen was standing in the front window, looking out.

"They're coming up the driveway," she said. "Five of them. There are more on the road."

"We're leaving, Jen. Let me help you outside."

She kept standing there.

"Come on, Jen. The truck is out by the front porch. Sara, are you ready to go? Everybody in the truck!"

I swept Jen up, and she looked at me with a blank expression.

"I don't want to leave anymore," she said.

Sara, Brian and I all had our hands full as we ran out on the porch. Sara and Brian put their boxes in the back of the truck and climbed inside. I put Jen in the passenger side and shut the door. I started around, but I was met by a grotesque creature. Its left eye hung out of its socket, and its bottom lip was completely missing, down to its chin. I pulled the .45 and blew its head open. Another came up behind me. They were everywhere. I backed away, firing. They started closing in. My only recourse was to run back into the house. They surrounded the truck. Sara, Brian and Jen were all trapped inside it, and I had the keys.

The windows on the truck began to fog up. I could see the fear on their faces as they realized the keys were not in there with them. Jen looked out at me. She mouthed the word "keys."

I pulled them from my pocket and showed them to her. I would need to do something quickly. These things were only trickling in, but the trickle was steady, and it would reach a point very soon where there would be no way to do anything.

Most of the guns were in the truck—the back of the truck. That included the AR-15. I had the .45 on me with two or three rounds left. The guns we'd left with Jen were still by the couch, and that .410 shotgun was still upstairs.

Come on! Quickly!

I grabbed the 12-gauge from beside the couch and the box of shells for it and ran back outside. I had no plan except to blow the hell out of everything until I got to the pickup.

The creatures were now three deep all around the truck. The trio inside looked worried but calm.

I lifted the shotgun to my shoulder.

Make 'em count. Don't think about it.

I did my best to stay calm. I put the bead on heads only.

Head shot. Pump out the empty shell. Head shot. Pump. Head shot. Pump. Reload.

I wasn't able to advance at all, and I couldn't get the weapon fully loaded. I managed to get two rounds into the gun before I was forced to use it again. The first one was off; it caught the woman in the chest just before she got to me. The second shot took off a man's face. No time to reload. I pulled the .45, fired wild, and went back into the house.

"Shit!"

I reloaded the shotgun and emerged again.

Head shot. Pump.

I jumped off the porch and ran out into the yard. Five of them came at me, but most of the crowd stayed with the truck.

Head shot. Pump.

I ran to the fence that surrounded the front pasture. Once on the other side, I reloaded. They weren't smart enough to climb over, the way I had. I didn't have enough rounds to get them all, and if I stayed there and shot them, more would come in to take their places.

I ran through the pasture, toward the road. I reached the partition fence, climbed it and kept running. I stopped near the road behind the hay truck, took out two of the monsters in the driveway, then climbed the fence to the driveway side. I headed straight for the bus.

A man came around the back of the bus. He was one of the fast ones, and he took me by surprise. I stopped when I saw him, and my feet slid in the gravel. I fell on my butt and elbow. Before I could recover, he was over me and coming down. I tried to roll, but I didn't make it in time. His mouth was right at my ear; his gurgling, clicking breath was hot. He stank, but not like death. I got my right forearm against his throat and held him away. His whole body was hot.

One of the three in the pickup got on the horn when they saw I was in trouble. It didn't distract him at all. I could see more feet coming in around me. The revolver was on my right hip, and I couldn't reach it. I did my best to angle the shotgun around toward him, but it was too long. The best I could do was shoot his leg with it. So I did.

I had the shotgun up under my left armpit. I pulled it back until the barrel lifted off the ground. I prayed it was lifted enough not to get me instead. I squeezed the trigger, and his whole body jerked and rolled off of me. I scrambled to my feet as quickly as I could. The blast had nearly taken off his leg just above the knee. He was trying to stand too.

Two women were there. One was wearing a flannel shirt and a denim skirt; the other was wearing nothing at all. They came in fast too. I pulled the .45 and hit the flannel woman in the face. I took aim on the other, but the hammer clicked. I was out. I'd have to reload the shotgun too. I holstered the .45 and turned the shotgun around like a club. One hit was enough to give me time to get into the bus.

Once inside, I pulled the lever to shut the door. It squeaked and folded shut, and then the naked woman slammed herself against it. I reloaded the shotgun and climbed in the driver's seat.

The pickup was completely covered. I got some speed on the bus and swung in as close as I could, raking them away from the driver's door. I continued toward the barns and turned the bus around in the wide patch of gravel in front of the buildings. I came in close again, so close, in fact, that I took the pickup's side mirror off. I stopped and opened the bus door.

It had been my intention for the three to come into the bus's door through the truck window, but Sara rolled her window down just enough to get her hand out. She wanted the keys.

I shot a girl who had clawed up to the roof of the truck, and I handed Sara the keys. Her window went up, and I shut the door. Up the driveway, a new group was approaching.

"Where the hell are they coming from?"

The pickup started up and began to move.

In my rearview mirror, I watched another group spill into the yard from the back pasture. Several in front of the pickup went down and then under as Sara attempted to bulldoze her way through.

She was crying, and Brian kept trying to take the wheel. The truck had made it no more than its own length when it could go no farther. She tried reverse, but just like in front, the bodies fell and were caught up underneath.

The creatures were far more interested in the pickup than the bus. I was able to pull away without much trouble, and decided to try plowing them aside like I had before. Sara, Jen and Brian needed to get in the bus if we were ever going to get away.

I reversed toward the barns, and then came back, scraping away the ones on the driver's side of the pickup with the front of the bus. There were so many, and they piled up so quickly, that the bus actually tilted as it went over them. That scared me. I didn't want to do that again.

I decided to try to push the truck out. I backed up again and returned. This time, I squared up the bus with the back of the truck. I didn't hit it hard, because I didn't want to hurt Jen, Sara and Brian, but I did hit it hard enough to mash the creatures between us. I couldn't actually connect with the rear of the truck, but instead made a zombie sandwich with arms and legs and heads sticking out.

I put the gas pedal to the floor. Sara helped on her end, but we couldn't dislodge them. So then it was back to the original plan. I put it in reverse, and then pulled alongside them once again, ramping up a little on the bodies.

Shotgun loaded, I opened the door to the bus. I shot two on the hood, then motioned for Sara to roll down her window. She cracked it.

"Come on, Sara! Roll it down!" I said. "You'll have to crawl over to me!"

"I can't! They're everywhere!"

I shot another one in the face when it started up onto the truck. The creatures were making an awful noise. It reminded me of the lowing of cattle.

"I have another idea," I said, reloading. I'd gone through half a box of ammunition. "I'm going to back up again. When I do, open your door. I'll pull back in fast and just take the door off. You'll be able to step right in."

"Bullshit!" Brian yelled at me. "That will never work."

"What else, then?" I said. "We don't have many options. Both of you are injured. You might be able to outrun them, but Jen ..."

I stopped and shot another one.

"Jen would never make it! The longer we sit here, the more come in."

Sara nodded.

"Go," she said. "Come back fast."

"No!" Brian said. "That door is the only thing between us and them."

I did it anyway. I backed up.

Don't open it too soon, Sara.

I put the vehicle in drive and barreled toward them. Just before I got to the truck, the driver's door opened. One of the creatures was right there. It started in. I smeared it against the side of the truck, and then slammed on the brakes to keep from overshooting them. The door didn't come off, but it bent back against the front fender. The two vehicles were only inches away from each other.

The twisted remains of the thing that had once been a woman were between us and still struggled to get in the cab. I opened the bus door and beat it down with the butt of my shotgun.

"Kill it!" Jen yelled.

I didn't want to shoot it this close.

"It'll splatter," I said.

"Do it anyway! Fast!"

I put the gun against its head and pulled the trigger. Gore sprayed out away from the blast like a giant sneeze.

We'd all be getting drunk that night if we made it out.

I helped Sara through to the bus. I had to shoot two of the things away before Brian could come through.

"Come on, Jen!"

She was having trouble scooting across the seat. I handed the shotgun to Brian and crawled into the cab. He fired the gun, but I didn't turn to see. I grabbed Jen and trusted Brian to keep the things off me.

"Sorry," Jen said.

"We're fine," I said. "Just try to help me."

She untied the straps that held the splint on her leg. She bent it and winced.

"Okay," she said. "But this is going to hurt."

She pushed herself toward me with her legs and cried out. Brian fired again. The empty red shell bounced off my back, then dropped to the space between the vehicles. Even in all the moaning and lowing, I could hear that hollow plastic sound as it rattled to the gravel below.

I was in the bus. I had Jen under her armpits. I slipped back against the bus steps, and Jen fell back on me. We were both on the bus, not fully, but enough. Sara had already shifted it into drive, and we were rolling. Jen and I had to pull our legs up in the air to keep from having them clipped off in the doorway.

Even after we cleared the front of the truck, we had to keep our legs up and out of reach of the clawing hands of the undead.

Brian tried to help us up, but we were already out of the driveway before both of us were completely in and the door was shut. The creatures pursued us. Some ran like wild things, others were barely more than ambulatory corpses.

They all funneled in down that long driveway between the white board fence, trying to catch us, but we were too fast.

"Everyone okay?" I said.

No one answered. They were alive, but that was all. Jen's wounds had opened up. There was blood soaking through her jeans.

CHAPTER 44

I know how these things are supposed to end. I've seen the movies; I've read the books. The little band of survivors is supposed to make a perilous trek to some supposed safe haven, only to find it overrun or deserted. Or they dig in and, standing back to back, engage in an epic battle with the horde that surrounds them.

Maybe somewhere in the world, those scenarios were playing out with different groups. In Grace County, Kentucky, just a few miles southeast of Clayfield, this particular little band of survivors just wanted a place to hide. Two of us were injured. We had only one working gun with ten rounds, no food or water and only the clothes on our backs. Supplies could be had for now, but a place to hide and truly be safe had been impossible to find.

For our group, there might never be a decisive end, just a dwindling—a dwindling of resources, health, people, hope and will to live.

* * *

Sara entered the little community of Farmtown. She took us through the shuffling crowd and abandoned cars with slow, serpentine turns. The bus swayed. Jen's jeans were down around her ankles, and she was wrapping her thigh with my t-shirt. The bandage she'd put around it that morning was completely soaked with blood.

"Has the bleeding stopped?" I asked.

"It will," she said. "But all my medicine is back at the truck."

"We'll give them time to leave, and I'll go back."

"What if they don't? Something was drawing them there."

"We're thinking the smoke from the fire," Brian said.

"We've always had a fire," she said. "Something changed."

"It's warmer today than it has been," I said. "It's also windy. Maybe they picked up our scent or something."

"I sure picked up their scent," Brian said.

"Do you think ..." Jen started, then stopped.

"What?"

"Never mind," she said. "It's silly."

She secured the bandage with her belt, then pulled her jeans back up.

"No," I said. "Nothing is silly. What are you thinking?"

"Well, I started my period last night. It's no big deal, but I've read before how some animals can pick up on that."

Brian shook his head.

"Urban legend," he said. "Or rural myth. Either way."

"Okay." Jen shrugged. "It must be the wind and smoke."

We passed through tiny Farmtown almost as quickly as we'd entered it, headed back toward Clayfield. Less than a mile away from the town was the Farmtown Elementary School on the right. On the large playground in front of the school was a crashed Chinook helicopter. It was bent in on itself, and the double propellers were tangled together. It looked like a massive sculpture. Bodies lay all around it.

"Sara," I said, "pull in. I want to check it for supplies."

She looked at me in the mirror, then pulled into the entrance to the school grounds.

"Stop right here," I said.

I made sure the shotgun was loaded, and then I stepped out of the bus. I turned and looked back up at Sara.

"Keep the engine running," I said. "I'll try to be quick."

* * *

Chinooks were troop transports. I'd seen them in the sky many times on their way to and from Fort Campbell. If no one else had gotten to the crash, there could be weapons on board and possibly food.

The helicopter looked like it came down on its tail. The cockpit area wasn't as damaged as the rear. There had been no fire, and the craft wasn't as mangled as one might expect. This led me to believe it hadn't fallen that hard. Maybe it hadn't been that far off the ground. The bodies on the ground all had head wounds. There were spent rifle and pistol casings everywhere.

There was a door toward the front, near the cockpit. It was open like the black entrance to a cave. It was about chest high and at an angle. I stepped up to it and stuck my head in, letting my eyes adjust to the low light. The cockpit was to my right. The bay was to my left. Both were tilted up in a gentle V shape because of the crash. There were still soldiers strapped in their seats in the transport bay. They were wearing green camouflage, helmets and goggles. They were no longer people. The two creatures—once a man and a woman—looked at me with curious expressions. The side of the male's face had been eaten away by the female. His bare jawbone was exposed.

The female reached for me and moaned.

They both had sidearms. There were rucksacks on the floor in front of them too, hooked somehow to keep them from falling. I looked up to the rear of the vehicle toward the large cargo door. There was a big tarp-covered crate back there, held in place with wide orange netting. On the floor, between the two soldiers and the cargo, was an M4 carbine. There was a square door in the floor, but it was closed.

I climbed inside.

First, I pulled myself forward to the cockpit. The seats were empty, but there was a map tucked into a slot next to the seat on the left. I took it. I eased myself back down, and then turned my attention to the things strapped in the seats. I wanted those rucksacks and guns. I could stay far enough away from them to get the M4, but I didn't know how to get the other things without shooting them. They were wearing helmets, which would make it more difficult. Plus, shooting them would be loud.

I was also very curious about that cargo container.

I'd have to do this as quickly and as quietly as possible.

A short honk on the bus's horn got my attention. There was a difference in the sound of the engine, and I heard it pull away. We must have attracted some. I didn't let it deter me from going after the stuff.

I secured my shotgun in one of the seats, then pulled myself along the wall opposite the soldiers. The female hissed and growled and strained against her shoulder harness. I made it to the M4, braced myself to keep from falling, and picked it up. The man on the roof at the high school probably had a similar weapon, possibly taken from this very craft.

I slung the rifle on my back and continued to pull myself up to the crushed rear of the helicopter. I hooked my fingers in the netting with one hand and reached in with the other, trying to open the container. I couldn't figure out how to get it open. The M4 and the rucksacks—if I could get them—would have to do.

As I made my way back down, I looked out the window, toward the school. The bus was driving slowly in the parking lot while four of the zombies followed.

The two in their seats were still watching me, probably waiting for me to slip. I made my way back down until I was directly across from them. I sat in one of the seats to steady myself. I could pass on the handguns, but I really wanted those bags. They probably held extra ammunition for the M4.

Using the rifle, I poked at the bag in front of the male. He wasn't as animated as the female, and I thought I had a better chance of getting his. The bag shifted, but not much. It was hooked to the front of his seat by a short strap.

The bus horn honked again. It was still near the school.

I climbed back up, then crossed over to the other side. I sat down two seats up from the male. He turned his head toward me, but that was all. I decided to go for it. I held onto the seat, squatted on the floor and reached for his bag. He made a gurgling sound but didn't try to reach for me. The female stretched for me. I could just touch the strap with the ends of my fingers. I would have to get closer.

The light changed. I looked down toward the door. A zombie was there in the doorway. Out the window, I could see more coming.

I edged closer and leaned in again. I grabbed the strap and fidgeted with the hook, all the while keeping my eyes on the male. He kept his eyes on me too, but he never made any attempt to even touch me.

The hook came loose, and the bag started to fall. I caught it, but it was heavy and threw off my balance. It slid down to the lowest point, pulling me with it. On impulse, I reached out to stop my fall and grabbed the female's ankle. An expression that could almost pass for delight came across her face. She still couldn't reach me; the shoulder harness kept her up in her seat.

I was stretched out there on the floor, both arms extended, a forty-pound rucksack in one hand, a zombie foot in the other. The creatures outside the door were clawing for me too, but there was no danger of them reaching me.

Despite my precarious position, I was feeling pretty confident. I was right there anyway. Why not get her bag too?

I dropped the bag I was holding so that it would slide down to the back wall, away from the door. Then I turned onto my belly and unhooked her bag. I let it slide down with the other.

She was beside herself with frustration. She actually let out a howl and stomped her feet. I scooted down with the bags. There were four infected right outside the door. I could see more in the distance. It was time to give that M4 a go. I held it sideways, looking it over, trying to see if I could figure out how to use it. Like the AR-15, it was very lightweight.

In movies, I'd always seen them pull back on that thing on the side, but I didn't know if that was how it should be done, or if it just looked good for the sake of the movie. Actors always pumped shotguns unnecessarily in movies to punctuate what they were saying.

The safety was already off. Maybe it was ready to go.

I pointed it outside, toward the nearest creature, and squeezed the trigger. It fired off three rounds before I knew what was happening. There wasn't that much recoil either. The target's head jerked backward, and it fell.

"Hot damn."

I put it to my shoulder and, careful to only fire one round at a time, took out the remaining creatures. The horn honked again, closer. Since I was making noise anyway, I turned the weapon on the two strapped inside. One each, right through their goggles. It had become so easy to do that. I almost didn't feel anything anymore. Once they'd slumped forward, I pulled myself up to them.

I removed their pistols and dropped them down to the bags. I also found an extra magazine on each of the infected for the M4. If I'd had the time, and if I could have gotten past the smell, I would have removed their body armor. But that was a big "no" on both counts.

I stuffed the pistols, map and magazines into the rucksacks, put both bags on my back, and hopped out of the helicopter with the shotgun in one hand and the M4 in the other. It felt like I was carrying at least 100 pounds of extra weight, and I went right to my knees when I hit the ground.

More of the monsters were coming in. Sara pulled the bus up as close to the playground as she could. I stood and moved as fast as I could to get aboard.

* * *

We found a big empty house between Farmtown and Clayfield to hide in for the night. When I say it was empty, I mean just that. It was completely empty, with a realty sign in the front yard. It did have gas logs and a big propane tank outside, so we'd be able to stay warm. Unfortunately, there would be no bathing. We all had varying amounts of blood splattered on us, and there was the lingering smell of decay.

There were MREs in the soldiers' bags, but Brian was the only one with any sort of appetite. We discussed whether we should return to the Lassiter house. We also discussed all the possible reasons why the infected would have come in such numbers so unexpectedly.

Jen's menstruation wasn't ruled out, particularly when Sara told us that the whole time she'd been surrounded in the church, she'd been on her period too. Jen also added that the blue house on Bragusberg Road as well as the building behind the courthouse were surrounded while women were inside. It could have been a coincidence, but there might have been something to it.

"The stories about animals pertained to pheromones," Brian said. "From what I've read, the pheromones of one kind of animal do not affect another kind. That's why I said what I said. Of course, we and they are of the same species, but in this situation, if it was indeed the reason, it might have been the blood itself. Jen's leg injury might have contributed to it too."

"Like sharks," Jen said.

"Yeah, maybe," Brian said.

"It all happened so quickly," I said. "I never asked ... Brian, did you and Sara update Jen on the other problem?"

"Yeah," Jen said. "They told me about the other survivors. They sound like a bunch of dicks."

"Probably the same group from Lowe's, so yeah," I said.

* * *

We took inventory of our haul from the Chinook. The contents of the bags were almost identical, except for the toiletry kits and the sizes of the clothing.

Each bag contained one t-shirt, two MREs, two pairs of socks, a gun-cleaning kit, night-vision goggles, a rain poncho, a plastic bag, one magazine for the M4, one magazine for the 9 mm handgun, a first-aid pouch, and a small toiletry kit. In addition to these items were the two 9 mm handguns, the map and two additional magazines for the M4.

"You did good," Jen said. I felt pretty good about myself, and was about to say something, but then she added, "Gun-wise. They'll come in handy. Of course, we'll need water and food pretty soon. I don't know if it was worth all the trouble if that's all you got."

"What about the night vision?" I asked. "That's going to be a huge help."

She shrugged, seemingly unimpressed.

"You and Sara better put them on," she said. "It's dark out, and we need booze."

"We can wait and drink tomorrow," I said. "We have a few hours before the fever kicks in."

"A few hours at most," Jen corrected.

"Do you think we'll have to live the rest of our lives like this?" Sara asked. She was already wearing the night-vision goggles, looking out the front window.

"By 'rest of our lives,' do you mean until we get old or until we die?" Brian said.

She tilted the lenses of the goggles up and turned around and sighed.

"I'm so tired," she said.

"Me too," he said. "Weary, actually. I'll go out to find alcohol. If all you need is a getaway driver, I think I can do that. You stay here with Jen and rest."

"No," she said. "I'm just being a baby. You're hurt. I can do it."

* * *

We left Brian and Jen with the shotgun and one pistol, along with the two extra magazines. I took the M4, and Sara got the other pistol. Sara and I took the night vision. There was no way to know how long we'd be gone. We could find something at the house next door, or we might have to drive around and search houses until morning.

I let Sara drive.

"We'll go house to house," I said. "You can stay with the bus. I'll go in and do the searches. Drive with the lights off and use the goggles."

The world was green. I thought maybe it would be better like this. Maybe the things would show up better. We pulled into the driveway of the first house, and I got out with an empty rucksack.

The door was locked, but there was a window right next to it. I broke the glass and reached in and turned the deadbolt. I didn't find any alcohol, but I got some canned goods, crackers and a two-liter bottle of Sprite.

At the next house, the door was standing wide open, and I surprised a family of raccoons who were in the kitchen, enjoying the box of Cheerios they'd knocked off the top of the refrigerator. They scrambled away, but soon came back and didn't seem to mind me being there. No alcohol there either.

We were out for more than two hours. I had to use the rifle three times. Finally, I broke into a house that had a box of Zinfandel in the refrigerator. The box was open, but still mostly full. I took it out to the bus. Sara had the radio on, listening to static.

"Got some," I said. "We can head back now."

She yawned and nodded, then put the bus in reverse.

"I'm tempted to drive us into town," she said, "find a house there and use the shower to get this gunk off me."

"It would be a very cold shower," I said.

"I don't care," she said. "I'm tired of smelling it. I don't know if I'll ever get the smell off."

"We'll go back, have some wine, get some sleep and go out first thing. We'll find a place where we can all get a hot bath."

"Really?" she said.

"Well ... a warm bath … Warm-ish."

When we got back to the house a few minutes later, we found Jen and Brian sleeping on the floor in front of the heater.

"Should we wake them?" Sara asked.

"Yeah," I said. "Jen would want to go ahead and drink something."

I went over to Jen and shook her awake. She opened her eyes. When she saw me, she gave me a little grin.

"We found some wine," I said. "Get up and have a glass or two. Then you can go back to sleep."

"You got glasses?" she said.

I stared at her.

"You didn't, did you?"

"I rely on you to think of stuff like that," I said. "Put your mouth under the spigot."

"Brian didn't try to shoot you, did he? He was a little jumpy right after you left."

"Brian is asleep. Sara is waking him."

Jen pushed herself up on her elbow.

"Brian Davies, you ass!" Jen said playfully. "Falling asleep on watch—you should be ashamed of yourself."

Sara was kneeling next to him. She looked up at us.

"He's hot with fever, and he's not waking up."

CHAPTER 45

Brian had done this before, but this time was different.

"It's too soon, isn't it?" Sara said.

"He's been out away from his house for a while. He might have contracted the virus during that time."

"Get some wine in him!" Jen said. "Maybe it isn't too late."

We couldn't wake him. He wouldn't even stir.

"Damn it!" Jen said. "Zach went real fast. Make him drink it!"

I propped Brian's head in my lap and gently opened his mouth. I put the spigot over his mouth and turned it just enough for a trickle. It filled his mouth and spilled over the side.

"He's not swallowing it," I said. "I'm afraid I'm going to drown him."

Jen dragged herself across the hardwood floors until she was next to him. She started stroking his throat.

"Brian!" she yelled. "Brian, swallow the damn wine!"

"He's burning up," I said. "Let's take him outside in the cold air."

I pulled him outside and lowered the night-vision goggles so I could see. I propped his head up in my lap again and gave him more wine. Again, it filled his mouth and spilled over. Sara came out with the shotgun and stood sentry in front of the porch. Jen pulled herself over the threshold, but it was so dark outside, I doubted she could see anything.

Then Brian coughed and sprayed wine in my face. His eyes opened. Through the night-vision goggles, it looked as if his eyes glowed like a demon's. He stared at me, coughing and trying to swallow the wine in his mouth.

"Sit up," I said. "You need to get as much down as you can."

I helped him to a sitting position. He slouched there, looking down at his lap.

"Head up, Brian," I said. "You need more. I'm going to let it run into your mouth."

His head came up slowly. He looked in my direction, blankly. It was very dark, so he couldn't see me, and he was likely delirious from the fever.

"It's okay," I said. "I can see you; I'm wearing the goggles. Just tilt your head back, and I'll get the wine into your mouth."

He just kept staring in my direction.

"Brian, do it," Jen said.

Jen looked a little clearer than Brian, because the faint glow of the gas logs reflected off of her.

"Is he doing it?" she said. "Brian, are you doing it?"

Then he made a sound. It started out as a whine, then built in volume while deepening in tone. It was like the growl of a cat. I scooted back away from him.

"Jen, get inside and shut the door," I whispered. "Sara and I will come in through the back."

"What happened?" she said. "Brian?"

Brian turned his head in the direction of Jen's voice. He was between me and her.

"Do it, Jen," I whispered.

I stood up and stepped backward.

"Sara, get around back. Jen will let you in."

Sara stood there on the lawn, staring at Brian. With the night-vision goggles on, she looked like something from a science fiction movie. Brian had turned toward my voice now.

"Jen, get inside. Now. He's ... gone."

"No," she said. "We have to ..."

"Both of you, get in the house!" I said, louder than I should have.

Sara took off in a sprint around the side of the house. Brian leaped to his feet, arms extended, trying to get his bearings in the dark. He growled again. Jen was pushing herself backward across the floor, crying. I had no weapon, just a box of wine.

"Get that door shut!" I said, backing away.

Brian took a step toward me, following my voice. There was steam coming off him. Jen groped for the door to swing it shut. Brian looked in her direction.

"No, Brian," I said. "Come on, now. Follow me. Damn it, Jen, shut the door!"

"I'm trying!"

Brian was fast. He darted inside the house.

"Jen!" I yelled.

I was close but not close enough. I ran across the porch. When I got to the door, he was on top of her. She was screaming. I hit him in the head as hard as I could with the box of wine. The box crushed in, but he remained unfazed. I hit him again and again and again. In the green light, I could see the dark wine dribbling out of the box and pooling on the floor.

I'd have to use something else; we were going to need that wine.

I kicked him off of her. He rolled away. The wine was everywhere.

But the wine shouldn't have been that dark.

It was blood. Brian's blood was on the box of wine; the blood on the floor belonged to Jen. Her throat was opened up, and her blood was smeared on Brian's cheek. He hissed and came at me.

"God, Brian, no."

I backed out of the house. He looked even more like a demon now, hunched forward, eyes glowing and arms out. Steam emanated off him like smoke, as if he'd just stepped out of Hell. I didn't think he'd be able to see me once I got into the yard. He stepped out onto the porch, looking around and listening for me. I felt so helpless. Jen was right there, so close, bleeding, and I couldn't get to her.

Sara rounded the corner of the house.

"I can't get it open," she said. "Jen hasn't unlocked …"

Brian ran toward her. Sara saw him coming. I could tell she was startled at first, but she quickly turned the 12-gauge and let one fly from the hip. There was a flash of bright green from the end of the weapon. The blast hit him in the chest and knocked him off his feet. He hit the ground and was still.

I ran into the house and knelt next to Jen. There was so much blood. I put my hand on her neck, trying to stop it. She couldn't speak, and I didn't know what to say to her. The blood still came, seeping between my fingers. I took off my bandana mask and put it over the wound, but I couldn't stop it.

I felt sick. I knocked the goggles away so I wouldn't have to see.

I heard Sara come into the house. She didn't say anything. My eyes had adjusted to dim light from the heater. I couldn't see much, but it was enough. Sara came in closer and put her hand on my shoulder.

"We can't stay here," she said softly. "They'll be here soon."

I nodded, but I couldn't find the strength to talk.

"Grab one of the bags, and go get in the bus," she said. "I'll take care of the rest."

I looked up at her. She was still wearing the goggles.

I nodded again and stood slowly. I don't really remember getting the bag, but I did. I felt empty and lost. I got on the bus, went back a couple of rows and sat. I don't know how much time passed, but finally, Sara came outside, carrying the other bag, the M4 and the shotgun. She climbed inside and stowed the things.

I checked out for a while. I know we drove around, and I know Sara got out of the bus a couple of times. The next thing I knew, she was standing in front of me.

"Come on," she said. "We'll stay here until daylight."

I looked out the window. We were parked in front of Nicholas Somerville's house. I looked at Sara.

"It's okay," she said. "We'll leave early in the morning. Besides, I doubt anyone will bother us here. They've already raided the houses on this street."

* * *

The water still worked. Sara heated some on the gas range, and we both took quick, chilly and much-needed baths. We changed into the t-shirts and socks from the rucksacks, and we found some pants and jackets to wear in the Somervilles' closet. They didn't fit, but at least they didn't smell like death and rot.

Sara had removed the plastic bladder from the box of wine. She pulled it from the rucksack and filled a glass for each of us. We righted the overturned couch in the living room and just sat.

"I'm sorry," she said.

"It wasn't his fault," I said absently. "He wasn't himself."

"I know," she said. "I'm sorry."

I nodded.

The house was cold. The Somervilles' gas furnace would never do us any good. It relied on an electric thermostat and electric blower.

I pulled the curtains off the window, and we used them like blankets.

"I don't want to leave Jen like that," I said. "I don't want to just leave her on the floor."

"We can go bury her tomorrow," she said.

That statement made me realize how final it was, and I got choked up. Sara took my hand.

"I'm sorry," she said.

"No. I ... I don't want to see her."

"I can do it."

"No," I said. "We'll go back when the sun is up and burn the house. Brian too. I don't want him getting up again."

We finished our glasses of wine and started on seconds. Sara eventually fell asleep with her head on my shoulder, but I didn't sleep at all. I just kept replaying the events of the evening, of the day, of the past two weeks—all of it.

I kept trying to tell myself not to get so upset. I had really only known Jen for a couple of weeks. If it had been a couple of "normal" weeks, we might have gone out on a date or two, but that would have been all. It felt like things had been accelerated and amplified since the virus. Certain emotions were unusually heightened, while others were unusually subdued.

I'd lost my mom too. My best friend, Blaine, and his beautiful family were gone. I hurt for them, but not the way I would have hurt before. It didn't seem right for me to feel such a great loss over Jen when I didn't feel it for these people whom I loved ... yet I still felt it.

It was comforting to have Sara's head on my shoulder and to listen to her sleep. The wine helped me not to hurt so badly, and I had more than I needed.

* * *

Dawn revealed a cloudy sky. I slipped away from Sara without waking her and stepped outside. It was cool out, but not cold. It looked like we'd have another warm, breezy day like the day before, with the possibility of rain.

The buzz from the wine had worn off, and I was left with a dull headache. I was surprised that I wanted to eat, but I wanted to put Jen and Brian to rest before the rain started. I went back in and woke Sara.

"Come on," I said. "It's time to go."

* * *

We drove back out to the house. The front door was still open. Brian's body was gone from the front lawn. I'd sort of expected that. We sat in the bus, staring at the house, trying to get up enough nerve to get out.

"I can't," I said. "I'm really sorry, but I don't want to see her."

"You don't have to," Sara said. "I'll get some sticks and build a fire in the kitchen, and then I'll throw some water on the gas logs. That will put the fire out, but the gas will keep running. Once the gas gets to the fire in the kitchen, that should take care of it."

"I can at least help you find some sticks," I said.

"You stay and keep watch for me," she said. "I'll be okay."

I watched her walking around under some large trees on the edge of the property. She seemed so much older than her years. Really, she was just a kid, but times like these could mature a person.

When she had a bundle, she went inside the house. I felt like such a baby for not being willing to go in there myself. She was in there for a while. I was just about to make myself go check on her when she came back out of the house, still holding the sticks. I stepped out of the bus.

"She's gone too," she said. "I checked the whole house."

I went as far as the front porch. There were at least three sets of bloody footprints going in and out of the house. For a moment, I thought that someone had carried her away, but then I realized that some of those footprints were mine and Sara's from the night before. The other set must have been Jen's.

This changed my understanding of things. I had tried to avoid admitting it, but I'd finally surrendered to the notion that the virus was bringing people back to life. However, seeing that Jen was missing added something new.

There were the infected. They were the ones with the fever who'd lost their minds. They were fast, albeit uncoordinated, and operating on animal instincts. Then there were the infected who had died—either through violence or from the virus itself—and had come back to "life." Jen's absence told of a third group. Jen hadn't had the virus before she died, yet because she'd been killed by the bite of one of the infected, she came back too.

This gave me pause about the possibility of a fourth group. What would happen to those who neither had the virus nor were killed by someone with the virus? Would they come back too?

"Do you want to look for her?" Sara asked, dropping the sticks.

"No," I said. "We might find her. Then what?"

"What do you want to do?" she asked.

I didn't know.

"Crawl in a hole somewhere," I said. "Pull it in on top of me."

She walked over to me and put her arm around my waist and her head on my chest.

* * *

We drove back by the stables. The crowd from the day before was mostly gone. There were just five left. We didn't want to shoot them because of the noise, so Sara pulled in close to the barns. We got out and found some farm tools—a shovel for Sara and an axe for me. We bludgeoned and chopped until they were all still, then we dragged their bodies into a pile.

There was a lone horse and two chickens left alive. The two chickens that made it did so by roosting in the rafters of the barn. We couldn't get them to come down. Pieces of the goat were strewn around the barn.

We unloaded the pickup and put the supplies from it into the bus. We then loaded it into the bus with everything we could carry from the house.

I went back in for one last pass and saw Jen's stack of magazines next to the couch, along with the golf club I'd left her for a cane. I almost lost it right then, but I kept my composure. I took the golf club.

I'd been going along with Jen on everything, and I had not really thought beyond that. My overall plan hadn't changed. I still thought it best to find a way to live here. I had no real desire to wander around the country, looking for someone to save me, but I knew I couldn't stay here at the stables. Sara had been right—staying at the Lassiter house was what Jen had wanted. It turned out not to be safe anyway.

When the bus was loaded, we poured kerosene on the bodies and set them on fire.

We drove down to the end of the driveway, where the hay truck was still parked askew. I stopped, and Sara got out.

"Where are we going?" she asked.

"I don't know," I said. "It almost doesn't matter."

She climbed back up on the steps.

"Listen, I know you're hurting, but we can't give up. They'll get us if we give up."

I nodded, staring out the windshield at nothing in particular.

"You said yourself that this is a chance for us to live however we want and wherever we want. Is there someplace you've ever wanted to live? Some place other than Clayfield?"

"Clayfield is home," I said.

"We could drive south and find us a nice place on the Gulf, right on the beach. How does that sound?"

"Is that what you want?" I said, looking at her.

She smiled and looked down at her feet, then back up at me.

"I'm with you."

I tried to smile back, but I couldn't.

"Okay," she said. "If we're going to stay around here, we're going to have to do better. We've just been reacting and hiding. I know that's what you and Jen wanted to do, but we can't live like that. I think the people at the high school had the right idea; they just went about it the wrong way. I think we need to take the town back. If that means we're exterminators, then so be it."

I nodded my agreement.

"Good," she said, hopping out of the bus. She climbed into the hay truck and motioned to me to lead the way.

Rain began to spot up the windshield. I switched on the wipers, pulled out of the driveway and turned the bus toward Clayfield.

PERMUTED PRESS

14

BY PETER CLINES

Padlocked doors. Strange light fixtures. Mutant cockroaches. There are some odd things about Nate's new apartment. Every room in this old brownstone has a mystery. Mysteries that stretch back over a hundred years. Some of them are in plain sight. Some are behind locked doors. And all together these mysteries could mean the end of Nate and his friends. Or the end of everything...

PERMUTEDPRESS.COM

THE FLU

BY JACQUELINE DRUGA

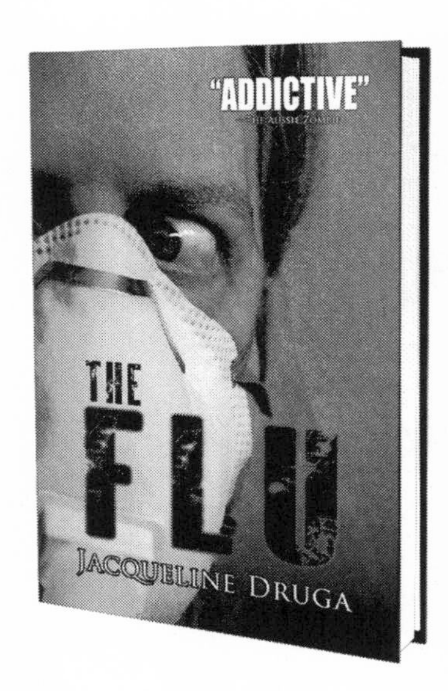

Throughout history there have been several thousand different strains of influenza. Each year hundreds are active. Chances are, this year, you will catch one of those strains. You will cough, sneeze, and your body will ache. Without a second thought, you'll take a double dose of green liquid, go to bed, and swear you'll feel better in the morning. Not this time.

PERMUTED PRESS

PERMUTED PRESS

DOMAIN OF THE DEAD
BY IAIN MCKINNON

The world is dead, devoured by a plague of reanimated corpses. Barricaded inside a warehouse with dwindling food, a group of survivors faces two possible deaths: creeping starvation, or the undead outside. In their darkest hour hope appears in the form of a helicopter approaching the city... but is it the salvation the survivors have been waiting for?

PERMUTEDPRESS.COM

REMAINS OF THE DEAD
BY IAIN MCKINNON

The world is dead. Cahz and his squad of veteran soldiers are tasked with flying into abandoned cities and retrieving zombies for scientific study. Then the unbelievable happens. After years of encountering nothing but the undead, the team discovers a handful of survivors in a fortified warehouse with dwindling supplies.

PERMUTED PRESS

ROADS LESS TRAVELED: THE PLAN
BY C. DULANEY

Ask yourself this: If the dead rise tomorrow, are you ready? Do you have a plan? Kasey, a strong-willed loner, has something she calls The Zombie Plan. But every plan has its weaknesses, and a freight train of tragedy is bearing down on Kasey and her friends. In the darkness that follows, Kasey's Plan slowly unravels: friends lost, family taken, their stronghold reduced to ashes.

MURPHY'S LAW (ROADS LESS TRAVELED BOOK 2)
BY C. DULANEY

Kasey and the gang were held together by a set of rules, their Zombie Plan. It kept them alive through the beginning of the End. But when the chaos faded, they became careless, and Murphy's Law decided to pay a long-overdue visit. Now the group is broken and scattered with no refuge in sight. Those remaining must make their way across West Virginia in search of those who were stolen from them.

SHADES OF GRAY (ROADS LESS TRAVELED BOOK 3)
BY C. DULANEY

Kasey and the gang have come full circle through the crumbling world. Working for the National Guard, they realize old friends and fellow survivors are disappearing. When the missing start to reappear as walking corpses, the group sets out on another journey to discover the truth. Their answers wait in the West Virginia Command Center.

PERMUTED PRESS

NEW ZED ORDER: SURVIVE
BY TODD SPRAGUE

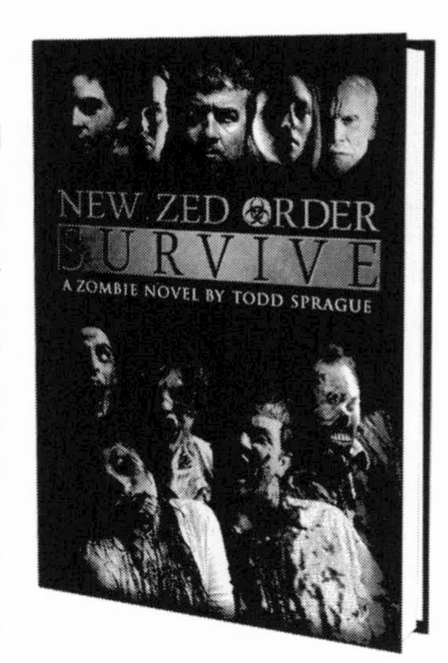

The dead have risen, and they are hungry. In Vermont, John Mason and his beautiful young wife Sara believe that family can survive anything. When the apocalypse arrives they pack food, clothing, and weapons, then hit the road seeking refuge in the mountains of John's youth. There they, together with family, friends, and neighbors, build a stronghold against the encroaching mass of the dead.

PERMUTEDPRESS.COM

THE JUNKIE QUATRAIN
BY PETER CLINES

Six months ago, the world ended. The Baugh Contagion swept across the planet. Its victims were left twitching, adrenalized cannibals that quickly became know as Junkies. THE JUNKIE QUATRAIN is four tales of survival, and four types of post-apocalypse story. Because the end of the world means different things for different people. Loss. Opportunity. Hope. Or maybe just another day on the job.

PERMUTED PRESS

THE UNDEAD SITUATION

BY ELOISE J. KNAPP

The dead are rising. People are dying. Civilization is collapsing. But Cyrus V. Sinclair couldn't care less; he's a sociopath. Amidst the chaos, Cyrus sits with little more emotion than one of the walking corpses… until he meets up with other inconvenient survivors who cramp his style and force him to re-evaluate his outlook on life. It's Armageddon, and things will definitely get messy.

THE UNDEAD HAZE

(THE UNDEAD SITUATION BOOK 2)

BY ELOISE J. KNAPP

When remorse drives Cyrus to abandon his hidden compound he doesn't realize what new dangers lurk in the undead world. He knows he must wade through the vilest remains of humanity and hordes of zombies to settle scores and find the one person who might understand him. But this time, it won't be so easy. Zombies and unpleasant survivors aren't the only thing Cyrus has to worry about.

PERMUTED PRESS

DEAD LIVING
BY GLENN BULLION

It didn't take long for the world to die. And it didn't take long, either, for the dead to rise. Aaron was born on the day the world ended. Kept in seclusion, his family teaches him the basics. How to read and write. How to survive. Then Aaron makes a shocking discovery. The undead, who desire nothing but flesh, ignore him. It's as if he's invisible to them.

AUTOBIOGRAPHY of a WEREWOLF HUNTER
BY BRIAN P. EASTON

After his mother is butchered by a werewolf, Sylvester James is taken in by a Cheyenne mystic. The boy trains to be a werewolf hunter, learning to block out pain, stalk, fight, and kill. As Sylvester sacrifices himself to the hunt, his hatred has become a monster all its own. As he follows his vendetta into the outlands of the occult, he learns it takes more than silver bullets to kill a werewolf.

INFECTION:
ALASKAN UNDEAD APOCALYPSE
BY SEAN SCHUBERT

Anchorage, Alaska: gateway to serene wilderness of The Last Frontier. No stranger to struggle, the city on the edge of the world is about to become even more isolated. When a plague strikes, Anchorage becomes a deadly trap for its citizens. The only two land routes out of the city are cut, forcing people to fight or die as the infection spreads.

PERMUTEDPRESS.COM

CONTAINMENT
(ALASKAN UNDEAD APOCALYPSE BOOK 2)
BY SEAN SCHUBERT

Running. Hiding. Surviving. Anchorage, once Alaska's largest city, has fallen. Now a threatening maze of death, the city is firmly in the cold grip of a growing zombie horde. Neil Jordan and Dr. Caldwell lead a small band of desperate survivors through the maelstrom. The group has one last hope: that this nightmare has been contained, and there still exists a sane world free of infection.

MAD SWINE: THE BEGINNING
BY STEVEN PAJAK

People refer to the infected as "zombies," but that's not what they really are. Zombie implies the infected have died and reanimated. The thing is, they didn't die. They're just not human anymore. As the infection spreads and crazed hordes--dubbed "Mad Swine"--take over the cities, the residents of Randall Oaks find themselves locked in a desperate struggle to survive in the new world.

PERMUTEDPRESS.COM

MAD SWINE: DEAD WINTER
BY STEVEN PAJAK

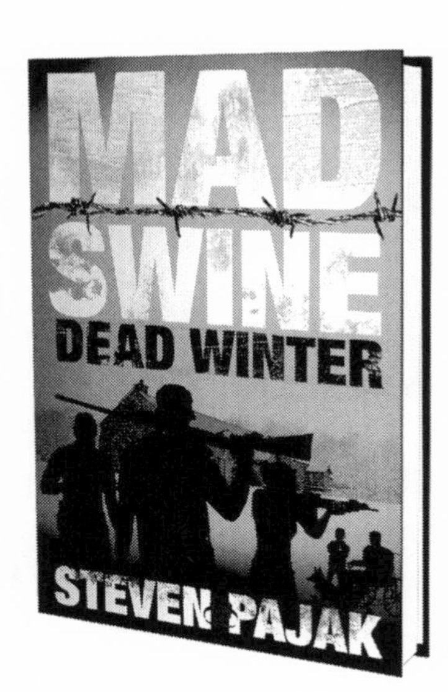

Three months after the beginning of the Mad Swine outbreak, the residents of Randall Oaks have reached their breaking point. After surviving the initial outbreak and a war waged with their neighboring community, Providence, their supplies are severely close to depletion. With hostile neighbors at their flanks and hordes of infected outside their walls, they have become prisoners within their own community.

PERMUTED PRESS

DEAD TIDE

BY STEPHEN A. NORTH

THE WORLD IS ENDING. BUT THERE ARE SURVIVORS. Nick Talaski is a hard-bitten, angry cop. Graham is a newly divorced cab driver. Bronte is a Gulf War veteran hunting his brother's killer. Janicea is a woman consumed by unflinching hate. Trish is a gentleman's club dancer. Morgan is a morgue janitor. The dead have risen and the citizens of St. Petersburg and Pinellas Park are trapped. The survivors are scattered, and options are few. And not all monsters are created by a bite. Some still have a mind of their own…

PERMUTEDPRESS.COM

DEAD TIDE RISING

BY STEPHEN A. NORTH

The sequel to Dead Tide continues the carnage in Pinellas Park near St. Pete, Florida. Follow all of the characters from the first book, Dead Tide, as they fight for survival in a world destroyed by the zombie apocalypse.

PERMUTED PRESS

PERMUTED PRESS

THE BECOMING
BY JESSICA MEIGS

The Michaluk Virus has escaped the CDC, and its effects are widespread and devastating. Most of the population of the southeastern United States have become homicidal cannibals. As society rapidly crumbles under the hordes of infected, three people--Ethan, a Memphis police officer; Cade, his best friend; and Brandt, a lieutenant in the US Marines--band together against the oncoming crush of death.

PERMUTEDPRESS.COM

THE BECOMING: GROUND ZERO (BOOK 2)
BY JESSICA MEIGS

After the Michaluk Virus decimated the southeast, Ethan and his companions became like family. But the arrival of a mysterious woman forces them to flee from the infected, and the cohesion the group cultivated is shattered. As members of the group succumb to the escalating dangers on their path, new alliances form, new loves develop, and old friendships crumble.

PERMUTEDPRESS.COM

THE BECOMING: REVELATIONS (BOOK 3)
BY JESSICA MEIGS

In a world ruled by the dead, Brandt Evans is floundering. Leadership of their dysfunctional group wasn't something he asked for or wanted. Their problems are numerous: Remy Angellette is grief-stricken and suicidal, Gray Carter is distant and reclusive, and Cade Alton is near death. And things only get worse.

PERMUTED PRESS

PAVLOV'S DOGS

BY D.L. SNELL & THOM BRANNAN

WEREWOLVES Dr. Crispin has engineered the saviors of mankind: soldiers capable of transforming into beasts. ZOMBIES Ken and Jorge get caught in a traffic jam on their way home from work. It's the first sign of a major outbreak. ARMAGEDDON Should Dr. Crisping send the Dogs out into the zombie apocalypse to rescue survivors? Or should they hoard their resources and post the Dogs as island guards?

PERMUTEDPRESS.COM

THE OMEGA DOG

BY D.L. SNELL & THOM BRANNAN

Twisting and turning through hordes of zombies, cartel territory, Mayan ruins, and the things that now inhabit them, a group of survivors must travel to save one man's family from a nightmarish third world gone to hell. But this time, even best friends have deadly secrets, and even allies can't be trusted - as a father's only hope of getting his kids out alive is the very thing that's hunting him down.

Made in the USA
Charleston, SC
12 December 2013